on EON

"A powerful, imaginative novel."   —*Library Journal*

"Bear pictures Axis City, and everything else for that matter, with astonishing clarity. . . . Bear's grasp is unfaltering, his control over the ramifying implications of his tale nearly perfect. . . . *Eon* may be the best-constructed hard SF epic yet."   —*The Washington Post Book World*

"The only word for it really is blockbuster. . . . It is big and breathtaking; the story and the concepts are ambitious to the point of mind-boggling."
                    —*Asimov's Science Fiction*

on ETERNITY

"As political rivals, inhuman alien intelligences, and travelers from alternate worlds meet in a corridor of possibilities, the destiny of the world hinges on the fragility of human choice. Showcasing Bear's imagination and considerable storytelling talent, this sequel to *Eon* is highly recommended."
                    —*Library Journal*

"[*Eternity*'s] portrait of the different responses of intricate, interlocking cultures is striking."   —*Publishers Weekly*

on LEGACY

"Hard science and human interest intersect ingeniously in the prequel to Bear's *Eon* and *Eternity*. . . . This is a stunning SF novel that extrapolates a scientifically complex future from the basic stuff of human nature."
                    —*Publishers Weekly* (starred review)

"A remarkable and utterly convincing feat of creation."
                    —*Kirkus Reviews* (starred review)

ALSO BY GREG BEAR

LEGACY

GREG BEAR

A TOM DOHERTY ASSOCIATES BOOK

NEW YORK

This is a work of fiction. All of the characters, organizations, and events portrayed in this novel are either products of the author's imagination or are used fictitiously.

LEGACY

Copyright © 1995 by Greg Bear

A Tor Book
Published by Tom Doherty Associates, LLC
175 Fifth Avenue
New York, NY 10010

www.tor-forge.com

Tor® is a registered trademark of Tom Doherty Associates, LLC.

Library of Congress Cataloging-in-Publication Data

Bear, Greg, 1951–
    Legacy / Greg Bear.—First trade paperback edition.
        p. cm.—(Eon ; 3)
    "A Tom Doherty Associates book."
    ISBN 978-0-7653-8050-0 (trade paperback)
    1. Space colonies—Fiction.   2. Space and time—Fiction.   I. Title.
    PS3552.E157 L43 2015
    813'.54—dc23

                                                                    2015023317

Our books may be purchased in bulk for promotional, educational, or business use. Please contact your local bookseller or the Macmillan Corporate and Premium Sales Department at (800) 221-7945, extension 5442, or by e-mail at Macmillan SpecialMarkets@macmillan.com.

First Edition: June 1995
First Trade Paperback Edition: November 2015

Printed in the United States of America

0 9 8 7 6 5 4 3 2 1

FOR BERTHA MERRIMAN
A PIONEER WHO LIVED IN A TOUGHER TIME . . .
WITH LOVE FROM A GRANDCHILD

LEGACY

PROLOGUE: JOURNEY YEAR 753

I stood on the lip of the southern bore hole, clutching a service line, and, for the first time in my life, stared beyond the mass of Thistledown at the stars. They spread through deep space as many and sharp as a cloud of crystal snow blown against black onyx. The uncharted constellations spun with a stately haste, betraying the asteroid's rotation around its long axis.

The worksuit performed its tasks silently, and for a time I seemed a point of crystal myself, at the center of the crystal empyrean, at peace. I looked for patterns in the stars, but before I could find any, my companion interrupted me.

"Olmy." She pulled herself carefully along the line and floated beside me.

"Just a moment," I said.

"We're done here. Parties await us, Olmy. Celebrations and diversions . . . but you're a bonded man, aren't you?"

I shook my head, annoyed. "Hard to believe that something as huge as Thistledown can shrink to nothing," I said.

Her expression, surveying the stars, was half worry, half distaste. Kerria Ap Kane had been my partner in Way Defense since basic, a good friend if not exactly a soulmate. I had so few soulmates. Not even my bond . . .

"Give me a minute, Kerria."

"I want to get back." She shrugged. "All right. A minute. But why look outward?"

Kerria would never have understood. To her, the asteroid starship was all and everything, a world of infinite social opportunities: work, friends, even dying for Way Defense if it came to that. The stars were outside, "far south," and meant nothing; only the confined infinity of the Way aroused wonder in her soul.

"It's pretty," she said flatly. "Do you think we'll ever get to Van Brugh?"

Van Brugh's star, still a hundred light-years distant, had been the original goal of Thistledown. For most of the ship's population of Naderites—my family included—it was the point of all our existences, a holy destination, and had been for seven hundred years' journey time.

"Can we see it from here, do you think?"

"No," I said. "It's visible from midline this year."

"Too bad," Kerria said. She clucked her tongue restlessly.

The ten-kilometer-wide crater at Thistledown's southern pole had once deflected and directed the pulses of the Beckmann drive motors. The motors had not been fired in four centuries. I took one last look beyond the lip of the bore hole, my eyes tracking outward along the honeycombed curve of the dimple at the center of the crater. Huge black many-limbed robots sat in the dimple around the lip of the bore hole, having arranged themselves for our inspection hours earlier.

"All right," I said to the massed robots. "Go home." I aimed the command transponder and the machines backed away, hooks and claws grabbing the spinning slope, returning to their duties on the asteroid's surface.

We turned and pulled ourselves along the line down the bore hole, toward the tuberider, an oblate grayness resting lightly against the dark rock and metal wall. Beyond the tuberider lay the massive prime dock, a cylinder within the bore hole designed to counterrotate and allow easier access to cargo vehicles. Tens of kilometers north glowed a small bright dot, the opening to the first chamber. We climbed into the tuberider, pressurized the cramped cabin, and collapsed our worksuits.

Kerria beamed a signal at the bore-hole mouth. Two massive shutters swung from the walls and came together like black-lipped jaws, sealing this end of Thistledown and blanking the stars.

"All clean and clear," she said. "Agreed?"

"All clear and clean," I said.

"Do the generals actually think the Jarts will get outside the Way and swing up our backside?" Kerria asked cheerfully.

"They surprised us once," I said. "They might do it again."

Kerria gave me a dubious grin. "Shall I drop you off at the sixth chamber?" she asked, lifting the vehicle away from the wall.

"I need to do some things in Thistledown City first."

"Ever the mystery man," Kerria said.

She had no idea.

We sped north down the tunnel. The kilometers to the end of the bore hole passed rapidly. The entrance to the first chamber yawned wide, and we flew into brilliant tubelight.

Fifty kilometers in diameter and thirty deep, the first chamber seemed to my recent interstellar perspective to be little more than the inside of a big, squat drum. Its true size was emphasized by the slowness with which our tuberider crossed to the bore hole in the chamber's northern cap.

Clouds decked the chamber floor, twenty-five kilometers below. The atmosphere in the chamber rose to a height of twenty kilometers, a sea of fluid lining the drum. I saw a small storm gathering on the floor overhead. No storm could touch us at the axis, riding as we were in almost perfect vacuum.

The first chamber was kept nearly deserted as a precaution against any breach of the comparatively thin walls of the asteroid at the southern end.

We traveled down the middle of the tube light, a translucent pipe of glowing plasma five kilometers wide and thirty long, generated at the chamber's northern and southern caps. We could see rapid pulses of light from our position along the axis, but on the chamber's floor, the tube presented a steady, yellow-white glow, day and night. So it was in all of the first six chambers.

The seventh chamber, of course, was different.

The bore hole seemed a pinprick in the gray, gently curved wall of asteroid rock ahead of us. "Shall I go manual and thread us in?" Kerria asked, grinning at me.

I smiled back but gave no answer. She was good enough to do it. She had piloted flawships and numerous other craft up and down the Way with expert ease.

"I'd rather relax," she said, peeved by my silence. "You would refuse to be impressed." She folded her arms back behind her head. "Besides, it's been a long day. I might miss."

"You never miss," I said.

"Damn right I don't."

Inspections were mandated by Hexamon law twice yearly. Way Defense had upped that to four times yearly, with special emphasis on sixth chamber security, inspection of reserve batteries in the ship's cold outer walls, and maintenance of the southern bore hole and external monitors. This time, Kerria and I had drawn inspection duty for the far south. We then had liberty for thirty days, and Kerria thought herself lucky: The Way's twenty-fifth anniversary celebration was just beginning.

But I had an unpleasant task ahead: betrayal, separation, putting an end to connections I no longer believed in but was not willing to mock.

The cap loomed, filling our forward view, and the second bore hole suddenly swallowed us. Kilometers away, the opening to the second chamber city, Alexandria, made another brilliant dot against the tunnel's unlighted blackness.

"Elevator, or shall I swoop down and drop you off somewhere?"

"Elevator," I said.

"My," Kerria said with a cluck. "Glum?"

"You sound like a chicken," I said.

"You've never seen a live chicken. How can you be glum with so much liberty ahead?"

"Even so."

We passed into the second chamber, the same size as the first, but filled with Thistledown's oldest city. Alexandria covered two-thirds of the second chamber floor, thirty-one-hundred square kilometers of glorious white and gold and bronze and green towers arrayed in spirals and stepped ranks, walls of blunt-faced black and gold cubes, ornately inscribed spheres rising from massive cradles themselves rich with colors and populations. Between the city and the southern cap stretched a blue-green "river," a kilometer wide and several meters deep, flowing beneath the graceful suspension bridges spaced at the floor's four quarters. In Thistledown's original designs, the parks along the capside bank did not exist; in their place had risen a "slosh" barrier one hundred meters higher than the opposite shore to mitigate the effects of the ship's acceleration. But in the early days of Thistledown's construction, that problem had been solved by the inertial damping machinery in the sixth chamber. The same machinery, centuries later, had allowed Konrad Korzenowski to contemplate creating the Way.

The chamber floor was flat, not banked; the park and the river formed bands of green and blue around the chamber's southern end.

Parks and forests covered the open spaces between neighborhoods. In plots scattered around the city, robots labored to finish structures destined to absorb the slowly growing population. Thistledown was ever young.

After seven centuries, the asteroid's inhabitants numbered seventy-five million. She had begun her voyage with five million.

Kerria clucked again and shook her head. We passed over Alexandria and into the third bore hole. Near the northern opening, she slowed the vehicle and sidled up against a raised entrance. A transfer passage reached across to the door of the tuberider and I disembarked. I waved to Kerria and stepped into the green and silver elevator. The air smelled of moisture and people, the clean but unmistakably human perfume of the city where I had lived two years of my youth.

"See you in a few days?" Kerria said, looking after me with some concern.

"Yeah."

"Cheers!"

I leaned my head to one side and said good-bye to her.

On the way down, I told my uniform to become civilian, standard day dress style one, mildly formal. I wanted to avoid attracting attention as a member of Way Defense, not all that common in the Naderite community.

The elevator took nine minutes to reach the chamber floor. I stepped out and walked down the short corridor into the chamber proper.

I crossed the Shahrazad bridge, listening to the whisper of the slender Fa River and the wind-blown rustle of thousands of long red ribbons blowing from the wires in the gentle breeze from the southern cap. Some neighborhood had chosen this decoration for the bridge, this month; in another month it might be crawling with tiny glowing robots.

Thistledown City had been built in the first two centuries after the starship's departure. With its chamber-spanning catenary cables, reaching from cap to cap and hung with slender white buildings, it seemed to dwarf Alexandria. It was obviously a Geshel showplace—and yet, in the worst conflicts between Geshels and Naderites on the starship, after the opening of the Way, many conservative and radical Naderites had been forced to move from their homes in Alexandria to new quarters in Thistledown

City. There were still strong Naderite neighborhoods near the southern cap. New construction was under way here as well, with arches being erected parallel to the caps, the greatest planned to be ten kilometers long.

A short walk took me to the tall cylindrical building where I had spent my early childhood. Through round hallways filled with sourceless illumination, my shadow forming and dissolving in random arcs around me, I returned to our old apartment.

My parents were away in Alexandria, to escape the celebrations—I had known that before coming here. I entered the apartment and sealed the door, then turned to the memory plaques in the living center.

For twenty-four years, I had kept one important secret, known to me and perhaps one other—the man or woman or being who had placed the old friend in this particular building, not anticipating that an inquisitive child might come upon him, almost by accident. I had come here to check up on a friend who had died before I was born, in his perfect hiding place, and make certain he was still hidden and undisturbed.

I—and no more than that one other, I was convinced—knew the last resting place of the great Konrad Korzenowski—the tomb not of his body but of what remained of his personality after his assassination by radical Naderites.

I connected with the building's memory, used a mouse agent to bypass personal sentries, as I had decades ago and at least once a year since, and dropped into the encrypted memory store.

Hello, I said.

The presence stirred. Even without a body, it seemed to smile. It was no longer human, half its character having been destroyed, but it could still interact and share warm memories. What remained of the great Korzenowski was vulnerably friendly. All of its caution removed, all of its self-protections destroyed, it could only be one thing—a giving and occasionally brilliant friend, ideal for a lonely young child unsure of himself. I kept this secret for one reason: damaged personalities could not be repaired, by Naderite law. If what remained of Korzenowski were to be discovered, it would be erased completely.

Hello, Olmy, it answered. *How is the Way?*

An hour later, I cabbed across the city to the mixed Geshel and Naderite "progressive" neighborhoods, favored by students and Way Defense members. There, in my small apartment, I linked with city memory, sent my planned locations for the next few days to the corps commanders, and removed my mutable uniform for purely civilian garb appropriate to the celebration: sky-blue pants, Earth-brown vest, pale green jacket, and light boots.

I returned to the train station.

As I joined the throng waiting on the platform, I looked for familiar faces and found none. Four years in service guarding against the Jarts on the extreme frontiers of the Way, four billion kilometers north of Thistledown, had given my Geshel acquaintances from university time to change not just partners and philosophies, but body patterns as well. If any of my student friends were in the crowd, I probably would not recognize them. I did not expect to find many Way Defenders here.

Except for raccoon stripes of pale blue around my eyes, I was still physically the same as I had been four years before. Arrogant, full of my own thoughts, headstrong and sometimes insensitive, judged brilliant by many of my peers and moody by many more—attractive to women in that strange way women are attracted to those who might hurt them—the only child of the most mannered and gracious of parents, praised frequently and punished seldom, I had reached my thirtieth year convinced of my courage from a minimum of testing, yet even more convinced there would be greater tests in store. I had abandoned the faith of my father and, in truth, had never understood the faith of my mother.

Thistledown, immense as it was, did not seem capable of containing my ambition. Even though I thought of myself as young, I certainly did not feel inexperienced. After all, I had served four years in Way Defense. I had participated in what seemed at the time to be important actions against the Jarts . . .

Yet now, caught up in crowds celebrating the silver anniversary of Thistledown's wedding with the Way, I seemed an anonymous bubble in a flowing stream, smaller than I had felt among the stars. What I was about to do dismayed me.

Music and pictures flowed over the largely Geshel crowd, narrative voices telling the details we all knew, Naderites and Geshels alike, by heart. Twenty-five years before, Korzenowski and his assistants had completed, connected, and opened the Way. From my childhood, the Way had beckoned, the only place—if *place* it could be called—likely to provide the tests I craved.

"In the history of humankind, has there ever been anything more auda-cious? Issuing from Thistledown's seventh chamber, the inside (there is no 'out-side') of an endless immaterial pipe fifty kilometers in diameter, smooth barren surface the color of newly cast bronze, the Way is a universe turned inside-out, threaded by an axial singularity called the flaw . . .

"And at regular intervals along the surface of the Way, potential open-ings to other places and times, histories and realities strung like beads . . ."

My parents—and most of my friends during my early youth—were devoted Naderites, of that semi-orthodox persuasion known as Voyagers. They believed it was simple destiny for humankind to have carved seven chambers out of the asteroid Juno, attached Beckmann drive motors, and converted the huge planetesimal into a starship, christened Thistledown. They believed—as did all but the extreme Naderites—that it was right and just to transport millions across the vast between the stars to settle fresh new worlds. Our family had lived for centuries in Alexandria, in the sec-ond and third chambers; we had all been born on Thistledown. We knew no other existence.

They simply did not believe in the creation of the Way. That, virtually all Naderites agreed, had been an abomination of the Korzenowski and the overly ambitious Geshels.

By releasing the bond between myself and the woman chosen for me in my youth at Ripen, I would finally end my life as a Naderite.

The trains arrived with a flourish as sheets of red and white arced over the train station. The crowd roared like a monstrous but happy animal, and pushed me across the platform to the doors spread wide to receive us. I was lost in a sea of faces smiling, grimacing, laughing, or just intent on keeping upright in the jostle.

We packed into the trains so closely we could scarcely move. A young woman jammed against me; she glanced up at me, face flushed, smiling hap-pily but a little scared. She wore Geshel fashion, but by the cut of her hair I saw she was from a Naderite family: rebelling, cutting loose, joining the

Geshel crowds on this least holy of celebrations—perhaps not caring in the least what the celebration was about.

"What's your name?" she asked, nibbling her lower lip, as if expecting some rebuff.

"Olmy," I said.

"You're lovely . . . with the mask. Did you do it yourself?"

I smiled down at her. She was perhaps five years younger than I, years past Ripen, an adult by any measure, Naderite or Geshel, but out of her place. She rubbed against me in the jostle, half deliberate. I felt little attraction to her, but some concern.

"You're going to see the Way? Visit Axis City?" I asked, bending to whisper in her ear.

"Yes!" she answered, eyes dancing. "And you?"

"Eventually. Family meeting you there?"

She flushed crimson. "No," she said.

"Bond meeting you there?"

"No."

"I'd think again," I said. "Geshels can get pretty wild when they party. The Way makes them drunk."

She drew back, blinking. "It's my hair, isn't it?" she said, lips flicking down suddenly. She fought to get away from me, pushing through the thick pack, glancing over her shoulder resentfully.

For the young—and at thirty, in a culture where one could live to be centuries, I could not think of myself as anything but very young—to be a Geshel was infinitely more exciting than being a Naderite. We all lived within a miracle of technology, and it seemed the soul of Thistledown had grown tired of confinement. The Geshels, who embraced the most extreme technologies and changes, offered the glamour of infinite adventure down the Way, contrasted with the weary certainty of centuries more in space, traveling with Thistledown in search of unknown planets around a single distant star.

Truly, we had outstripped the goals of our ancestors. To many of us, it seemed irrational to cling to an outmoded philosophy.

Yet something tugged at me, a lost sense of comfort and certainty . . .

The train passed through the asteroid rock beneath Thistledown City, more news of the celebration projected over the faces of the passengers. Stylized songs and histories flowed over and around us:

"For twenty-five years, the Way has beckoned to pioneers, an infinite frontier, filled with inexhaustible mystery—and danger. Though created by the citizens of Thistledown, even before it was opened, the Way was parasitized by intelligences both violent and ingenious, the Jarts. With the Jart influence now pushed back beyond the first two billion kilometers of the Way, gates have been opened at a steady pace, and new worlds discovered—"

I pressed through the crowd and left the train in the fourth chamber. The open-air platform held only a few sightseers, mostly Naderites, fleeing to the countryside of forests and waterways and deserts and mountains to escape the celebration. But even here the sky that filled the cylindrical chamber flashed with bright colors. The yellow-white tubelight that spanned the chamber's axis had been transformed into a pulsing work of art.

"They're overstepping it," grumbled an older Naderite man on the platform, dignified in his gray and blue robes. His wife nodded agreement. Twenty kilometers above us, the tubelight sparkled and glittered green and red. Snakelike lines of intense white writhed within the glow.

Forests rose on all sides of the station and resort buildings. From the floor, the chamber's immensity revealed itself with deceptive gradualness. For five kilometers on each side, as one stared along a parallel to the flat gray walls of asteroid rock and metal capping the cylinder, the landscape appeared flat, as it might have seemed on Earth. But the cylinder's curve lofted the land into a bridge that met high overhead, fifty kilometers away, lakes and forest and mountains suspended in a haze of atmosphere, transected by the unusual gaiety of the tubelight.

In the early days, the chambers had been called "squirrel cages"; though immense, they were roughly of the same proportions. The entire ship spun around its long axis, centrifugal force pressing things to the chamber floors with an acceleration of six-tenths' Earth's gravity.

My heart felt dull as lead. The station platform was just a few kilometers from the Vishnu Forest, where my bond would be waiting for me.

I walked, glad for the delay and the exercise.

Uleysa Ram Donnell stood alone by the outside rail beneath the pavilion where we had once jointly celebrated our Ripen. We had been ten then. She leaned against the wooden railing, backed by the giant trunks of redwood trees as old as Thistledown, a small black figure on the deserted dance floor. The high white dome shielded her from the rainbow flows of the tubelight. I walked up the steps slowly, and she watched with arms folded, face going quickly from pleasure at seeing me to concern. We had spent enough time together to prepare for being man and wife; we knew each other well enough to sense moods.

We embraced under the high white pine dome. "You've been neglectful," she said. "I've missed you." Uleysa was as tall as I and after we kissed, she regarded me at a level, large black eyes steady and a little narrowed by lids drawn with unspoken suspicion. Her face was lovely, clearly marked by intelligence and concern, nose gently arced, chin rounded and slightly withdrawn.

Our bond was special to our parents. They hoped for a strong Naderite union leading into city and perhaps even shipwide politics; her parents had spoken of our becoming Hexamon representatives, joint administers, part of the resurgence in Naderite leadership . . .

"You've changed," Uleysa said. "Your postings—" For a moment I saw something like little-girl panic in her eyes.

I said what I had to say, not proudly and not too quickly. My numbness grew into a kind of shock.

"Where will you go?" she asked. "What will you do?"

"Another life," I said.

"Do I bore you so much?"

"You have never *bored* me," I said with some anger. "The flaws are mine."

"Yes," she said, eyes slitted, teeth clenched. "I think they must be . . . *all* yours."

I wanted to kiss her, to thank her for the time we had had, the growing up, but I should have done that before I spoke. She pushed me away, held out her hands, and shook her head quickly.

I walked from beneath that dome feeling at once miserable and free.

Back on still another crowded train to the sixth chamber, I simply felt empty.

Uleysa had not cried. I had not expected her to. She was strong and proud and would have no difficulty finding another bond. But we both knew one thing: I had betrayed her, and the plans of our families.

I intended to sink myself wholeheartedly into the celebrations. Getting off the train in the sixth chamber, standing in the Korzenowski Center with other celebrants waiting to be carried by construction cars to the seventh, I watched patters of rain fall from thick clouds onto the transparent roof.

It almost always rained in the sixth chamber. The carpets of machinery that covered most of the chamber, transferring and shaping forces that were beyond my own comprehension, created heat that needed to be drained away, and this ancient method had proved best.

I thought of Uleysa's face, her narrowed eyes, and an unexpected stab of grief hit me. My awareness of where I was, and who I was, curled inward like a snail's horns. Implants did not stop me from having negative emotions . . . And I did not try to blank them. Uleysa had no affect controls. I deserved my own share of suffering.

Someone touched me, and I thought for a moment I was blocking a line into the cars. But the cars had not yet arrived. I turned and saw Yanosh Ap Kesler. "You look all beaten up," he said. "Without the bruises."

I smiled grimly. "It's my own fault," I said.

He wore around his neck the pictor then becoming fashionable, though he did not speak in picts with me. Otherwise his dress was of the style called atonic, mildly conservative, blue and beige midwaist, black leggings, charcoal gray slippers, all fabrics flat, lacking image inlays.

"Yes, well, I've been trying to reach you for two days now."

"I've been on duty," I said. Yanosh was an old friend. We had met as youths at the Naderite Union College in Alexandria; I had performed favors, not too difficult, that obscured some of his less discreet escapades. All in all he had been a better judge of circumstance and character and had risen in his career much more rapidly than I. But I was in no real mood for companionship, even his.

"That's how I traced you. I convinced someone I needed to learn your whereabouts . . . *desperately.*"

"Rank hath its privileges," I said.

He frowned and half twisted his upper body before turning to shoot back at me, "Stop being so damned opaque. Where are you going?"

"To the seventh chamber."

"Axis City?"

"Eventually."

"Join me. No need to wait in line."

Four months before, Yanosh had been elected as third administer for the seventh chamber and the Way. He had come to this center of power and activity from a background similar to mine. Son of devout Naderites, he had gravitated to the Geshels shortly after the opening of the Way, as so many others had.

We all respected the philosophy of the Good Man, crusader and wary critic of the technology that had brought on the Death, but that had been ten centuries before.

"More privilege?" I asked.

"Just friendship," Yanosh said.

"You haven't spoken to me in a year."

"You haven't exactly made yourself accessible," Yanosh said.

"I might prefer crowds now."

"It's important," Yanosh said. He took my arm. I hung back, but he tightened his grip. Rather than be dragged, I relented and walked beside him. He palmed his way through a security door and we walked down a chill hallway to a maintenance shaft. Lights formed a line down a long, wide tunnel, vanishing north into darkness.

"What could be so important?"

"You can listen to something incredible, as a favor," Yanosh said. "And maybe I can save your career." He whistled and a small sleek cab with Nexus markings came out of the shadows, floating a few centimeters above the gritty black floor.

"You're being investigated by the Naderites," Yanosh told me as the cab traversed the tunnel in the wall between the sixth and seventh chambers.

"Why?" I asked, smiling ironically. "I'm in Way Defense. I've just cut myself off from the last Naderite ritual in my life—"

"I know," he said. "Poor Uleysa. If I were you, I'd have tried to convince her to come with me. She's a fine woman."

"I wouldn't do that to her," I said, staring through the window at the flashing maintenance lights. Lumbering dark robots moved aside to allow our quick passage. "She tolerated my lapses. She didn't agree with them."

"Still, she might have appreciated being tempted. Should I look her up and console her?" Yanosh asked. "It's about time I found a family triad."

I shrugged, but some tic of my expression amused him.

"Much as I need to renew my connections with the Voyagers now, I wouldn't be so rude," he said. "The Naderites are going to push for control of the Nexus in a few weeks. They'll probably get it. The cost of pushing back the Jarts is drawing grumbles even among the hardiest Geshel administers. If Naderites take over, the Nexus changes its face—and all us juniors get drudge work for a decade. My administer's career is hanging by a few thin threads. And, I might add, the Way could be in peril."

I stared at him, genuinely shocked. "They couldn't put together the coalition to do that."

"Never underestimate the people who made us."

The cab emerged on a straight highway beneath brilliant pearly light, tan and snow-colored sand on either side. We were five kilometers spinward from the public access to the seventh chamber. Behind us, the gray heights of the seventh chamber's southern cap receded, an immense cliff wall.

Ahead, there was no cap . . . No end.

The Way stretched on forever, or at least into incomprehensible and immeasurable distances. This was what Korzenowski had done—making the Thistledown bigger on the inside than the outside, opening up endless potential and adventure and danger, and for that, he had been assassinated shortly after the Way's opening.

He could not have known about the Jarts.

"It's a matter of economic stability, to be sure," Yanosh said. "But some high passions have been engaged in the past twenty-five years."

"There are gates being opened. Naderites are signing up to immigrate."

"Politics isn't a rational art," Yanosh said, "even on Thistledown. We have too much of Earth in us."

I looked up. In the center of the tubelight that flowed from the southern cap, a thin line made itself visible more as an uncanny absence. The creation of the Way had by some metaphysical necessity I only half understood made a singularity that ran the length of Korzenowski's pipe-shaped universe: the flaw. Threaded on the flaw, sixty kilometers from the southern cap's bore hole, a suspended city was being built a section at a time.

Spinward, a new section lay on the empty white sand, covered by robots like ants on a huge sugar cake; it would become the remaining half of Axis Nader, a concession to those forces that did not even believe in the Way. Three previously threaded sections or precincts of the Axis City already floated over us, white and steel and gray, great cylindrical monuments studded with towers that reached a kilometer and more from their main bodies. The city gleamed, startlingly clear seen through the thinner atmosphere that covered the floor of this section of the Way.

At the end of the highway, sixty kilometers from the southern cap, a private cable hung from the city overhead. The cab stopped beside the cable's gondola.

"What do they think I've done?" I asked Yanosh.

"I don't know. Nobody does. It's something not even the First Administer of Alexandria is willing to talk about."

"I'm a small soldier in a very big army," I said. "A lowly rank seven. Not worth the fuss."

"That's what the sensible folk are saying . . . this month. Secret allegations too dire to be spoken, among extremists who are not supposed to have a voice even with the radicals . . ." He turned to me as the door to the gondola opened. "Make any sense?"

It did, but I could never tell him, or anyone else for that matter. Korzenowski, in theory, could be revived if Geshels changed the laws. He could become a very powerful symbol. Perhaps the only other who knew had had a change of heart, or had been indiscreet.

"No," I said.

"We'll talk more in my office."

Yanosh's office opened to an outer wall of the finished first precinct of Axis Nader. Nexus offices clustered like quartz crystals in this external neighborhood.

"Let me counter one absurdity by relating another," Yanosh said. "This one's more important by far, actually. Have you heard of Jaime Carr Lenk?"

He perched on the edge of his narrow workboard. Details of Axis City construction flashed in display around and behind him.

"He headed a group of radical Naderites, calling themselves divaricates. He disappeared," I said.

"We know where he's gone," Yanosh said. "He took four thousand followers—divaricates—and a few humble machines and went off to make Utopia."

I wondered if Yanosh was joking. He loved stories of human folly. "Where?" I asked.

"Wrong first question," Yanosh said. He studied my face intently.

The limits of Thistledown were well known. Hiding places could be found . . . But not for so many. Then the enormity of this disappearance struck me: first, the sheer numbers, four thousand citizens, and next, the fact that their disappearance had gone unnoticed and unpublicized. I became at once intensely interested and wary.

"*How*, then?" I asked.

"Their devotion to Lenk was complete. They even adopted his name and gave him honorifics, like Nader himself. Each carefully laid a trail of deception. Individually, or as a family or group, they claimed to be off on a knowledge retreat, in one chamber or another, in one city or another, under the laws of the coalition, not to be pursued or questioned by Nexus agencies until they returned to secular life. As well, Lenk chose whole families, husbands with their wives, children with parents, triad groupings together . . . No loose fragments. They vanished and left nary a ripple, five years ago. Only Lenk himself was reported missing. The others . . ." Yanosh shrugged.

"Where did he take them?" I asked.

"Down the Way," Yanosh said. "With the complicity of two apprentice gate openers, he created an illegal passage in a geometry stack."

"No one knew?" My amazement grew to incredulity. I was relieved not to have to think about my other predicament . . . if it was a predicament, and not a false alarm.

Yanosh shrugged again. "We've been distracted, needless to say, but that's a weak excuse. They chose a stack region near the frontier, close to Jart boundaries. They used the conflict of 748 as a cover. Slipped in behind defense forces . . . Disguised themselves as a support unit. Nobody detected them. They had help—and we're still investigating.

"Lenk had connections, apparently," Yanosh said. "Somebody told him about Lamarckia."

"Lamarckia?" The name sounded exotic.

"A closely held secret."

"The Nexus?" I asked, mocking dismay. "Keeping secrets?"

Yanosh hardly blinked. "An extraordinary world was discovered by the first gate prospectors about twelve years ago. Very terrestrial. They named it Lamarckia. There was little time to explore, so after making a brief survey, they closed the gate, marked a node, and saved it for future study. All such discoveries have been kept secret, to prevent just such occurrences as this."

"How do we know about Lenk, after all this time?" I asked.

"One of the immigrants returned," Yanosh said. "He stole one of two clavicles in Lenk's possession and came back through a tangle of world-lines in the stack. A defense flawship found him more than half dead in a depleted pressure suit. It brought him here."

Yanosh stared through the transparent floor at the immense cranes and webs of cables and flowing strings of purple and green tracting fields lifting pieces of the new precinct from the floor of the Way. "Some say we may never be able to return to Lamarckia, because of what they've done," he said. "Others I trust more say it may be difficult, but not impossible. The gate openers are disturbed that a clavicle could fall into Jart hands—if they have hands. We could lose control of that region at any time. The Nexus has agreed to send a mid-rank gate opener to check out the damage. They've asked for a single investigator to accompany him. Your name came up. I wasn't the one who brought it up."

"Oh?" I smiled, disbelieving. He did not return my smile.

"It may be the most beautiful world we've yet found. Some Geshels privately speculated Lamarckia might become our refuge if we lost the war." He lifted an eyebrow critically. "It's the most Earthlike of the ten worlds we've had time to open."

"Why didn't we develop it?"

"Could we have held it if we did?" Yanosh asked. "The Jarts pushed us beyond that stack, and we pushed them. Back and forth three times since its discovery."

Little or nothing was known about Jart anatomy, psychology, or history.

Even less was known about how they had made their own *reversed* gate just after the Way's creation, and before it had been opened and attached to *Thistledown*.

The Jarts had begun a furious surprise offensive at the moment of the opening, killing thousands. Ever since, the war had been waged unmercifully by both sides, using all the weapons available—including the physics of the Way itself. Those who had built it, and who accessed its many realities strung like beads, could also make large stretches of it inhospitable to anything living.

Yanosh looked at me squarely, intense green eyes challenging. "The Nexus would like someone to cross to Lamarckia and retrieve the remaining clavicle. While that someone is there, he might as well investigate the planet more thoroughly. We know little—a slim surveyor's report. Lamarckia appears to be a paradise, but its biology is unusual. We need to learn what damage Lenk has done."

"You didn't suggest me immediately?"

Yanosh smiled.

I shook my head dubiously. "My reputation is that of a stubborn but capable renegade. I doubt my division commanders would recommend me."

"They asked me about you, and I said you could do it—might even relish something like this. But frankly, this isn't an assignment I'd give to an old friend."

Yanosh suspected I was bored as a simple soldier and needed a chance to excel; he knew without my telling him that my personality chafed in Way Defense. The Jart situation had settled for the time being into a drawn-out stalemate. Being brought into a Nexus action—and a difficult action at that—was a guarantee of rapid advancement, if I succeeded.

Yanosh knew I had once had some social connections with divaricates. My mother and father had known a number of them; I had once met Jaime Car Lenk fifteen years before. I knew their ways.

"Lamarckia has been dropped into my lap by the Geshel leaders in the Nexus," Yanosh said. "It's my own kind of trial by fire. And a test. If you agree and succeed, we both benefit . . . So I said I would ask, but I did not specifically back you."

"And the immigrants?"

"Bringing them back will be politically difficult. Divaricates are peculiar in their attitude toward the Way. They abhor it, but they think they can use it. They have always spoken of a homeland away from Thistledown and the Geshels. A new, fresh Earth. But in truth, for the time being the Geshels are still in power in the Nexus, and we're more interested in the planet than in the people. If they've interfered, and it seems inevitable that they would—being who they are—then we'll bring them back, and Lenk will stand trial. It would give the radicals a bad stain on their record."

"That's grim," I said.

Yanosh did not disagree. "It's a grand assignment for somebody," he said. "An entire planet, yours to explore. Not that it's going to be easy. I have to admit, in some ways, it suits you, Olmy."

I wondered if I was being too sensitive about my secret. I had not spent the last five years just soldiering; and Yanosh, or the people behind him, were not the first outside of Way Defense to find me useful. This, however, was well beyond my proven capabilities.

"Are there other reasons I've been chosen?" I asked.

"Whatever you've done to displease the Naderites, this gets you out of the political war zone. The mission could be a kind of oubliette, actually, a tight little closet where nobody can reach you, until we sort out the political situation. Whatever it is you're involved in . . ."

"I've never been other than loyal to the Hexamon," I said.

"The Nexus appreciates loyalty as well."

"You make fine distinctions," I said. "Power comes and goes. I render unto the caesars."

Yanosh looked away, eyelids lowered with sudden weariness. "You've become an enigma to most of our friends. Where *do* your loyalties lie—with Geshels, or with Naderites?"

"Korzenowski was a Naderite," I said, "and he built the Way."

"He paid for his presumption," Yanosh said.

"Where do *yours* lie?"

"You didn't answer my question."

"Fortunately for us all, we don't have to reveal our loyalties to serve in defense, or in the Nexus. I've served Geshel ends for years."

"But Uleysa . . ." Yanosh raised an eyebrow, significant of so many things unsaid, all that had happened since we last met. Throughout our friendship, there had been moments—quite a few of them—when Yanosh's perceptiveness irritated me.

"A mistake," I said. "Not political. Personal. But if the Nexus wants something done—why send just one?"

Yanosh's look intensified, as if he would see through me. "Your face. Your eyes. You've never tried to blend in, have you?"

"I've never had to."

"It's more than that." He shook his head. "Never mind." He sighed. "I wish I had been born before the Hexamon opened the Way. Things were much simpler."

"And more boring. I wonder how much confidence you have in me."

"To tell the truth, I was maneuvered into agreeing to interview you," Yanosh said. "By skilled tacticians whose motives are never clear. I think you can do the job, of course; I don't think it's *my* hide they're after. And if you agree, you'll take considerable pressure off me."

"Somebody values Lamarckia."

"The presiding minister herself," Yanosh said. "So I hear. She wants to know more about Lamarckia, but can't push a major expedition through the Nexus just now. Jarts must be our main concern. In a way, you're a chip in a massive gamble. The presiding minister will gamble that they can place you on Lamarckia, alone, to gather information and make judgments. When she convinces the Nexus that a larger team should be sent, their mission will go all the more smoothly. They connect with you, you fill them in, and together, we all lay a stronger claim on Lamarckia."

"I see," I said.

"I believe she'll win the gamble, even if the Naderites take control of the Nexus. Her arguments are unassailable. In a few weeks or months, if the geometry stack cooperates, you'll have lots of company."

"And if they can't get Nexus approval, and the gate can't be opened?"

"You'll have to find Lenk's second clavicle and open your own gate."

"That does sound like an oubliette," I said.

"Nobody believes the mission will be safe or easy."

To me, that sounded like a challenge, as much as Yanosh's flickering enthusiasm. "Perfect," I said. In that small office, with its spectacular view, crowded with perspectives of progress on Axis City, I smiled at my old friend. "Of course, I'm interested," I said.

"Interest isn't enough, I fear," Yanosh said, pulling back and folding his hands. "I need an answer. Soon."

My first instinct was to refuse the assignment. Despite recent setbacks and confusions, I did have my plans, and they had a certain elegance. I also had my responsibilities . . . Which made me far more important and valuable than I seemed, than even Yanosh or anyone in the Nexus could know.

But I was acutely aware of my lack of experience. My time spent in Way Defense had largely been wasted. *I will be nothing unless I am tested and tempered.* The counter-argument sounded much more compelling: *You'll certainly be nothing if you're dead, or lost and forgotten on a world closed off from the Way.*

The voice of reason was about to prevail. But another voice leaped ahead and answered for me, the voice my father had warned me about and my mother deplored.

"I'll go," I said.

Yanosh gave me a shrewd look, then leaned forward and grabbed my shoulder firmly. "Grand impetuosity. It's what I expected."

I had become more than a little cynical, with my torn loyalties. I did not know who I was any longer. Getting away—completely away—seemed a real solution. My secret would keep, perhaps be in less peril if I was gone.

This is the way history sometimes works. Simple connections, simple decisions, with untold consequences.

I studied the secret Dalgesh report, made by three surveyors immediately after Lamarckia's discovery. Lamarckia was the second planet of a yellow sun, born in a relatively metal-poor galactic region, not correlated with any known place in our own galaxy. The surveyors had barely had two days to do their work before the gate was closed, and so their findings were incomplete. They had left three monitors on the largest continent but had launched no satellites. The photos and recordings showed a world at once familiar and extraordinary.

I was particularly interested in Jaime Carr Lenk's logistics planning. The Good Lenk had selectively abandoned divaricate restrictions to make the immigration possible. There were no tested and confirmed native foodstuffs on Lamarckia, and of course no support for machines beyond what the immigrants themselves could transport. The expedition had carried six months' food and personal water purification systems. They also took selected traditional seed stock—grains, some fruit and lumber trees, a few herbs and ornamentals. Though Lamarckia lacked the complex terrestrial ecosystem to make farming easy, these monoculture crops had been designed by humans to need nothing more than human-supplied chemicals. In effect, humans were their essential ecosystem. The chemicals, the immigrants believed, could be found or synthesized on Lamarckia.

The immigrants took no animals. For machines, they transported three small factories for making tools and electronics, and twenty multipurpose tractors, all capable of self-repair.

In one way, Lenk had stuck to his divaricate beliefs: The immigrants had refused to take nutriphores, highly efficient artificial organics that could easily have fed them indefinitely. Nutriphores, however, had not existed in Nader's time; and the Good Man had been highly suspicious of genetic engineering.

Yanosh accompanied me to the chambers in Axis Nader where the informer now resided. His name was Darrow Jan Fima. He was a small, worried man, dressed in simple dun-colored clothes. Now that he had regained his health—in decidedly advanced medical conditions not favored by divaricates—he was eager to tell his story again, to provide all the details he knew.

He told Yanosh and me of Moonrise, the village and ferry landing near his point of exit—the most likely place for the emergence of a new gate; of the towns and travel routes by river and sea, the short history of the Lenk immigrants—privations, arguments over the planning of this one-way voyage, rivalries between quickly split factions, the unavoidable politics of any group of people of that size . . . And more about Lamarckia's biology, what little Lenk's immigrants had come to understand.

At the last, contrite, weeping, perhaps only half rational, the informer had told us of the Adventists, an opposition group formed to resist Lenk's rule. They had never been very effective; they waited for the Hexamon to send people to bring them back to Thistledown. In each village, he said, they had placed an operative to prepare the way for the Hexamon. Rumors of Hexamon investigators had acquired the status of folk myth. But nobody had come.

Darrow Jan Fima had argued with his fellow Adventists, broken ranks, pretended to serve Lenk, worked his way over a year into Lenk's inner council . . .

And stolen the clavicle.

"Why did you take so long?" the informer asked plaintively. "I had to lie, to do so many evil things." Finally, he whispered his confession to the sins of his people. "We have sullied the many mothers of life."

Then, smiling as if about to give me a gift, "Lamarckia is not a bad place to die . . ."

I did not believe that. He had left, after all.

I began my training. Yanosh accorded me all the resources I needed. And I made appointments to have all my supplements removed.

That would have pleased my mother, but of course she would not know.

The spindle-shaped silver flawship coursed down the center of the Way at three hundred kilometers per second. I sat in one of two well-padded white seats in the ship's nose blister and stared ahead into a funnel-shaped brightness that seemed full of eerie promise. I was caught between numbness, exaltation, and simple terror.

I fingered the pink patches at the base of my skull and on my wrist, feeling a new loneliness. Since the death of my father, I had given myself a variety of mental enhancements not condoned by him: tiny devices in my head and neck that sped thoughts, improved memory, gave me certain abilities and knowledge bases, and also made direct internal connections to city memory, to millions of individuals and thousands of libraries.

To pass undetected among the Lenk divaricates, who carried no such implants, I had been stripped of my extra voices and eyes and minds. Within my thoughts there was only my own self now. I felt a peculiar embarrassment: I was naked in a way that had nothing to do with clothing or revealed flesh.

The flawship began its long, gentle deceleration. Barely four meters from where I sat, the flaw glowed pink, brightening as the clamps spaced within the middle of the ship applied pressure. It was not friction that slowed the ship, but the clamps' intrusion into a forbidden region of space-time.

"Greetings, Ser Olmy Ap Sennon." Gate opener Frederik Ry Ornis, tall and thin as a praying mantis, stretched and bent himself into the blister beside me, slid his trunk into the seat and let its plush white cushions enfold his hips and chest. "How long since you've hugged the flaw?"

Whatever my concessions to progressive Geshel fashions and technologies, I had at least kept my natural body plan. Ry Ornis was of the new breed that explored more radical shapes.

"A few years. And never this far north," I said.

"Not many of us have been this far," Ry Ornis said with a rueful look. "Not recently. The Jarts are less than a million kilometers from here." He stretched a long, five-jointed finger and pointed elegantly ahead.

Gate openers such as Ry Ornis had acquired immense power and prestige. Part of me envied him.

"One hour until we go down to the wall," Ry Ornis said. "I'm not looking forward to this."

"Why?" I asked.

Ry Ornis gave me a dour glance. "Anxious to begin your first mission?" he asked.

"I suppose," I said, grinning.

"Ready to show your loyalty to the Hexamon Nexus . . . Ripe for adventure?"

My grin faded at his sardonic tone. I shrugged against the green and purple glow of the tracting fields.

"You don't have to *find* this place again," Ry Ornis complained. He grimaced ruefully. "It's been accessed by amateurs. I can imagine what they did to isolate and pull up the right world-line. They've probably mangled the embryonic gate and reduced our accesses to at most three or four. So . . . I have no room for error. If I fumble a few world-lines, it's a one-way trip for you, and Lamarckia is of no use to anybody."

I did not like Ry Ornis much; most gate openers made me nervous. Their talents were on such a different plane, their personalities radically opposed to my own.

The minutes stretched. Ry Ornis seemed mesmerized by the endless spectacle outside the blister. He leaned across the gap between our seats. "Frankly, the council members and administers have too much on their minds. If Lamarckia was really important, don't you think they'd have expended more effort than sending just you?"

My emotions burst forth in a wry laugh. "The thought's occurred to me," I admitted.

"Why did you agree to do this?"

"It suits me," I said. "Why did you?"

Ry Ornis grimaced again, his face contorting like a circus mask. "Among the gate openers, advancement comes at the expense of obedience. Is it the same in Way Defense?"

"I don't know," I said, not entirely truthful. "I'm only a seven."

Ry Ornis stared at me. "Even so," he said.

"Can you get me to Lamarckia?"

"Blunt questions deserve blunt answers," he said. He took a deep breath. "Unfortunately, I don't know." The flawship had slowed to a few thousand kilometers an hour; soon it would come to a complete stop. "It's not an exact science. Every gate opener has illusions. My illusion is that the more I know about a place, the better I'm able to sniff out its world-lines."

"In some ways, it resembles Earth," I said.

"I've read the Dalgesh report. I know the size and rough characteristics. I'm asking for a personal opinion. What makes it so *interesting*?"

I didn't understand what he was getting at. "There are humans on it now . . ."

"The story about our being able to sniff out humanoid life is quite wrong. That's not what a gate opener looks for. We look for *interest*."

"What do you think is interesting?" I asked.

Ry Ornis leaned his head to one side. The tracting fields had withdrawn. We were moving at less than a hundred kilometers an hour and the flaw no longer glowed. "Lamarckia defies all we've learned of evolution and the origins of life."

"The informer seems to think it does. He called it a 'New Mother.' He thought the immigrants would destroy it."

"Now that's *interest*." Ry Ornis nodded approval. "Big events mark world-lines. If Lenk's people are going to reshape the history of a planet . . . I'll get you there," he said.

The flawship pilot pulled herself forward and poked her head between us. "Enjoying the view?" she asked.

"Immensely," I said.

"We're both nervous," Ry Ornis said.

The pilot bent her lips and cocked her head with an expression of regret. "Well, this won't reassure you. The Jarts know we're here—no surprise—and we have maybe thirty minutes before they investigate. The borders here are flexible." She gave us an appraising look. "Not a top-priority mission, I take it?"

I lifted myself from the seat and went aft. Ry Ornis followed, staring at the pilot with feigned affront. "Some of us might disagree," he said haughtily.

I found that a clownish response. *Perhaps I deserve no better than him. We are, after all, the agents of a measured response—a gamble. Not top-priority.*

Ry Ornis and I descended from the flawship in a small transfer craft. The journey took less than ten minutes. The deltoid vehicle maneuvered in a cautious spiral. The closer it came to the wall, the more weight it acquired. And, contrary to its name, the wall behaved more like a floor—a gravitating surface. The craft landed lightly, with no discernible jolt.

Ry Ornis and I put on light pressure suits. He picked up a box not much larger than his head and tucked it under his arm. We nodded to an eye conveying our images to the pilot waiting in the flawship above; then we stepped outside.

Beneath our boots, the wall felt as hard as rock. Ry Ornis immediately set out across the bare bronze surface, long legs carrying him two meters with each stride. He removed a clavicle from the box, dropped the box carelessly, and immediately gripped the bars of the device, swinging it back and forth ahead of him. I had read of old-fashioned dowsing rods, once a fad on Earth; Ry Ornis wielded his clavicle in much the same way as an ancient seeker after water.

Beneath us lay one of the fabled, fearful regions called geometry stacks, where the Way's physics adjusted itself unpredictably—often compared to a wrinkle in the skin of a many-dimensional worm. I did not like the comparison.

"This whole region is knotted," the gate opener said, voice rough, his tone between wonder and disgust. "What color is it? My God, what does it *smell* like?"

Puzzled by the questions, I did not answer. Best not to interrupt, I decided.

Ry Ornis continued, "Do you know a geometry stack *hurts*? When we search it? It gives us colossal headaches that are tough to cure. Somebody's clearly been here before us, though. They've left their own kind of dirty fingerprints: bulges; world-lines pulled out of place; accesses ruined. My God, what *amateurs*."

I followed him at a measured pace. I carried nothing; I would take nothing with me but the clothes beneath my pressure suit. All of my baggage was internal—weeks of training and education, the careful transfer of relevant knowledge from my supplements to biological memory. . . .

The pilot's voice sounded in our helmets. "The Jarts are painting us every few seconds. I'd be happier if I could leave soon."

Ry Ornis said, "I can't guarantee putting you on Lamarckia at any particular time." His voice dripped disgust. "It'll be very difficult to get you to within a decade of when the informer made his temporary gate. Lenk must have left a nipple, a node, or the informer could never have returned at all. But that's gone now."

The gate opener stood straight, his tall, emaciated figure and white suit a startling contrast to our surroundings. Light played tricks in this immense featureless, shadowless pipe. To stand and stare at the distant curve of the wall, rising above the flat nearness until it arched high overhead, disoriented me even more. I squinted up at the plasma tube, running the length of the flaw to a dazzling blur of brightness in the south, illuminating the Way for millions of kilometers . . . But ending not far north of where we stood, leaving the Jarts in a darkness all their own.

I looked down to keep from getting dizzy. My body had no help overcoming feelings of vertigo. Naked *inside*.

The gate opener bent over, gripping the bars of the clavicle, passing its spherical head a few centimeters above the surface. "Found something," he announced. "Knots retied. Some attempt to renormalize, to heal, apparently."

"Heal?" I asked.

Ry Ornis did not hear, or simply ignored me. "Most of these lines pour out into empty expanse. So much desolation, measure without interest.

Makes us all very lonely. Here a solitary star, there an airless ball of rock. So easy to be attracted by false worlds, dreams of futures not yet accessible, not yet quite real. Ten years, twenty years . . . Maybe two dozen years. No guarantees. I might drop you before Lenk's immigrants arrived. Wouldn't want that. And no way to return, for any of you . . . must be careful to leave a few more accesses."

"Please do," I said, shivering. I had pictured this time as a trouble-free interlude, a brief moment watching the precise and even inhuman work of a master gate opener. Instead, the assistants to the presiding minister had assigned this stick figure, this insect man with his long face and propensity to babble. *Perhaps they really do want to lose me.*

"Found something. Come here, Ser Olmy." Ry Ornis beckoned for me to step closer and watch.

I walked up beside him and peered at the cryptic display between the bars of his clavicle.

Ry Ornis drew his gloved finger lightly over the colors on the display. "See this?" I saw only twisted lines, flashing fields of green and blue. "An access. It tells me it's a locus of extreme *interest*. Nothing around it . . . No doubt that's Lamarckia. And it follows chronologically what must be the Lenk access. But where do I shift it? Where do I drop you in Lamarckia's world-line? Here to here," sketching across the display with his finger, "comparative boredom, boredom, nothing . . . but here." He smiled radiantly behind his visor. "These are exquisite loci. I look for things of interest to humans, Ser Olmy, and I find them. If Lamarckia is of interest all by itself, then these points on its world-line are even more interesting to us. To you and to me. Understand?"

"No," I said.

Ry Ornis shifted his finger again, waving the clavicle gently. "Loci of large human-centered events. Lamarckia is a huge event behind them, unfamiliar . . . But definitely ready to change. Shall I place you at one of the most fascinating loci, Ser Olmy?"

"Just get me there," I said. I bit my lower lip, trying to still my growing anxiety. Courage seemed a sorry abstraction.

"Within a decade or two of Lenk's access. Can't be certain. It's really the best I can do."

"Do it. Please, just *do it*." I had already disgraced my family and the memory of my father by cleaving to the progressive Geshels and putting unnatural devices within my body, by signing up in Way Defense, by rejecting the woman I had pledged to. I did not want to disgrace myself again by failing here and now.

"No reason to be nervous. No gate will open if I can't put you someplace truly *interesting*."

I wanted to hit the man.

"So I spread my carpet here . . . And dub this gate number thirty-two, of stack region twelve . . ." Ry Ornis traced a glowing red line on the wall with the sphere of the clavicle. "Stand aside."

I stood aside.

A bump rose from the surface of the Way, five meters wide with a dimple in the middle. Red and green lines danced across its fresh surface, vibrated rapidly, and became the familiar color of fresh bronze. Ry Ornis spread it by backing away, trailing the clavicle behind him. A disk-shaped canopy grew over the new gate.

Mouth dry as stone, head cold as ice, I climbed the side of the bump on hands and knees, perched on the rim of the dimple, and stared down into a storm of fluid darkness.

"It'll take you where you need to go," Ry Ornis said. "And it will vanish after you."

I stood erect on the lip of the gate, pushed by the very last of my limited courage. I would walk straight ahead, in a straight line, and come out where the informer had left Lamarckia.

"Just walk," the gate opener said, voice hollow in my helmet. "Don't forget to remove your suit halfway across. There will be air from Lamarckia in the gate at that point."

"All right," I said.

"Only two more accesses left, I judge. How you'll come back, I don't know. Good luck."

I looked over my shoulder, saw the gaunt white-suited figure, the eye-twisting uniformity beyond and above . . . turned, and met another kind of illusion, even more extreme.

Here, there were no straight lines, would never be any unswerving paths. In the gate, I would crawl through a hole punched into all possible worlds, a fistula between the Way and somewhere else . . .

I had to put complete faith in Ry Ornis. My body did not think that was wise. I clenched my teeth, pushed one leg forward, then the other. Felt the pressure build around me. I removed the suit and dropped its pieces on the gate's slope behind me. I now wore only the clothes that might be worn by one of Lenk's immigrants.

I could no longer see the Way or Ry Ornis.

"Gate's pressurized. *Hurry.*" The gate opener's voice echoed around me like the buzz of an insect, issuing from the discarded suit. Ahead, I saw a swirl of purple and red and black, bands of blue and a bright arc of yellow-orange: my destination, viewed through the distorting lens of the gate.

I closed my eyes, held out my arms, made one last step forward . . .

And fell feet-first into lumpy wet soil, spattering my boots and brown pants. For a moment I thought I would fall over. I held out my hands, knelt with boots firm in the muck, and steadied myself. Behind me, the wheeling darkness dilated to a point, sucked at my coat's fabric, and abandoned me in a tiny eddy of air.

CHAPTER ONE

The sun hung two handspans above the horizon. Late morning, early evening: I could not judge. I stood on the crest of a low hill, between thick black trunks smooth as glass. Behind me, a dense enclosure of more black trunks. And ahead . . . detail rushed upon me; I sucked it in with frantic need.

Red and purple forest pushed over low boxy hills, fading to pink and lavender as the hills receded toward the horizon. Mist curled languidly between. Immense trees like the skeletons of cathedral towers punctuated the forest every few hundred meters, pink crowns perched atop four slender vaulting legs, rising high over the rest of the forest. Above the hills, sky beckoned crystal blue with mottled patches of more red and purple, as if reflecting the forest. In fact, the forest inhabited the sky: tethered gas-filled balloons ascended from the distant stands of black-trunked trees into thin shredded-ribbon clouds.

Everything glowed with serene yellow light and brilliant blood-hued life. Everything, related. For as far as the eye could see—what Darrow Jan Fima had called Elizabeth's Zone, one creature, one *thing*.

From where I stood, at the top of a rise overlooking the broad, dark olive Terra Nova River, Lamarckia hardly seemed *violated*. Not a human in sight, not a curl of smoke or rise of structure. Somewhere below, hidden in the tangle of smooth black trunks, huge round leaves, and purple fans, the ferry landing was supposed to be . . . And inland a few hundred meters along a dirt and gravel path, both hidden in the dense pack, the village of Moonrise.

I touched my clothes self-consciously. How out-of-place would I look?

I realized I had been holding my breath. I inhaled deeply. It was a sweet and startling breath. The air smelled of fresh water, grapes, tea leaves, and a variety of odors I can only describe as skunky-sweet. Rich aromas wafted from nearby extrusions resembling broad purple flowers, with fleshy centers. They smelled like bananas, spicy as cinnamon. The extrusions opened and closed, twitching at the end of each cycle. Then they withdrew altogether with thin, high chirps.

I reached out my hand to stroke the smooth black curve of a trunk. At my touch, the bark parted to form a kind of stoma, red and pink pulp within. A drop of translucent white fluid oozed from the gash, which quickly closed when I lifted my hand.

"Not a tree," I murmured. The Dalgesh report—by the original surveyors—had called them "arborid scions." And this was not a forest, but a *silva*.

There were no plants or animals as such on Lamarckia. The first surveyors, in the single day they had spent on the planet, had determined that within certain zones, all apparently individual organisms, called scions, in fact belonged to a larger organism, which they had called an ecos. No scion could breed by itself; they did not act alone. An ecos was a single genetic organism, creating within itself all the diverse parts of an ecosystem, spread over large areas—in some cases, dominating entire continents.

Each ecos was ruled, the surveyors had theorized, by what they called a seed mistress, or queen. Neither the surveyors—nor the immigrants, according to Jan Fima—had ever seen such a queen, however; understanding of Lamarckian biology and planetary science in general had still been primitive among the immigrants when the informer left.

Above, the black trunks spread great round parasol-leaves, broad as outstretched arms, powdery gray at their perimeters, rose and bloodred in their centers. The parasols rubbed edges in a canopy-clinging current of air, making a gentle shushing noise, like a mother calming an infant. Black granular dust fell in thin drifts on my head; not pollen, certainly not ash. I rubbed some between my fingers, smelled it, but did not taste.

The last light of the orange sun warmed my face. So this was not morning but evening; the day was ending. I savored the glow. It felt wonderfully, thrillingly familiar; but it was the first sunlight I had ever directly experienced. Until now, I had spent my whole life within Thistledown and the Way.

My terror passed into numb ecstasy. The sense of alien newness, of unfamiliar beauty, hit me like a drug; I was actually walking on a *planet*, a world like Earth, not within a hollowed-out rock.

Reluctantly, I turned from the sun's warmth and walked in shadow down an overgrown trail. If I had come out in the right place, this trail would lead to the Terra Nova River and the landing that served the village of Moonrise. Here, I had been told, I might catch a riverboat and travel to Calcutta, the largest town on the continent of Elizabeth's Land.

I wondered what sort of people I would meet. I imagined feral wretches, barely social, clustered in dark little towns, immersed in their own superstitions. Then I regretted the thought. Perhaps I had spent too much time among the Geshels, having so little respect for my own kind. But of course Lenk's people had gone beyond my own kind. Yanosh had characterized them as fanatic.

The moist air of the river valley sighed around me, like an invisible chilly flood. Picking my footsteps carefully, avoiding lines of finger-sized orange worms topped by feathery blue crests, I listened for any sounds, heard only the rubbed-silk hiss of air and the liquid mumble of the river.

The trail at least had once been traveled by humans. Dropped between the trunks, in a tangle of stone-hard "roots," I spotted a small scrap of crumpled plastic and knelt to pick it up. Spread open by my fingers, it was a blank page from an erasable notebook.

At least, I realized with considerably relief, I had not arrived *before* the human intruders. That would have meant I was truly trapped here, with no chance of returning until they arrived . . . Or someone came from the Hexamon to get me.

I pocketed the scrap. I still could not be sure how much time had passed since the arrival of Lenk and his followers.

Four thousand one hundred and fourteen illegal immigrants; as much as three decades between my arrival and theirs. What could they have done to Lamarckia in that time?

I pushed through a tangle of purple helixed blades. My feet sank into a grainy, boggy humus littered with pink shells and pebbles. No landing visible; no lights, no sign of river traffic. For a moment, I knelt and dug my fingers into the soil. It felt gritty and resilient at once—grains of sand and spongy corklike cubes half a centimeter on a side, suspended in inky fluid that globbed immiscibly amid drops of clear water. It looked for all the world like gardener's potting soil mixed with viscous ink.

I picked up a pink shell. Spiral, flat, like an ancient Earth ammonite, four or five centimeters across. I sniffed it; clean and sweet, with a watery, dusty smell backed by a ghost of roses and bananas. I poked it with a finger; it crushed easily.

More black powder fell in thin curtains nearby. I glanced up and saw what looked like an immense reddish-brown snake, banded with deep midnight blue, dozens of meters long and as thick across as my own body, twisted around and draped across the trunks and leaves above. It wriggled slowly, peristaltically. I could see neither its head nor its tail. With a clamping sensation in my throat and chest, I trotted down the trail, trying to get out from under the serpent.

The trail became thicker, overgrown by smaller red and purple plantlike forms, *phytids*, filling in between the arborids. I lost my way and had to listen for the sound of the river to orient myself.

Several minutes passed before I realized I was smelling something out of place, rich and gassy. During my walk, I had not once smelled mold or methane, not once felt the squelch of dead vegetation. Plants, trees—convenient words only—grew from soil that might have been prepared by diligent and cleanly gardeners. Only the pink shells, mired in the mud, gave a hint that anything here lived, then died, and in dying, left remains—

And this fresh scent of decay.

I thrashed down to the bank again and stared over the deep brownish water to the black silhouette of the opposite shore. Faint, broad patches of blue glow sprang up between the trees across the river. They sputtered and went out again. I could not be sure I had seen them. Then, high above, the undersides of the broad parasols flashed blue. Somewhere, high-pitched tuneless whistling. A flutter beneath the parasols: dark winged things carrying fibrous scraps. Something small and red darted past my face with an audible sniff.

The wind died. The night air sank. Fog danced and twisted in the middle of the river. With the silence came another whiff of decay. Animal flesh, rotting. I was sure of that much.

I followed the scent. Back up the bank, stepping gingerly over writhing purple creepers, guided by faint blue flashes through the undergrowth, I found the remains of the trail.

Something made a sound between a squeak and a sigh and scuttled on three legs out of the undergrowth: a pasty white creature the size of a small dog, triangular in shape. It stood by a black trunk and regarded me through patient, empty eye-spots mounted along a red central line. It pulsed and made tiny whistling sounds. Its skin crawled in what I took to be disgust at my presence. But apparently disgust was only disapproval—or something else entirely—for it did not retreat. Instead, it slowly clasped and crawled its way up a trunk, opened a stoma with a tap of its pointed tail-foot, and began to suck milky fluid. I watched in fascination as its white body swelled. Then, half again as large as before, the creature dropped from the trunk, landed in the dirt with a rubbery plop, and crabbed away with a half circling gait on the down-bent points of its triangle.

Twilight was quickly obscuring everything. A double oxbow of stars pricked through the thin clouds. Ahead, a flickering orange light drew my attention: a torch or flame. I pushed toward the orange light and found the landing and the dirt road that pointed inland to Moonrise.

The landing began as a broad platform at the end of the road, then narrowed to a long pier. On the platform a figure squatted beside a lantern: human, small. Other dark shapes sprawled on their backs or stomachs on the landing and the pier.

In the broad smear of starlight and the lantern's dim glow, I saw that the dark shapes were also human, and still. Their stillness, and the careless way they sprawled on the dock platform, told me they were not alive. They had been dead for some time. Lying in blotches of dried blood, they had bloated in the sun and now strained at their clothes, as if having surrendered themselves to a feast of violence.

My eyes abruptly filled with a sheen of tears. I had expected anything but this.

The figure near the lamp wore a tattered mud-spattered brown shirt and long skirt. Its head was bowed and its breath came harsh and shallow.

My foot made a hollow thud on the platform. The figure turned quickly, with surprising grace, and raised a long-barreled black pistol. It was a woman, brown face muddy and pinched, eyes slitted. The lamp probably half-blinded her. She could only see my outline.

"Who are you?" she asked, voice quavering.

"I've come to take the ferry," I said. I put a strident note into my voice. "Star, Fate and Pneuma, what happened?"

The woman laughed softly, bitterly, and pointed the pistol squarely at my chest. "My *husband*," she said. "He went with Beys."

"Please," I said. "Tell me what happened."

"Do you know him? Janos Strik? My husband? Do you know Beys?"

"No," I said. Neither of those names had been on the list of immigrants, I was sure.

"You can't be anybody. Didn't know my husband. He was very *important* around here."

"I'm frightened," I said, trying for her sympathy. "I don't know what happened here."

"They'll kill us all." She stood slowly, pushing on her knee with one hand as if it pained her. The gun remained pointed at my chest. Her eyes were wild, light gray perhaps, yellow in the lantern-light. She seemed ancient, face cramped with pain, streaked with tears and mud and dried blood. "You must be one of *them*," she said sharply, and pulled back the hammer.

"One of who?" I asked plaintively, not having to work to sound frightened. It could all end here, before I was fairly started. *It could all really end.*

"I'll keep you here," the woman said with a note of weary decision. "Someone will come soon from the north. They took our radios."

The divaricates had not brought weapons with them, the informer had said, yet this gun was metal, heavy, smoothly machined to judge by the sound. Bullets probably charged with explosive powder. A primitive but very effective weapon. Her language was recognizably first-century Trade, common in Thistledown, but the accent sounded marginally different.

I kept my hands visible. The woman shifted from foot to foot, eyes straying to look into the darkness beyond the lantern's circle.

"Who killed them?" I asked.

"The Brionists," she said. "You dress like them."

"I'm not one of them," I said. "I've been in the forest studying Calder's Zone, south of here. Zone two. I didn't know about this."

The woman squinted, held the gun higher. "Don't be stupid," she said.

I tried to shrug congenially, an ignorant stranger, if it was possible to be congenial under the circumstances. The woman was more than suspicious; she had been through hell, and it took some strength of character—or some deep reluctance to add to the carnage—to keep from pulling the trigger and killing me, if only to avoid having to think.

"I haven't heard of Calder's Zone in years," she said. "It gave in to Elizabeth's Zone. They sexed and fluxed when I was a child."

Years had passed, perhaps decades. My information was seriously out of date. "Are you a biologist?" I asked. She did not seem so tired or unskilled that her bullets would miss. And I had none of my medical machinery to save me if the gun did tear me open, not even a memory pack to store my thoughts and personality.

"I'm no biologist and neither are you," the woman said. "You don't even *talk* like anyone I know. Why do you call it a *forest*?" Her eyes glittered in the lamplight. The gun barrel dropped a few centimeters. "But I don't think you're a Brionist. You said you've been in the silva—out there—a long time?"

"Two years."

"Studying?"

I nodded.

"A researcher?"

"I hope to become one."

"You didn't fight when they came?"

"I didn't see it. I didn't know it was happening."

"The best ones fought. You're a coward. You stayed in the silva." She shook her head slowly. "That's my cousin, Gennadia." She pointed a shaky finger at the nearest of the corpses. "And that's Johann, her husband. That's

Nkwanno, the village synthesist. Janos went to Calcutta and then crossed to Naderville to join the Brionists. He left me here." She rubbed her nose and inspected the back of her hand. "He told them we had magnesium and tin and copper and some iron. They came to see. Janos came back with them. He wouldn't even look at me. We told them they would have to consult with Able Lenk."

I thought perhaps Lenk had had a son, until I realized by her intonation that the first name was an honorific.

"They said we could not refuse them. They took our radios. They said Beys had his orders. The mayor told them to leave. They killed the mayor, and some of the men tried to fight. They killed . . . all except me. I hid in the silva. They'll come back soon and take over everything." She laughed with girlish glee. "I'm a coward, too. Not much left."

"Terrible," I said. Nkwanno—that name had been on the list. I had once met the scholar named Nkwanno—a devout Naderite student who had studied under my uncle.

She picked up the lantern and raised it above her head, stepping closer. She shined the fitful beam on my clothes. "You've only been in the silva a few hours. Elizabeth covers all visitors with her dust. But the boats left days ago. You're hardly black at all." Her eyes burned. "Are you real?"

"I bathed in the river," I said.

She issued a half whine, half laugh, raised the gun as if to fire into the air, and pulled the trigger. The hammer fell on an empty chamber. Then she released the gun, letting it dangle from one finger before it fell to the boards with a heavy thump. She dropped to her knees. "I don't care," she said. "I'd just as soon die. The whole world is a lie now. We've made it a lie."

With a shudder, she lay down, curling up her arms and legs into a fetal ball, and abruptly closed her eyes.

I stood for a while, heart thumping, mouth dry, uncertain where to begin. Finally, with a jerk, I walked over to the woman and knelt beside her. She seemed to be asleep. My breath came fast from having the gun held on me. This proof of my weakness—nearly dying within a few minutes of my arrival—made me angry at myself, at everything.

Teeth clenched, I picked up the gun, slipped it into my waistband, and stepped around her to examine the bodies. Two men and a woman. I found the smell unfamiliar and offensive. I had never smelled dead bodies undergoing natural decay except in entertainments and training; conflict with the Jarts in the Way did not have such crudities.

I suspected the decay had progressed in unfamiliar ways; no external bacteria, I thought, only internal, and those carefully selected centuries ago for the populations of Thistledown. A peculiarly artificial and unnatural way to return to the soil—if Lamarckia could be said to have soil.

With a shudder, I bent over to examine Nkwanno first. A tall, dark-skinned male, face almost unrecognizable; but in the discolored features I saw a resemblance to the young, vital student who had worked with my father's brother in Alexandria. But this man was much older than the Nkwanno I knew would have been . . .

The hastily opened gate had pushed me decades along Lamarckia's world-line.

For a long moment I could only stare, all my thoughts in confusion. Then I steeled myself and searched through the corpse's pockets. I found a few coins and a thin pouch containing paper money, a small, elegantly tooled slate, and a stale piece of bread wrapped in waxy paper. I examined the money, then returned it to the corpse.

Divaricates preferred twentieth-century modes of economic exchange. In my own pocket, I carried some money copied from samples provided by the informer. The money bore little resemblance to that which I found on Nkwanno. More than likely, it would be useless here.

I could not bring myself to steal money from corpses. The slate was another matter. I needed information desperately. I slipped it into my pants pocket.

I sat beside the sleeping woman, thinking. The breeze had died to nothing and the blunt, sweet stink of death hung in the air. I closed my eyes, pinched my nose against the smell.

Jan Fima had said he was part of a faction opposed to Lenk's policies. This faction regretted Lenk's decision to migrate illegally, with limited resources, and foresaw much trouble in the future. Apparently the trouble had begun. Perhaps it had been going on for some time. Jan Fima had supposed there would be an individual in Moonrise who would have supplies and information for a Nexus representative . . . But how *patient* an individual?

I cursed under my breath and rubbed my eyes. Two small moons rose within the hour, each a quarter of a degree wide, and chased each other slowly overhead. Their light threw mercurial roads across the river's smooth currents.

Large dark humps rose in the river, several dozen meters from the bank. Moonlight danced around them in ghostly sparkles. I did not know what the humps were. *Your ignorance will kill you. And here . . . it could all really end.*

The woman slept soundly, like a child, breath even and shallow, with occasional twitches and grumbles. I was reluctant to leave her, but there did not appear to be any more trouble in the offing. I could not let her stay on the dock, however. I lifted her and carried her away from the corpses, laying her gently on the soft dirt adjacent to the landing. I took off my coat and made a pillow for her. She grumbled faintly, twitched, and settled onto the cushion, gripping the folded coat with long, dirty fingers.

You had it all and it wasn't enough. Restless, searching, you threw it all away . . . You went to the Geshels, gravitated to their power. Begged for assignments. Glory of fighting the Jarts. Then they sent you here. A grand assignment, Yanosh told you. An entire world, and all the glory yours. But a kind of oubliette. A mere sideslip in one's career.

To shut up the whining voice, I pulled Nkwanno's slate from my pocket. It was an anachronism—a late twentieth-century design favored by the divaricates, who shunned all later technology.

I sat. The illuminated screen cast a glow across my face remarkably similar to that from the moons above. Searching the memory, I found a number of Nkwanno's personal files, some of them extensive, but all locked. I searched through the library on the slate, and found a directory with files created on Lamarckia, dated by a calendar established after the immigration.

A scholar named Redhill had begun a fairly extensive local encyclopedia, and I was able to learn much about this part of Lamarckia in the space of an hour. Reading and scrolling and playing back videos, I lost myself in new knowledge, and my confidence began to return.

Thirty-seven Lamarckian years had passed since the arrival of the immigrants. The gate-keepers had been off more than they knew; it was possible I could never return to the Way, even if I located the other clavicle, and that no one in the Way could ever find Lamarckia through the stack again.

The humps in the river sank with soft gurgling sounds. The encyclopedia called them river vines and said they were intrusions from zone five, Petain's Zone, scions of another ecos; the river was only lightly utilized by zone one, Elizabeth's Zone, which apparently did not like riparian or pelagic environments.

So much to learn. I searched with an inward lick of thought for the elements that had once enhanced and accelerated my mind. The gaps left by their removal felt like missing limbs, still having a kind of phantom presence. I kept darting back and forth between exhilaration and fear amounting to despair that I would fail. In my dread lurked a strong sexual need. My erection seemed more than inappropriate in these surroundings. With the smell of decay, such a response struck me as obscene.

I frowned and quelled the impulse. Others had spoken of danger arousing such reactions; no reason, yet, to be ashamed.

With a few minutes to calm down, I felt my confidence return. I had been well-trained and well-educated for this mission. Using what the informer knew, I had created an inference map of talents necessary to survive and travel on Lamarckia: technologies, attitudes, language shifts.

But no one had expected slaughter, or wholesale war.

A fine mist crossed the river, out of place in these conditions; I realized after a moment that the mist was a scented aerosol, not just water vapor: something in the ecos conveying information to something else. I visualized all of zone one, all of Elizabeth, as an organic processor, a vast, sensate organizer not quite as primitive as a hive, not as swift and connected as a mind, but aware of all its tiny forms, sending them messages on chemical winds, a huge mother directing many billions of children.

Redhill brought me up to date on what progress had been made in Lamarckian studies in almost four decades. The encyclopedia postulated that life had first arisen on Lamarckia three hundred million years ago. The star was young, barely four billion years old; the planet still retained a great deal of primordial heat, which supplemented the star's relatively weak insolation.

On all of Lamarckia, only one hundred and nine genetically different organisms had been discovered, all ecoi, seven of them on Elizabeth's Land. Ecoi in the different zones rarely preyed on scions of other ecoi, but frequently *observed and copied*, or captured them for more detailed study. The ecoi sent swift samplers, sometimes called spies or thieves—flying or running or swimming scions—to recover and return bites of tissue or whole scions. If the designs were found useful, the ecoi incorporated them, modifying some or all of their own scions or replacing them with new forms. Observed, stolen, and copied, as well as inherited, traits were passed on to subsequent generations.

Inheritance of acquired traits, a largely discredited theory of Earth's evolution, had been postulated almost nine hundred years ago by the French biologist Jean Baptiste de Lamarck . . . So the original surveyors had given his name to the planet.

When the immigrants had first arrived, Elizabeth's silva had been mostly orange and gray. The encyclopedia said that an ecos could "flux" or alter much of its character suddenly, in as little time as two days and without warning. During a flux, many if not all types of scions were absorbed and recycled into scions with new designs. This had last happened in zone two twenty-eight years before, as the woman had said; Calder's Zone, had "sexed"—become receptive to a complete genetic merger. Elizabeth's Zone had accepted this proposal. The two had merged and all of the scions of both ecoi had been recalled. The new single ecos had then "fluxed," recreating itself.

This had been a time of extraordinary hardship for the immigrants.

Elizabeth's Zone had dominated, taken over Calder's Zone, and now occupied a stretch of Elizabeth's Land from the center to the northern coast, two thousand kilometers at its widest extent east to west. Where it met with other zones—three, four, five, and now six, denuded "truce lines" formed stark white barriers like lines on a map. Altogether, five zones now covered the continent of Elizabeth's Land.

In the south, I learned, a group of large islands filled a crowded sea bounded by Cape Magellan, and on these islands, zones three and four divided territories, with one island occupied by a much smaller zone, little explored and called simply zone seven.

Zone five, called Petain's Zone, lay east of Elizabeth's Zone and along the eastern coast. It was an adapted pelagic—an oceangoing zone that had adapted to land perhaps a million years before. Few zones occupied large areas of both land and water. It was zone five's huge vines that rose three times a day from the river that flowed past Moonrise.

I pinched the bridge of my nose and shut off the slate. I had used these primitive displays in training and had become proficient, but they still hurt my eyes.

After a few minutes, listening to the lapping of the river against the piles of the pier and the woman's steady breathing, I returned to the slate again. I found a citizens' list, two years old, and searched for the village of Moonrise, found the woman's picture, and connected it with a name: Larisa Cachemou, born to Sers Hakim Cachemou and Belinda Bichon-Cachemou thirty-two Lamarckian years ago. Married into the Strik triad. Janos Strik, husband. In divaricate society, and in most orthodox Naderite arrangements, triad families did not exchange mates—monogamy was the rule—but families shared finances and the raising of children.

Larisa Strik-Cachemou was in fact not much older than I. Stress and disaster had made her seem ancient.

I slipped the slate into my pants pocket and took the woman's lantern. Time to find out what had happened in Moonrise; time to begin this work, however unpleasant.

CHAPTER TWO

The road from the dock was irregularly paved with stones and gravel. Fresh broad-tread wheel tracks had been cut into the roadbed, making a mess of the gravel. Twisted scraps of mud on the dock could have fallen from tire treads. I concluded that someone had moved large equipment down the road and onto the dock.

Shining the light across the silva, I noticed holes and splintered gouges in the trunks of a few arborids near the road. Poking my finger a few centimeters into one hole, I felt a hard object at its bottom: a bullet. I looked back at the bodies on the landing, trying to put all this evidence together.

I dismissed the possibility that Larisa had killed the people on the dock. For the moment, that made no sense at all. The only other conclusion possible was that shots had been fired from boats on the river.

Narrow pipes mounted on iron rods lined the road. I bent to examine the pipes, felt a moisture dripping from their lower halves. Tiny holes pierced the pipes, pointing outward toward the silva. I sniffed a drop on my finger.

The fluid in the pipes was redolent with a sour skunkiness. I guessed that the pipes sprayed something the scions found unpleasant, one way to keep the roads and village from being overgrown—or invaded.

Something large and indistinct stirred trunks and made gentle sucking sounds in the undergrowth. Against the bright stars, two long, sinuous arms or necks rose black against the trees, plucking at the parasols and fans; not grazing, but wiping with long shussing sounds and pruning with quick snicks of faintly luminous blue teeth. I raised the lantern high, but the unfocused beam revealed little. Each arm rose from a dark central body and extended six or seven meters above my head. The whole was as large as two adult giraffes.

I picked up my pace, again feeling my arm hairs prickle.

The road broadened and then ran up against a round tower of ochre stone, rising above the silva. The road split and skirted the edge of a clearing beyond. In the clearing sat the center of the village of Moonrise. Twin two-story square stone buildings with peaked slate roofs, like dormitories, flanked a quadrangle north of the tower.

I crossed the square, shining the broad, dim beam right and left. More bodies lay on the square. In the middle, I paused beside one of the bodies, a woman, age uncertain, a bullet through her forehead. In the square, which covered perhaps a quarter hectare, I grimly counted twenty-two bodies. They had all been shot with low-caliber kinetic weapons: guns somewhat less powerful than the one now tucked in my waistband.

I stood in the middle of the square, working to stay calm. Gentle wind and the rhythmic creaking of a door. Cool moist air, bodies, silence, bright double arc of star clouds and spray of brighter stars, gave me a moment of giddy vertigo. I controlled that quickly but found the burn of anger less easy to snuff.

Away from centuries of culture and political experience, away from all restraints and the enforced patterns of tens of millions of fellow citizens, the immigrants had reverted. The old human pattern of violent conflict had started again. But my instructions did not include salvation for the divaricate immigrants.

Lamarckia was my main concern. *I didn't come here to get involved in a stupid war.*

I crossed the quadrangle diagonally and reached the north end of the closest dormitory. I climbed the steps quietly and peered into the open door. My fingers felt the door's strong, smooth-grained material as I waved the lantern at the dark and empty hall beyond. In Redhill's encyclopedia, zone one's most common "trees" were called lizboo—Elizabeth's bamboo. The door was made from *xyla*, the immigrant word for woody material taken from arborids—in this case of lizboo trunk sheet, unwound from the spiral growth. One could simply fell the trunk, lop off the crown and low-growth parasols, grab the edge of lizboo in one's hands and unwind it.

I shook my head. Old habits—mind happily displaying fresh knowledge, like a shield.

I entered the building and searched, not for bodies—though I found twelve more of those—but for information. The buildings had been fully wired and had electric lights. I looked through desks and chests of drawers, carefully replacing everything. I picked through the pockets and belongings of the corpses, grimacing at the ghoulish task, hoping to find more slates. I found none.

Robbing corpses had not been specified in my instructions, but it was not entirely dishonorable under the circumstances. On the second floor, I entered the mayor's office and found a primitive message board covered with village records. Charts for monoculture crop growth and harvest yields, a chart of the village's population over the last twenty years—pegged at its highest, one hundred and fifty, in the last year—and a map of the village. I touched the thornlike pins holding the map and saw that another, more recent map had been torn off, leaving corners. The older map, heavily penciled, had been revealed.

I emerged from the building and looked at the dark sky. Clouds had sailed in, thin parallel lines of irregular fluff high across the stars. Both moons were down.

It would be dawn soon.

Before searching the next dormitory, I walked to the greenhouses and fields farther north, beyond the water plant. Two white ceramic pipes carried water from the river to the plant, where it was filtered, but not boiled or otherwise treated. Lamarckia had no indigenous microbes that would bother humans. Human-carried microbes (the few that had survived purging and translation to Thistledown) seemed not to thrive on Lamarckia. The biological niches were either too restricted or already occupied.

The power plant employed simple technologies. Two hectares of silva had been felled and cleared and lizboo trunks now supported sheets of electrolysis membrane. Hydrogen was rapidly and efficiently stripped from water by sunlight and stored in fuel cells. The sheets also created electricity directly—bilayer technology, simple to manufacture from raw organic materials.

I lifted the lantern, sniffed at it. Not oil or some other liquid fuel, but an ion discharge coil that flickered much as a flame would. The liquid was a supercharged chemical solution. Pretty, but not efficient. Perhaps it had hung as a decoration outside a house. I had seen no other lanterns, and the town's power had been cut at its source—the fuel cell and transformer shed. Cells, generators, and other heavy equipment had been removed.

As had the village's children, apparently. I found no bodies of inhabitants younger than twenty.

So equipment and children had been stolen. Carried downriver, perhaps. The raiders—Brionists, the woman called them—were hungry for metal. Lamarckia was short of high-quality metal ores, and the immigrants evidently had not gone in for large-scale mining or big smelters.

The village's communications center had once occupied a small house thirty meters west of the power shed. The equipment—simple radios, judging by the marks and few implements left behind—had been removed. Three bodies sprawled on the porch.

I studied the dark greenhouse and crop fields, a hundred hectares of cleared land cut out of the silva. The raiders had left behind a number of wagons but taken the village's electric tractors. That explained the wheel ruts on the gravel road to the dock. They had probably used the tractors to haul the transformers, generators, and other stolen goods from the village.

I pictured a wagon full of children, crying and screaming. Teeth clenched harder, I walked to the second dormitory.

Inside, the halls were piled high with bodies. Streaks of blood up the walkways and steps showed the course of action taken against Moonrise. Clearly the raiders had meant to torch this building and all the bodies in it. Somehow, they had failed to finish their task, leaving the bodies on the quadrangle and in the other dormitory, perhaps in the houses as well. Someone had apparently decided it was more expedient to take the equipment and children and get away before others arrived.

Bullets in the trees.

Perhaps a few—Larisa, her cousin, Nkwanno, and one other—had survived the attacks and gone to the docks. I pictured a lone boat left behind to pick off survivors as they came out of the jungle.

Or they might have been the first to die, as the boats arrived.

Then I thought of Nkwanno's slate. Slates would be valued here. I had found no other slates among the bodies, yet they had left his. That convinced me Nkwanno, Gennadia, and the other had been killed last.

This level of violence was a new thing on Lamarckia.

I picked my way through and over the bodies at the end of the hall, keeping my lantern beam high, boots sinking into soft flesh, arms and legs and torsos sliding, chests expelling bizarre moans as they shifted. I refused to look into their blank rotten-fruit faces. My eyes already filled with tears and my stomach spasmed at the extraordinary smell. Never in my life had I been exposed to so much intimate, concentrated death. I climbed to the second floor and leaned against a wall. I could not remember the last time I had felt a need to vomit.

The feeling passed. I stood upright again.

A sound came from a side room. I stopped, listened, rapped the wall with my knuckles.

"Who are you?" a weak male voice responded. "Oh, kill me and damn you."

"Are you armed?" I asked.

No reply. I got to my hands and knees and placed the lantern in the doorway. Nobody shot at it. I peered around the corner, saw a room filled with crates and boxes, and lying against the boxes, a man. Only his legs were visible from where I squatted, pants torn, dried blood caking the cloth. I stood and entered slowly.

The man lay with arms spread wide in a pile of books and papers, eyes focused on the ceiling. He appeared to be seventy-five or eighty years old, hair white, face gaunt with more than age. He clutched a bottle of water and a dark gnawed piece of something—bread perhaps. I hunkered beside him. The man turned his head into the beam of the lantern, squinted, and said, "Did you see? Have you brought them?"

"I'm alone," I said.

The man reached up and felt my sleeve. "They left us behind," he said. "Are you a—?" His lips couldn't make the word.

"I'm a researcher. I just got here."

"On a boat?"

I shook my head.

"No other boats? No disciplinary?"

"Not yet. Are you badly hurt?"

"Bad enough," the man said. "I'm going to die. I really need to die."

He had been shot in the chest and arm and seemed to have been cut across his arms and breast by knives. I could do nothing for him. No water left in the village plumbing, no electricity, no medical supplies. I asked if he could describe his attackers.

"Everything we predicted," the man murmured, shrugging free of my fingers. "Everything I told them." His lips worked again, managed the word he had been trying for. "Brionists, of course. General Beys. Who else?"

"From where?"

"Nearby. Beys sailed from Naderville in Hsia and made a base. His ships send boats upriver at night. They lie low during the day. They look for ore and metal and machines. Everything goes east to Hsia." Hsia was a massive continent northeast of Elizabeth's Land, across two thousand kilometers of the Darwin Sea.

"Children?" I asked.

The man's face wrinkled in distress. "All," the man said. "Beys wants them for Brion."

"What's your name?"

"Fitch." He licked his lips. "Sander Darcy Fitch. A doctor. They took all the medicine. All the equipment."

"Why did they kill so many?"

"Except me," Fitch said.

"And a woman."

"Who?"

"Larisa Strik-Cachemou."

Even in his pain, he managed to make a face. "Crazy bitch. Her husband thought we could deal with the Brionists."

"Why kill everybody?"

"Oh, there will be *mansions* and *riches* and Lamarckia will bow to their *will*." The man started to sing in an undertone. His eyes shut tight, he rocked back and forth, making the box upon which he leaned creak and rustle. Suddenly he convulsed, then opened his eyes again and reached up to me.

"Secret," he said. "Very secret."

"What?"

"The Hexamon will come. Do you believe?"

"It's inevitable," I said.

"I have disguises and supplies. Old clothes. Cast-offs. Right here. I run the charity. That's why I hid instead of fighting. I thought they would come, seeing this. They can have their pick. Of course, if they send thousands . . . not enough."

"You've been waiting?" I asked.

"He's been gone thirty-seven years," Fitch said. "He took the clavicle and just went away. Maybe he didn't make it." Fitch coughed and shuddered again. "Smells so bad. Secret. Please, I have to tell now."

"It's all right," I said.

The old man reached up, brushed his filth-caked fingers on my face. "Don't know you, or anyone like you," he said, looking me over, my thin shirt and baggy tan pants. "You dress the old style, like when we arrived. And you look different." A light grew in his eyes. His mouth opened wide. "Take these clothes. Yours are all wrong. By the Good Man, do I make you out of air?"

I shook my head. He struggled to rise but fell back, legs kicking like shaken sticks.

"Star, Fate, and Breath," he croaked, licking his lips, "be kind to me, preserve me from the pride of the hand. Star, source of all life, to which I will return to be remade, erase my sins . . ."

My eyes moistened again, hearing the old prayer, and I echoed the old man. Together:

". . . *and purify, bind my atoms to something higher, send my light far to others who truly see. In the arms of great galaxies there lies salvation, and we there will go, to dance in endless joy the innocent dance free of the hand.*" The old man's voice faded, and I finished, "*In the name of the Good Man, the secrets of Logos, of Fate and Breath and Soul, so be it through deep time.*"

"You," Fitch said, grasping my arm weakly. "Are you alone?"

Tears streamed down my cheeks. "Yes," I said.

"Take the clothes. Save us from what we've done. May the memory of the Good Man serve you."

Fitch's breath stopped. Here, that was enough. He was dead. The bottle of water rolled and spilled. I set it upright, then sprinkled water on the old man's face. *Free of the hand and its toils. Absolution.* I kneeled beside the body, lips set tight.

After some minutes, I stood, nerves ragged. As Fitch had suggested, I searched through the boxes of old clothes and cast-off goods. I exchanged my new clothes for sturdy, if frayed, trousers and shirt, but kept my boots. A cloth rucksack served to hold the slate and a few other clothes.

Outside, in the courtyard, away from the trails of blood, I smeared my boots with mud. Then I returned to the river.

CHAPTER THREE

In the east, sun peeked pale yellow between the immense trunks and parasols and fan-leaves behind the dock. The woman stirred. She opened her eyes, saw me, and closed them again, as if resigned.

"Nobody's come," she murmured.

"Not yet," I said. "Feel better?"

"I haven't eaten in days."

"I'm pretty hungry myself," I said. "Is there food anywhere?"

She shook her head. "They looted the town."

"The Brionists."

"Yes."

"You're expecting somebody to come. A boat."

"I don't know who's alive. Beys sent big boats filled with troops. Maybe they took Calcutta, too. They shot . . . when Nkwanno and Gennadia and Ganna . . ." She lifted her head, jaw thrusting and neck straining at the memory. "Missed me."

"Are there any boats nearby? Another village?" I asked.

She pointed upriver with her nose. "They should have been here yester-day. I waited and they didn't come." She walked to the shore. I stood and followed. She glanced over her shoulder. "Go away, whoever you are," she said. "I'm tired. I'm a dead person."

"What's your name?" I asked, though I knew already.

"Larisa," the woman said, stopping again, hunching her shoulders as if I were a buzzing insect that might sting.

"My name is Olmy," I said. "I'm from the triad family of Datchetong."

"I've heard of them," Larisa said. "Lenk disenfranchised them." She rubbed her nose and raised her eyes to my face. "I know you're a liar," she said, eyes narrowed. "Maybe the silva made you."

I shook my head.

"I'll believe anything now. Nothing matters," she said. With a shake of her head and a shiver, she led me away from the river, back to the village.

I walked beside her. She took each step with a wide-eyed deliberation, forcing herself on. Her lips worked silently.

"We're almost there," she said.

The broad red fans and black trunks closed overhead. We walked in shadow. Something—a flying ribbon—darted in front of my face, undulated, stung me on the cheek, flashed away before I could swipe at it. Larisa stared at me listlessly.

"Samplers only bite once here. Then Liz knows you."

I wiped a small smear of blood from my cheek.

Larisa trudged on.

"When were *you* bitten?" I asked.

"When I was a little girl, I suppose. I forget."

We neared the tower. From the direction of the river came a sound of motors. Larisa slowed, eyes wild, breath coming in jerks. I stopped and took hold of her arm. She looked up at me like a child. "They're back," she said.

"Stay here. I'll see," I said. I held her shoulders as if to plant her feet on the spot, but felt sure, once I was gone, she would run and hide. I returned along the path, looked over my shoulder, saw her standing beside the tower like a stunned animal.

By the dock, I hid behind a thick black lizboo trunk and peered north, downriver. Four small launches moved slowly against the current, their hulls chalk white against the river's dawn gray-blue. Each launch carried ten or twelve passengers, all in uniform. I frowned. Black dust fell from above, coating like soot. I absently rubbed some between my fingers. It felt fine as rouge and clung to my skin. There was some commotion on the boats; I heard their voices across the water, angry and concerned. The launches were within a hundred meters of the dock and observers in their prows had already seen the bodies. The motors cut back and the boats edged toward the shore. I saw rifles held at ready.

They did not appear to be invading soldiers. Very likely the boats carried police—a disciplinary and officers—from Calcutta. I considered whether to meet them here or at the village.

Larisa decided for me. She stepped up behind me and walked onto the dock. Her footsteps echoed on the planks in the morning stillness.

"You're late," she shouted to the boats.

A thick-bodied, balding man with a narrow, closely-trimmed beard stood in the bow of the leading boat. "Who are you?" he called back. He tossed her a rope and she took it, sidestepping her cousin's body to tie it. She stood, brushing black dust from her hands on her pants, and said in clear, accusing tones, "Why didn't you come earlier?"

I stepped from behind the trunk and stood on the dock. The men and women regarded us both warily. All wore uniforms, but of varying colors, some ill-cut; homemade, I thought, hand-sewn.

The balding, bearded man climbed from the first boat. "We didn't get any radio calls for a day and a half. We saw unknown boats going upriver . . . raiders, Brionists, we presumed. The citizens rank thought maybe a disciplinary should have a look." He approached, squinting at her. "Larisa, aren't you? Larisa . . . Strik-Cachemou? What happened here?"

"They killed us," she answered. "Then *he* came." She pointed to me. I stepped forward and pulled the pistol from my waistband, holding it by the barrel. "It's hers," I said. The balding man took the pistol and handed it to one of his officers, who placed it in a cloth bag. "My name is Olmy Ap Datchetong."

"Elevi Bar Thomas. Disciplinary at Calcutta." He did not offer to shake my hand. "I don't recognize you. Where are you from?" he asked.

"I've been in the silva, traveling and studying," I said. "I just arrived."

"He's a liar," Larisa confided, as if it might ingratiate her with the older man. He gave her a wary glance, sensing something was not quite right.

"Did you see what happened?" he asked me.

"No," I said.

All but three of the men and women in gray marched along the trail toward the village. One man with a heavy, long-barreled rifle stood guard over the boats. The disciplinary examined the bodies on the dock. One woman, short and powerfully built, with auburn hair cut short beneath a loose gray cap, pulled tarps from the boat lockers and spread them beside the corpses. "We didn't bring a doctor," she reminded Thomas.

He could not take his eyes from the bodies. His broad, fleshy face showed taut pale lines. "In the name of the Good Man, why?"

"Passion," Larisa said, lips curling with hate. "They have a lot of *passion*."

In the empty village refectory, where all the inhabitants of Moonrise would have sat in communion for lunch and dinner, the disciplinary spun a chair around and sat on it front to back. I sat across from him, on the opposite side of a round table.

"You're lucky you weren't involved, aren't you?" Thomas didn't wait for my answer. "The whole village had maybe three guns. They've lived peacefully here for thirty-nine years. They had twenty-seven children. All gone. We haven't found a one of them." Thomas scratched his nose reflectively. "I've heard Beys is taking all the children, that the Brionists want to raise them to think as they do. I hope that's true. They wouldn't just kill them, would they? Take them away and then kill them?"

I shook my head, ignorant.

"You can't tell me anything?" he asked in an undertone.

I summed Thomas up quickly: chosen by the citizens rank and heads of triad families of his district to act as chief disciplinary, a kind of constable. The disciplinary would choose new citizen deputies every three years, a tradition in divaricate communes. He had arrived late, I judged, because there would have been nothing he could have done. He had seen the boats, known them for what they were, and . . .

Or perhaps I misjudged.

"I've only been in the village since yesterday evening," I said. "Larisa says they had a dispute over minerals."

"What do they lack in their zone? An innocuous village, no reason for it to be *slaughtered*. One hundred twenty-four dead." Thomas's face wrinkled into an ugly scowl and he seemed ready to spit. "Not much high-grade ore on Lamarckia, not out in the open. A little here . . . Ten kilometers through the silva. Just beginning to think about mining it. Brion lusts for metal, enough to kill for it. What can we do? We have few weapons. Just bury the bodies." Thomas leaned forward. "The woman calls you a liar. Something's taken a chunk out of your cheek. A sampler?"

I had hoped to have more time to blend in. I could only stick with my story, however thin—and hope to get away in Calcutta.

"It wasn't the first time I've been sampled," I said. "I discovered a sub-zone and spent some time in it. Looking for signs of a new flux." Subzones, Redhill's encyclopedia said, were regions of peculiar specialization within an ecos, where scions of unfamiliar characteristics sometimes emerged. Some scholars speculated that changes in subzones could be harbingers of fluxes. Others maintained subzones were actually small ecoi in themselves, serving specific needs for the larger zones in a symbiotic relationship.

I hoped the encyclopedia was not hopelessly out of date.

Thomas considered this answer, then shrugged. "I try to stay out of zone studies. People interest me." Thomas raised his own slate. "I have no track on you. Census of five years ago. Twenty-two thousand of us on Lamarckia, ten thousand on Elizabeth's Land. I have no birth records for a man named Olmy of the Datchetong. I *do* have a record for a Darrow Jan Fima, of the Datchetong extended triad . . . He stole something pretty important—it doesn't say what—thirty-seven years ago. He was never caught. Case not pursued."

My respect for the disciplinary jumped several notches. Darrow Jan Fima was the informer who had returned to the Way. I suddenly connected his theft of a clavicle with Larisa's comment that the Datchetong had been disenfranchised. *Wrong name*, I told myself. *They proscribed the whole triad.*

Thomas rocked on his chair, then stood and pocketed his slate. "I knew Nkwanno well. An intelligent, kind man. He came to lecture every few months downriver in Calcutta. We found the body of the encyclopedist, Redhill himself. Did you know he lived here? He put Moonrise on the map, so to speak. They shot him in the head." Thomas raised his eyes and met mine squarely. He stood. "Quite a few distinguished citizens, for so small a village."

I watched him closely, saying nothing.

"Time to finish. Bury the bodies and leave. We've recorded the scene. Nothing more I can do now."

"The silva will take over inside a week," said Thomas's second, the tough-faced, stocky woman, Bruni. She stood by the tower and scrutinized the liz-boo trunks and one foot of a cathedral tree beyond the pipes. One of her eyelids twitched reflexively. She turned and regarded me curiously, but was leaving all questions to Thomas.

I accompanied Thomas and four others down to the river. I took one end of a stretcher, Thomas the other, and we carried Nkwanno's body, the last, from the dock. Larisa watched as we approached the other bodies lined up in the quadrangle. "Thank Logos I have no children," she murmured, falling in step behind.

We all dug four long trench-graves in the hard-packed soil of the quadrangle, very different from the rich chunky loam in the silva. The spades bit into the dead and chalky dirt with short singing barks.

Until arriving in Moonrise, I had never had human mortality shoved in my face with such visceral force, and so often. I had never buried anyone before. Conflicts with the Jarts in the Way were altogether swifter and more deadly, leaving few traces . . .

The sharp intakes of breath and heavy panting of the men and women working around me, the stamps of defiant individuality on their faces, awoke a hazy, difficult emotion, horror and pride commingled.

I dug with a will.

One women stopped to wipe away tears. A man joined her, shovel in hand, arm around her shoulder, and offered her a handkerchief.

We finished a trench intended for thirty of the dead. The first was a small thin body. The tarp was removed and I saw a woman of perhaps sixty or seventy years. *Natural* years, lived without extraordinary medical assistance or rejuvenation. She had been shot in the neck and chest by a projectile weapon. The wounds looked ugly, purple and puffy like old meat. That was what they had made of her: old meat. The woman's swollen brown and purple face seemed rudely, disdainfully peaceful.

I looked at my fellow diggers: a strong young man with broad bull-shoulders and fat cheeks, the auburn-haired strong-bodied woman Bruni, a slender middle-aged man with a permanently worried expression, a young woman whose face stayed flushed all the time we dug. Individual. No acquiescence to artificial beauty; no reconstruction. The bull-shouldered young man put down his shovel and stared at the dead woman. He seemed reluctant to do what had to be done.

I bent and closed the old woman's eyes with two fingers. I had once seen that in an entertainment about times long past, on distant Earth. The touch of her skin, cold and moist, and the sticky push of her eyelids against sunken eyeballs made my flesh crawl. The young man nodded gratitude and approval. We put the woman into the shroud again, making a sling, and lowered her into the grave. Others arranged more bodies—young men, old men, two more older women. They lowered the other bodies into the hole. Working in synch, we filled in the grave. I observed the faces around me, grim, eyes a little wild; some dream dying inside.

Sunset. The quadrangle bathed in orange light from a passing cloud, glorious in the sun.

Dusk loomed when we finished.

Thomas spoke a few words from the Prayer of Common Place over the rows of long graves. Others finished their lists and maps of what remained of the village. A female officer conferred with Thomas about a list of missing children taken from records in the mayor's office.

Then Thomas took me back to the tower. He pulled a bar of sweetened gum from his coat pocket, broke it in half, offered half to me, and I took it, interested in maintaining a friendly connection with this man.

We climbed the tower and looked down on the darkening silva and village, the empty buildings and houses, the pale tan scars of fresh graves in the grayish-brown quadrangle, the small greenhouse farm and large tanks, paddles motionless inside brown sewage, no longer converting waste directly to food. I could not see the dock, but the far bank of the river was visible. Parasols and fans folded and furled, withdrawing for the night. A cloud of black dust shot up from the silva a hundred meters off, drifted. I smelled citrus and spice.

"Tell me more about why you're here," Thomas said.

"I came here to catch a riverboat. I've spent much of my life the last few years alone in the silva. I'm not used to violence. I don't know what more I can do or say."

Thomas rubbed his balding head with a chalky hand. "I said years ago citizens should be forced to carry papers." He lifted his eyebrows and glared at the horizon. "'Oh, no, not that,'" he mimicked. "'This is a place where we can all be free.' We'll take you to Calcutta. You'll tell what you know to the committee of citizens rank. If you're one of the Brionists and they left you here by accident—or left you here to spy—I'll personally see you to a full citizen trial in Athenai."

There was nothing I could say.

I still did not need to sleep. No one wanted to sleep in the buildings. I lay with the others in one corner of the quadrangle, where no bodies had fallen and the soil was not stained with blood, under the broad clear sky, tracing patterns in the stars. The double oxbow was not visible. Now, the sky was marked by tiny puffs of dim color—purples and pinks. The shrouds of dead suns. I felt a dizzying moment of complete disorientation. These stars probably occupied the same universe, but not necessarily the same galaxy, or even the same period of time. In the Way's geometry stacks, distance and time could become as tangled as an infinity of threads tossed into a box.

I was among humans, but that gave little comfort. If I died here, who would know me well enough to connect the thread of my pneuma to any comprehensible past?

The burial and service had moved me more profoundly than I thought possible. I had largely abandoned my spiritual beliefs since joining Way Defense, concentrating on a different kind of personal development: devotion to concept, to large-scale social and not metaphysical issues. Devotion to fighting off the menace of the Jarts, devils beyond the conception of any human before the opening of the Way.

Now I faced a much smaller problem, but more personal, and challenging to the point of almost certain defeat. What I saw in the stars now were the faces of my mother and father, and all they stood for, suddenly become diseased, *wrong.*

Not many slept that night, however tired.

The boats prepared to depart at dawn. They would move much more quickly with the river current, but it would still take a day to get back to Calcutta. I listened to the officers talking among themselves; they had segregated me at the stern of the last boat, leaving me two meters of space, as if I were a pariah. No family, no known origin, rumors passing quickly; monkeys shying from a stranger to the communal tree. I felt a brief flash of anger at their stupidity, then wondered what I would do in their place.

Before Thomas could give the order to leave, however, we all heard the distant sound of another small engine. Larisa, in the cabin of the largest boat, let out a sharp wail and struggled, pushing aside the startled men and women around her. She leaped ashore with surprising dexterity and ran up the road to the village.

The few deputies who had rifles lifted them, aiming them upriver where the sounds came. A single eight-meter launch was drifting downriver with the current, its internal combustion engine idling, bow cutting through swaths of morning fog. In the launch, two men squatted at stern and prow, both staring at the four boats arranged around the dock and shore. Neither of them appeared to be armed.

The disciplinary came aft and stood beside me to get a better view of the boat. "It's Randall," he said. "Erwin Randall and someone else—Matthew Shatro, I think." Thomas seemed to know everyone on the river. He ordered the rifles lowered. "They're not Brionists. They're researchers." He shouted to the crew of his second boat, "Go get that woman, damn her."

The launch came alongside and a tall, loose-limbed man with a thin face and long nose and somber brown eyes waved to Thomas, adding a half hearted flick of the hand to the others. "What happened here?" he asked.

"Dead," Thomas said.

"Fate and Breath," Randall said. Shatro, at the rear, frowned and drew up his jacket collar. "All of them?"

"All but the missing," Thomas said.

"There are seven boats upriver," Randall said, pointing. "They must be the ones. Three flatboats. They didn't even bother shooting us."

"Good to see you're healthy," Thomas said without irony.

"I passed a radio message down to Calcutta," Randall said. He ran his hand through thick, straw-colored hair. "You know Matthew Shatro, my assistant. We've been surveying Liz up to Lake Mareotis."

Thomas seemed in a quandary and not happy to see these men. He stood with foot on the lead boat's gunwale, glanced at me with a puzzled expression, and then looked to his boats and deputies. "They came past Calcutta at night. They must have a base somewhere . . . We should go after them."

"We passed a camp on the way down. They're about thirty kilometers upriver by now, and the camp's empty. Everything cleared out. I think they'll make a run downriver in the next few days."

"If I know where they are . . . then we must respond." Thomas sounded regretful.

Randall sympathized. "They're all armed—over fifty men and women. We'll go with you . . ." He held out his empty arms. "But without guns we're not much use."

"No need for that," Thomas said. "I have two people who need to get downriver. This man here, his name is Olmy Ap Datchetong, and a woman from the village. She's been through a lot and she's easily frightened. Her name is Larisa Strik-Cachemou."

"I know of her," Randall said. He nodded to me and fixed me with a curious stare. Everybody knew everybody and I did not fit in.

"Can you take them to Calcutta and deliver them to the citizens rank for depositions?"

Randall's eyes, it seemed, would permanently record all that was important. "Of course," he said. Shatro, a well-muscled, short fellow with pale skin and cropped blond hair, began to rearrange boxes and bags in the launch.

Randall and Thomas stood awkwardly in their boats, both realizing that the news had put Thomas and his deputies into a quandary. As disciplinary, Thomas had a duty to confront the attackers. Yet a small party such as this, armed with only eight rifles and a few pistols, would not do well against such opposition. Randall's face grew red, and he stammered, "I don't think it would be a good idea for you to take them on—"

Thomas coughed and waved a hand. "That's my decision," he said. "We'll call downriver and ask for more boats, and for citizens to be on the lookout. Nobody wants them to get away after all they've done on the north coast. They can't sneak so many boats past us if we're watching night and day."

"They may divide their forces and send their stolen goods down first," Randall said. "One of the flatboats was heavy in the water."

"Loaded with tractors and scrap metal," Thomas surmised. He shook his head sharply, not wanting to hear news that would make him angrier, or fix him more firmly in his duty. "Pull your launch in and take these people, and we'll be on our way."

Larisa returned to the dock in the firm arms of two women. Thomas explained the situation to her, and she listened with little birdlike nods, eyes wide. We climbed into Randall's boat and I thanked Thomas for all he had done.

"I've done nothing for you," Thomas said, a little coldly. "When you get to Calcutta, tell the truth, and tell them what I'm doing here. If nobody sends help, or even if they do, we may not come back. I'm not asking for pity. It's just the damned truth."

The deputies in the boats stared at us owlishly as we pulled away and headed downriver. Shatro unfolded a rough blanket for Larisa, and Randall took the tiller, pushing us out to the middle, avoiding a few river vine humps. The bottom of the boat was filled with boxes packed with glass jars. The jars contained chunks of mottled tissue: specimens.

"You weren't in Moonrise when it happened, then?" Randall asked. I shook my head. Larisa began to chatter nervously, telling the two men all she had told Thomas and me, and adding her suspicions that I was a liar. Randall listened intently but did not seem to share her concern or disapproval.

The banks of the river revealed an immense monotony of silva, with little change in color or elevation. Red and black, browns and purples, no green. Tens of kilometers from the banks, mountains rose, and silva balloons clustered along the base of the mountains; but from this distance, a hundred meters from either shore, I could see little more than black trunks, parasols and fans, and the legs and pink crowns of cathedral trees.

The river smelled of pure fresh water, bland but invigorating. Peering into the dark clarity, I saw dappled silver blurs move flash and undulate us. Redhill's encyclopedia said that creatures of Petain's Zone, zone five, dominated the Terra Nova to its roots deep in Elizabeth's Land. Some of the riparian scions were as large as whales, easily capable of toppling a boat. A picture showed a sinuous monstrosity, twenty meters in length, crude eyes arrayed in a cross on its flat forehead, blunt tusks mounted on nose, no mouth. Its function within the river, its use to the zone five ecos, was not known.

I imagined such a thing sliding beneath our boat in the deep blue water and actually enjoyed the shiver I felt. Awe at nature was a much cleaner emotion than any I had been feeling lately.

Larisa fell asleep, head lolling with mouth open. Randall sat on a bench beside me, letting Shatro take the tiller, and offered me a bar of gum. Chewing gum seemed quite the habit here.

"Ser Cachemou is known up and down the river," Randall said in a low voice. "A loud and foolish woman. If her husband left her to go to Hsia, he may have had better reason than most." He confided a wry grimace. "What were you doing in the silva?"

"I've always wanted to do research," I said. "Science" was a word rarely used by divaricates. "I've spent the last two years studying on my own." I felt very vulnerable with this man; he probably knew more about the silva than anyone on the river, and certainly more than I could have gleaned from Jan Fima, the Dalgesh report, and Redhill's encyclopedia. "It's not been easy. I should have studied more . . . Before going into the silva."

Randall chuckled. "Very likely. Did you really get sampled?"

The small prick on my chin had almost healed. "She says I did. Something flying struck me in the dark and drew blood, but Liz doesn't do that twice, does she?"

"No," Randall said. He smiled and went aft to rig a shade for the woman.

Left to myself, with nothing to do but study the river and the endless silva, I took out Nkwanno's slate and resumed my study. I still could not access the scholar's personal records, but judging from clues left in several small open files, Nkwanno had used a few key words that he changed every few months. I wondered who he thought would read his private documents. I could not put the right words together yet, but all his public references were open to me.

As we drifted downriver, I searched for a history, and found several, all unfinished, all with the hallmarks of enthusiastic amateurs.

The immigrants had come here, thirty-seven Lamarckian years before, emerging from a gate near the present site of Calcutta. Lenk named their landfall (its measure then unknown) after his wife, Elizabeth. They had been woefully unprepared. It took months to sort out Lamarckia's possible contributions to diet and the need for raw materials. For the first ten years, starvation was a major problem.

I punched through dozens of stills of gaunt, hollow-eyed settlers clearing lizboo scions, planting grains and fruit trees and vines, toppling cathedral trees for their strong, light, woody trunks. Lenk's recordists made videos of determined mothers and fathers carrying the first children born on Lamarckia, babies wrapped in worn cloth, parents in rags.

Among the four thousand had been seven doctors with less than a ton of medical supplies, little of it advanced; here, Lenk had insisted on doctrinal purity. Some, apparently, had ignored or interpreted his instructions, but not enough to avert serious medical problems, including fatal allergic reactions to certain scions. Hungry, desperate people had eaten many things without going through proper procedures.

The faces in the pictures and movies haunted me: gaunt, frightened but steadfast, sure of themselves. All Thistledown's citizens regarded themselves as pioneers and explorers, but Lenk's people had embarked on an adventure qualitatively different from Thistledown's journey, and with far less chance of success.

Along the banks on both sides, black and brown pipes several meters wide reached down to the river, mouths half submerged. Booming, sucking sounds came across the water, enormous organic pumps at work, drawing water from the river and transporting it inland. Every few kilometers we passed these pipes, part of Liz's immense hydraulic system, circulating water for all of her scions.

Ten hours into the journey, Randall divided a loaf of bread between the four of us. "Wine?" he asked, offering a small ceramic jug. Larisa ate her bread in delicate nibbles, staring at the far shore, but refused the wine, scooping water from the river instead.

I accepted a cup. The wine was heavy and sweet, with a bitter aftertaste. I carefully did not make a face. Randall, focused on my reaction, seemed dissatisfied.

"You didn't say where you studied . . . Though I assume at Jakarta, since that's where most of the Datchetongs have lived since Lenk brought us here."

"I studied independently," I said.

Randall squinted. "I'm as fond of Liz as anyone . . . But I can't imagine being alone in the silva for years. I'd go slaps. What was it like?"

"Hard," I said. I grinned. "I almost did go slaps."

"You're a cautious man, Ser Olmy."

"Being alone does it," I said.

He shaded his eyes, searching the overgrown banks. "There are a couple of camps along here. Prospectors, small crop farmers, gatherers. Characters. I promised to look in on one. Kimon Giorgios is his name. He likes being alone, too."

I followed Randall's gaze to the western bank. The lizboo arborids were hung with orange sausage-shaped pods as much as two meters long, dangling over the water like a thickly tasseled fringe. Through the fringe, I saw a pale brown smudge hidden among the shiny black trunks. "Is that a house?" I asked.

Randall rose to a crouch, hands on his knees, and murmured, "Yesss. Sharp eyes, Olmy."

The boat pushed slowly into a narrow branch of the main river. Amid lizboo and thick clumps of phytids, five cathedral trees surrounded a small clearing. An elegantly crafted small house stood in the clearing. Hinged window covers raised on stakes propped up in the dirt gave it the appearance of an old, crippled bird trying valiantly to fly.

Shrill whistling broke out on the opposite shore and was taken up by the silva around the house. The sound bothered neither Randall nor Shatro, so I did not act surprised, either.

Randall hailed the house. No one answered. He gestured for Shatro to take us in closer. We pushed up onto the bank beside the clearing.

"Giorgios has been up and down this river for years," Randall said. "He knows it better than anyone. Someone looking for a guide . . . like Janos Strik . . ." He didn't finish his thought. We stepped off the prow and walked up the bank, listening to whistles echo back into the depths of the silva. Larisa stayed under the shade Randall had rigged, peering out at us like a small, frightened animal. Randall and Shatro walked around the house and Randall called Giorgio's name. Still no answer.

Randall entered the house through the front door. A startled curse was followed by a relieved chuckle. A scion the size of a cat, tubular red body mounted on three long, thin legs, stalked through the front door with slow dignity, pointed what might have been its head at the shore and the boat, and turned to walk into the jungle.

Randall came out of the house shaking his head. "He's been gone for days. Liz is starting to move in." He climbed into the launch. Shatro and I pushed the boat off the bank and climbed in after him. Randall took the tiller and guided us back to the middle of the main body of the river.

Randall nodded as if keeping time with some inner tune. "He'd have shut the house up if he'd left voluntarily. Never left it open for longlegs. He's well-known on the river. Everyone knows he's the best guide upstream."

Larisa shouted, "They took him!" Her voice rang across the river and was met with more high whistling from both shores.

"If they were smart, they probably did," Randall said.

Shatro sat in the bow and said little, but scanned the river constantly.

Twelve kilometers from Calcutta, the banks of the Terra Nova grew in height and narrowed to form a deep gorge only fifty meters wide. The launch rushed through the gorge with thrilling speed. Randall took the tiller, and we avoided the few rocks and quick, broad eddies without mishap.

I observed large pink parasols waving like huge hands on the rims of the gorge. Black and electric blue creepers hung down the sheer, mist-shiny black walls, pulsing as they pumped water from the river to the silva above. After several kilometers, the walls dropped again and we passed through low, flat countryside, populated by thick canopies of lizboo and punctuated by the ubiquitous cathedral trees.

"Did you see any heliophiles this far south?" Randall asked. We had been quiet since leaving the deserted cabin, and he seemed to want to break the grim mood. I did not know what heliophiles were, so I shook my head.

"Some years they travel south of Moonrise, but I haven't seen them recently. They're taking a different role in Liz's scheme, I think . . . You must have relied on diospuros."

"Kept me alive most of the time," I said. Edible after soaking in water and cooking, high in usable protein and sugars, sweet and meaty to the taste, diospuros had been one of the first phytids used successfully for food. If Randall was testing me, however, he would soon catch me up.

"Did you see whitehat feeding on diospuros?"

"No," I said. "I saw them sucking on lizboo."

"That's their habit this far north. South of here, where we haven't depleted them, they seem to prefer diospuros." Randall seemed satisfied with this, and kept silent for the next few kilometers.

The sun felt good on my hands as I clasped the launch's gunwale. Much of the time, the sky was veiled by thin, high ice-crystal clouds, diffusing the sun's hot disk into an incandescent pearl. I shifted forward and leaned back, closing my eyes in the bright, milky glare. My neck muscles had bunched with something . . . tension, I supposed. I could not remember having felt *tense* in years—if ever. The implants and supplements I had given up for this mission had smoothed so many of my body's basic reactions; I seemed to be experiencing a new kind of existence, or at least one largely forgotten.

My vision blurred and I drifted into a musing doze, also a novel experience.

I jerked and lifted my head, blinking at a shadow leaning over me.

Shatro handed me a tin of biscuits. He spoke softly, diffidently. "We'll see Calcutta in an hour."

The river broadened and the current slowed again. Larisa came out from under the shade and sat well apart from me, staring at nothing in particular but away from the boat, lips pursed, brows elevated as if in unending surprise. On Thistledown, her family would take her in for a mental refresh. Even divaricates recognized mental dysfunction.

Randall joined me with his own tin of biscuits. "You've not heard much news recently, then."

I liked Randall, felt that he was sympathetic, but I was not looking for more conversation. I needed much more time to study, to avoid being caught up in stupid mistakes. "Yes," I said. "I apologize for my ignorance."

He smiled and shook his head. "The political situation has changed since you left . . . Calcutta?"

"Calcutta," I said.

"Passed through Moonrise."

"On my way upriver, yes."

"Brion sent his dogs out to savage the north coast last year. They've ran-sacked seven villages and stolen everything they could get their hands on . . . including children."

"Why take children?" Shatro asked, shaking his head. "It doesn't figure, a hungry community stealing children."

"They may not be hungry anymore, if the stories are to be trusted. We don't talk with Naderville much now," Randall said. "Somebody in Naderville may have made some calculations and realized we'll outstrip them in population and influence in the next generation. Their women are exhausted and they can't make their baby machines work. Stealing kids in populations as small as ours makes sense, if you can feed and raise them."

I had heard nothing about baby machines. Nkwanno's references did not mention them either. Divaricates had never believed in ex utero gestation and birth. "Nobody's fought back?" I asked.

Randall gave me one of his appraising looks. "Lenk doesn't seem to have the stomach for a war. I think he hopes Naderville will just fade away. But they've regained a lot of strength in the last year. Of course, when they com-municate with us at all, they publicly disavow General Beys . . . But he delivers his goods to Naderville, all the same."

We sat in silence for a moment. Then Randall said, "Do you have any-place to stay in Calcutta?"

"Hospice," I said. "No money."

"No need to stay in hospice. Why not stay with my family while you wait to testify? Might be a couple of days."

"Thanks," I said. "I'm not very presentable. I've been on my own for so long . . ."

"We've been down south on the Terra Nova for the last two weeks," Ran-dall said. "I'm sure you've seen interesting things, even if you don't know how to interpret them. There aren't enough researchers on this planet that we can afford not to talk with each other."

Six kilometers above Calcutta, the geology changed abruptly. The land became bumpy and rugged. The silva thinned, leaving cathedral trees and a few scattered lizboos rising like game markers on a low rolling carpet of vivid purple and sky blue. Pale gray granite hills rose to the west, capped by thick, violet phytids.

"Look at the color on the hills this spring," Randall said. "Brightest I've seen in many years. Wonder if Liz has changed a specification or two?"

Shatro examined the hills through a pair of binoculars. He saw my interest and loaned them to me. I looked at the hills, a clump of lizboo two hundred meters from the bank, and saw a group of two-necked cleaners working on the arborids' parasols and fans. Their eyeless heads swept from leaf to leaf with slow, sure motions, reminding me both of dinosaurs and microscopic tardigrades. I returned the binoculars to Shatro.

"Ser Randall and I found seven more varieties of lizboo, all specialized to different mineral conditions," Shatro said. "We've been measuring oxygen production in the deep silva."

"Impressive," I said.

"Elementary, really," Randall said. "Lenk gave us a commission to make sure Liz isn't headed toward another flux. The silva really isn't an important source of oxygen. Negligible, actually. Most of it comes from the coastal oceans. Dissociation of water, we presume—though we don't know. But oxygen levels in the silva could point to changes in the scion mix. It's important work, but rather dull."

I began to wonder how long I could hold out in conversation, as a visitor in Randall's house, without being unveiled as a complete fraud.

I wondered when the Brionists would return to Moonrise and stake their claim. Would the disciplinary or the citizens of Calcutta oppose them? I tried to imagine this Brion, about whom there was nothing in Redhill: an ambitious petty dictator, I guessed, clothed in a ridiculous uniform.

Shatro cut the motor and the launch drifted with the stream. Breezes carried unfamiliar scents—tomato juice, ginger.

From the south, upriver, I heard the thin, flat whine of more motors. Three large flat-bottom boats were gaining on us. Clutching a half eaten biscuit, Randall stepped aft and stared at them. With disgust, he crumpled the biscuit and threw it between the thwarts. "Here they come, the bold bastards," he growled.

Soon the three boats were less than a hundred meters away. Uniformed men crowded their decks, perhaps a hundred in all. Each flatboat was about fifteen meters long and six or seven across the beam, with shallow drafts and long, wide cabins large enough to store farm and other equipment. No women were visible on deck. *They would all be back home*, I thought, *rearing more children for Brion.*

The men standing around the cabins were mostly brown, a few blacks and whites, the familiar Thistledown mix. They wore tan trousers and loose-fitting white shirts. Most carried their large rifles prominently. Some smiled and talked in low voices as the boats passed the launch. The rest said nothing and just stared at us, rifles poised.

"What do you know about a village upriver, called Moonrise?" Randall called to the boats. His face reddened as he got no answer. Larisa retreated to the shade and lay down, covering her face with her hands.

A slight restless milling on the flatboats. We were very close. They could kill us all if they chose.

"What about a citizen named Giorgios? Kimon Giorgios?"

The boats motored ahead of us. We faced the men on the rear, faces young and old, all indifferent.

"Where are the rest of you?" Randall called, a little foolishly, I thought. We sat waiting for an answer, but nobody replied in words. Instead, the men on the boats lifted their rifles and pointed them just over our heads, teeth shining behind the glistening black barrels.

A high, ululating shout rose from the boats. The men lifted their hands and rifles and sang out again, voices echoing from the edge of the silva. The gray boats' harmonizing electric whines sounded like a leftover taunt.

"They're going to pass through Calcutta in broad daylight, and ahead of us," Shatro said.

"We're about six kilometers south of Calcutta," Randall said. "Won't even talk with us. Absolute contempt. The bastards."

The silva grew lush again, lizboo with fringes of pods packed thick along both sides. On the northern bank, a glistening black sand beach pushed into the silva and along the river. A party of picnickers lazed over their midday meal, watching us. The men waved politely. They might have waved at the gray boats as well; they did not seem concerned. Three naked children splashed in the river, their musical shouts and screams rising above the liquid lapping of the river against the boat hulls. I wondered if the children had been called in to hide when the flatboats passed.

Everybody seemed unconcerned, relaxed . . .

I dropped one arm over the side and dabbled my fingers. The water was cold, but not bone-chilling. Before I could react, a silvery creature the size of a small trout swifted from the depths and plunged something sharp into my thumb. Jerking, clamping my jaw to still a startled yelp, I yanked my hand out, sucked away a drop of blood, and wiped the thumb quickly on my dark socks. A prick; nothing more. Nobody had noticed. I thought, *The river knows me, as well, now.*

The sky gleamed like old polished silver at zenith, bluing only above the horizon. Farther downriver, buildings appeared in more clearings, closely attended by lizboo: boathouses, some sort of small factory with smoke pouring from a thin black stack and men marching across a clearing in black aprons, loading wagons. I saw only a few tractors, and of course there would be no horses or oxen; the Lenk group had brought no animals with them.

A small farm nestled between walls of lizboo like a brown postage stamp on red and purple and black paisley. Silos, but no barns. Out of place, my mind said, but it actually looked quite lovely, familiar in my gut, though I had never seen such a thing in actual experience. I imagined fields of crops—grain and vegetables, biomass ponds—inland, away from the river, perhaps scattered between or spread across the low plateaus northeast of Calcutta, as Redhill described: human intrusions that Liz apparently tolerated. As we passed the farm, a young man in blue and brown workits—overalls of an ancient cut—came out on a small dock and waved to us. Randall and Shatro returned his wave.

"There's a reception downriver, above Calcutta," the young man shouted, his voice cracking with youth and excitement. "I'd pull in and wait it out."

"What kind of reception?" Randall asked.

"Enough said. You might be spies."

Randall shook his head and waved his thanks for the slender warning, but we did not pull in.

"A reception?" Shatro asked nervously.

"I think he means Calcutta isn't going to let the flatboats pass," Randall said.

"What can they do?"

"I'd like to find out."

Shatro started to object, but shut his mouth and lowered his head. Randall stood at the bow, glaring downriver. We all listened. Larisa moaned beneath the shade.

"We should land the woman," Shatro said.

Randall did not seem to hear him.

"Perhaps Ser Olmy would like to get out, too," Shatro added.

I shook my head. I was as curious as Randall to see what sort of response the town might mount.

A few shots like snapping sticks sounded down the river. We all jumped as one.

Randall told Shatro to bring the launch about and run the motor at quarter speed, letting us drift with the current, but more slowly. An island covered with pure black lizboo split the Terra Nova half a kilometer ahead. "That's where I would do it," Randall said. "Which way . . . right or left?"

"I would take my flatboats around both sides," I said.

"Both sides flow deep," Randall said. "But the best side is to the east, left. It's the widest. A lazy, self-assured pilot would go to the left . . . And that's where I'd put my pickets and lay my traps. The Brionists are arrogant bastards, Ser Olmy. They think they know more than we do. They think we've become sheep."

More wide-spaced shots, then a steady series of *crackcrack-crack-crack*, frantic shouting, a boom. A puff of smoke rose above the trees, whirling. "Left," Randall called out, and Shatro turned the tiller to veer us east of the island.

In the silva along the left bank, men and women stood peering downriver, talking. Some waved and grinned like fools as we passed; others shouted warnings. "Skirmish ahead! Pull in!"

Randall shook his head and ignored them. Shatro was becoming more and more agitated, sweat standing out on his pale face. He stared grimly forward with his pale blue eyes as if expecting the boat to be swallowed.

We rounded a stand of lizboo on a narrow sand spit. Randall increased the turns on the motor. At less than a kilometer an hour, we descended toward the three Brionist flatboats. Nets and ropes had been strung across the river and the flatboats were caught in them. Men had been pulled off into the water by the ropes and swam around their boats, heads bobbing in the current. One man hung from a sagging rope, feet dragging in the river, dead. On the eastern bank, shots rang out from behind cover of small shacks and lizboo trunks. The men on the flatboats were returning fire as best they could, but they were exposed, and more and more of them were falling to the deck or into the water. The air filled with more cries and shouting.

From the shore came war whoops and more shots. A sizzling pipe bomb flew over the river and bounced on the deck of the leftmost flatboat, rolled into the water, and exploded, sending up a plume of spray. Another landed squarely on the cabin, rolled to the starboard side, blew up, and propelled a cloud of splinters high into the air. Yet a third landed on the middle boat and a man plucked it up to toss it away. It exploded in his hand and his arm and head vanished. On the shore, mingled cries of horror and cheers met this sight, and more cheers as the headless body crumpled and slid off the deck.

I felt a sick excitement. My stomach knotted and I clenched sweaty hands. I smelled gunpowder and burning and something else—I presumed it was blood. My skin crawled and my throat closed and I choked at the thought of breathing the vapor of somebody else's blood.

All three flatboats were hopelessly caught. From their decks now came cries of surrender, and a few men stood with hands raised, throwing their weapons into the water.

"No quarter!" someone bellowed from the shore, no doubt a student of history. Shots continued, but fewer in number. The rightmost of the flatboats was taking on water and listing badly. Other sounds came to us, muffled, like trapped animals crying out. Randall stood in the bow, brow creased. "Fates and Breath," he said. "There are prisoners in that boat."

He walked aft, took the tiller from Shatro, swung the launch around again and propelled us at full speed down the river, directly toward the fight. Shatro scrambled to the middle of the launch. "Where are we going?" he shouted.

"That boat is going to founder," Randall said.

Shatro sat beside Larisa, who stared straight ahead like a doll, frightened out of her wits.

The cries from inside the listing flatboat came louder now. A few bullets zizzed past our heads until voices on the banks shouted that we were not Brionists. The river was backing up behind the flatboats, fifteen meters ahead, and we began to yaw in an eddy. Randall took advantage of the eddy and steered us to the right. The rightmost flatboat, heeling onto its starboard side, suddenly threw open its cabin hatches and seemed to erupt. Heads, arms, legs poured onto the deck: children, I saw, over two dozen of them.

I could not help crying out, and Randall nodded grimly, tears on his cheeks falling in twin glittering streams. The children leaped and fell off the tilting deck into the water. A man carrying two babies lost his balance and also fell. For a moment, he held the babies up, then let them go and swam to save himself.

I thought of ants falling from a floating leaf.

The water was filled with bobbing heads: a few Brionist soldiers, but mostly children of all ages. Our boat moved in among them and Shatro and I immediately began grabbing arms, legs, heads, pulling children into the boat, five, six, eight, nine, I lost count. Larisa remained rooted to her seat, staring left and right like an antique toy. A young girl with slick wet hair climbed over her, crying out, "I know you! I know you!" and tried to hug her. Larisa pushed her away with frightened disgust.

More boats came from the shore now, dinghies and smacks and canoes. The river filled with boats.

A crouching soldier on the flatboat mechanically aimed and shot his rifle into the rescuers. As if in a dream, I watched him take aim, fire, and turned to see a splash of water beside a boat, or a man scream and grab his chest, lurching backward. The soldier's expression was calm, indifferent. I stared at him for what seemed minutes but could only have been a few seconds.

A small body came out of the water in Randall's arms and he passed it to me. I immediately laid it on the forward bench and began artificial respiration. It was a young boy. His skin was warm and his eyes open, staring. I dreaded he was already dead. But after a few of my puffed breaths he shut his eyes tight, coughed up water and vomited, and started to breathe, and then to scream and thrash. I spat the sour taste of vomit from my mouth and handed him to an older boy, who cradled him in a skinny lap.

I looked up, took another child from Shatro, and then another, and saw that our launch held too many, was in danger of tipping over itself. We had drifted with the current past the flatboats. A few men still huddled on the decks, but most had retreated within the cabins.

The soldier with the rifle had been shot and lay over the gunwale, blood dripping from his ruined head into the river.

A few shots still rang out, from the boats and from the shore, but the children were the main concern of most of the citizens.

Randall gave Shatro the tiller again and shouted at Larisa to help keep the children calm. She did not move. The launch carried perhaps twenty-five boys and girls, the youngest barely two, the oldest twelve or thirteen, all terrified, pasty white or olive green with shock. A small boy's body lay in the bottom of the boat, staring with the slack empty look of the dead. The boat smelled of fear and urine and vomit. "Put in to shore," Randall told Shatro. "Olmy, help me get these children to the port side . . . to the left." I helped rearrange five of the youngsters, moving them bodily if they were too stunned or frightened to respond.

The launch ran up onto a small black sand beach, nearly knocking me off my feet. A tall, wiry older girl fell into the water and clambered ashore on her own, hair streaming sand and water, face set with determination to stay alive and get away from the madness.

Three women and two men came out of the silva behind the beach and helped us unload the children.

"Where are they from?" a matronly, tall woman with graying hair asked. She gripped two children by their arms. One kicked his feet in the water and began to scream.

"I don't know," Shatro answered.

"From Moonrise, perhaps," Randall suggested.

How many villages had had their children stolen?

A man in soaked brown pants and clinging white shirt swam to the beach and stood in the shallows, lurching ashore. He glanced at us, saw we were busy tending to the children, and tried to run into the silva, but two strong young men in workits carrying large sticks blocked his path. "Who are you?" one asked him.

"I give up," he said breathlessly.

They took him away, whacking him on the shoulders and back with their fists.

The children were led or walked on their own back into the silva, and the launch bobbed gently in the water now that it was lighter, beginning to come around stern first and pull off the beach. A single boy of five or six had stayed in the boat. He gripped the gunwale with both hands and looked over his shoulder at me.

"My name is Daniel Harrin," he said. "My family is dead. Where do I go?"

Other than the dead boy still in the bottom, he was the last in our care. I sat beside him and put an arm around his shoulder. "We'll find you a place, Daniel," I said.

Larisa had somehow managed to get ashore, where she squatted on the sand, as helpless and useless as ever. I felt a sudden flash of hate mixed with pity for her. So many primitive emotions in one hour; I felt drained.

Randall moored the boat with a line and anchor, and stood in the water beside us, staring at me and at the boy.

"Where have we gone so wrong?" he asked.

CHAPTER FOUR

Calcutta rose along the scallops and harbors of the west bank like a magnificent card castle, more lovely than I expected. Yellow and white walls rose from the surrounding red and black and pink silva. The late-afternoon sun burnished the tops of the low, planar, angular buildings like white gold. The walls merged with steps descending past level parks and warehouses to the river, where the waters slopped and slid.

As the boat cruised past the outlying sections of the city—if it could be called a city, having less than five thousand residents—I saw that most of the buildings were made of painted xyla, probably lizboo or cathedral tree. Foundations and retaining walls were concrete and granite. Of steel and plastic I saw little. Broad glass windows faced the east and the river. That meant furnaces and manufacturing.

The launch passed a few other boats. Shatro and Randall sat in the rear, Larisa back beneath the shade, and I took the bench near the bow. We had been relieved of the dead boy and we had cleaned the bottom of the boat as best we could with buckets of water and rags.

I could not clear my head of the sounds and smells. Vomit from the boy I had breathed life back into stained my shirt and pants. Parts of me still saw and analyzed, but the center of my thoughts was a numb grayness. I could not sleep yet but I wanted to fall asleep. The closest I could come to sleep was to sit on the bench and stare and try not to remember too clearly.

I had never felt strong parental instincts until I saw the children in the water. Now, behind the grayness, flashes of horror and unconditional love for the children, and animal hatred, the urge to wrap my hands around the necks of the Brionists, all came and went like lightning behind clouds.

I would have to work hard to keep my objectivity. My mission was to study Lamarckia, not to become involved in immigrant politics.

The tallest building rose from the city's center on a low hill, four rounded stories, each eccentric from a central axis, beneath cantilevered pagoda roofs and porches that to me seemed lovely if ancient: *Frank Lloyd Wright, Richard Neutra*, I thought, *a touch of Tibet, Shangri-la*, trying to remember fragments of terrestrial art history that I had explored before all my memory supplements had been removed.

The missing information bothered me. I shuddered slightly, stumbling onto a lapse in some personal wisdom based on memory no longer accessible, like a missing molar. I hated that sensation. It made me feel reduced, less capable; it shook my confidence. What if I lurched into a crucial gap during an emergency?

But none of this really mattered compared to what we had just experienced.

The launch slid smoothly into a covered berth at the municipal dock. As Shatro secured the lines, I climbed out of the boat and took a deep breath, turned, and found Randall staring at me blankly. Suddenly he smiled. He looked like a wolf.

"We did some good back there," he said. "We'll go to the court tomorrow and let them know you're here. You can stay with my family tonight."

Larisa came out from under the shade, stiff with dignity or perhaps exhaustion. She barely looked at us. "I have family here," she said. "I do not need your help."

"Thomas wants you at the court," Randall reminded her.

She nodded. "I will be there." She glared at me. Her eyelids drew together and her face seemed full of hatred. "I do not need your help."

We walked through the center of Calcutta to Randall's home. Shatro said his farewells and went off to his own home. He was unbonded, Randall said, and lived with an older man and woman in the Karpos neighborhood. "They raise fruits there. Pears and apples do well if you grind up lizboo parasols for fertilizer. They naturally give up the right nutrients for those trees. It's a luxury crop, but that's nothing against it."

The courthouse, center of the district's legal proceedings, sat just below the elegant tower on Calcutta's highest hill. We walked up a long winding flight of steps lined with homes and shops. The tower, Randall said, was the Lenk Hub, seat of cross-district government and home of Lenk himself when he chose to come to Calcutta.

"It's really quite spare quarters for such a fine man," Randall said.

"Do you know him?" I asked.

"Through Captain Keyser-Bach."

The broad steps were caught in afternoon shadow, which seemed richly brown, almost golden beneath the silver sky. The city smelled of cooking food, mostly yeasty bread smells and rich molasses smells, dust from carts rolling on the busy street below, orange and tomato and spice from the silva never completely absent. Children ran laughing and shrieking down the steps beside us, boys and girls from late infancy to middle childhood, wearing red shorts and white vests with green vertical stripes, tended by a young man with a bemused look, no doubt junior husband in a triad. Otherwise, the streets were quiet, the citizens polite, their clothes muted, generally browns and grays or greens, each however with one splash of color, a scarf or sash or belt, signifying solemnity within living joy. These traditions had held up well on Lamarckia.

I was relieved that not everything had fallen into chaos. After all I had heard of famine and hardship, I was surprised that Calcutta looked prosperous and its citizens well-fed.

At the top of the stairs, in a shaded courtyard graced with a single terrestrial tree—an ash, I thought, its limbs bare, not faring very well—we turned into a narrow alley. The houses that rose on either side were made of cut reddish lava held together by dark gray cement. An anonymous xyla doorway no different from the others pushed open with a creak at Randall's touch, and we entered cool shadow.

"Randall?" a woman called eagerly. "Erwin, is that you?

"That's me," Randall said. He smiled shyly, the wolf look gone. "That's my wife, Raytha. Head of family. I'm an infrequent extra here."

Randall's family totaled seven: four children, age two to twelve, two younger girls and two older boys, who flocked around him with broad smiles and big eyes, simply glad to see their father; his wife Raytha, a plump, pretty woman the same age as he; and her mother, Kaytai Kim-Jastro. Ser Kim-Jastro was tall and straight and gray and formidable, and she did not hug Randall, but instead shook his hand and welcomed him back with deep gravity.

The children gathered around me when they were finished welcoming their father. They asked where I was from and whether I was married and had any children, and why their father had brought me home with him. Randall answered the last question by saying, "He's a researcher and he's our guest. He's not used to a lot of company, so please give him some room until after dinner at least."

The two older boys stayed to hear Randall's stories, but the younger girls went with their mother and grandmother into another room down the hall. I heard other voices in that room: a communal kitchen. Men from another family in the triad were cooking today. "Nothing fancy," Raytha said as she walked down the hall flanked by her girls. "But it's food."

"More gray piscids and flockweed paste," Randall said when she had left, and confided another grimace. He led me into a room he said was his own, and his alone, but he did not object when the boys followed. This tiny cubicle had a window high in one wall to the outside, through which a cool evening breeze was blowing. A small electric lantern hung in one corner, casting a dim yellow light over shelves packed with crudely bound books.

"Father, what happened at the river?" the older of the two boys asked as we settled onto woven fiber chairs. "The teacher dismissed us early today and went to the river . . . He said he was joining a committee."

"There was a fight," Randall said, lines growing deeper in his face. He did not like describing this to his sons.

"Did anybody get killed?" the younger boy asked. He reminded me of the boy I had saved by breathing life back into him. His eyes danced with intense interest. My stomach knotted with the remembered love and hate all over again.

"A lot of people were killed, mostly pirates," Randall said. He did not volunteer information about the children in the boats. A bell jangled near the alleyway door and Randall got up to answer it. After a conversation of several minutes, during which time the boys sat in the room alone with me, biting their lips and staring at each other for support, but saying nothing, Randall returned.

"A representative of the citizens rank, welcoming me back," Randall said. "Thomas radioed them from upriver. They will indeed expect us tomorrow."

"Any more news?" the older boy asked.

"Ser Olmy, let me name these chatty ones for you," he said, patting their heads. "This is Nebulon, and this is Carl. Carl is a year and a half younger than his brother."

"I made my mother a little sick," Carl said. "That's why our sisters are so new and we're not."

"There's more news, yes," Randall said, eyes half closed with exhaustion. "Go help your mother and grandmother. I'll tell you later."

"Now!" Carl insisted, but Randall gently and firmly packed them out of the room and drew the curtains once they were down the hall and out of hearing.

"There were thirty-seven children on the boat," Randall said. "Thirty of them were saved. We had most of them in our boat. Twelve of the Brionists died and twenty were wounded. Sixty are in custody. Nobody knows what to do with them. They'll probably be sent to Athenai for Lenk to decide. We can't afford to keep them here." He took a deep breath and lifted his arms. "Pardon me. I'm acting as if we're old friends."

"We've been through a lot," I said.

"But I don't know you. That's unusual around here. Most people know each other along the Terra Nova."

"I've been a loner most of my life."

"Because your family was proscribed?"

I put on an air of ignoring this, and Randall assumed he had touched on a sensitive issue.

"You showed real courage on the river today," he said. "Even more than Shatro. You seem accustomed to this kind of incident."

"I'm not," I said, truthfully. "And I wouldn't call it courage."

"Um." Randall muttered and sat down in his chair, stretching his legs out in the small, close, brown, and shadowy room. "Still, you impressed me. What prospects do you have, what plans, if I may continue this ungrateful prying?"

"I need to get to Athenai at some point," I said.

"How soon?" Randall asked.

"I'm not sure."

"I'm asking because my partner, Captain Keyser-Bach . . ." He paused to gauge my reaction to that name. I pursed my lips and widened my eyes, and that seemed to satisfy him. ". . . And I . . . are about to begin a very ambitious journey by ship. We've overcome many difficulties and many kinds of reluctance, both to get this journey financed and approved, and to find the right people to go with us."

I saw that the name of Captain Keyser-Bach was meant to impress me, but though he had mentioned it once before, I knew nothing about this person. I decided to behave as if I were impressed. "A journey to where?" I asked.

"A circumnavigation," Randall said. "We hope to finish the voyage Jiddermeyer and Baker and Shulago never completed. To Jakarta first, then to Wallace Station to pick up Ser Mansur Salap and more researchers, then across the Darwin Sea northeast to Martha's Island . . . That's just the beginning. A circumnavigation from east to west. We'll end up in Athenai, but it might take us three years."

I felt my chest tighten. "That's a grand voyage," I said. "A scientific expedition?"

Randall cringed, and I realized my mistake too late. "The captain uses that word much too often, and in the wrong company," he said. "For us, it is always *research*, and we are *researchers*. But it amounts to the same thing. We've studied Liz enough for the time being. She's a wonderful ecos, peaceful and nurturing, once we knew her ways, but she's a little bland and uniform for our tastes. It's time to make comparisons and draw broad conclusions. Otherwise, both the captain and I firmly believe, in time Lamarckia is going to kill us." He lowered his voice. "We came here ignorant and unprepared, and it has taken all these decades to even begin to climb out of the hole." Now he stared at me earnestly, large liquid eyes penetrating, measuring, still more than a little doubtful.

"Whom will you report to," I asked, "when you've finished the voyage?"

"To Able Lenk himself," Randall said.

I stared at my hands, almost too tired and numb to realize my fortune. Ry Ornis had truly put me at a locus of extreme interest.

"If it fits within your plans, you're welcome to interview with the captain, and I'll back you up. But no need to answer right away. We both need rest. And you have to testify tomorrow."

"The offer is very interesting," I said.

"That's enough for now," Randall said, lifting his hands from the arm of the woven chair. "We should wash ourselves before dinner. We deserve a brave meal and a few glasses of wine."

As I splashed water on my face from a ceramic bowl in a cramped washroom, I saw clearly again the Brionist soldier on the flatboat, kneeling and taking careful aim at the rescuers in their canoes and dinghies. His expression haunted me more than his death, which I did not witness. He seemed perfectly content to be killing people, even those who were not trying to kill him. He squinted one eye and aimed his pitiful rifle, as if it might be the most powerful weapon in the universe.

For the people he killed, of course, it was.

But I had seen weapons that could scour a million hectares and reduce matter to blue-violet plasma . . .

I looked up at the little unframed mirror on the wall and wondered just why this thought had occurred to me. The soldier on the flatboat had become a tool and this man, this dead man, had been content to be such a tool. He did not think whether it was right or wrong to shoot men and women in boats trying to save children he himself had kidnapped.

I wondered whether there was not a little of him in me. What would I do with this anger, this wish that I myself had put my hands around the man's neck and strangled him, watching his flat, contented eyes go blank and slack as the eyes of the boy in the bottom of the boat?

"Not your job," I whispered to the image in the mirror: black hair, sharp eyes, sharp nose, large lips that seemed a little insolent even to me. "Just learn what you can, get the clavicle, go home."

The eight of us sat down at a long lizboo table to ladle helpings from several bowls of flockweed paste and baked piscids from the river: gray-skinned mouthless fishlike creatures with translucent fringed tails, three black eye-spots, and a body about twenty centimeters long. They consisted almost entirely of ropy muscle-like proteins that were nourishing but tasteless. Various sauces concocted from a private herb garden added some zest to a very bland meal.

It was apparent within the first few minutes of dinner that Ser Kaytai Kim-Jastro thought she was the head of this branch of the triad. Randall and his wife treated her with quiet deference, and the children did likewise; but it was obvious that nobody treated her quite as well as she thought she deserved. As we settled down to eat, she picked at her food with sad dignity, like deposed royalty dreaming of past feasts. This did not seem to bother Raytha, who had not cooked the food this day, taking the family's share from the communal kitchen.

There was little talk of the action on the river. Instead, Raytha asked her husband about the journey upriver and what they had found. Randall described twelve previously uncataloged scions. "Not new ones—they don't have the marks of prototypes or test cases—but we've just never observed served them and recorded them at the same time. We made a great many oxygen measurements. No signs of a fluxing."

"Was it worthwhile, as a trip?" Raytha asked.

"I think so. Not nearly as worthwhile as the big voyage, of course . . . But good exercise."

"My husband gets restless if he spends more than a few days a month at home," Raytha said to me cheerfully.

Randall smiled and inclined his head, as if showing modesty at some compliment. "My wife gets restless if I'm underfoot," he responded.

"We like having Da home," the youngest boy, Carl, said. Carl was eating very little. I found the children's faces mesmerizing. The girls in particular were enchanting—little mimics of the adult women, lisps and childish accents like music. The children in the river had affected me more deeply than I realized.

"Why are you staring at us?" the oldest girl, Sasti, asked after a few minutes.

"I've been out in the silva for so long . . ." I said. "Not many young, beautiful faces out there."

"Our children *are* very attractive," Raytha said proudly. "Not well-behaved all the time, but attractive."

"Thank you, Mima," Sasti said primly.

"Would it be polite to ask about your work?" Raytha asked me.

"Much like Ser Randall's, only less educated and much less directed. Largely a waste of two years, actually."

Randall gave a quick warning look to Raytha, who caught it and redirected her line of questioning. "And your present plans?"

"I need to find work. I thought I would go to Athenai."

Raytha's mother shook her head. "A snobbish town if ever there was one. Everybody bows to Able Lenk. I came here from Athenai to be with my daughter when her children were born. My husband is still there."

"Kaytai's views are a bit harsh," Raytha said. "She lived close to the throne too long."

Randall said in an undertone, "Be kind. Remember, we have the funding and approval."

"Yes, well, it took Good Lenk seven years to give it to you," Kaytai said. "I don't fear spies. I know Lenk doesn't go in for them, for one thing—this is not a police state, and I give him credit where it's due—and besides, Ser Olmy does not have the look of an informer."

"I wouldn't know who to talk to," I said. "I don't know much about politics in Athenai."

"It's a political town, but that's hardly abnormal," Kaytai continued. "Few criticize Good Lenk, even when there is much to criticize. If more criticism had been given at the beginning, perhaps we wouldn't have experienced so much hardship and tragedy."

"The crossing through the Way was very difficult to arrange," Raytha said with a hint of piety. "So I understand, of course. I hadn't been born."

"Tell us more about Thistledown and the Way, Granmee," Nebulon said, but she ignored him.

"I was an adult," Kaytai said. "I should have known what I was getting into. But living in Thistledown was a dream of luxury and we weren't prepared. Nobody knew what to expect. Least of all did we know we'd be turned into baby machines."

That phrase again.

"Law of nature," Randall said dryly.

"Easy for men to say," Kaytai continued, warming to her subject. "And for Lenk to expect of us. And we agreed! It sounded dramatic and powerful, to become mothers to a new and cleaner society. But what happened on the river today—was that *clean* or honorable?"

"What the defenders did was honorable," Raytha said, cheeks pinking. She glanced at Randall, but he was used to his in-law, apparently, and was studiously taking no offense.

"Did you see all bravery and no foolishness, Ser Olmy?" Kaytai asked.

"I saw bravery and a lot of foolishness," I said.

"A lot of foolishness, that's true enough. We need to be brave with so much foolishness." She sat silent for a while, and we finished the dinner with little but the chatter of the children. Nebulon described Thistledown and the Way for me, and Carl added telling details. They thought it was a fabulous place, full of cold pounding machines and people who no longer looked like people.

Kaytai picked up where she had left off as herb tea was served. "I remember Thistledown well," she said. "Nobody else here remembers it at all."

"I was three years old," Randall said. "Not very clear memories."

"It was not what Lenk portrays, nor what Carl and Nebulon make up. It was not a corrupting place of technological hubris. It was wonderfully comfortable and fulfilling. I did not realize it at the time. I was a young idealist. My husband was a devoted follower of Good Lenk. Everything my husband believed, I believed. And for his sake, I crossed. Three of my children died in the first three years. I bore those children in misery and pain and they died. On Thistledown their births would have been much easier, and they would not have died . . ."

"The price we paid was high," Raytha said softly, sipping from her ceramic cup and staring at the top of the table. "But we've gained a beautiful world, a young world."

She seemed embarrassed by her mother's talk, but was not going to cut it short. I wondered how much she agreed with it—and how much Randall agreed, and how much the general population of immigrants resented the difficulties of the past few decades.

"How many worlds have been opened in the Way by now? Almost forty years! We might have each found a paradise . . ."

Kaytai thought that time passed on Thistledown as it did here.

"But we hated the technology. We feared it. We feared it so much we left most of it behind, even the machines that would have kept our children alive. Everything fell upon the women. Making babies and watching them die. The old ways, forgotten by all of us. We were not prepared for them. I remember."

"The Way was monstrous," Raytha said.

"Lenk used the Way, didn't he?" Kaytai said.

"Mother, our guest has had a very difficult day . . . And so has Erwin. We should find other things to talk about."

"The day's difficulties are part of what I . . . I can't even begin to express. Someday it will all be set right, but I do not know how. I apologize, Ser Olmy, if I've upset you."

"Not upset at all," I said.

Kaytai gave me the first smile I had seen on her face. "I'd like to tell you about Thistledown, sometime," she said. "You're much too young to remember, and there's so much distortion of the facts. I remember the way it really was. When I was a girl, before I met my husband . . ."

Randall and Raytha prepared a cot for me in the study. "Feel free to consult the books," Randall said.

"We often have scholars stay with us," Raytha said. "Randall likes to show off his library."

"Not many as good outside of Athenai or Jakarta," Randall said. "Almost everything known about Lamarckia." He shook his head ruefully. "Obviously, there's a lot left to learn."

The family retired a few minutes later, and the apartment fell quiet. My exhaustion had passed, and I sat up on the cot, wide awake. I had the entire evening ahead of me while the family slept.

Fingers tapped lightly on the frame beside the drawn curtain. I pulled the curtain aside. Kaytai stood in the hall, fingers to her lips, gray eyes glistening in the dark. "You seem sympathetic," she said. "I get so little sympathy here. Oh, there's much love, but nobody seems to understand."

Irritated that I might have less time to study the slate or the books, I pulled the curtain aside and invited her in.

"I do feel I have something to tell," she said stiffly, glancing at the walls of books with no interest whatsoever. "Erwin will take you away tomorrow and I'll probably not have another chance.

"You spent two years in the silva. I have no doubt you found it fascinating and maybe even beautiful. It is beautiful, I can't deny that. But on Thistledown, there were chambers filled with terrestrial forests, animals, insects . . . Rich and dense and complete. When I was a girl we would spend weeks in the forests, and unless we looked up into the sky, we could pretend we were back on Earth . . . Lovely, lovely places.

"My husband told me Lamarckia would be a paradise. He assured me Lenk knew everything, and that we would live in pristine wilderness never visited by humans. I don't think even he understood what that would mean. Lenk told us to procreate. I spent the first ten years here having babies and watching most of them die. Raytha was my fourth, and the first to live. The soil was poor in cobalt and selenium and magnesium. None of our crops grew properly. We didn't know which things to eat on Lamarckia. The food was wrong. Adults became sick as well, but not as often as the children. Their little bodies didn't seem to know how to fit in. Those were terrible times . . . We suffered diseases never known on Thistledown. We were not prepared."

Raytha stood in the doorway. "Mother," she said gently. "Please. Our guest is very tired."

"I just wanted to tell him," Kaytai said.

"I'm sorry, Ser Olmy," Raytha said, putting her arm around her mother's shoulder. She turned her head to look at me. "I don't disagree with my mother, but there are better times to talk. And we haven't even asked what your views are."

"He's young," Kaytai said. "He should know. Who will tell him?"

Raytha drew the curtain and the apartment became quiet again.

I took Nkwanno's slate from the backpack. The walls of books were too formidable. High-level texts, papers written by researchers for other researchers. I had to prepare myself with basic knowledge before I tackled them. But by morning, I had to be ready for further conversations with Randall and with his friend, the important and well-known Captain Keyser-Bach.

I studied Nkwanno's personal files again, trying to piece together the clues to unravel his code. There were many bookmarks in texts by Henry David Thoreau, laid in with quotes from Henry Place, the head ecologist during the construction of Thistledown. I tried combinations of these names and of various titles as keys, without success. Then, half by accident, I found a highlighted passage from Thoreau:

> What is a country without rabbits and partridges? They are among the most simple and indigenous animal products; ancient and venerable families known to antiquity as to modern times; of the very hue and substance of Nature, nearest allied to leaves and to the ground.

After the quote, a laid-in note from Nkwanno: "*Thoreau has the Earth in him. 'Unless you know where you are, you don't know who you are.'*"

"Place," I thought. "Rabbits, partridges. Place . . . Country. Thoreau. Rabbits . . ."

Thoreau has the Earth in him. Not had, but *has*.

I tapped the slate against my knee, getting more and more irritated. It was right in front of me. I knew it . . .

Earth. Thoreau.

I saw the letters, and matched them name to name. Thoreau did indeed contain Earth, with O and U left over. UO. OU. Ou. I checked the dictionaries in the slate for O and U and U and O. *Ou*, the slate told me, was French for *where*. "*Unless you know where you are, you don't know who you are.*" That was a quote from a twentieth-century author named Wendell Berry, often used by citizens of Thistledown.

The slate's simple computer was tracking my searches, a small icon revealed. I felt as if Nkwanno watched over my shoulder as I riddled his little puzzle.

I keyed in, "Earth. Where. Place. Thoreau. Berry."

A box suddenly popped up on the screen of the slate. "Do you know the place where Thoreau is buried?"

I entered, " 'Earth.' "

The box wrote in new text:

"Thoreau is in the Earth. The Earth is in Thoreau. But where is Thoreau buried?"

I went to the old *Greater Starship Encyclopedia* that had come as standard issue with these slates when they had been made—reproductions of twentieth-century antiques—for divaricates on Thistledown. The slate had lasted all these years; I wondered how many twentieth-century batteries had been brought with the immigrants, for their special humble slates, but there was no place to remove batteries and replace them. As I searched the encyclopedia for entries on Thoreau, I realized that the slates must have been equipped with contemporary power supplies, which could last centuries. Divaricates often made such choices, after careful consideration with their philosophical leaders. The usual dispensation for modern technology was given following the phrase, "The Good Man would have approved of this, for it is human-centered and does not make us less than what we are."

I could not disagree that Nkwanno's slate was human-centered.

There was no specific answer as to where Thoreau was buried in the encyclopedia, or anywhere else in the slate's references, but it did say that he had last lived in Boston. I keyed in, " 'Boston, Massachusetts.' "

"Access given," the slate replied.

I now had Nkwanno's personal journals open to me. I remembered his smooth, musical conversation, when I had met him as a child on Thistledown, and even then, his keen intellect had impressed me. I knew I would find some of the perspective and clues I needed.

I began with entries from more than thirty Lamarckian years before:

Crossing 4. Fall 67.
Much discussion today about Lenk's plan to formalize our search for edible scions. From his perch in Jakarta, Lenk listens to his various lieutenants, and suddenly realizes how hungry we at the edge of the human territories are . . . Everybody is hungry. The crops do not grow fast enough, nor in sufficient quantity. Harvests are poor. The soil is metal-poor, and that includes trace minerals. We eat scions in des-

peration, and some of us have sickened and died. We know that whitehats—so we have named the slow, flat, three-cornered scions that walk on their downturned tips—are not edible, yet two of Moonrise's children have died in the last week trying to eat one.

Some successes. For a long time, we have trimmed mat fiber from low-growth broadfan epidendrids, which prosper near Moonrise, and used it as a kind of tea and in making fabric. Chewing it provides some satisfaction—it contains a mild elevant, not yet isolated by our chemists—but little nutrition. The most successful food we've discovered so far is a pulpy paste made from the thick pelt of purple and red tendrils on the so-called asparagus phytid. The pelt regrows quickly, the paste tastes like mild fish, and it provides substantial protein. No one has yet analyzed all the phytids, and it is likely that some of what we eat may hurt us later—but for now, hunger rules, especially in places like Moonrise, on the edge of Lenk's domain.

Crossing 7. Spring 78.

The first two years after Able Lenk brought us all here, I remember the silva would sing every night. It sang a gentle whistling, whooping song, the arborids drawing air through slits on parasol leaves, other scions making their own unique sounds, like instruments in an orchestra. Nobody knew why the silva sang. It just did, and we accepted it, and grew used to it.

But as the years passed, the nightsong declined. Some nights, the silva would produce only a few scattered sounds, haunting and lonely. Some nights there would be no singing at all. Now, the silva sings perhaps once every ten days. I think I understand why it sings, but I do not know why it does so less frequently.

The ecos must have many ways to keep track of its scions. We have seen speeders on their accustomed trails through the silva, like three-legged greyhounds, zipping between the phytids and arborids at speeds up to thirty kilometers an hour. We know some of the paths of gliders and avids, who swoop above the silva. I believe (and I'm not alone) that all of these creatures play a role in the ecos's internal communication. Like messengers, they carry information . . . perhaps about conditions in the south, or the north, about intrusions from other zones, or just general gossip. They carry them somewhere. Something listens, considers, contemplates . . .

Or so I hope. I would like to meet the heart and mind of an ecos. I have many questions to ask of her—or it.

Crossing 8. Spring 43.

Today saw a herd of parasol sweepers, like great two-headed giraffes, pushing through the silva half a kilometer outside Moonrise and a few dozen meters from the river. Infrequently see them in daylight, and never in such numbers, and of such size—one was tall enough to touch the brushes of a cathedral tree! I wondered if the ecos was reassigning them to another region. They move on three parallel tracks, like the feet of slugs. On close inspection (when Hilaire killed a small one by accident with a tractor one night) each track reveals itself as a parade of thousands of sucker-tipped feet, each no more than an inch long, yet supporting the weight of these creatures large as Earth's dinosaurs . . . And bearing them some resemblance.

They do not ingest—I hesitate to say "eat"—the parasols or fan-leaves unless the stalks have been injured—perhaps by wind—or are otherwise not functioning. When we first arrived, some of us thought these were herbivores, as we might expect on an Earth savanna or in a jungle. Now we know much more about them, yet not nearly enough.

Also today saw many whitehats feeding from a lizboo, like aphids on a rose stem. They remained there for hours, but usually feed in a few seconds, then leave. No one knows what purpose the whitehats serve.

Received a package of documents from Jakarta today. The recon-vened Research Standards convention has finally decided on classifi-cations and nomenclature for Lamarckian biology. We must deviate substantially from old terrestrial standards, for obvious reasons.

There seems to be no higher classification than an ecos. Ecoi will be described and defined by geographic location or the name of the dis-coverer, and a zone number (e.g., Elizabeth's Zone or Zone One). De-termination of boundaries and proof of relationship to an ecos will depend on observations and genetic analysis, the latter still crude and uncertain. Observation seems to be the principal and most reliable method for the time being.

Clades within ecoi come next. Arborids or treelike clades, phytids, annulids, polygonids, etc., define these groups of scions. Next come related scions, or forms, that vary little in design. Thus, whitehats are classified as Elizabethae Polygonon Trigonichos.

No doubt the classifications and nomenclature will change and improve, but at least we have reached some agreement on how to begin.

I skipped ahead, scrolling rapidly through the hundreds of pages of text:

Crossing 22. Winter 34.
My wife has been dead for almost twenty years, and I have not remarried. I began this journal when she died. Women have borne the brunt of our coming to Lamarckia. We live our philosophies with a vengeance now, and deep are the hurts and regrets. Some say deeper still the satisfactions. But I remember my wife, and her gentle ways, and the dismay on her face at the pain of birthing our first child. I felt so much pain myself, that my lust, my insistence, should put her in this state. There was of course her recovery and joy after . . . But I can't help but think the women look back on our time in Thistledown, and feel regret at what they left behind. It is because of their true courage that they don't complain more.

My wife's time came far too early. Something failed within her, and she just died. Death can arrive a simple friend for those who die. It is never simple for those who survive.

Crossing 23. Summer 7.
With the village children from the Lenk School, I have walked through the silva. We have captured scions and brought them back to the school for study, always releasing them within a few hours. The most poignant capture for me was last week. William Tass Fenney, age eight, found a small six-legged transporter with seven young phytids. At this early stage, Elizabeth's phytids—especially the smaller ones we call sprouts—are little more than blobs of dark gray or purple gelatin the

size of a finger, filled throughout with tiny white threads. William brought the transporter back to our school in a cart. We looked at the wriggling bowl with its leathery lid, and at the young phytids within, and made our notes. I then told William to take it back to where he had found it, and he said, "But I don't remember where that was."

We tried to walk back along some trail into the silva, but William had left few marks, and his cart's wheel tracks had vanished in the springy soil. Finally, with less and less of the day to spare, and lessons on other subjects beginning soon, we placed the transporter and its cargo on the silva floor. It turned in a circle several times, emitted a small sigh, and fell to the ground. Then it dumped its load of phytids. They lay like finger-sized worms, wriggling on the dark, clumpy earth.

Angela called from the school building, so I took the children back, but vowed to return as soon as I could. A few hours later, I found the transporter in a morbid condition, and all the young phytids desiccated and crumbling.

We had interfered with the transporter's simple instructions, or removed it from a track scented or otherwise marked, and replaced it where it did not belong.

I think often of that carrier. What of our own children, removed from their track?

Crossing 25. Winter 15.
Joseph Visal visits again from Calcutta. He came from Athenai and arrived in Calcutta just yesterday, then took the Wednesday boat immediately to Moonrise. We have spent many hours the past evenings catching up. In the daytime he travels with his researcher friends farther south along the river, but they always return by dusk. I fear none of them are more than dilettantes. But they take joy in their small discoveries, some of which may be valuable . . .

He brings more details of the attempted assassination of Able Lenk, news of which horrified us all two weeks ago, when we first heard it on the radio. The would-be assassin belongs to the Gaians, a group much rumored and about which little has ever been learned, making me think perhaps they are more legend than fact; but this would-be *assassin, Daw Tone Kunsler, whom I have never met, claims to be of them. Joseph tells me that the Gaians are active everywhere, and know each other by secret signs.*

Quaint. We left Thistledown to create a new kind of heaven, and instead find ourselves on roads to old, insipid hells.

Joseph also brings word that Lenk is approving a new research program, against the advice of his counselors, particularly Allrica Fassid, a small woman who is a formidable adversary. For once Lenk does not listen to her. The program will be called the Lamarckian Year, and all communities will participate—by which they must mean allocate resources to some central distribution point. There will be much protest. Our resources are still scarce, though the famine has passed.

I suppose we may sacrifice a tractor and send it to Athenai.

A new exploring expedition will begin, led by Baker and Shulago, two of my former students at Jakarta. They are brilliant but argumentative and I fear they may not be good leaders.

After a dozen entries in Nkwanno's journals, I went to the shelves of books and found two thick volumes, introductory texts that were not filled with technical terms and words I could not easily cross-reference. They would serve well enough as introductions to what the immigrants knew about Lamarckia, or at least about Liz.

I read all that night, until just before dawn, when I grew restless and my muscles began to cramp. As in Thistledown, there were no locks on the doors. I stole out quietly and walked north up the alley. I needed to see Calcutta alone and think about what I had read.

I had not counted on the profound darkness of Calcutta in the early-morning hours. No electric lights burned along the alley or on the streets outside, and only a few were visible on the hills below. Clouds had moved in over the river delta and not even the starlight helped. I felt my way back down the alley, counting doors, fingers scuffing rough lava brick and the grain of the lizboo in the door posts and doors, until I came back to what I thought must be Randall's.

With some relief, I lay on my cot in the library and considered all the simple things I would have to learn.

CHAPTER FIVE

Randall accompanied me the half kilometer from his house to the court building below the Lenk Hub. We passed through a crowd of angry, curious citizens. Some of them recognized Randall and me from the engagement on the river and clapped us on our backs, expressing their thanks and congratulations. We came to a cordon of court security guards, and the officer in charge checked our names and let us through.

Outside the main courtroom, a group of five citizens rank, two grim-faced older men and three women past childbearing years, greeted us stiffly. Before hearing our testimony, they were taking a short break in the annex, standing in their dark gray robes and sipping mat fiber tea. They had been busy since dawn that morning ruling on how and when to send the captured Brionists to Athenai for Lenk's disposition.

Larisa Strik-Cachemou sat on a bench nearby, alone and silent.

The last of the Brionists to be arraigned that day were led out of the court as we arrived, seven men and a woman, all wearing the clothes they had worn the day before though dried and cleaned for them, all trussed neck to neck and foot to foot with thick ropes. Iron and steel were too valuable for chains, and I suspected there was little need for chains in Calcutta.

The crowd outside began to shout and jeer as the prisoners came in sight. Their guards guided them swiftly down an open alley and away from the hub complex.

A few minutes after we arrived, the disciplinary Elevi Bar Thomas and two of his deputies walked into the annex. Thomas nodded at Randall, Larisa, and me, and walked closer. "I hear we both had a skirmish," he said. "We met the three flatboats snagged above Calcutta. They passed us upriver. A few shots were fired, but we knew we couldn't stop them."

"Did you wait for the other boats?" Randall asked.

"Until last night. Then I decided it was useless and we came back to Calcutta."

Randall was not impressed by this story, but he did not say anything critical.

"The citizens did well here," Thomas said. "I wish I could have been here to help them."

After five minutes, the clerk announced the citizens rank would reconvene. Randall excused himself and invited me to come down to the *Vigilant* at the docks after and meet Captain Keyser-Bach. The rest of us moved into an interior, windowless room, brightly illuminated by electric incandescents. Here the city smells lapsed into mustiness and stale air. The citizens rank took five chairs on a low dais. Thomas stood beside them, facing Larisa and me. Larisa rose from her cot and sat gingerly on a chair.

"What are her injuries?" asked the eldest woman with a sympathetic tone. Her name was Sulamit Faye-Chinmoi. Small, lean-faced, her hands wrinkled and bones showing in fine ridges beneath ivory skin, she focused her attention on Larisa, brow wrinkled in concern.

"Grief and shock," Larisa replied sharply. "Betrayal."

"Exhaustion," Thomas added. "Days without food."

"Are you strong enough to tell your story?"

Larisa rolled her eyes and clenched her jaw muscles. "I've told already. It hurts to chew on it again and again."

"We understand," the eldest woman said. "Do you recognize me, Larisa Strik-Cachemou?"

"No," Larisa said.

"I married you to your husband ten years ago."

"Then I curse you," Larisa said.

The woman drew back in some surprise. "We should identify ourselves formally," she said. One by one, the citizens rank gave their names and residences in the city. The youngest male, a broad-hipped, narrow-shouldered man with a pinched, nosy face and searching, deep-set eyes, said he was from Jakarta, servant in courtesy to Calcutta by rank exchange. His name was Terence Ry Pascal, and he seemed particularly interested in me.

"Please tell your story to us," said a tall, long-fingered man with thick black hair and large blue eyes, Kenneth du Chamet of south city, a farmer. "And remember, under the creed of the Good Man and Lenk's law, every citizen speaks before a legally convened five as if sworn under sacred oath."

"The oath assumed, that none should ever feel free to lie," I remembered.

That I would almost certainly violate this brought a sudden and unexpected pang.

Larisa gave her testimony slowly, painfully. She drew herself upright in her chair several times as she told of her husband's meeting with the Brionists and of his leaving with them two seasons before. Then she spoke of the boats that returned and of the Brionist soldiers—she used the old term of disdain, *soldaters*, creoled just after the Death ten centuries before—and her words hissed forth like air from a deflating balloon. Weak, exhausted, she slumped in the chair, face twisted and wet with tears.

"The mayor turned down the representative of General Beys. I hid when they came. I knew they would do bad things."

Drawing herself up again, she spoke of searching the village, finding no one alive, hiding again for a time, then wandering to the river to wait for boats. There she had found the last victims, Nkwanno, her cousin Gennadia, and the other two. Then she described my appearance on the dock. "He came out of nowhere. Everything he said was a lie."

She asked forcefully why the boats had not come earlier.

Faye-Chinmoi said in reedy tones, "Because your village was not missed until radios went unanswered for a day and a half. Normally boats go there from Calcutta once every five days."

"We've explained this to her," Thomas said in an undertone.

"Don't condescend to me! I am a thinking human being!" Larisa erupted, rising. I looked away, feeling a quick flush on my cheeks—distress at her distress, at this whole proceeding. Why did these people affect me so? I felt as if I were looking back nine centuries in time, to the Recovery; falling into an older kind of history, the adolescence of humanity, with all its snares and barbs.

"And your story, Ser Olmy?" Kenneth du Chamet asked. "Your name and location, please. And remember—"

"The oath assumed," I said. "My name is Olmy Ap Datchetong, of Jakarta by birth."

"And how did you come to Moonrise?"

"I walked. I've been studying in the silva."

"Ser Thomas indicates in his report that you claim to have been in the silva for two years. Is that correct?"

"Yes."

"Under what grant or institution?"

"On my own."

"And how were you qualified for such research?" asked Faye-Chinmoi.

I looked puzzled. I certainly did not want to answer unnecessary questions.

"Your education."

"I don't see how that's important," I said.

The woman leaned back, glanced at her colleagues, then leaned forward again. "You must have gone to an institution after Lenk schooling."

"No," I said. "I'm an independent." I walked on loose ground. How had divaricate society changed since Lenk brought them here? Were independents—those who chose to avoid formal schooling—still tolerated?

"Did you witness the attack?" Faye-Chinmoi asked.

"No."

"Did you hear it while it happened?"

"I was several kilometers from the river."

Larisa stood again, a length of hair falling into her eyes. "He couldn't have been in the silva for more than a few hours. I saw a sampler bite him. And he called it a *forest*."

Du Chamet looked up at the ceiling in exasperation. "We must focus on the village and incidents surrounding the attack," he said.

They questioned me for another hour. Thomas listened carefully to my answers, no doubt weighing them against what I had already told him.

"I don't feel as if we've gotten the whole truth here," Faye-Chinmoi said after the end of testimony. "However, there is no evidence linking anyone other than boatloads of renegades who may or may not be Brionists, and the only immediate witness to that effect is Ser Larisa Strik-Cachemou, and perhaps this Kimon Giorgios, if he can be found. I understand that Ser Olmy took part in the skirmish with the Brionist flatboats, and helped to save most of the children from the boat that sank. We express our gratitude to you, Ser Olmy. You are free to go, but we request you stay in Calcutta and make yourself available for further testimony, until we release you of that obligation. We have to report to Athenai and Jakarta by radio. We are damnably spread out on this planet, as a bureaucracy." She sniffed.

Larisa had fixed her gaze on me for some minutes now.

"I think," du Chamet said, "that we're going to have to become much more efficient, soon. This is the ninth such raid on Elizabeth's Land, and by far the worst, although the first in our district. The north coast towns have been taking the brunt. They are more accessible than towns and villages along the Terra Nova."

Sulamit Faye-Chinmoi concluded: "For the first time, we have a number of prisoners to use in negotiations. I don't know what good they'll do us, but if Brion's General Beys is in desperate need of children, how much more desperate will he be for trained soldiers?"

"Who will protest to the Brionists?" Thomas asked.

The citizens rank glanced at each other, then du Chamet said, "I'll report to the district administer through the mayor's radio. We'll ship the prisoners to Athenai tomorrow."

Thomas followed me to the bottom of the steps and the main street leading from the river to west Calcutta. I saw tall poles in the direction of the river, rising between a gap in a row of shops. Yards and rigging crossed the poles—masts, I realized. Sailing ships in the main harbor. A fair number of them, judging by the number of masts. That was where I would meet Randall. For some reason not clear to me—a kind of instinct—I did not want to explain all this to Thomas.

"Where to now, Ser Olmy?" he asked.

"I'm supposed to stay here," I said. "That was my impression . . ."

Thomas closed one eye and smoothed his crown's shortcut stubble with a thick, strong hand. "But what will you *do* here?"

"When I'm free, continue with my studies."

"You *will* wait?" Thomas seemed doubtful. "You won't just vanish back into the silva?"

"I don't seem to satisfy you, Ser Thomas. Not that you're alone. My poor mother had higher hopes for me."

Thomas acknowledged the shadow wit with a nod and a small smile. "My mother wanted me to be a farmer. I preferred keeping an eye on people, making sure they were all right. Well, I haven't done much of that recently. In truth, Ser Olmy, you've shown more courage than I have." Thomas straightened and clasped his hands in front of him, stretched his arms and shrugged his shoulders. "Cause no harm, eh, Ser Olmy? That's what I ask of you while you're here."

I smiled and held out my hand. Perhaps because of his suspicions, I liked Thomas. He reminded me of instructors I had had in Defense School. He took my hand and shook it firmly.

"No harm," I said.

Thomas stared after me as I walked away. When I had gone half a dozen meters, he said, voice raised only slightly, "You are not what you say you are, Ser Olmy. I don't know what your purpose is, but I hope to."

I wanted to see more of Calcutta before I met up again with Randall. I doubted that I would get lost in bright daylight. I strode down the stone-paved streets, walking north between shops and the blank fronts of houses painted white and light gray and yellow, smelling the dust and pervasive odor of lizboo like dry dusty ginger. I walked beside a long straight road flanked by freestanding houses, well-maintained frame structures whose porches and decks had been allowed to weather to a natural wheaten color, the black edges and stoma-marks of lizboo exterior layers inlaid in simple floral patterns.

No street signs were evident, and no maps; Calcutta was not built for strangers. I ate lunch in a small, dark restaurant at the end of the main north-south street. The cook and waiter, a thin young woman who kept her gaze on the brightness of the single small window, described the menu to me: three kinds of grain bread they had baked that morning, Liz cherries and hookvine paste—both from epidendrids, forms *adenophora* and *ampelopsis*—and fried flockweed patties. I ordered patties and bread and a single Liz cherry. She looked at my ticket for a long moment, frowned, and walked off to get my food.

The bread was chewy, like sponge, but tasted good. The Liz cherry was extremely tart with the characteristic bitter undertaste of all phytid fruit. Some phytids created nutritional packets for mobile scions on long journeys, and these were generally what passed as fruit in Elizabeth's Zone. Liz cherries were one of the most common. They were not highly nutritious, but contained usable sugars, some vitamins, and few allergens or toxins.

After eating, I stopped by a small park overlooking the river and sat on a stone bench. I took out Nkwanno's slate and returned to a history of the years just after the Crossing.

"*Among some who came with Lenk to Lamarckia,*" the history continued,

> a substantial conspiracy arose. Where it began, and how large it was when it began, is not known; but it is assumed it began in Thistledown, and there were eventually several hundred of the conspirators who joined Lenk's secret expedition. They regarded Lamarckia as an opportunity all their own. They would follow Lenk, they would pretend fealty, but they had their own plans and goals.
>
> Upon arriving in Lamarckia, this conspiracy had no strength. Its parts and individuals could not agree on specific goals. Lamarckia, they thought, would be theirs, but which of the splinters would grow the new tree, none could decide. What was decided almost from the beginning, apparently, was Lenk's unsuitability to rule.
>
> Yet within a few years of the Crossing, most of the splinters gave up their grand plans, discouraged by the extreme difficulty of maintaining conspiracies within a grander and much-divided conspiracy.
>
> The last of the splinters, and the most persistent, was the most hidden and thoroughly disguised. For there soon arose a faction that had no Naderite leanings whatsoever. Technophilic, aristocratic, the Urbanists followed a persuasive woman named Hezebia Hoagland, who quickly professed Geshel teachings. Hoagland believed in the necessity of female control of technology. "Only through knowledge can women rise above patriarchy," she proclaimed. "Naderites, and particularly Lenk's divaricates, have tried to return us to patriarchal servitude: to keep us constantly pregnant, in order to populate a new world with babies in the most primitive conditions imaginable; quite against the teachings of their supposed mentor, the Good Man Nader. Who was, of course, a man . . ."
>
> Hoagland took seventy-seven followers—twenty men and fifty-seven women—and crossed the Darwin Sea to Hsia. There, on a rugged coastline, they found a relatively sheltered harbor and began a settlement in conditions far cruder and more primitive than those at Jakarta or the newly founded Calcutta. Initially, the settlement was called Godwin.

At Godwin, conditions improved very quickly, and population grew at a rate double that of the settlements on Elizabeth's Land. Some have said that the Godwinians took charge of secretly smuggled advanced medical equipment—or the resources for making such equipment— allowing ex utero births.

Soon, the hopes of many of the discouraged turned to Godwin, a golden land across the sea, where conditions—so it was said—were ideal, where no one starved, and where technological harmony with the zones of Hsia had been achieved without predation upon scions. Here, it was claimed, vast tracts of land left open by the ecoi, unused, were "ceded" to human farming, and "seeded" with fast-growing grains.

By this time, grainlands had been cleared in Tasman, and Able Lenk had moved his government to the newly founded port of Athenai to oversee food production. But the attractions of Hsia and Godwin were immense. Four hundred and five women and ninety-three men shipped across the Darwin, causing crises in Calcutta and Jakarta.

The remaining splinter groups finally united behind a strong and able leader, born on Lamarckia, named Emile Brion. A quondam ecologist with some training in agriculture, Brion early in life showed a remarkable talent to convince and organize. This attracted the attention of Lenk's assistants, who could not, however, recruit him to Able Lenk's cause. Some say pressure was applied that Brion deeply resented.

At age twenty (Lamarckian years), Brion traveled in secret (some say in female disguise) to Godwin.

I looked up from the slate and watched part of a triad family walk through the park: two fathers with their respective wives; three girls and two boys in late infancy; and two adolescents, one boy and one girl. Most adults dressed in dull clothes with bright sashes or scarves, and most children in happy tatters of play clothes.

I felt a wave of homesickness for the parks of Thistledown, and wondered if I would ever serve as father in a triad, or have any children at all.

One of the fathers, the younger of the two, limped. He walked on one leg with a hip-swing motion that showed it was a centimeter shorter. He had been injured and the injury had been imperfectly repaired.

The family passed, self-absorbed. The man with the limp had survived his injury and adapted to it. Perhaps they simply took these last few peaceful years as relaxation between challenges, a time to walk in parks and raise children. Life was made of challenges and distortions.

What Brion and his acolytes found in the secret and largely closed society of Godwin was chaos. By fiat of Hoagland, more females than males had been born. Hoagland believed that a society consisting of nine women to every man would be ideal. She wrote that women who lived together in harmony could do quite well with many fewer men. Oddly, most of the men in Godwin did not object.

After five years of comparative peace, the plan went awry when several hundred young women, led by a young engineer named Caitla Chung, formed their own political group, calling themselves the True Sisters. The True Sisters disapproved of what they referred to as the Matriarchy, claiming it reduced all women to workers, giving them no say in the character of the children they raised, not to mention no way to exercise natural urges and desires.

A kind of religious rebellion occurred, instigated by the True Sisters—none of them older than eighteen—perhaps with Brion's help. Hoagland committed suicide, though some claim she was murdered. Both men and women dismantled—some say destroyed—the advanced machines, and perhaps also the miniature factories that could be used to make more machines.

The fields went unharvested, and starvation became widespread in the land of alleged plenty.

I rubbed the bridge of my nose and eyes, then went to a stone fountain and dipped water to drink. The water I drank tasted sweet and pure; even if there was contamination from human sewage, it wouldn't matter. All remaining human disease had been eradicated on the Thistledown during the first years of the journey, long before my birth. Mutation of microorganisms into potential disease-causing forms had been eliminated by supplements implanted in all children—even divaricate children—during infancy. The Good Man had never disapproved of immunization, and these supplements were, so orthodox Naderites ruled, merely elaborate forms of immunization.

What mutation of bacteria and viruses that occurred in such a small population as inhabited Lamarckia would easily be handled by these supplements and by natural defenses. The reservoirs of disease were simply not there. Whether Lamarckia's living things could produce disease—or could be infected by human pathogens—was still an open question, but most experts thought it unlikely.

The human pathogens of Lamarckia were cultural and philosophical, not biological.

I searched the slate, trying to find updates of the last ten years, but there was nothing more about Brion and Hsia. Apparently Brion had renamed Godwin, calling it Naderville.

My ignorance felt like a deadly itch I could not scratch fast enough.

I walked to a bare stretch of dirt surrounding a half dead elm tree. Digging my fingers through the tough, hard-packed soil, peering at the grains in my palm, I found bits of fiber, grains of black sand, a dry dark powder— but none of the living vibrancy of the dirt in the silva.

Clearly, this was human ground.

The sky grayed again in the afternoon and a gentle rain fell.

The showers stopped and the clouds passed, blowing slowly eastward. I walked along the waterfront, past long covered docks and warehouses, stone and concrete steps.

I shouldered my rucksack and walked beside the brick and stone wall, through which steps broke every fifty meters to lead down to the water. In a small building near the main warehouses, adolescent boys and girls in ill-fitting black uniforms stood in rows, listening to a large man with beefy arms and fists like gnarled tree roots explain riverboat handling and sailing skills. Seven small boats and a ten-meter single-masted yacht were moored near the building alongside short floating piers. I stopped to listen for a moment, until the large man noticed my presence, then moved on.

A riverside market was just closing for the day. A few men with a wagon traded the last of their terrestrial produce to a vendor cleaning out a stall.

I saw river catch in the buckets and on tables covered with mostly melted ice: small silvery "smelty piscids" from zone five; river celery, purple tubes as thick as my arm; piles of apple-sized shining balls the color of unbaked bread, called, reasonably enough, lumpfruit. From my reading I knew that these came from dashers, scions that crossed large tracts of Liz for purposes unknown, but which supplied themselves with lumpfruit along the way. Where the lumpfruit originated, or whether the dashers actually made them, was not known.

Coming into the margin of the main harbor, separated from the Terra Nova by a curving wall, I saw the two Brionist flatboats tied up. Tractors and other equipment were being offloaded on ramps and with small cranes. Farther along, the largest ship in port was a full-rigged vessel about forty meters long, with three masts and two cylindrical slatted windmills for generating power. Two gangplanks linked the ship with the pier, and men carried boxes along the planks, loading them onto the ship. More sailing ships—three-masted schooners, barques, a small ketch, all with elegant sharp prows, all wide in the beam—lay at anchor. One of these ships, a barque with a single low, large canvas windmill mounted astern, glowed along its rigging and rails with hundreds of little electric lights, and, as if that might not be enough, additional gas lanterns hissed port and starboard.

As I watched from the dockside, a sailor walked along the deck, extinguishing the lanterns. She walked aft, reached into a box, and the electric lights went out.

I smiled in anticipation. Here at last was something I thought I might be competent to handle. I had sailed many times in the fourth chamber waterways on Thistledown and had studied sailing ships extensively for this mission, clued by the informer's description of travel and commerce. I knew the nautical terms—what I did not know was which terms the immigrants had retained in the decades since the informant had made his gate and left, and what they had added. Nkwanno's slate had little to say about ships or travel on Lamarckia's oceans and waterways.

I walked a few dozen meters along the pier, to the next vessel, a full-rigged ship. A tall, lank, discouraged-looking man stood by a pile of lizboo-plank boxes wrapped in nets, waiting for a short, thick crane to lift the assemblage and convey it into the ship's hold. I approached. "I'd like to find Erwin Randall's ship—I mean, Captain Keyser-Bach's ship."

The man looked me over woefully. "I'm the chandler's assistant," he said. "This is the *Vigilant*."

"Keyser-Bach?" I persisted.

"He's the captain, yes."

"Where's Ser Randall?"

The discouraged-looking man curled his lip. "I'm not *from the ship*, man. I deal with supplies."

"Who would I talk to?"

"I don't want to judge, but by your dress . . . You've not had work in some time." He chuckled and shook his head. "She's an eccentric ship, the *Vigilant*. There's a shortage of seamen here, but you don't look the grade." The man sucked in his cheeks. "I don't spread tales, besides, but Captain Keyser-Bach is not the man I'd sail under. A thinking man's thinking man, and what kind of a sailor would that make him? All wrapped in charts and studies." He tapped his head meaningfully.

I thanked him and waited for someone to disembark the *Vigilant*. Within a few minutes, a man of middle years in long brown breeches and a light coat, chest bare between two half tied strings, picked his way along the plank with grace. I said, "I'm looking for Ser Randall."

"Not a passenger ship," the man said, regarding me curiously. "I don't know you." He waited for a moment, then began to move off again before adding, "Not that I know *everybody* here."

"Ser Randall told me to report to Captain Keyser-Bach."

The man turned and spent more time looking me over. "Name's French. Navigation and meteorology. Randall isn't back yet. Here's what you do. You go to the researcher's mate—he's in that little shed with the black lizzie fringe. He's seen Randall recently and he might know something. But beware. He's arguing with the chief chandler and he's in a viney mood, right?"

I crossed the yard to the shed, and entered. Inside, bare dim bulbs cast a waxy yellow glow over a dusty desk. Two men argued across the desk, one sitting behind it on a battered stool, the other, a chunky blond, standing, leaning on the desk with thick arms. It was Shatro. He looked surprised to see me. The man behind the desk looked up, fixed me with sharp blue eyes, and said, "Ship? Needs?" His narrow face and thin cheeks gave him a skeletal appearance.

"Randall told me to report to the ship," I said to Shatro.

"I'm chandler here," the seated man said, a broad if not convincing smile displaying fine teeth under his long pale nose. "Do you know—"

"I know this man," Shatro said. "Why did he tell you to come here?"

I did not really want to explain myself to Shatro and did not understand why he asked the question. "He did, and I'm here. Where is Ser Randall?"

"He hasn't reported in yet," Shatro said. He gestured for me to go away, but I stood my ground and he turned back to the chandler with a look of one more weight laid upon his shoulders.

The argument between the two continued. The chandler's prices had gone up twice in the past year, against Lenk's economic suggestions, Shatro claimed. The chandler calmly responded that with seven ships lost in that year and metal at a premium, it stood to reason gear would cost, and especially gear useful for research. "Good-quality jars and steel receptacles are at a special premium," the chandler said.

Shatro faced me in exasperation. "We're putting foam on the beard tomorrow morning, and this . . . *man*, cares nothing for science." But the argument seemed to have lost its momentum. Shatro sighed and stood back from the desk. "I can't believe Ser Randall told you any such thing," he said to me in a pointed undertone. "Our crew is select. We need Lenk schooling and strong secondary training. Seamanship desirable. Forgive me, but you don't look it."

"I have many skills. Technical training and experience. And I'm strong."

The chandler looked between us with some amusement. "Everybody's *strong*, now," he said with a low hoot of humor. "Just a few years ago, now—"

"Been under sail?" Shatro asked.

I nodded.

"You certainly don't look it," the chandler said, shaking his head sadly.

"He wants you to be a ship's hand, right?" Shatro asked. "We're short of hands, but not that short. Excuse me, Ser Costa," he said to the man behind the desk. "Charge what your conscience suggests. You can serve all knowledge, bring honor to your children, and share the adventure, or you can prosper on our hunger."

The chandler received this with a broad smile and squint. "I trust the next ship you serve on—if there is a next ship—you'll be back with a better argument." He swiveled on the stool to look more closely at me. "I suggest you find yourself a less ambitious vessel."

Shatro walked heavily from the shed, across the stone paving. I followed, and behind, the chandler began to crow with laughter.

"You must have misunderstood Ser Randall," Shatro said. "He's master of the *Vigilant*, but the captain chooses the crew. We've been in Calcutta six months waiting for funding from Athenai and trying to put together a scientific team. How can you help us?"

I crab-gated, almost skipped beside him, yet spoke firmly—to appear at once youthfully obsequious and competent, assured. Shatro, I judged, lacked the basic elements of self-confidence. Somehow or other, I posed a threat to him. "I know physics and the principles of meteorology. I know the basics of ships and the sea. And I'm a quick learner."

Shatro stopped, held up his hands with palms toward me, and said, "Let me add to the chandler's poor description of our itinerary."

"Ser Randall explained—"

"I doubt he gave you the whole itinerary. It's going to be a difficult voyage, to say the least. We'll go east along the Sumner Coast, then swing south-southeast around Mount Pascal, drop in to Jakarta to pick up some more real researchers, then south to Wallace Station for another load of researchers. Along the way, we might study the pins in the Chefla Lava Waste, then sail out to Martha's Island. A journey of eight thousand nautical miles, fourteen thousand eight hundred kilometers to you. After Martha's Island, we'll head south to Cape Magellan, make landfall there and study zone six, then round the cape and run west with the Kangxi current, *if* it exists, around the unknown side of Lamarckia, We hope to reach Basilica and Nihon, if *they* exist, and touch Hsia from the eastern side. Then we slip through the Cook Straits. An additional twelve thousand nautical miles. And still we won't be home. We'll cross the Darwin Sea at the lowest longitudes to La Pèrouse Land. Only then will we turn north for Athenai, if our ship lasts so long. So, would-be sailor, how many days do we have left before we miss the spring northers and the southeasters from the Walking Sticks?"

"I don't know," I said.

"Right," he said, suspicions confirmed. He turned and boarded the ship. "Ser Randall will be here any moment. It's really up to the captain, and to him."

I took a deep breath and spent the next twenty minutes sitting on a bench at the head of the pier where *Vigilant* was moored, watching men and women come and go. A small electric tractor pulled a wagon of foodstuffs in casks and boxes to the side of the ship. There it was left, to be loaded aboard later.

Randall came down to the docks with several other men. He saw me sitting on the bench, gave me a curt nod, and continued about his business, walking along the pier, examining *Vigilant*, exchanging remarks with his companions, pointing, nodding heads. I had seen men everywhere do this—a ritual of checking and measuring and reassuring, liberally punctuated with outstretched arms and fingers.

When the men departed, still talking and pointing, Randall stood by the *Vigilant*'s gangplank and waved for me to join him.

"Still no luggage, eh, Ser Olmy?" he asked as I approached. "Thomas will think you're a man without roots."

"I am," I said.

"Sorry to keep you waiting. Have you been here long?"

"Not long," I said. "I had a talk with Ser Shatro."

"Oh?"

"I don't think he approves of me."

Randall grinned. "The captain makes the choices," he said.

"That's what Ser Shatro told me."

"Shall we get on with it?" Randall asked. We crossed the gangplank and went aboard the ship.

A small, knobby man with darting eyes, quick stringy fingers, and a high forehead topped by thick red hair, Captain Keyser-Bach gave me a look of pinched concern. The mate and Shatro bustled in and out of his cabin, bringing forms on paper for signing, a printed newspaper (I had never seen one before), a box of manuals and texts, also on paper, and in the midst of this, his right hand wielding a pen and his left pushing signed forms into a folder held open by one aide, the captain said, "I assume the respectable master has given you some idea what we're facing."

"Yes, Ser."

" 'Captain,' " Randall said.

"Captain." I examined the cabin, walls of white-painted cathedral tree with lizboo trim, xyla floor with brass cleats, ceramic gutters beneath a small lab table, a wall covered by rolled charts and a case filled with large, thick books. A single slate hung in a sleeve from the bulkhead beside the captain's narrow bed. The air smelled of ethanol and other chemicals, arrayed on a table beside an optical microscope. The microscope occupied the focus of the room, like an icon; I did not doubt such instruments were far rarer than slates, and that Randall and the captain had fought for permission to take one on the voyage.

Slices of a small unidentified scion were laid out on a board, pinned and labeled. But for their clothes—long shirts tied up with belts, loose pants, and sandals—we might have been in a late nineteenth-century Earth laboratory.

"No one at Athenai is enthusiastic about this expedition. Some profess interest, some give encouragement, none show enthusiasm. Lenk himself wonders about its utility." The captain finished signing and took up the newspaper. "Some of us at least have rediscovered ambition. What's *your* ambition?"

I said, "To learn about the ecoi and our place among them, Captain."

"If the master says you're adequate, I won't contradict him. We'll sail short three hands—short ten, if we count seasoned sailors and A.B.s. But by Fate and Logos, we'll sail." He plucked a sheet from the folder and waved it for Randall's benefit. "Received this while you were up the Terra Nova. Permission from the Administer of Science and Metallurgy at Athenai. Should have been here three months ago. We are forbidden to 'risk the metal-containing ship *Vigilant* unnecessarily, or to report findings to anyone other than the officers and ministers of Able Lenk.' 'Science and Metallurgy' indeed. As if the ship's metal is more important than crew or mission . . ." The captain thrust the permission form into the folder again. He shook the newspaper, turned the headline toward Randall, who bent to read it. "Villages raided on the north coast and around Jakarta, and upriver here at Moonrise. Ships taken. Crews let off in boats or rafts." He drew up his cheeks, squeezing his eyes to slits, and sucked on his teeth, then straightened and lifted one hand, as if after all this meant very little.

"I've a hunger for knowledge," I said. "I need passage for experience. I need to reach Athenai eventually—that's all. My mother and father told me to go where I can be educated. Apprenticed."

"How old are you?" the captain asked. He had an odd habit of touching the prominent knob of his chin with his fingers and tugging until he had a space of one or two centimeters between his teeth, all the time keeping his jaw muscles clenched as if in defiance.

"Twenty," I said.

"Family?"

"Datchetong. A branch not reassigned."

"Proscribed, with no education, then?" the captain asked. I appeared distressed, nodded.

"Bonded or linked?"

"No triad connections," I said. "I've been in the silva for a couple of years, on my own. Trying to study."

"Then at least you have some survival skills . . . Shall I check with the disciplinary and make sure you're not fleeing his wrath?"

"We've both met the disciplinary," Randall said quietly.

The captain leaned closer, eyes penetrating. "You know nothing about our expedition?"

"More now than I did a few days ago," I admitted.

"Two years in the silva—Elizabeth's Zone? Breath of Logos, you're the *mystery man*, aren't you? From Moonrise?" He swung around on his seat to face Randall. "You didn't tell me that, Erwin."

"I didn't want to prejudice you. We traveled back together."

"I should have guessed . . . And the disciplinary gives him a fair mark?"

"So far," Randall said.

Keyser-Bach pulled his chin vigorously, glancing between Randall and me. "They say the Brionists and General Beys in particular are working several sea routes, commandeering ships. I don't believe them—I think the Brionists are blamed overmuch—but we can't afford not to be—"

"Vigilant," I said.

Randall seemed to enjoy such cheek. The captain seemed less amused.

"This expedition has been in the making for ten years, and it starts without the enthusiastic support of anybody in power. We set out with faith and strong drive and not much more." He puffed out his cheeks. "You'd be shocked at the youth around here, and the courage of our seagoing breed.

"But if the master thinks you're fit, we'll sign you on as an apprentice. Don't expect to do a lot of science. Expect calluses and shouting."

———

I made my way around the boat before the assembling of the crew, and made my own assessment. In their decades on Lamarckia, the immigrants who had taken to these seas had pushed the words for things nautical this way and that, deleted or elided, added and compressed, but still, most were recognizable. Recognizable as well was the design of the *Vigilant*, a forty-meter three-masted full-rigged ship made largely of xyla, with brass and steel trim. A few details would have startled sailors on Earth (or in the fourth chamber of Thistledown, where a replica clipper ship had once plied the Lake of Winds): broad in the beam, forecastle prominent, the bow sharp but with a bulbous protrusion at the waterline. Seen from above, the over-all outline of the ship would have resembled a short chisel with a drop of paint hanging from the angled tip. Two canvas-vaned windscrews rose abaft and slanted outboard of the sails, their rotors connected to generators within the hull.

What I knew of the Crossing showed that Lenk had handicapped his flock deliberately, choosing the most dedicated radical Naderites—who would, of course, eschew the fine technologies of the contemporary Hexamon. Certain instruments and technologies not available in the twentieth century—the batteries within the slates, for example—had been accepted by fiat among the divaricates. But with the significant exceptions noted in the history on Nkwanno's slate, the immigrants had come to Lamarckia remarkably innocent of such skills as engineering, mathematics, and physics, beyond the most basic sort.

Perhaps nautical engineering had not yet recovered from Lenk's choices. In strong winds, with a high forecastle and elevated poopdeck, the *Vigilant* would tend to roll; the windscrews seemed pasted on, and sailing down-wind, or with the wind fine on the starboard or port quarter, could steal from the courses.

The dearness of iron showed. The *Vigilant* was xyla-hulled and solid enough, but with very few iron or steel parts; aluminum, bronze and brass, tin and copper were used sparingly. Sails and masts were suspended from and supported by a mix of rope and wire stays and braces; shrouds alternated rope and wire, and all ratlines were rope or lizboo. Where wire was used, and where rope, seemed to vary with whim; the main backstay being rope, forestay wire; and yet the backstay took the strain of the following wind. I felt a sudden shadow of worry. I hoped I was wrong, but for the *Vigilant* I judged there would be trouble at sea: continuous, nagging trouble.

Which could explain the loss of so many ships. As for the crew: thirty-one men to twelve women, the youngest apprentices delivered by their triad families to a sea trial, failures perhaps at Lenk school (despite the captain's speech to me); the eldest, largely able-bodied seamen or A.B.s, hired from the rejects of the none-too-large merchant fleets. Even with twenty thousand inhabitants, commerce was slow, sea travel haphazard and hazardous besides.

I saw more clearly why the captain had taken me on with so little resistance.

The sun hung within a few degrees of the hills behind Calcutta. After the last of our food and equipment had been lowered into the hold and stowed securely, the mate, a blocky, red-faced man of forty with the auspicious name of Salvator Soterio, assembled the crew on the deck before the wheelhouse. Randall sat on the capstan, arms folded, a roll of lizboo parasol under one arm. The sunset cast ship, crew, docks, and warehouses in a fiery glow; black dust from the silvas, blown far out to sea from the continent, made for spectacular day's-end colors.

Waiting for the captain, I stood among the apprentices and A.B.s, who, shuffling their feet, those who knew each other murmuring and exchanging knowing glances, ignored me but for sideling glances and occasional gruff instructions, one of them being to "Watch his way, watch your way. Learn and be meshed." By which they meant, follow the example of experienced crew members and fit into the way of the ship.

The mate called us to respectful attention. The captain emerged from his quarters and gazed at the setting sun with a squint as if he were some bug emerging from under a rock. He came to the rail and swept his eye over the crew on the quarterdeck.

"We've received our orders and confirmed our mission," Keyser-Bach began. "With first light tomorrow, we put out to sea. Most of you are new to the *Vigilant*. New to me and the master, as well. You've signed on from Tasman grain ships and merchant vessels and a few from pleasure boats, and you should know the *Vigilant* runs a different course. We are out for learning, not for trade. We will circumnavigate for the glory of knowledge.

"We'll chart the life of Lamarckia in its most extreme forms. It's been tried before . . . Two missions, four ships, two of them sunk, Fate be kind and the winds rest above them. There are hazards enough where we'll go, some known, some not.

"We are as infants on the face of Lamarckia. I've spent twenty years on these seas and still know them only poorly. And half the world has yet to be seen at all. This voyage depends on all of us to keep our senses sharp.

"Because what is taught in Lenk schools, even in secondary, is so tentative and inadequate, I feel it is my duty to train you all to a finer sense of nature. That makes this as much a schoolship as a research and exploration vessel.

"Some of you will think me eccentric. And if my eccentricities spread rumor along the dock, and make me a laughingstock, so be it.

"So now all of you know my style. Fairness follows performance. We'll all make history, if we mind our weather and keep eyes bright and straight ahead."

The gloom of the past few days was lifting. I glanced at the crew around me, at Randall. The master's face seemed to take on a new light, his weariness fading. They truly were in their early age of exploration here, hazards enough for any adventurer. I looked on the *Vigilant*, with all her eccentricities and inadequacies, with blossoming affection.

I was the last of the new crew. The navigator and provisions mate, French, whom I had met earlier, wrote me into the crew list and the supplies roster, gave me a thick oiled canvas coat and pants, a pair of boots more appropriate to shipboard duties, and took me to my assigned berth in the forecastle.

Thick-jawed, pouch-cheeked, with enormous shoulders and unforgiving black eyes, Soterio, the mate, called the crew together before sunset on the foredeck. Randall watched with little apparent interest, leaning on the starboard rail. I took my place with the apprentices, scrawny fellows, little more than gangling, uneasy boys.

"Good evening," Soterio said, forcing what could be mistaken for an amiable smile.

"Good evening," we murmured.

"It looks to be a glorious one, too," he said, his face betraying no great enthusiasm. "I'll leave talk about pride and accomplishment to the master and the captain. I'm practical, myself, and care only for my life, my ship, and my crew, in whatever order you find most comforting." He huffed out his cheeks, shook his head. "But there's rules we lay down here and now."

He paced before us, thick arms crossed over his chest, jaw thrust forward.

"What the master tells me, I tell you, and you do. No flarking, no stumping about, nothing lax. Flark and I'm on you. There's no ship on this world that runs herself, and none so complicated a fool can't learn her, but learn we must." He huffed again. "This is no *yacht*, so put your days at Lenk school or wherever behind you. The Great Darwin is no lake, it's a sea, foaming and thick, as unforgiving as any sailed by man or woman on any world." He glared at us through those cold black marbles.

"Yes, Ser," we responded.

"And when the voyage begins, none of this 'Ser' stuff. It's the 'sir' of many seagoing centuries and not for *politesse*."

"Yes, *sir*."

"Some have sailed before, some a lot, most not. Some have sailed under the master and me. But all will follow me around the deck this evening and learn this ship and her ways."

Soterio then took us around the boat, stem to stern, talking rapidly for an hour. All that I had studied of ships and seamanship for this mission only began to prepare me for the shift of language, for the invention of the immigrants. Many sailing terms used by the mate were familiar, but the immigrants had built their ships without benefit of years at sea, using only what references they found in the slates they had brought with them. There were differences, and mixtures of nautical terms across the centuries.

The *Vigilant* was three-masted, full-rigged, by old Earth standards, yet here she was called a *spankered three-tree*. The masts, in the mate's lingo, were all *trees* and he named them *foretree, maintree, and mizzen*. The names of the major sails were easy enough to adjust to, the lowermost called courses and named after their trees—fore course, main course, but then, on the mizzen, the *christian*, called crojack or crossjack traditionally; the next pair, gallant and topgallant; above them, upper and lower topsails became *hightop* and *lowtop*. But the jibs from bowsprit and jibboom to foremast were called *bellies*, the outermost called (without a single smile among the apprentices) the *flying belly*. The seldom-used royals, above the hightops, took the name *skysails*. Stays supporting the masts remained stays, and the sails sometimes hung from them, staysails. Studding sails, however, were called *wings*, bent or fastened to extensions of the yards called *outbrooms*. "So it is," the mate said, "when the *Vigilant*'s going to *sweep with the wind up her ass*, we beat with our *wings, bellies* in the breeze, clear?"

He dared anyone to smile.

The halyards, braces, sheets and other rigging working all these reflected such changes. I labored to memorize—and to forget some of what I had learned on the Lake of the Winds.

Fortunately, on the upper decks and belowdecks, the names had changed little. Fore and aft still applied: bow, midships, stern; forecastle, foredeck or maindeck, quarterdeck aft of the maintree, but the poop aft of the mizzen had reverted to the original Latin, *puppis*. The long superstructure on the puppis, which appeared top-heavy to me, was called, with affection, the *pupcastle*. On the *Vigilant*, the captain, master, doctor, and researchers kept quarters here, and the two laboratories were also in the pupcastle.

The ship's craft rates—Story Meissner, the dark, sepulchral sailmaker; the small, dour female carpenter Varia Gusmao; William French the navigator; stooped, grizzled and wrinkled Pyotr Khovansk the engineer; and Shatro, the only researcher already on board—bunked in the pupcastle as well, sharing a common cabin, or adjacent to their work-cabins. The able-bodied seamen or A.B.s, and apprentices (sometimes called monkeys, since they spent much of their time in the trees) were each allotted a bunk in the forecastle.

All below the craft rates served watches, four hours on and four off, divided into port and starboard. Each craft rate and A.B. and apprentice received three meals a day. Grain from Jakarta and Tasman provided the staple, supplemented by flockweed flour. The mainstay was *freechunk*, a paste made of soy and flockweed, served up fried or baked, or ground into flour and made into bread. Packed and dried river celery and diospuros served for essential vitamins. Fresh terrestrial fruits and vegetables, grown on plantations outside Calcutta, served as treats. Sailors it seemed did not favor scion fruits such as Liz cherries, and seagoing or pelagic scions, whatever ecos they came from, were by and large inedible, unlike their riparian counterparts, which could at times be nutritious and not provoke immune challenges.

There were plans (Soterio told us darkly) to feed the crew occasionally on land scions deemed edible by the cook—with the second opinion of the captain and the chief researcher, the mate added. This was obviously something of a sore point with the more experienced crew, since nearly all—according to whispers—had eaten one or another type of non-Liz scion that had not agreed with them.

The tour finished with a brief lecture from Soterio on discipline. "Each is expected to do his work. Favoritism of any sort is considered flarking." The mate used the word "flarking" constantly, to describe anything in opposition to the ship's established order. Now, his brows almost obscured his black marble eyes, and he crooked his mouth as if remembering a bitter taste. "There is to be no sex between crew members at sea. No need to explain why. We are all equally valuable here, and such leads to serious disputes. Phylactics," meaning drugs to dampen sexual drive, an interesting misuse of a word, "are available from the medical."

The mate concluded this lecture with a list of punishments. "First-time offense, four hours at the skysail top. Second, confinement in stores antechamber for a time deemed sufficient by the captain and master. Third, we put you off at the next settlement landfall and take aboard someone more suited."

The crew was then sent to arrange their personal effects. There would be no dinner served aboard this evening; instead, the crew could spend their last night in town.

In the forecastle, all had been assigned their bunks by number, but the A.B.s quietly and with little resistance traded assignments with the others for a section of their own. The social weaving took perhaps ten minutes, with the apprentices left a step behind, somewhat bewildered.

Talya Ry Diem, the senior female A.B., a grizzled, stocky woman with thick, well-muscled arms and legs and a bulldog countenance, took it upon herself to explain. "There's rates and there's ranks, even on a free citizen's ship. More experience, more time at sea, more privileges. The A.B.s know enough to keep you from killing yourselves. It's only right. And what's more, it puts *me* in a better bunk."

A curtain was drawn forming a partition for the twelve women. All the women were A.B.s, and they commandeered a portion of the elite section and put an angle in the curtain to mark their special territory. As there were no female apprentices, we could divide no farther, and received the least desirable berths—with so little difference between them that arguing was useless.

Names were exchanged again for the benefit of the newer crew members. I shook hands with my shipmates, a pot of Tasman tea was set boiling, and sweet biscuits passed around from Ry Diem's chest. "These are especially for the new ones, who don't know how this kind of ship works," Ry Diem said. "We all have to get along in a special way—a sea-going way, that works across months or years without much in the way of fighting. If you have any questions or problems, you can come to me, or to Ser Shankara. Or to Meissner, the sail-maker. He's a good man. He and I have sailed before."

The apprentices, after trying to brighten the picture of being closest to the bow, in the tightest spaces and with the smallest bunks, set to displaying and describing their few valued possessions, that all would know who might have stolen from whom. Already, two likely characters had been singled out as potential thieves: the youngest and scrawniest, both with narrow, lackadaisical faces, Uwe Kissbegh and Uri Ridjel, who seemed to wear perpetual smiles of shocked innocence.

A tall boy of eighteen, with a thick shock of brown hair, shaven thin at the sides, shook my hand with extra conviction. "My name's Algis Bas Shimchisko. My first ship. Yours, too?"

I smiled and nodded.

"Apprentices have to stick together," Shimchisko said. "The A.B.s lord it if we don't. From Calcutta?"

"Jakarta," I said.

"Meet Miszta Ibert," Shimchisko said, putting his arm around the wide shoulders of a thin boy of sixteen or seventeen, with a small, mouselike face and short foxfur hair. Ibert smiled. "We joined together. We've both taken science at the Lenk schools. We spent five months in the depths of Liz."

"Inland from Cape Zhuraitis," Ibert said. "We think we know Liz very well."

"What does she think of *you*?" I asked.

The boys laughed loudly. Shimchisko slapped his knee. "We think she *favors* us, of course. All the women do."

Among the other faces, I paid immediate attention to Ellis Shankara, senior male A.B., a quiet, dark-skinned man with humored eyes, large and examining, but a stern mouth. Shankara's alert expression and calm manner impressed me. I spent a few minutes watching a short-legged, round-faced woman A.B. with a quick, birdlike manner, whom I found oddly attractive, but whose name I did not then catch.

Kissbegh and Ridjel took it upon themselves to play an ill-timed jape as we put our valuables away in shallow drawers beside the bunks. Kissbegh leaped about in seeming abandon, claiming to perform a farewell dance to the land. Ridjel tootled him along with a raucous lip-warble, and as if by accident, Kissbegh swooped down upon, and fell through, the curtain separating our bow space from the space set aside for the female A.B.s. Hair on end like a furious cat, Talya Ry Diem yanked Kissbegh up with two strong hands around his jaw and ears and dragged him until she jammed him against the forward fiber locker. "I'm kind," she growled, "but I'll kick your ass if you don't act the man."

Saying not another word, glaring fiercely, she left him there minus his smile.

I liked all of this. It seemed very alive and boisterous. I might slip smoothly into the immigrant culture after all. Despite my earlier misgivings, and whatever their skills, and however isolated, these people seemed at heart decent and hard-working. They wished to learn what they could, and they were willing to take obvious risks to do so.

I could cheerfully go to sea with these people, work with them, learn what I could; I could even forget, for a time, what my mission was.

Before all introductions could be finished, with the crew's opinions of each other given an early shape, the mate returned. "You'll stare at every block and line for the next few years," he chided. "Grab the shore for one more night."

All but one of the women chose to stay aboard, boiling their own free-chunk over a small stove, stringing mat fiber ropes to air their clothes. Most of the male A.B.s and apprentices, and several of the ranks, left the *Vigilant* just before sundown and took the Hill Step Road up and over a low rise, to that part of Calcutta where all sailors were supposed to go.

The nightlife of Calcutta had been walled off, concentrated and capped in a district of town away from the center, surrounded by high stone walls, a dreary, river-damp set of narrow streets and low, ramshackle buildings the color of dust and cloudy sky. Here the cobbles had gaping holes—I saw a suspicious congeries of holes before an empty building with broken windows, a broken sign over the door reading ADVE—and the gutters had not been swept. It smelled anciently human, yet seemed quiet. The crews of several vessels wandered these few streets, mostly male. Without the women, the men became restless, peering into windows, making dull, unenthusiastic remarks, trying out their sailor's gaits, broad steps and arms swinging confidently, coming upon each other every third turn, looking for cheer and something to brace up their spirits for the coming absence from shore. Little cheer or support was to be found.

A brief flame of sunset turned our faces and the low, false-fronted buildings orange. Dusk followed quickly, gray and dismal. The fitful lighting, dim lamps on xyla poles at corners, made us all shadows. Three scattered knots of searchers, twenty in all—eight from the *Vigilant* including Shimchisko and Ibert; the eldest among us, Shankara; and the round-faced young female apprentice, Shirl or Shirla—went from a small bar with five stools and two tables, serving bitter rum, to a larger establishment reputed to serve food, to the largest place of all, which the most experienced men seemed to avoid with dark faces. But this, the walk-in known as the Fishless Sea, was where we ended up.

Here was entertainment, the most perverse (and therefore fatally attractive) that the divaricate city could offer. Here a half dozen blank-faced women and a few pale men offered themselves for conversation or dancing or turns in the rooms upstairs. It was fairly ritualized and acceptable; divaricates had never been prudes. But something else hung in the air of the Fishless Sea, a restless, guilty anticipation made half of dread and half of curiosity. The best entertainment in this establishment, the older hands said, was supplied by Lamarckia itself.

Shankara led us through thick xyla doors into cool air, a small, dark room at the very rear, the sounds of the kitchen coming from someplace to my left. The rum buzzed in me, a novel and not unpleasant sensation.

I sat with my shipmates before a low stage daubed with tarry black paint. A short, slender woman with long brown hair and a fixed gaze, who some said was the owner, came on stage and stood beneath a bright spot. Her voice was deep and sandy and she did not look at her audience.

Some chewed mat fiber, tasteless but scented of sweetness and garlic and filled with a mild stimulant, and others drank more rum. The young, round-faced female A.B. sat beside Shankara and balanced a plate of indifferent gruel on her lap, eating slowly, staring up with doubtful but wide eyes.

"We've all lived our lives in the shadow of the silva," the woman said in a breathless monotone. "We've been sampled, and the silva knows us. But can we ever know the silva? There are *curiosities . . . peculiarities.* The zones, rich with life, do they resent us? Do they notice our existence? Can they truly see and think, or are they blind as stones? Sometimes we feel we are wrapped in the depths of a heedless mother, and we cry out in our sleep like children. There are mysteries no one will ever fathom. Absurd mysteries, unexplainable phenomena. How many have heard stories?"

A few hands rose, then others, taking encouragement in numbers.

"*I've* heard stories," the woman continued, nodding to herself, her tone confessional, and then darkly mysterious. "Stories not to be believed. Terrifying, strange, but not . . . *surprising.* Does anything surprise us on this, our chosen world?" An edge of weary resentment in her words now, eyebrow raised, a flip of the long brown hair.

I sat with my hands gripping the sides of the seat of my chair. A fog of unreality stole over me, caused not by the rum, but by the sour animal smell of bodies in the close room, the rough lizboo between my fingers, the floor strewn with bits of dried parasol leaf to soak up spilled liquid. The cloying smell of mat drifted through the air, sweet and garlicky.

"When my husband vanished in Eastern Tasman, hunting curiosities in Baker's Zone, I took off to search for him. Long weeks and months by boat, then through thick swamp, over tall mountains—"

"Get on with it," grumbled a bearded man near me, swaying slightly in his chair, jaw working a clump of mat.

"To find . . . *something.*"

"Something!" the crowd shouted in derision. "Show us!"

"Not pickled," the woman said, leaning toward the crowd, hands sweeping out, fingers pointing, enjoying her own melodrama. "Not stuck in a bottle."

"Not like us," a man shouted, and the crowd laughed at itself, in a perverse humor.

"Not in a bottle. Alive. *Alive and away from its land, and so very lonely,*" she chanted.

"Like us," several voices sang out. Nervous laughter now.

"Strange," the woman said, "to stare into what it uses for its eyes, and wonder . . . Does it think? Does it miss its home, thousands of kilometers away? Does it miss its *queen*, whom no one has ever seen? Was I cruel, to bring it here . . . Was I seeking to avenge my husband?"

"Be cruel, be *cruel*," a drunken man, not of our ship, shouted from the front.

This is the dream, Lenk's dream, I thought. *Get his people away from Thistledown, from people no longer shaped like people, from the blasphemous Way* . . .

The rum fogged and distorted and was no longer pleasant. I set my glass down, half empty, and drank no more.

Two brawny men in aprons rolled a large crate onto the stage. Liquid slopped from between the boards and ran thick and brown over the black tarry floor, lapping up against the raised edge, the *fiddle* I thought, testing out a nautical term, like old port spilled on a ship's table. Within the crate, a sigh, a clatter of sticks or branches.

"What possible use to its zone, to its queen?" the woman asked dreamily. "Such a monster, perhaps no use at all. A *sport*, a dream gone bad, a nightmare. The silva dreams and twitches in its sleep. We hear it, breathing its black breath across the land, over our heads, in our skin and hair. We cut its trees, harvest its leaves, fence its helpers and attendants . . . Will it not someday know what we are, and hate us? What will it make next? Perhaps this is a *test*. Something that will eventually grow large, and attack . . . Let's take a look, and perhaps see *our future* . . . "

"Naah," a man sneered from the rear of the room, waving a hand. He stood and pushed through the thick xyla door. The woman on stage watched him leave with sad, tired eyes. The cool air settled again. The woman reached out for the crate, challenging the audience with a piercing stare . . .

Her hands fumbled at a corroded brass latch, opened the front of the crate wide with a groaning creak . . .

One of the burly men stood beside a stagelight and dropped a colored gel over the bulb. The stage became green, dark and cold.

"From the north," the woman moaned, as if mourning. "It might have killed my husband. It wants to kill *me* and go home. A monster, a queen's own nightmare. Look upon it."

The door swung all the way, and within, restrained by iron bars, a cage within the crate, long thin black legs, dozens of them, with red joints.

The round-faced woman leaned forward, eyes even wider. The audience fell silent. A chair leg racketed on the floor, several feet shuffled. "Fate and Pneuma," said one voice.

"Hoping to kill us all," the woman on stage suggested dreamily.

Lights switched on overhead, bathing the cage in brighter green and yellow. The form in the cage stirred, legs twitching. The woman pulled a large key on a brass ring from the folds of her dress, slipped it into a prominent lock on the cage within the crate, turned the key, and pulled open the cage door with a ghastly unoiled screech. The sailors in the first row of the theater pushed their chairs back with a clatter until outthrust arms and legs from the people behind would let them push no farther.

"What would we do if they freely walked among us?" the woman asked, spinning out her story, making herself a potential victim as the legs stretched reflexively across the stage toward her, flat cup-claw feet spatting into the leaking brown liquid. One sailor, a young fellow not from the *Vigilant*, bolted. Shankara looked after him and gave me a knowing smile.

The creature squeezed and squirmed slowly from its cage and stood in the sickly light, rising three meters in height, gangly, loose. I tried to discern its shape in the glare: thick trunk or abdomen dragging, thin upper body, disks half rotating at its shoulders, and emerging from the edges of the disks the long, half limp legs. It had no head, but a long stalk pushed up from the trunk and arched over the form, and from this hung two transparent globes—eyes, perhaps—that slowly rotated, black oblate pupils absorbing the sight of the crowd. It sighed, thorax expanding alarmingly, then shivered its legs together. The audience as one groaned and backed away, tables and chairs bunching, overturning.

The scion and the woman seemed to regard each other with equal detachment. "What is it you wish, *monster*?" the woman asked coldly.

The form lifted its legs as if beckoning.

"*Me?*" the woman asked, voice rising to a kind of cheery glee. "*Me*, as well as my husband?"

"Stop it!" shouted the man half seated in front of me. "For the love of God, it's just a scion! A silvan child! Let it be!"

The woman ignored him. The audience had come here for rough entertainment; she was determined to give it to them. The long pleats of her dress contained many things, apparently. She lowered one hand gracefully and brought out a machete. "Which is it to be?" she asked us. "Revenge . . . or forgiveness? Respect, or anger given an edge?"

My own anger suddenly flared and I restrained myself with an effort. The woman's face fairly glowed with enthusiasm. She seemed half committed to chopping the form to bits; in the cloud of rum, I thought, *No act, this*. But the burly men emerged from the wings and restrained her, one grabbing the arm with the machete, both bodily lifting her, suddenly rigid as a board. The slow spidery creature, left alone on the stage, sighed, bunched its legs up and sidled back into its cage.

The stagehands returned without the woman and raised and locked the door of the crate, then lowered the curtains. The audience sat stunned for a moment; *that was all? No exit music, no announcements?*

Grumbling, disheartened, we passed through the glass doors to the bar. I stayed behind, stunned and heartsick, slumped in my chair. Somehow, this seemed almost as wrong and perverse as the slaughter at Moonrise.

The round-faced woman, Shirl or Shirla, put aside her unfinished bowl of gruel and stood before the stage and curtains. She wore a kerchief around her head topped with a small black hat. Her face seemed childlike in the half light. She turned to Shankara. "What is it?" she asked.

"Nothing but a Tasman western scion," Shankara said, half in contempt, half in pity. "Not eastern. Not from Baker. Probably from Kandinski's Zone. But I'm just guessing."

"We'll see more like that?" the woman asked distantly.

Shankara gave a brief, hollow laugh and looked at me with dark brown eyes. "Shocking, eh? We live in the most boring zone on Lamarckia. We have to *import* our monsters."

"It was wonderful," the round-faced woman said, and seemed genuinely to mean it. "Poor thing. What does it do?"

"A mulcher, I'd guess," he said. "Something that cleans arborid roots and prepares soil. About as dangerous as a cricket. I've served on merchant ships going to Tasman and seen stranger than that."

We walked toward the door past the small tables and overturned chairs. "Your name is Olmy, isn't it?" Shankara asked.

"Yes," I said. I looked at the young-faced woman. Her eyes flicked to meet mine, like a bird's.

"This is Shirla," Shankara said.

"Shirla Ap Nam," the woman added. "Junior A.B." She picked something from her teeth with one finger and shook her head as we pushed through the heavy doors. "You know," she said, "if we had a zoo or something . . ."

"The captain has a zoo," Shankara said. "A small one, in bottles."

"Not what I mean," Shirla said. "If we could go *see* all the parts, all the scions, we wouldn't act like such damn fools."

By midnight, beneath a cloudless sky filled with the double arc of stars and one small, lantern-bright moon, the crews wended their ways back to the docks and ships, neither wholly drunk nor satisfied. I walked a few meters behind Shankara and Shirla and the rest of the group from the *Vigilant*. Shirla kept glancing over her shoulder at me, as if I might be stalking her. With her last glance, she gave a little shiver and frowned in apparent disapproval. Somehow, this completed my sadness.

As they rounded a corner ahead of me, a man stepped from the shadows and held up an arm. I gave him a wide berth by instinct, but the man spoke my name. It was the disciplinary, Thomas. He wore a dull green overcoat and a small cloth cap with a tail that fell down his neck, into his collar.

"I had hoped you would stick around long enough to answer my questions. Now, you'll put out to sea . . . On a research ship, no less."

"Is that suspicious?" I asked. I stuffed my hands in my pockets. "I'm interested in the zones. I always have been."

Thomas looked at me with a bland, patient expression. "I've had time enough to run my checks. No birth records for an Olmy of the Datchetong. No Lenk school or residence records. Unless you come from Hsia, or some unregistered community, you don't exist."

I felt distinctly uncomfortable. Then I took a chance. "Ser Thomas, nobody has complete records anymore." I stood in the dark beside Thomas, and silence fell between us for several seconds. Finally, he looked away, then down at the stone paving. "I don't believe you're a Brionist. That doesn't make sense, judging from your behavior . . . and how we met. You would have faded into the silva and taken a passenger boat later, or made your own. I've given a lot of thought to you. I think perhaps I will leave you alone and let you go where you wish."

"Thank you," I said.

"There was a small group of people, years ago, that kept a secret vigil. They called themselves Adventists. They were waiting for someone from the Hexamon to arrive."

"Sounds Christian," I said.

"'Advent' means the coming of something big, something momentous. Nothing to do with Christians. Not all of them made their views known. One of them stole something and vanished. Nobody knows the details except perhaps Lenk himself. I had heard there was an Adventist in Moonrise. Was there?"

"I don't know," I said.

"Is it a crazy idea?"

"Why didn't they come years ago?" I asked.

Thomas smiled. "Now *that* I don't know, either. Some say we erased the path to Lamarckia and we'll be here forever, alone."

"Suits me," I said.

Thomas's bland expression returned. "If they did come, they would try to take us all back to the Way. That's the general opinion. I'm not so sure, now that we've been here so long, and we've grown in numbers. We own this world as much as any human owns anything."

"We don't own the zones," I said, trying to reestablish some fragment of my role.

"No-oo," Thomas said thoughtfully. "Promise me this, will you? Someday, if there's time, and if you can, unravel a few mysteries for me."

I shook my head, grinned, looked away, as if to say, *Crazy notions.*

Thomas raised his hands, clasped them, and rubbed his palms together.

"The citizens rank made their decision earlier this evening. Brionists or their renegades killed the citizens at Moonrise. Naderville will claim it was renegades. It's for the rank at Athenai to decide what to do. No need for more testimony from you. You're free to go wherever you please."

With a curt nod, Thomas turned and walked up the street, past a feeble streetlamp and into shadows.

Calcutta was a dull town indeed, I thought to myself as I walked up the gangway to the *Vigilant*; at least as far as its vices were concerned. Divaricates had no flair for debauchery.

I was eager to get to sea.

I stood sleepless by the taffrail, staring astern at the cold black waters and the night, half clouded, the void between black clouds thick-studded with stars. I thought about Lamarckia's sun and her five sister planets, about which I found very little in Redhill other than what the original surveyors had recorded—a remarkable lapse on the immigrant's part, or an oversight on Redhill's, I thought.

What I could see between the clouds, by eye alone, was tantalizing. Just a few degrees east of the main skysail yard shone one very bright bluish point surrounded by smaller points just outside its concentrated light: Pacifica, a gas giant with many moons that seemed to move as the minutes passed. High above the western horizon gleamed a yellowish point that I was fairly sure must be another planet, probably Aurum. All around shimmered the volumes and volumes of stars, including the double oxbow—part of the encompassing galaxy, analogous to the Milky Way seen from Earth. Randall's few books on astronomy called this blurred twin loop by several names: the Hills, the Kraken, or the Tetons. No astronomical authorities had authorized a final name, apparently. I preferred the Tetons myself. I hoped to find out more by examining the ship's chartroom.

I left my mates in their bunks in the forecastle when all seemed to sleep soundly. William French, the navigator, was snoring in his pupcastle cabin. The contents of the deserted chartroom, books and maps opened or drawn down quietly, lighted only by a single dim lantern, added much to what I needed to know about the immigrants' present state of knowledge.

There were no complete and accurate charts of Lamarckia. No one had ever seen the planet from space; no satellites had ever been put into orbit, and the immigrants had much left to explore, including the entire hemisphere opposite Elizabeth's Land, called the Deep West by some cartographers, the Far East by others.

The star charts were fairly thorough, and some improvements had been made by the immigrants on the surveyor's originals. Ephemeris data was kept in several thick volumes in the chartroom, much amended by French's hand, and probably on the captain's slate as well. (Nkwanno's had no such data.) The sailors on Lamarckia did not lack knowledge of how to find their way around, and how to calculate latitudes and longitudes. Working with the planet's magnetic field was relatively simple: there were few compass deviations in this hemisphere, and those well understood.

Still, any sailor on Earth at the time of Thistledown's launch—or even by the close of the twentieth century—would have been appalled at the prospect of using such limited and inaccurate means. What little of Lamarckia had been charted in detail, had been explored by brave men and women indeed.

Lenk's first Captain of Voyages, Alphonse Jiddermeyer, with two sailing ships, had set off from new-founded Calcutta five years after the immigrants' arrival. His two-year journey took him along the Sumner Coast, named after his first mate, to the northeast point of Elizabeth's Land, then south, discovering the violently volcanic Agni Islands that lay four hundred miles from the continent's eastern coast. (Those islands did not figure on later charts. Some of the histories mentioned enormous blasts heard fifteen years ago, and clouds of ash settling across southeastern Elizabeth's Land, the Darwin Sea, and even Hsia. Enormous waves had struck the eastern Cheng Ho Coast and Jakarta, causing considerable damage to the human settlement, and the islands were not seen again by merchant ships or later explorers. Penciled on the *Vigilant*'s charts were specks in that general region, and question marks.)

After leaving these islands, Jiddermeyer's ships were relentlessly blown south by southwest, back to the southern extremities of Elizabeth's Land. Jiddermeyer and his researchers charted the visible boundaries of what later became known as zones five and six, Petain and Magellan. They sailed around Cape Magellan, depending in a drawn-up curve from the main body of Elizabeth like a giant fang in the upper jaw of a sabertooth cat, and found the Kupe Islands. Here, a storm sank one boat, and the second—with Jiddermeyer and two thirds of both crews—continued south. They found two long strips of land, named them the Alicias after the sailor who first sighted them, and then were blown swiftly west to the environs of the southern polar continent, La Pérouse Land, seen only as a distant blue coast backed by huge mountains and glaciers.

Here, they had encountered vicious westerly winds they called the Ice Knives. The winds blew them east along La Pérouse Land, the cold, stormy bottom of the world. This ended Jiddermeyer's plans of circumnavigating Lamarckia. Exhausted, Jiddermeyer slipped free of the Ice Knives, repaired his ship on Southern Alicia, and sailed due north, close-hauled against the seasonal northerlies. Their last discovery, all by chance, was Martha's Island, with its sterile surrounding sea and fertile, varied lone ecos. Thereafter, they turned southwest and put into port at Jakarta.

Jiddermeyer had taken an awful chance. No one knew whether edible scions existed in any of the zones away from Tasman or Elizabeth's Land. Indeed, no one was quite sure that the basic biology of these two continents would also be replicated in other territories. Jiddermeyer's head researcher, Kia Ry Lenk—Jaime Carr Lenk's sister—believed they would find only ecoi on Lamarckia. Others disagreed.

But she had been correct, and no other scheme of life had been discovered. And wherever they went, they found no scions willing to eat *them*—but sufficient edible forms to sustain the crew. The voyage had been horrific, nonetheless—improper nutritional balances and immune challenges had played havoc with the health of the expedition.

In the end, out of two ships and two hundred and five men and women, one ship and sixty-five had returned to Jakarta. The sinking of the second ship had drowned many of the crew, including Kia Ry Lenk and her husband and two sons.

Exploration lost its charms for Able Lenk. He never quite recovered from the death of his sister. He departed from Jakarta, sailing north to the smaller continent of Tasman, discovered three years earlier by merchant ships. There, he founded what was now Lamarckia's second largest city, Athenai.

He had not since returned to Jakarta or Calcutta. This had left Elizabeth's Land to an uneasy kind of independence.

Shortly after, Hoagland and her splinter group had sailed for Hsia and founded Godwin, later Naderville.

Only one other expedition—led by Dassin Ry Baker and Lucius Shulago—had carried on from Jiddermeyer's example. Twenty-five years after the Crossing, they sailed from Jakarta across the Darwin Sea to Hsia, then down to the Cook Straits and Cook Islands, between Efhraia's Land and Hsia. They rounded Efhraia's Land, returned to the Darwin Sea, and sailed north until they reencountered Martha's Island, quite by accident. They headed south again, and one ship turned back, carrying all the records from that expedition. On the far side of Hsia, in an ocean still almost completely unknown, in search of two small continents rumored to have been seen by merchant ships blown astray—Basilica and Nihon—Baker and Shulago and the second ship vanished, after sending a weak radio signal that all was well.

Dawn began as a thin pink line against the eastern sky, much of it obscured by the low arborid-crowned hills directly east of Calcutta. The silva's great four-legged cathedral trees stood against the morning glow like sentinels, feathery fronds below their crowns waving gently with intermittent puffs of breeze that had not yet reached the harbor. The pink horizon turned briefly red, then pale violet; the stars gave way, and the entire sky began to fill with rays of gray and shallow blue.

I stretched and swung my arms, working the chill out of my body, then ran around the deck as warm-up, joining French the navigator and three others similarly engaged.

The sun stood half above the headland when wakeup was announced by the ringing of a brass bell.

Belowdecks, I joined the rest of the crew at the mess. The cook, Leo Frey, a peaceful-looking man of about forty with a thin body but a prominent belly and fat face, and the cook's sour-looking, heavy-set assistant, called simply Passey, dolloped gruel into xyla bowls and handed each of us a thick slice of river celery. Officers shared the same lines and ate the same food, but sat at a separate table in the officers' mess beyond a narrow open doorway. The rest of the crew—including the navigator, the engineer, the sailmaker, and other craft rates—sat around rough-planed tables in the crew mess in no particular order. The crew went through morning routine in stolid silence punctuated only by half awake grunts.

When breakfast was finished, in less than ten minutes, the crew lined up again to drop their bowls into a pot of boiling, frothing water outside the galley. A few minutes attending to personal hygiene (this was a clean ship, with a clean crew, for which I was grateful) and they all gathered on the upper deck to receive the captain's words, inaugurating the voyage.

Captain Keyser-Bach stood on the puppis, looking down on the crew with bright eyes. He stepped to the rail, smiling confidently, and his hands gripped the smoothly turned xyla. "Today we begin our journey to the extremities of this world, and to understand the life upon it. We bow, all of us, to Jiddermeyer, and to Baker and Shulago, but we will not repeat their mistakes. We add also years more experience on the seas, a better ship, and I am certain, a better crew." He spread his feet wide, balancing from one to the other, clasped his hands, and bowed his head. The crew did likewise. "We set our faith in the lines drawn by Star and Fate, that all of our worlds here conjoin to make one rope, each strand a man or woman, all pulling in unison for the joy of life well-lived. In the name of Star, Fate, and Breath, illuminated by Logos, inspired by the example of the Good Man, we will not fail in our duties, though the seas roar and mountains shoot flame." He added, in a voice barely audible, "And though our own kindred set against us." With a shrug of his shoulder, three fingers rubbing his chin vigorously, he turned to Randall and said, "Set our slates for ship's time. We depart in fifteen minutes."

The occasional puffs of breeze had finally come to the harbor in greater strength, united as a westerly blowing steady at five to seven knots. On the sea, distance and speed here as on Earth were measured in nautical miles and knots, or nautical miles per hour. For Lamarckia, with its radius of 5931 kilometers, a nautical mile came to about 1725 meters.

I took to the shrouds of the fore and main trees with the least senior apprentices—those who had been aboard the ship a month or less, six in all—and two junior A.B.s. My group of four set the fore course. Others unfurled the main course and main lower topsail. We then set the upper top-sails and lower topgallants, and three of us—myself included—descended to the deck and forward to bend and raise the outer and inner bellies. With the breeze blowing across the beam—perpendicular to the ship—the captain and mate skillfully ordered us here and there, pulling on this halyard and that, and the ship began to work about, pushing from the dock in gradual zigs and zags.

On the dock, wives, children, family, and friends—a fair crowd of about two hundred—sat waving hands or hats or handkerchiefs, again in somber dignity, with few cheers. However momentous this occasion, however mon-umental the import of this expedition, the citizens of Calcutta did not reveal their emotions.

I remembered wedding or funeral gatherings on Thistledown among or-thodox Naderites—emotion aplenty locked in each breast; but a strong, dedicated face to the world. That restraint had always made me uneasy. As a youngster, dreaming of glory and challenges, I had always wished for a more appreciative farewell from family and friends.

The *Vigilant* sailed with dreamlike smoothness toward the middle of the river. Both port and starboard watches were busy on the deck and in the rigging. The captain stood at the bow with one foot on the bowsprit, inspect-ing every meter of the water ahead.

I scrambled high up the ratlines, muscles aching, to adjust a jammed block. For a brief moment, I looked across the river and silva from a top, hands aching, toes and insteps of my feet feeling as if they had been bro-ken. Then as quickly back down; on deck, dizzy with the height, I pulled on halyards with my team to raise the christian on the mizzen and secured them to belaying pins. Then we all scrambled aloft again.

The waters spread wide in the delta, flowing around dozens of sandy black islands. Beaches sparkled like diamonds against velvet in shafts of light breaking through the thick clouds. Avoiding darker shifting shallows and gnarls of rivervine required more deft maneuvering.

After an hour, we saw lines of breakers fighting through thick tangles of vine, an open channel forty meters deep and a hundred wide, and be-yond that, blue-gray and finally slate gray, the Darwin Sea.

As we crossed to brackish and finally ocean water, the air took on a sharp tang. Captain Keyser-Bach remained on the bow, thin nose pointing due west. The breeze had stiffened to twelve knots and we were moving very briskly. "Shorten sail, Mr. Randall," he instructed. "Take the main courses up two points, the fore topgallants two points, and let's loose and stow the windscrews for the time being. Steer her northeast by east until we cross the Sticks. Then due east."

Hanging on to a yard, helping five other seamen lift and tie the points on the fore tree's upper topgallant, I felt the touch of a new kind of wind and air, and my skin prickled. The mix of minerals in these waters was not the same as in Earth's seas, not familiar to my blood; less sodium salt, more potassium, more dissolved silicates and carbon dioxide and oxygen. Yet despite the constant faint hiss of oxygen bubbles in the water, like a gassy soda, this was undeniably an ocean.

Later, as the wind strengthened even more, the captain amended, "Take in all but main and lower topsails. Once we're out in open sea we'll set for our best speed, and keep well away from shore."

"Yes, sir," Randall responded, and called the apprentices out again.

Twenty miles and two and a half hours out of the delta, the foam of oxygen bubbles subsided. Surrounding Lamarckia's continents, and in many huge patches throughout the oceans, microscopic scions of pelagic ecoi dissociated seawater into hydrogen and oxygen. Reducing metabolisms had been chosen here, very early in life's history, as on Earth—the routes and processes were substantially different, however.

Ahead, spread across our course like thick straight fingers, five tall dirty-brown towers stuck up from the sea, each over a hundred meters high. Huge purple and red "sails" ballooned out from the tops of the towers, light-absorbing tissues each perhaps a hectare in area. From where I caught a few moment's rest on a top, I saw the towers were shot through with man-high tunnels.

"The Sticks. Bunyan's walking sticks," A.B. Shankara said, clinging to the mast. "From zone five. The captain will thread them for luck, then we'll head east."

The ship slipped between the southernmost two giants. We watched the waves swell and beat against their immense bases, sucking and booming through the worm-hole tunnels. Bulbous black shapes the size of cow's heads poked from some of the narrower tunnels, sporting three rows of eyes gleaming in the late-afternoon light as the sun flashed beneath a thickening deck of clouds. Shankara had something to say about them, too. "Sirens," he shouted over the flapping of the sails and hum of wind, as we hung from a yard, tying reef points. "They watch all the time, everything. They watch our ships come and go. Spies for their zone. Their bodies . . ."

I held my breath against a sudden whoop of wind that sang through the braces and forced the sails aback, nearly knocking our boots loose from the footropes.

"They twist all through the insides, like worms," he continued. "That's what I'm told. I've never explored the holes."

"You think they're intelligent?" I yelled back at him.

"Hell, no!" Shankara said. "They just *watch*. Who knows what they *see*?"

"Work, don't flark!" the mate shouted from below.

A hundred miles out of Calcutta, the westerly picked up again, blowing at fifteen and then twenty knots, driving strong seas beneath night sky covered with a ceiling of black clouds. We rigged for a steady blow. The dinner was cold for the fifth watch—Leo Frey decided not to risk cooking fires in such a wind or drain the batteries with hotplates. Seven of the starboard watch and I descended to the mess as our watch ended, sitting to eat with stiff fingers our plates of freechunk and fruit, heads drooping in abject exhaustion. With the windscrews stowed, and the ship on backup batteries, the electric lights glowed fitfully and in alternation, first three on one side, then three on the other, as if trading duty. They cast long alternating flickers of brown shadow around us while we tried to eat.

With sails properly rigged, a storm watch was called, and the rest of the crew retired to take their dinner as well.

Randall stood at a podium forward of the tables and rang a small bell. Heavy heads rose, mouths doggedly chewing, and Randall announced that the captain wished to give a short lecture. The captain took the podium, grabbing it with both hands as a swell lifted and then dropped the ship.

"Each night," he began, "I hope to continue our education on the goals of this journey, to discuss the nature of the ecoi and their benefits and potential dangers . . ."

Many of the newer members of the crew—myself included—did not yet have their sea legs, or rather, their sea lungs. It took some time to get used to the combination of the ship's motion and the invigorating but initially upsetting smell of Lamarckia's sea spray. One by one, cold paste heavy on our stomachs, but perhaps not heavy enough, the newer sailors begged the captain's pardon and retreated, either to go topside or to the heads, two fore and one aft. I counted six desertions as the ship pitched and rolled. My own stomach felt none too calm as the seas became rougher. The air was beginning to smell peculiar, like an old orange.

"Yes," the captain said, watching his audience decline. Then, "Yes," again, and finally he gave it up, postponing the talk until the morning.

"He's a good captain, really," said Algis Bas Shimchisko. "The best on Lamarckia, I bet. A true seaman."

Miszta Ibert went for a second helping of paste and brought it back, grinning as if he'd won a prize. "He's a *very* good captain," young Ibert agreed, forking the paste hungrily. "Just enthusiastic, and who's to judge against that?"

I watched him eat and felt my insides quiver.

"Hooo," said Shimchisko. "Lost a few this evening, haven't we, Mish?"

"A few," Ibert said. "No more than I expected."

"They'll get right after tomorrow. It's the sea," Shimchisko explained. "Sometimes when even a good sailor spends some time ashore, the smell of the sea, the *broad* foaming sea, gets them."

"You all right?" Ibert asked me.

"Never better," I said. I refused to go topside.

Once my body had been equipped to handle almost any emergency, any illness, any unease. I was truly on my own now, this naked and natural body as unfamiliar as somebody else's, a complete stranger's, might have been.

The days passed in a way I had never experienced before. Time took on a new quality. The ship became a world unto itself; I had difficulty imagining anything else, especially during watches, when one assigned task succeeded another in dizzying succession. Steady, exhausting work, day and night, clutching ratlines or hanging onto yards during driving rain storms and rugged seas, watching foam-ribboned billows as high as the courses on each side . . . Flat calms when *Vigilant* drifted motionless or slid ahead slowly on a single screw driven by her reserve batteries. Up the shrouds, into the tops and out on the yards, reefing or furling, setting 'brooms to take advantage of running downwind, bending new sails when the old needed repair, manning the winches when the electric motors failed (as they did more often than not).

Greasing the trees, the lowest and thickest trees consisting of three straight legs of a cathedral tree strapped together with thick iron bands; pulling mat fiber strands from great wads of junk and spinning them into twine; drawing the standing rigging taut as it stretched with use. Rubbing down the rippled patterns on the xyla deck with pumice holystones, raising a faint scent of cloves and garlic; performing the daily ablution of all deck surfaces . . .

Only as I rolled into my bunk, lost in an almost spiritual state of physical exhaustion, did I think of any prior life, of immense chambers within an asteroid and the dreamlike infinity of the Way. None of that seemed real. And yet I still did not feel firmly established on Lamarckia. It seemed anyone around me—wise old Shankara, nonchalant Ibert, clownish Kissbegh and Ridjel, cynical but intelligent Shimchisko, round-faced Shirla—could tell just by looking at me that *I wasn't real.*

Only the sensual details, minute by minute, gave my self a solidity memory could not corroborate: the invigorating smell of charged air as we sailed the edge of a brewing storm; towering cumulus clouds swelling into massive anvils over the flat sandy prairies and setback mesas of the Sumner Coast, the crimsons and siennas of vivid sunsets over the stern.

Under the chafing of ropes and wires, the press of capstan spokes, the palming of marlinspike, my hands became a maze of cuts, scratches, and bruises, until they seemed little more than bloody claws; what would have healed in minutes or hours on Thistledown, now took days. Still, they toughened, and I no longer flinched from actions that, in my inexperience of days before, might have caused me painful injury. I dodged, grappled, hung, pulled, shifted, learned when to groan and when to swear.

The sun burned bright most days and I tanned to pale chocolate. The skin on my arms flaked and peeled, and I followed the example of the experienced A.B.s and smeared my cheeks and arms with thick, milky lizboo sap scooped from ceramic jugs. To cut the glare, I smeared my lower eyelids with blackrouge—the fine powder that fell from all arborid scions in Liz's silva. My hair dried to a stiff wiry brush, crusted between infrequent fresh-water rinses with a residue of salt spray.

Ibert loaned me a pocket mirror. I did not recognize myself: white eyes underscored by blackrouge, dark-skinned, brushy-haired. A pirate.

I had not spoken much with Randall since being assigned to my berth.

After dinner, when weather permitted, the captain told us more about Jiddermeyer and Baker and Shulago's visit to Martha's Island. Martha's Island differed greatly from most of Elizabeth's Land. Volcanic, isolated from other landmasses by a thousand miles of ocean, a thriving ecos at the center of a sterile sea, it was a perfect site for Keyser-Bach's science. Little was known about most of the island; and over a decade had passed since Baker and Shulago's journey. Few ships crossed now between Hsia and Elizabeth or Tasman; none had passed Martha's Island since the visit by Baker and Shulago.

"We are engaged in primary science," the captain enthused, standing before the lecture board, raising and fastening his sheets of illustrations from Shulago's artists, reproductions of photographs from Baker's cameras.

I examined the photographs of Martha's scions, and Shulago's drawings, with a growing bewilderment. Snakes without mouths, arborids that picked up their roots every few days and slunk across the rugged landscape like immense slugs; entire silvas migrating from one side of the island to the other in a few day's time. Hard-carapaced guardians rolling on dozens of tough calcareous wheels propelled by vigorous tiny cilia, searching the beaches for intruders, "sniffing up" humans but paying them little attention . . .

Who could ever make sense of such diversity? The captain sometimes expressed his ideas of ecos organization, of hierarchies, but was reluctant to explain in detail. "All tentative," Keyser-Bach said at the end of one lecture, answering questions from the researchers and crew. "We know some things . . . but not nearly enough." And behind it all, the unproven theory of central queens or seed-mothers, perhaps reflecting human needs for answers more than any reality.

After a few days, I relaxed completely and let the process of my absorp-

tion into the crew become complete. I quickly learned respect for nearly everybody on board, and for the ship itself, which I had underestimated. It
gave us few problems at sea, or no more than any ship made of inadequate
and primitive materials. Only Shatro, the researcher, continued to leave
me unimpressed. Bulky, with large but soft muscles, shorter than me, with
a boyish face on a wide head, he was prone to worries and enthusiasms,
suspicions and confidences, in equal measure. He seldom spoke to me, but
I could never tell whether he would treat me with suspicion or say something light and cheerful. He never said anything of much consequence,
either way. He had a habit of stating the obvious and then being embarrassed about it.

I could not yet judge his scientific ability.

While at sea, the crew followed the first mate's rules about sex scrupulously,
but flirting was rampant, and some couples were beginning to pair off in
ways that might as well have involved sex. Men took on women's tasks, and
women conferred grooming favors: cutting hair, tending to slight wounds.
Some men actually hid their cuts and contusions from Shatro, who acted
as ship's doctor, and revealed them to sympathetic female friends in privacy. I learned quickly that many of the women had brought aboard
special bags or small trunks containing medicines and sweet or pickled
treats, which they doled out to the men they favored.

Shirla Ap Nam, the round-faced A.B., reserved most of her attentions
for me, and it would have been out of character, not to say rude, for me to
decline. In time, I decided to relax about these matters as well. I was
young, my body was in command of its own reactions and not buffered
by implants. The flow of time complemented the flow of my hormones, and
I realized, with some surprise, that socializing was a bodily function, regu-
lated by deep instincts.

Aboard *Thistledown*, most of us—and nearly all in the Geshel
communities—had acquired so many layers of conscious control and sup-
plemental intervention that it seemed, from my new perspective, we might
have lost sight of our true animal natures. And that of course had been the
point. We had risen above our instincts and the rough grind of history; we
had given human society a new and smoother character.

The immigrants had both the best and the worst of their own unenhanced natures.

At first I found Shirla attractive, but not deeply so. I would as soon have had the attentions of one or two of the other women, but did not encourage them. Shirla was pleasant, however, and her conversation interesting enough. She did not seem to take our flirtation with deep seriousness, so we avoided private admonishments from Talya Ry Diem, who regarded it as her duty to keep the younger women from being hurt, as apparently she had been years before, by shipboard trysts, even unconsummated ones. For the ship was small enough (and the mate rat-nosed enough) that sneaking off in privacy for anything more was almost impossible.

Randall and the first mate often deferred male-female disciplinary problems to Ry Diem. And partly through her vigilance, the mate did not have to follow through on his muttered threats to put various over-demonstrative couples into compartments in the bilge.

To my surprise, Ry Diem took Kissbegh and Ridjel directly in hand. Soterio was glad to leave the two problem children to her half tender mercies. Ry Diem, Sonia Chung, Seima Ap Monash, and the other women A.B.s gave the crew its final social structure—that of an extended family, with Ry Diem as surrogate mother and finally, Shankara and Meissner as surrogate fathers. The captain became a tough taskmaster, combination peculiar god and professor, and more than once did I hear Ry Diem threaten Kissbegh with a tree hearing—being called up before Keyser-Bach for whatever infractions had most recently occurred. Kissbegh always relented.

We traveled for three days in the sea-chopping westerly, then turned south southeast, coming within a mile of the eastern Sumner Coast, though still sailing in deep water. So little of the coast had been explored or named, that a thousand miles of it, filled with shallow bays and backed by deserts and hills, carried only one designation: Sumner, after Lenk's second economist, Abba Sumner, who had also laid out Calcutta.

The currents flowed dark and rich beneath the *Vigilant*, and in what little time I had to spare, I stood by the rail peering into the clear water. Keyser-Bach had finally gotten the crew used to a nightly round of lectures, and most recently we had discussed zone five pelagic scions. I saw them swimming close to the surface: massive piscids called eggplant sharks, ten to fifteen meters long, deep purple-blue with white spots, thick-bodied and trilaterally symmetric, with blunt mouthless noses and lines of knife-shaped bony fins sweeping from nose to screwlike tails. They spun slowly in the water as they glided beneath the *Vigilant*. We also saw bowfish like gigantic tied ribbons floating on a gift-wrapped sea, long red streamers trailing from their winglike fins fifteen or twenty meters behind. Tangled masses of arm-thick vine seemed substantial as rope, yet parted like soapsuds as the ship passed through them, and regrouped in our wake.

A storm inland had broken loose balloon-trees, close relatives of lizboo, according to Randall; on the third day, the gas-bag of one floated off the starboard beam, twisting slowly, rumpled and half deflated, in the currents. As I watched, coiling ropes and splicing a broken line with a marlinspike, piscids the size and rough shape of harbor seals but black and silver in color tore at the balloon vigorously with external fangs, called thorn-teeth by the captain, then sucked the shredded fragments into orifices along their sides. Getting a closer look at one near the ship, I saw no head or mouth as such, only broad paddle-shaped fins with sharp white claws, and in a line on each side, the little mouthlike openings with sky-blue interior tissues revealed. They swam swiftly both backward and forward with rapid swishes, reversing their fins. Some, Shimchisko and Ibert among them, believed the cucumber sharks and other large piscids would eat anything tossed into the water. Shankara believed they acted more as clean-up crews, and did not actually digest the fragments they swallowed, but carried them to special stations where they were processed.

According to the captain, predation between ecoi was rare between Elizabeth's Land and Petain, or at least quite formalized. "They watch, they spy constantly, sending thieves or samplers, usually in the air but also underground, or skimming across the river or ocean. Between zones, the boundaries are clearly marked, but on rare occasion, parties of mobile scions will cross in a tight herd, grab what they can of arborids or phytids, and return . . . We do not know why. Perhaps the zones need to challenge each other. Perhaps it is a kind of sport . . ."

Shirla equated it with love bites, but I could not tell if she was serious.

CHAPTER SIX

As evening approached and my watch ended, with the day's work done and the ship rigged to slice on a beam reach across the strengthening northerlies, I leaned on the starboard rail amidships and studied the shore from our distance of five nautical miles. The high cliffs of this part of the eastern Sumner Coast were split with deep U-shaped grooves that spilled boulder-strewn floors into the sea, then thrust sinuously inland. I judged glaciers had once cut these grooves. A scattering of rangy short arborids covered the mesas and plains, and between them, a velvety, patchy carpet of blue and brown phytids spread in gentle mounds like fuzz on a rotting peach. The sun had reached its vernal zenith four hours before and now fled steadily westward, gently warming my face and hands, brightening the cloudless skies to a chalky enamel blue, almost white above Elizabeth's Land. The air smelled round and sweet, unlike any air I had ever breathed before, and the ocean sang its liquid rhythms against the hull, a metronomic slap of waves and hissing trill of swirling waters. Our wake fell astern in steady white smeared curves with a shiny roiling smoothness between, vanishing when the ship had advanced a few miles.

Randall strolled beside me and leaned on the rail, in a mood to talk. "We've been at sea a week," he said. "The mate and I have kept our eyes on you."

I nodded, unsure what to say.

"You told me you'd catch on fast, and you have. I'd swear you've sailed before."

"I've dreamed of sailing all my life," I said.

"You're the best apprentice on board, better than Shimchisko, even, and he's a decent fellow, though he does have a sharp tongue. You could go for your A.B. rate in short order if you wanted. I also notice you attend the captain's lectures no matter how tired you are."

"They're fascinating."

"Yes, well, he's a fine captain, but maybe the best scientist on Lamarckia . . . Or a close tie with Mansur Salap. We've traveled Tasman and Elizabeth and the Kupe Islands together for ten years now, at sea and ashore." He let silence sit between us for several minutes, the sweet wind providing enough distraction. "It's your face that interests me, Ser Olmy. The apprentices, the A.B.s, they're familiar faces to me. I know their types. I have to judge people, and I think I'm good at it, but I cannot by face or Breath or Fate judge you." He looked at me directly, elbows on the rail, hands clasped. "I swear you're older than you look and know more than you say."

I raised my eyebrows to acknowledge these unwanted observations. First Larisa, then Thomas, now Randall. I seemed particularly transparent to these people.

"How do you feel you fit in with the crew?" he asked.

"Sir?"

"You don't scuffle, you don't argue, and you certainly don't aspire to a sailor's top bunk. You're calm and humble, Ser Olmy."

"Thank you, sir," I said. "I've made friends and taken advice. Listening makes me popular, I suppose."

He laughed. "But you're hiding something."

"Sir?"

"I suppose having your family proscribed does something to your spirit. Two years in the heart of Liz. Witness to atrocity." He shook his head, then clucked his tongue in sympathy. "No easy way to return to the bosom of society. What I'm coming round to, Ser Olmy, is that when we put into Jakarta and Wallace Station and pick up Mansur Salap and our researchers, there will be a lot of work that requires more than a sailor's skills. We are short of trainable assistants, with sharp eyes and sharp minds. From the moment we picked up the children above Calcutta, you've impressed me. I'll watch you the next few days—don't let it make you nervous—and after we pass through Jakarta, I'll consider suggesting that you become an assistant to the researchers. I think we understand each other." He nodded as if greeting the coast and said, "I love this stretch. So different from the silva around Calcutta."

As the starboard watch ended, Shirla and Talya Ry Diem called together a circle of apprentices and A.B.s. Shirla took my elbow and pulled me into the circle, and Meissner brought out two long stringed instruments, each with two parallel rows of four strings suspended above two adjacent resonating hemispheres made from dried phytid fruit. These were kimbors, developed by the immigrants in the first few years after the Crossing. Meissner handed one to Ry Diem and began to tune one himself. Ry Diem hummed and sang a sequence of clear notes on a pentatonic scale, and all around the circle, others joined in, tuning themselves to the instruments and Ry Diem. Their voices seemed to cut through the wind.

Shirla put a xyla shoe on one bare foot, took Ry Diem's kimbor, set up a steady beat on the deck with the toe of the shoe, and thumbed the lower bole with her fingers. Immediately the crew in the circle began a high, singing chant. Meissner provided a booming bass line, sounding like a talented bullfrog. Shimchisko stood with hands outstretched and began a falsetto vocal. The hair on my neck stood up; I'd never heard anything like this. It sounded primeval, but very complex. I had no idea the Lamarckian immigrants had developed such a different style of music.

Shimchisko sang a list of names, starting with the people in the circle, then growing more and more exotic, until they became nonsense words. Others picked up with words that pleased them, and soon twelve voices wove in and out around each other, until the whole became far too complicated. The song collapsed in laughter, and Shirla thumped the deck rapidly five times with her shoe.

Next came a quiet ballad, sung by Shirla and Meissner, in clear words describing the sweet romance between a young lad and the personified Queen of Elizabeth's Zone. This was an old song, apparently, and its sentiment struck Shimchisko and several others deeply. Meissner's eyes filled with tears as Shirla described the inevitable end of the queen's love, and the suicide of the boy, who leaped from a cliff into the depths of an unknown silva.

The singing went on for two hours, punctuated by sips from a jug of mat fiber beer. Randall joined in toward the last, singing a song his mother had taught him, about children naming the scions they met in a newly settled silva. His voice was gravelly but well-modulated; they all sang well.

The evening ended with Leo Frey serving small sweet cakes. Keyser-Bach came down from the puppis, and Gusmao—the reclusive carpenter—joined us also, which brought a toast from Soterio to the craft rates. A.B.s toasted the captain and master, and Randall offered a toast to the apprentices, "Just growing in the ways of Lamarckia's seas." Kissbegh in turned toasted Talya Ry Diem, "Who cracked my head early, and gives this ship spirit!"

Ry Diem actually blushed.

The stars came out from behind thin clouds. Head filled with the music, I rolled into my bunk.

The ship sailed around a barren, wind-whipped promontory called Cape Sadness. Five ships had been wrecked there, I heard from Shimchisko. The captain surveyed the cape with a telescope, looking for scion activity. The winds and sea were favorable this day, and we rounded the cape without incident.

Fifty miles south of Cape Sadness, with Jakarta only a hundred miles away, the captain came on deck, swearing and waving the ship's slate. "We're warned off!" he cried out to Randall and the mate. "I've just spoken to the disciplinary and the port rank. They say they've spotted raiding parties off the Magellan shore. They *say* the parties are looking to come in by night and fire the town, and they'll take any ship they find at sea. They're refusing all ships for the next few days . . . just in case the town comes under siege. Damn them all . . . that's just not *pure!*"

I listened from the mizzen top. The trio conferred, joined by the sailmaker, Meissner, and the senior A.B.s. I was distracted by a silver sparkle to starboard: pterids, glittering scions shaped like boomerangs and trailing long fringes, swooped and flapped over the blue foam-streaked waves, dipping their wings and fringes in the water, flipping, miraculously recovering their flight, zipping on to the next wave.

"We can sail on to Wallace Station," Randall suggested, but the captain was not willing to settle for that.

"We have supplies and two more researchers waiting for us," he said. "I'll be damned if I'll let a bunch of flip-chipping bureaucrats keep us out of port!" He clapped his hands together, face red and eyes reduced to angry slits. Then, as if with a passing storm, the captain's face cleared. He forcibly put his hands at his sides and said, "Even so, I'd hate to run into one of Beys' ships at this stage—or any stage." His pacing grew more purposeful, energetic; he nodded, then grinned. "Yes, yesss," he said. The men talked in lower voices, heads together, then retired to the puppis and below to the captain's quarters. The mate, Soterio, came on deck to take the master's place and stared at the apprentices and junior A.B.s with a dour eye.

I and three apprentices descended the ratlines and stood on deck, awaiting further orders.

"You know what *that* means, don't you?" Ibert cried out, slinging a rope end sharply at the deck.

Shirla slapped the young apprentice soundly on one arm and told him to keep his voice down. "We signed on for years at sea," she said. "Don't ache for a last day or two on land."

"Not that at all," Ibert grumbled, shouldering a coil of mat fiber rope.

"What, then?" Shirla asked.

"The best damned theater on Lamarckia," Ibert said, stalking off. "And now I'll never see it."

Shimchisko slung his leg over a spare yard. "Ibert loves the theater," he said. "Live theater. Jakarta's famous for it."

"I *know* that," Shirla said, face screwed in irritation. "Such infants."

The master emerged and conferred with the mate. "Close-haul!" Soterio shouted. "We'll anchor in the redwater at Sloveny Caldera."

"Captain's going to wait them out," Shimchisko said with some satisfaction. "Myself, I don't see why the towns are so aquiver."

"You haven't been in a town that's been raided," Kissbegh said.

"Have *you*?" Shimchisko asked, rushing for the shrouds at the master's second bellow.

"No," Kissbegh said. "But I hear Ser Olmy has . . ."

I joined the apprentices aloft.

"Redwater," moaned Shimchisko, hanging from the futtock shrouds upside down beneath the top. "Smells like a sewer in redwater."

The ship sailed with the wind on the port quarter. We swiftly rounded a sea-jutting mountain covered with layered stripes of purple and red, as if painted with contours from an old topological map. The mountain, visible at sea for fifty miles, was cleft on its southwestern flank by an immense crater that seemed filled with thick, slowly waving hair; clouds streamed from the high, jagged rim of the crater. I did not have time to examine this sight in detail. The captain was on deck again, French the navigator by his side, steering the ship through narrow alleys between wave-smashed vine reefs. The sea swirled and sucked alarmingly just a few dozen meters from where the ship passed. Vines thrust above the waves and spread broad fans and bright red petals twenty or thirty meters wide, like enormous water lilies. The crew called them "castle flowers."

"If we wreck ourselves, swim for the castle flowers. There's fresh water in their insides," Shankara called out across the deck as we leaned into halyards.

"There'll be no wrecking of this ship," Soterio grumbled, but he stared overside nervously.

We cleared the vine reefs. The port watch rushed around the deck under the barking orders of the mate. The steady wind was finally fading into bursts of light breeze, leaving calm water. A sour scent began to fill the air; even the cat's-paws couldn't clear it. The water alongside seemed quieter, less effervescent. We half drifted, half sailed into the mountain's afternoon shadow.

With some respite from hauling on the braces, I gulped great lungfuls of the lightly tainted air. "Get it while you can," the master advised from the puppis. "It's going to stink like a sour paste pot."

It soon became obvious that the mountain was merely a little sister, a parasite on the flanks of the massive Sloveny Caldera. The caldera sat a kilometer lower than the mountain but spread over eight kilometers in diameter. Its eastern flank had collapsed centuries ago and ocean had rushed in.

We passed under the clouds streaming from the higher, smaller sister, Mount Pascal, and the sea took a purple tinge in the shadow. The farther we drifted into the outlines of the bowl, the redder the water became, and the stronger the smell of hydrogen sulfide, until I spotted a solid mass of what looked like flame lying ahead, filling the western curve of the natural harbor. The air did indeed stink now, and flakes of red bobbed in the waves like lost chips of paint. With the sloping western wall of the caldera less than a hundred meters off, *Vigilant* set a sea anchor; the depth here was at least three hundred meters.

I helped the crew furl sails, then all scrambled down to the deck at the mate's orders and stood in rows on the main deck. The captain and

Randall came aft and stood before the crew. Shatro joined them. Randall stepped forward. "I'll need twelve hands for a shore party. The captain proposes to go ashore and make observations, put our time to practical use until we can get in to Jakarta. I doubt any other ships will follow us here—it's not easy to get in or out, and it smells bad. The captain's been here before, as have I; the dangers are minimal, so long as we exercise caution. Ser Shatro and I, of course, will go. Volunteers?"

I raised my hand. Ibert scowled at me from one side. "It is a most unpleasant region," Shimchisko whispered from the opposite side. Shirla, three places down in the same line, volunteered as well, and Shankara. Grimacing at me out of the sight of the master and the captain, Shimchisko stepped forward, followed quickly by Ibert. In a few seconds, the captain had his list. Kissbegh and Ridjel seemed relieved.

The two boats pulled through the red-spackled and odoriferous waters with all but the captain, Randall, and Shatro taking turns at the oars. Between strokes of my oar, I saw the red flakes as more than just patches of pigment. They floated atop the waves with the insouciance of jelly fish—but these blood-colored scions were flat, fringed with tiny cilia that somehow steadied them and separated them from their fellows.

The captain directed us to a defile opened in the western wall thousands of years ago, through which a thin trickle of water now flowed, leaving a white and yellow mark on the black and brown rock. The boats were secured to outcropping rocks near a rugged, small, rock-strewn beach, and all but the two who were left behind to guard—Shimchisko and Ibert—waded ashore.

The sea water here felt rough between my fingers and curled around my waist with an unpleasant tingle. Once on shore, Randall offered all of us a bulb filled with white powder to puff on our clothes and skin. "Sodium bicarbonate," he explained. "The water here is mildly acid, and while you are still damp, it is best to neutralize."

The job was performed in a few minutes. Clothes still fizzing slightly, we formed a line, led by the captain and master, and marched up the cleft.

On all sides, the rock was covered with clusters of sulfur flowers. No life was visible; the air reeked and breathing was not pleasant. "Bear up, fellows," the captain said. "It's only for a few hours."

His cheer was not infectious. I felt my eyes sting and my lungs burn. Coming up behind, Shirla favored me with a smile of encouragement. "No worse than the latrines on ship," she offered.

The defile led gradually to the top of the massive main body of the old volcano. Here, a broad black lava plain of broken chunks mingled with smooth rivers of once-molten rock. Open pits blew forth steam and clouds of yellow vapor. The wind drove these clouds away from the defile, but I worried the wind would shift and we would asphyxiate.

Randall and Keyser-Bach climbed to the crest of a pressure ridge and surveyed the terrain beyond with field glasses. The rest of the crew and I sat, catching our breath between the wafts of sulfurous gas. Shirla coughed into her fist and wiped her eyes with a small cloth.

Shankara, always calm, folded his leg, braced his foot against the rock on which he sat, and wrapped his fingers around his knee. "Don't rub your eyes," he told Shirla. "It won't help; it could hurt."

"You've been here before?" she asked.

"I've been near volcanoes before, in the west. Interesting places. Where I lived, the only mobile scions that survived around volcanoes were fume dogs," he offered blandly.

"What did they look like?" one of the younger apprentices, a blocky, bright-faced fellow named Cham, asked. He kept his face covered with a noserag.

"The size of a young child. Bright red, like everything else alive around there. Long, six or seven legs—the last legs large, for jumping—covered with fur, with three or four eyes on the back or on the 'head.' They harvest fume fruit—florid scions clustered around fumaroles. Very sparse—just the dogs and the fruit."

"Why is everything called a 'dog'?" Cham asked. "I've never even *seen* a dog."

Shankara turned his attention to me, seated across from him on another black rock sloppily daubed with yellow and white.

We all held our breath as a cloud of sulfur stench wafted uncomfortably close. "My people were all intellectuals," he said. "Not enough call for *thinkers* here, let alone researchers. So we work where we can. The same for you, I'd judge."

"Um," I said, adopting the best nonchalant nasal tone of Shimchisko or Kissbegh.

"You have the air of a man who wanders free from his family. I make it a study also to learn the people around me. By the end of the voyage, I'll know the crew as well as they know themselves." His tear-streaked cheek, constant winking, and stoic forebearance gave him an odd, Lewis Carroll aspect. He said, "I wish the captain would return."

Randall, Shatro, and Keyser-Bach had dropped out of sight on the other side of the ridge. The master's head appeared first, and he quickly climbed to the crest, waving to attract our attention. "Up here!" he shouted. "Bring the equipment."

We got to our feet with little enthusiasm, shouldered the bags, and hefted the boxes. I followed Shirla and Cham; Shankara followed me, and Shimchisko and Ibert trailed. We wound between chunks of lava and vents oozing viscous yellow smoke to join Randall. Beyond Randall, the captain and Shatro stood in a small depression that widened to the east into a larger valley.

"It's still here!" the captain shouted. "Just as I remember!"

The valley beyond was filled with large, bright red jug-shaped scions, the largest eight to ten meters across and twenty high. They protruded from the ground, mostly upright, like squat bowling pins stuck in the black sand.

We followed Randall, Shatro, and the captain between the red pins, deeper into the shallow valley. A smelly yellow ooze dripped from gashes in the side of the pins like sulfurous honey and gathered in pools to suck at our feet.

"It's the simplest sub-zone on record," Keyser-Bach explained, forging ahead, pushing and slapping the red bulks as he passed them, like a light-hearted Samson. "This is where Jiddermeyer worked out his final theory. He reported his theory to Lenk twenty-four years ago today. It's worth celebrating."

Randall struggled to pull his boot from a particularly obstinate patch of muck.

The pins grew higher toward the middle of the valley, and now cast considerable shade. Yellow mists drifted between the looming red scions. "Can you reason it, Ser Shatro?" the captain called over his shoulder.

"I've read about it in your books, sir."

"Of course. But my books don't explain the mystery. Anybody care to reason it? Ser Randall . . . Shankara . . ." The captain stopped and surveyed us with a devilish, almost leering grin. "Ser Olmy?"

"Ah, Olmy," Shatro murmured, sticking hands in pockets and turning as if bored at this masque. "So good at theory."

"I haven't seen enough yet, sir," I replied. The question unanswered, we pushed over the thick, slowly sweeping scimitar-shaped roots, the yellow fluid swept along by their motion spilling over our boots and staining them.

Shirla passed by and muttered, "You'll soon help the captain peel scions and Randall pickle their guts. We'll miss you when you graduate, Olmy, *sir!*" She gave me a cheeky salute.

Ahead, I saw a clearing between the pins, a pool of standing water in the middle of the valley. We climbed on a platform of layered lava, above the sweep and slop of the yellow fluid.

Around the pool, built-up deposits formed an irregular wall that kept out most of the flow from the scimitar roots. In three places around the pool perimeter, purple and black valves laced with ornate red bands filled gaps in the wall, allowing dribbles of the yellow fluid into the pool.

I stared at the pool's glassy surface. Beneath the surface, layers of red and yellow minerals formed broad fans. Where the water intercepted the dribbles of yellow muck passed by the valves, oily sheens spread, casting rainbows where the sun struck them between the shadows of the surrounding pins. I felt uncomfortable here, and not just because of the smell.

"The puzzle isn't complete, by any means," the captain admitted. "Harsh conditions force simplicity on an ecos. It hasn't the evolutionary versatility, the immense runs of time, the *lack of concern* for its offspring, that describe our evolutionary upbringing. There's energy here, nutrients to be had, but specialization is the key. And here's the miracle—these scions, the pins, belong to no ecos. They form a subzone of their very own, adjacent to and dependent on both Petain and Elizabeth . . . And in a moment, if we're lucky, we'll see what Jiddermeyer saw. It happens every day, even in the worst weather."

The captain told us to place our bags and boxes on the platform, above the yellow muck. "So human," the captain mused, pulling glass jars and a metal tube from one box. "They are truly social, the zones. But they are also individuals. We are concerned for our arms and legs, as well as for our children—concerned for our friends and neighbors. The ecoi feel similar concerns for their scions. Now we wait for a few minutes. Something *interesting* will come by."

I was struck by the similarity between the way Keyser-Bach and the gate opener Ry Ornis uttered that word, *interesting*. For the captain—even more so than for Randall—life was a steady succession of puzzles to be solved and eventually linked together.

A muffling quiet surrounded us, nothing but the sighs of wind through the bizarre colonnades, my breath harsh in an irritated throat, shufflings and whispers and grunts as we helped the captain take samples from the muck and the pool.

The captain had filled two jars and was examining them with immense satisfaction when a buzzing sound became audible at the far end of the valley. The captain and Shatro immediately pulled out box cameras and tripods, setting them up in the black sand and muck. "Bees, you'd think, coming to suck up the honey of these immense flowers," the captain said, face glowing with enthusiasm. "Perhaps not so far wrong."

I listened to the buzzing apprehensively. If they were bees, they sounded like very large bees. We all stared up at the sky above the tops of the huge red pins. The plume of cloud from the higher crater had shifted and now streamed over us, its contorted rolls of moisture arrayed in crosscurrents of higher winds like fibers in the muscle of a fish. The plume blocked the sun, casting the valley and its scions in a cool half light.

The stench was almost unbearable now. Shatro bent over the pool, inserted a thick metal pipette, and drew up a sample of the minerals beneath the glassy slick.

"Here they come," the captain said. "Harvesters. Damnedest things you ever saw."

The buzzing rose to a high, slapping drone, as if a hundred children were whacking long sticks together. Three furry black saucers like flattened beetles flew into view above the pool and hovered. Each was about a meter wide and sported two long thin limbs at the front, and a kind of tail at the rear, which flicked a few centimeters side to side with every adjustment in their hovering. One descended to the tallest squat pin-shaped scion on the edge of the pool and raised itself, limbs uppermost, tail drawn back delicately. The red surface of the pin abruptly split and formed five deep horizontal gashes—stomata. The saucer inserted its two limbs into the highest stoma and settled in, its buzzing subsiding to intermittent clacking. The remaining two saucer beetles did the same with other pins around the pool. Piston noises surrounded us, and fine drops of yellow, stinking sulfurous dew sprayed over us, sticking to our faces and arms, our clothing.

"Wonderful!" the captain cried. Shatro snapped pictures quickly, adjusting the tripods. I held up a bag of instruments to protect my face from the spray. Peering from under the bag, trying to see how they flew without visible wings, I observed the leading edge of one saucer beetle. Eight or nine white rectangular apertures opened and shut rapidly, producing the buzzing, slapping noise. Somewhere within the flat carapaces, the saucer beetles pumped the air and ejected it from the rear.

"They're dirigibles," I said, revelation coming upon me.

"Very good!" the captain said. "Any one of us could lift them like feathers. And they're not just here to suck out what they need—they *feed* the pins. Mutual needs met, from a sub-zone to each of at least two zones!"

Dozens more saucer beetles came blowing over the valley with a steady westerly breeze. As they hovered, darting back and forth with considerable dexterity, their companions, mounted on the pins, suddenly leaped back, leveled off in flight, and buzzed away. With a sidling motion, the pins whose production had been harvested pulled back slowly, a stately retreat that allowed other pins to come forward and take their places by the pool.

"We presume they fly back to some interior region, perhaps around a seed-mother, and drop their cargoes," the captain shouted over the buzzing. "We've never traced their paths. I've always longed for a good airplane or helicopter to follow them. Perhaps we'd find our first queen!"

A fog of vapor now filled the valley with an almost unbearable smell. Everyone began to cough uncontrollably. Shatro grabbed his camera and retreated.

"All right, enough," Randall cried, swiping his hands at the smoke.

The captain hesitated, said something about waiting for the next flight, but the vapor became unbearably thick. Coughing, he agreed. We picked up the bags and walked as fast as we could back to the caldera and the sea.

CHAPTER SEVEN

Unable to sleep, head resting on folded hands, I lay on my side in my bunk aboard the *Vigilant*, listening to an incessant spectral hooting from the mainland. A deep booming sound underscored the hooting and was itself topped by fluting trills.

We had weighed anchor in the early evening and sailed several miles southeast, out of the tricky waters in the shadow of Mount Pascal. We had then dropped anchor once more in a calm patch of ocean a mile outside the boundary of the sunken caldera.

The captain had been too tired that evening to give his customary lamplight lecture. If his lungs were feeling as tight and reluctant as mine, I didn't see how he *could* lecture. Here, the air at least was sweeter.

I took up Nkwanno's slate and scrolled to the last section I had read in his journals. The soft glow of the slate screen filled my curtained bunk with false moonlight.

Crossing 29, 125
We have survived this long, so many disasters, and have just begun to feel confident, and now the rules are changing and all that we have learned may become useless.

For weeks there have been rumors from trekkers and small villages in south Liz and at the head of the Terra Nova that something is happening in the truce between Liz and Calder's zone, where few of us live. Thief activity has increased across the truce, according to harvesters at Lake Mareotis, and the lake itself changed color from blue to orange along the east shore.

Yesterday, a delegation of Lenk's ministers—two men and one woman—returned from Mareotis and stopped here for the evening to rest. I went down to the docks with Johanna Ry Presby and met them walking up the path. They appeared tired and downcast and refused to answer questions at first. Johanna invited them to the refectory and we fed them a late cold meal. Their gloom seemed to deepen as they ate.

I tried to pry information from them. They were adamant about saying nothing, which angered us. "We should know, if it's something important, to give us time to prepare," I insisted. "Keeping secrets will do no good." The woman had tears in her eyes but no one would talk. "It will come out soon," she said. They thanked us for our food and left early the next morning.

Radio messages from Athenai and Jakarta have been received, most in Lenk's code, but some have been open. The crisis has gradually been unveiled. From here and there, we are putting together rough pictures of a disaster—not truly a disaster, but momentous change, disastrous perhaps for us—but in truth we have no words yet to describe what is happening.

Crossing 29, 128
I have been invited to accompany Redhill and Shevkoti to Mareotis. Shevkoti became the village agro upon Ser Murai's death last winter. With Mayor Presby's blessing, we will go upriver and examine the truce near Mareotis, in hopes of learning for ourselves what the problems may be. We have become discouraged about learning from Athenai in time to prepare Moonrise for whatever may be happening.

Crossing 29, 134
At Mareotis for a day now. At some peril, we have hiked along the truce and seen wonderful, terrible things. The truce boundary—white dead soil between the ecoi—has become invaded with soil preparers, including what I am calling Tillers, a scion either unseen until now or new. These are massive and crudely made forms as much as eight meters long and five high, resembling wheeled spiders, that roll and crawl methodically—

I had been reading about wheeled scions but until now had not considered how seriously improbable such creatures were. With a little cross-referencing, I found a small piece in Redhill's encyclopedia about scions with wheels:

Wheeled forms defy practical explanation in terms of terrestrial biology. We must not forget, however, that scions are very likely not created from seeds containing their own genetic instructions, but are assembled in biological factories. Wheels and the creatures that bear them may not be made all at once and together, but at different times and separately. The difficulties of imagining a creature that can grow and maintain its own wheels are overcome. The wheels may even be thought of as separate scions, or as constructs made of organic materials, but no longer alive.

Observations from Kandinsky's Zone in Tasman point to wheeled scions that may actually create their wheels from recycled, compacted arborid or phytid tissues, replacing or repairing worn wheels as needed . . .

I returned to Nkwanno's journal:

—churning the soil and preparing it for occupation. But among these forms dart many varieties of thieves and defenders, some sighted in the silva—though infrequently—and others never seen before.

The thieves and defenders do what they have always done, but on a scale and with a frequency never witnessed before. Defenders— serpents and arthropods, translucent five-legged ursids with shining glassy saber-teeth on the leading and trailing edges of their forelimbs— keep behind the old boundary of the truce, grabbing and dispatching scions that cross from the opposite side. But more and more scions cross, and the defenders are overwhelmed. We have seen worn-out defenders, sitting in the redefined silva like exhausted warriors, twitching and spilling their fluids from torn joints—and all around them, foreign scions pass, as if in glee at new freedom. Yet dead scions litter the silvas on both sides. It seems that here, a war is being combined with an orgy.

Crossing 29, 136
Our food has run out, and we risk starving before we return to Moon-
rise. We stay nevertheless.

The carnage has increased to such a level that we can't imagine
the outcome. Are the ecoi caught in a struggle to the death? Has one
seed-mother or queen taken offense at the actions of its neighbor, and
declared destruction that must inevitably become mutual?

What Shevkoti fears—and his fears translate easily to us, hungry
and terrified—is that all of Liz's scions we have come to identify as
edible or useful will be destroyed, leaving us with a much-reduced food
supply.

Crossing 29, 137
New transporter forms have arrived and are carrying away dead and
dying scions. The once-fertile stretches along the truce and around
Mareotis are denuded, or covered with a sad wreckage of scions, which
of course will not decay. Pink worms cluster on many of Liz's casual-
ties, consuming much of the remains, but then the worms themselves
die and litter the ground . . . The process is never completed, and we
can see only endless hectares of destruction and waste.

Crossing 29, 139
We have begun to scavenge dead scions ourselves. With our small
radio, we have kept in touch with Moonrise, and the destruction is
happening there, as well. The villagers are terrified. We have actu-
ally fought against defenders and transporters trying to remove edible
scions, but scavengers the size of ants enter our larders and remove
any scion foodstuffs, however processed they may be. This is a purge,
and all of the old forms must go.

I have sickened myself trying to chew on remains of scions we have
collected as samples. Fortunately I have eaten nothing that has done
more than make me violently nauseated, and I have recovered quickly.
Shevkoti is less fortunate, and the lining of his mouth and his gums
have become blistered and hang in shreds.

It is as if we begin all over again, in a new Lamarckia, with new
perils.

Smaller transporters have begun to arrive, filled with young immobile scions whose eventual forms we can only guess at. Shevkoti, even in his agony, has discovered young arborids and classified them as combinations of elements from Liz's arborids and Calder's. He believes that in this conflict, Liz has predominated, however; we see many new scions that are quite familiar, though with some changes in design.

Crossing 29, 141

We must return to Moonrise to share our fates with those of our neighbors. We can't eat even the most familiar of the new scions, which are growing rapidly and replenishing the silva. In a few days we will die if we stay.

The truce has been erased. Zone one and zone two seem to have united. From Moonrise by radio we hear that Athenai's scientists believe this may be a kind of sexual act. They are describing this event as a sexing and a fluxing.

Our fields in Moonrise have been trampled by marauding scions, and our orchards destroyed. Buildings within the village itself have been damaged. I think this may be the end, unless we can somehow remove all the inhabitants of Elizabeth's Land to Tasman. But that will be an impossible task.

I turned off the slate and sat in the darkness for a few minutes, thinking of the terrors and hardships Lenk's people had passed through. I knew in rough outline the outcome of the sexing and fluxing between Liz and Calder. There were no complete explanations of what had actually happened, but Calder no longer existed, and Liz was forever altered.

I clasped the slate with an emotion I had never experienced in my brief and inadequate life: something like reverence. The body on the dock had been a powerful and experienced man, in some respects a better man than I. Yet he had been ruthlessly slaughtered.

I could not absorb it all. My mind was crowded and I felt half sick with sadness and confusion.

But they survived. Without my help, without the help of the Hexamon, Lenk's people survived and returned to a kind of prosperity.

Sleep, it seemed, would finally come to me. I drifted in a dark, cloudy void, neither comfortable nor particularly concerned about comfort, thoughts flitting in and out of my awareness, which was fading into something deeper and more basic. I had not slept in many years, and the sensation was more unnerving than the sounds from the shore, or what I had just read in Nkwanno's journals.

I heard a rapping nearby, thought for a moment it was a group of friends in my apartment in Alexandria, in Thistledown, trying to fix a broken toy by striking it gently on the edge of a table . . . And then I opened my eyes. Shirla's round face peered at me, half hidden by the drape of my bunk's curtain. "Good," she said. "You're awake. Randall and Shankara and the mate and a few others are talking on deck. They thought you'd like to join us."

I foggily wondered if I was about to be drawn into a conspiracy to mutiny. The day had not been *that* miserable, however, and the captain had certainly not shown himself to be unfit for duty . . . I crawled out of the bunk, slipped on my pants while Shirla waited, and followed her up the ladder to the forecastle deck.

A group of nine stood around two electric lanterns: Randall, Shatro, and the mate, the sailmaker Meissner representing the craft rates, Talya Ry Diem and Shankara for the A.B.s, and I supposed, Shimchisko and myself for the apprentices. Beyond the ship's bow, outlined by stars and clouds glowing dimly in the light of a single small moon, rose the distant black shadow of Mount Pascal. Having brought me on deck, at Ry Diem's request, Shirla stood to one side, out of the lantern light.

"The captain's asleep," Randall said. "He's had a bit of a setback . . . He overdid his stay on Mount Pascal, I'm afraid. He's asked me and Ser Soterio and Ser Shatro to talk about what we'll do if we can't finish this voyage, if Jakarta's taken, in short, what if the Brionists move in to Elizabeth's Land in force."

"Which many think may happen soon," Shatro said somberly.

Randall cleared his throat. His own voice sounded hoarse. "The captain's put his personal fortune into this ship. I've contributed what little I can spare. The rest of you get an adequate wage, but . . . if we put out to sea, and nothing's certain on land, we could come back, find our money's no good—Brion's appropriated everything, shifted currency . . . We don't know, because frankly, we don't have much experience with this sort of thing. So we've brought some of you together, members of the crew we place trust in, as intelligent types, to start sounding out individuals, see whether this voyage is feasible. If we can't go on beyond Jakarta, we need to know now."

Shatro stepped to the center of the group and said, "Some of the crew may even sympathize with Brion and hope to join his forces." He shifted his glance from face to face, lingered on mine, squinted, and moved on.

"I don't know much about Brion, except that he's taken over Hsia and been thieving and killing," Ry Diem said softly, glancing around the circle.

"The captain had hoped we could spend a few days exploring the Chefla waste," Randall said, "waiting to see if the Brionists left. Then put into Jakarta and pick up the supplies and the researchers. That's not possible. Seems the Brionists are in for a long blockade, to force some sort of settlement. Jakarta advises we just clear out. It might mean war."

"We're not equipped for a war," Soterio said in an undertone.

"We should get on to Wallace Station and pick up Ser Salap," Ry Diem said wearily. "We should get on and do what we can."

"That's what the captain thinks," Randall said after a pause.

Shatro considered that for a moment. "Makes sense," he agreed.

"But it puts us critically short of researchers," Randall observed.

"Salap and I can do the work," Shatro said. "Perhaps he can spare a few others from Wallace to come with us." Clearly, Shatro regarded this as an opportunity. A junior, he might quickly advance. Ser Randall seemed less convinced.

"You think the crew will agree . . . that we proceed down the coast to Wallace Station, and plot our course from there?"

Ry Diem shook her stiff, graying shag. "We're not amateurs," she said. "Speaking for the A.B.s. We do our work. It seems worthwhile work to me."

Shimchisko and I glanced at each other, and he nodded. "The apprentices have no other pressing duties," he said. "Wherever we go, there might be war."

"I agree," I said.

Randall seemed relieved. "I'll tell the captain in the morning," he said.

CHAPTER EIGHT

During our trip south, skirting Jakarta and sailing along the shaggy black and brown Cheng Ho Coast, the captain kept in constant radio communication with Salap at Wallace, less frequently receiving instructions or bulletins from Jakarta and Athenai. He shared these snatches of information only rarely, passing something along to Randall or Soterio for the consumption of the rest of the crew. None of the news sounded good. Perhaps Keyser-Bach wanted us to feel isolated from the unfolding history in Jakarta. He succeeded in part; we kept our focus on handling the *Vigilant*, though we always kept a sharp eye out for Brionist ships.

South of Jakarta, we saw no ships at all. There was little commerce in these waters. The coast north and south of Jakarta lay in Petain's Zone, which had been explored by harvesters and mineral prospectors under the leadership of Jorge São Petain just months after the immigrants' arrival. They had sailed in crude boats along the Cheng Ho Coast south from Jakarta, venturing inland every few dozen miles, finding little of interest from the point of view of ores and mineral resources.

While Elizabeth's Zone, blessed with steady rainfall, seemed to concentrate on thick silva with four main types of arborid scions and perhaps thirty types of phytids, Petain's Zone, with many different climates, showed considerable variety, both on land and in the sea, which it favored. Most of Petain's variety was found in seas and rivers. The land south of Jakarta it covered with a desultory and uniform carpet of small black bushy phytids called sootbrush, seldom reaching waist-high. The captain, when he resumed his lectures, showed us photographs and drawings of these forms, and their attendants: blue crowflies—pterids the size of a human hand, which functioned as cleaners, scavengers, and defenders—; deadeye trees, covered with shrunken white or gray berries that served as nutrients for various small arthropod scions, including crowflies; and a dozen or more others, none as large or widespread as the pelagic forms.

It had been Jiddermeyer's main triumph to prove the original survey-ors' theory—using specimens returned by Petain, analyzed with standard medical equipment—that zone one was one individual organism and zone five another.

Jiddermeyer had first stated the firm principles of Lamarckia's biosphere, toppling centuries of evolutionary theory—for that was all it took, one ex-ception to the established rules. There was no competition between what he first called "scions" within an ecos because they were in fact parts of one organism, one genetic individual, grown or created in some unknown fash-ion to play specific roles and accomplish certain tasks.

His colleagues and students—including young Baker and Shulago—had tried to chart the life cycles of scions, traveling deep into the silvas to find the fount, the birthplace or places of all scions. They had never succeeded. They had learned that arborids and phytids began as blue-gray sluglike forms, called pre-scions or neonatals, which traveled or were carried across hun-dreds or even thousands of kilometers, led by the silva's status singing to find sick or dying scions and replace them. Arborids and phytids per-formed the function of Earth plants, and made up ninety-eight percent of scions by count in Liz. Mobile scions, which fed from special stomata rather than consuming their comrades, tended the silvas, cleaning up the envi-rons, consuming and removing dead scions, preparing the soil and grow-ing beds, and in general acting the role of expert gardeners.

Other mobile scions, Jiddermeyer believed, acted as scouts, the eyes and ears of the hypothetical "queens" or "seed-mistresses." Still others—such as samplers—monitored scion activities, searched for intrusions from other zones, or crossed zone boundaries to act as spies. Jiddermeyer first found and described examples of disguised intruders, boundary-crossing scions, the carcasses of failed mimics being cleaned up by processors and gardeners, or on several occasions successful mimics discovered quite by accident.

Each zone had managed, without direct competition, without obviously obeying the laws of survival of the fittest, to fill all the major niches available, to take complete advantage of sun, air, water, and minerals—Lamarckia's environmental qualities and resources.

The zones received their human-assigned numbers by order of discov-ery, not identification as separate organisms. Explorers heading upriver from Calcutta had first discovered zones two and three, followed by zone four along the western coast. Petain's expedition had set out shortly thereafter. What had astonished the early explorers—all searching desperately for good farmland and resources—was the *lack* of variety in the various zones. Most zones contained less than a thousand types of scions—including microscopic varieties. Even more astonishing had been the apparent lack of competition between scions, except at zone boundaries, where a kind of long-term "cold war" went on.

The evening before our arrival at the station, about half a day's sail if the wind maintained its present direction and speed, we saw the edge of a huge storm. As the sun burnished the storm's leading edge, turning it into a distant red and gold temple of clouds, the captain paced on deck, scowling deeply. He watched the storm closely through binoculars, swinging them east to west repeatedly.

True to his word, Randall invited me into the captain's study and lab for a conference among Shatro, the captain, and himself. I sensed my delicate position, having no established role in the proceedings yet, and listened attentively.

The captain was still agitated. He marched back and forth in front of the wall-mounted cages containing boxes of empty jars and shelves of books, arms swinging loosely at his sides. "We had hoped for time and purity of concentration," he said. "We may have neither. Athenai may recall all shipping . . . unless talks begin soon with Naderville. Good Lenk can't afford to lose his ships—whether to storms or pirates."

Keyser-Bach stopped his pacing to peer through the small window on the wide cabin's port side. The storm clearly worried him. "Ser Salap wants us to spend two weeks at Wallace, so he can put a cap on this portion of his work there. He cares little for the Brionist troubles. I wish I could afford his nonchalance, but we can't spend more than two days at the station, much less two weeks."

"Then our course is clear," Shatro said firmly. His eyes shifted around the room, looking for the flow of consensus. "We need to pick up Sers Salap and Thornwheel and Cassir . . . and get on with our voyage."

The captain shrugged and turned away, staring again through the window at the wall of grayness beyond the horizon. "In this atmosphere, no storm should last decades." He tapped his fingers on the sill. "We could be out of range of recall in a matter of weeks. Radio reception has always been chancy below these latitudes."

"Not that chancy," Randall said.

"A problem, Erwin?" the captain asked.

"I dislike avoiding or ignoring orders," Randall said.

"As do I," Shatro hastened to add. Then, unsure whom he might displease most, he stumbled on, "But the . . . reception does fade now and then. South, below—"

"Not a matter of disobeying orders," the captain said tightly. "More a matter of riding ahead of the storm. I am an Ahab with two white whales, but I don't seek them out, I flee *from* them." He flashed a grin at this conceit. "One is politics, which has bitten one leg off, and which I shun at every opportunity—"

"Unless it furnishes your ship," Randall said gloomily, hoping to head off this clumsy metaphor.

"And the other is that *storm*." The captain pointed emphatically out the window. "It nearly overtook me when I dropped off Salap at his station two years ago. Which of my white whales is worse?"

Shatro shook his head, unable to follow the captain. "Sir, I am unclear about the promotion of Ser Olmy."

"No doubt," Keyser-Bach said with an acid tone. "I understand this young fellow is bright, and we are short of researchers. Salap tells me on the radio that he cannot spare more than two from Wallace to accompany us." He held out his hand as if to cue Randall. "But how will Ser Olmy serve?"

"I leave that up to Salap," Randall said. "I would like to have as many capable minds as possible at work on this expedition, and at the chief researcher's disposal."

"How does one more *mind* help?" Shatro asked with a sniff.

"This expedition should not face the same problem we all face on this planet," Randall said. "We came here knowing we would be a small group, and completely isolated. We did not understand what that would cost us intellectually and culturally."

"What does culture have to do with it?" Shatro asked.

"I understand what Erwin is saying," the captain said. "We face a huge puzzle that would challenge our greatest minds, even if they had access to all the resources of Thistledown. But we don't have access to those resources. And this ship—all due respect to all aboard at present—is not filled to overflowing with creative geniuses. Right, Erwin?"

"Though by no means a ship of fools," Randall said, waggling one hand slowly.

"By no means," the captain echoed, eyes half lidded.

Shatro shrugged and puffed out his cheeks.

"I recognized that Olmy was bright the day he came aboard," the captain said. "But I feel little sympathy for those so-called explorers who launch themselves into the silva, uneducated and ill-prepared. I've seen too many of them come back wild-eyed mystics, if they come back at all. Did the silva give you a fit of *vastitude*, Ser Olmy?"

"I felt lost in it, sir," I said. "Overwhelmed. But I came back still myself, if that's what you mean."

"All right," the captain said. "I will go along with this promotion, with Salap's approval, so long as we do not have to sail with one less hand."

"I'll enjoy my work either way, sir," I said, trying for the proper humility. Shatro scowled, then resumed his mask of patent neutrality.

"I'd like to be securely moored at the station by tomorrow morning," the captain said.

Night had obscured the ocean and the coast as I came up on deck, but looking north, I saw bright flashes, orange and pink, dozens of miles away in the general darkness: the captain's immortal storm.

By morning, the storm had moved out of sight, and tension on the *Vigilant* eased. The wind held, and we sailed smoothly over deep blue water, beneath a sky filled with cotton-puff clouds and high, fleecy cirrus.

The land at the southeastern extreme of the Cheng Ho Coast consisted of a line of low, intermittent cliffs, dotted by granite domes, against which the sea broke in thin lines of breakers. Inland, what first caught the eye were twisted, squat towers like immense, thick thorn bushes trimmed by giant gardeners. As we sailed closer to the shore, these towers resolved themselves as thickly intertwined trunks spreading across several hectares of ground, rising to heights of more than a hundred and fifty meters, and crowned with brilliant red discus-shaped leaves as much as ten meters in diameter.

Between the towers, a pale tan uniformity painted the low, gently rolling hills, giving the impression of featureless sand stretching to infinity. This was not sand, however, but Petain's prairie, which covered thousands of square kilometers south of the sootbrush country. The prairie was made not of dried grasslands, which might have been a second guess, but of a thick, shiny surface dotted every few meters with dimples deep enough to hide a human.

I performed my sailor's duties on the starboard morning watch with the other A.B.s and apprentices. Shirla had been part of the night watch, and passed me on deck with a weary, satirical grin. "Kiss-up," she whispered. "Now you'll get the best duty. Never hang off a yard again . . ."

"Not so lucky," I said. "You're stuck with me for a while."

She stopped, surveyed me with an expression of mock disdain, hands on hips. "I hardly feel worthy of your company."

I gave in to a flush of irritation. "Shirla, I am what I am. I can't help being interested in what the captain and Shatro study. Are you mad at me?"

She sneered. "Don't *presume* that you arouse such strong emotions, *Sir* Olmy. It doesn't become you."

"No more sweets?" I asked. Now it was her turn to blush.

"Flirts with a higher rate are *doomed*, you know," she said.

"We've been so involved," I chided.

Her expression fell then, no mocking, and I realized I had caused genuine pain. "Screw that," she said, and turned to go below.

The first mate glared at me, but before he could speak, I was down by the mizzen with Ibert and Riddle, unfurling the christian and raising the spanker before putting in to the cove near the station.

The captain came on deck with Randall and stationed Shimchisko and Cham fore and aft to drop depth lines and report. Ibert and Kissbegh climbed to the tops to look for shifting vine reefs, always a danger around Petain. Three miles ahead, five low brown huts stood on the beach above the wave line—there were hardly any tides on Lamarckia—while a few small boats bobbed offshore in the regular, gentle surf. The wind blew offshore at two or three knots, complicating our maneuvers; we tacked back and forth across several miles before dropping anchor in sixteen meters of effervescent water, about two hundred meters off the beach.

The captain ordered the longboat lowered. Randall and Shatro supervised the loading of boxes of provisions for the crew that would remain at the station and the packet of mail. It had been three months since the last ship visited this cove.

Shimchisko, Shirla, Ry Diem, Shankara, and I crewed the longboat. All but Randall and the captain pulled on the oars across the short distance. Ry Diem and I leaped out into the foaming, hissing waves, pushed through a thick line of sea crust—dried foam with the consistency of baked meringue—and tugged the boat onto the beach, tying the rope to a thick woody stem of sea vine rooted deep in the sand. We walked up the beach in line of rank.

Shirla pointedly said nothing, lips set tight. I wondered how much of this sea flirtation was a kind of hidden courtship, and what rules I had violated.

Five men and four women met us on the beach. The chief researcher, Mansur Salap, stepped forward and embraced Keyser-Bach with a warm smile. Salap was the eldest of the station's nine personnel, fifty-seven years of age, streaks of gray in his close-cropped black hair and narrow goatee. Dressed in loose black pants, black shirt, with a long black coat draped over them, feet shod in fiber sandals, he was smaller than the captain, and a touch thinner, though his thinness seemed more in proportion. In truth he was an elegant fellow, not a movement wasted, his long fingers on feminine hands making small, precise gestures as he spoke in a pleasant tenor, explaining the nature of their work the past few weeks. The captain walked beside him, chin in hand, nodding and frowning in concentration.

Thornwheel and Cassir, two of Salap's assistants at the station, were younger than I, though we appeared about the same age. Youth passed more quickly on Lamarckia than in Thistledown. The captain preceded us into the main lab building. The walls were made of thin frames covered with dark leathery sheets; the roof was thatched sea vine strips.

The captain took a seat and Salap gave us a tour of the apparatus on the tables within the lab, relating the outcomes of some of his most recent experiments. "The prairie is not just one continuous scion, as we thought a year ago . . . It consists of at least five different types, adapted from one form across centuries or even millennia, a new kind of growth and development in our experience . . . Instead of recalling and reshaping the scions at some point far from their habitat, the ecos provides them with modified templates and they change themselves."

The captain listened attentively, clearly feeling at ease with Salap, and fascinated by his discoveries, but not eager to speak his mind.

"With the equipment on *Vigilant*, we could easily understand the prairie's relations to the sea vines and other pelagic scions. There is a reciprocal arrangement, of course, as Jiddermeyer thought—a constant for all ecoi— but the nature of the arrangement between land-dwellers and the pelagic or riparian scions has not been clearly established. Here, we've charted the deliveries of nutrients from the sea, measured and estimated the rates of exchange and what gets returned to the sea . . . We begin to understand the metabolism, as it were, of all Petain."

"Very good," the captain said, tapping his chin with one finger.

Salap folded his arms. "Something you wish to say, Captain?" he asked coolly.

"We can't stay long. Two days at most—"

"Because of the troubles," Salap said.

"Randall agrees with me," the captain said, as if there might be a debate, and he wished to squelch it early.

The master sat on a stool across from the captain. He raised his eyebrows and smiled uneasily.

"Do you think it will be war?" Salap asked.

"It's going to be a bureaucratic nightmare, whatever it is," Randall said. "We've endured enough of those."

"We'll need as many researchers as you can spare," the captain said. "Erwin's already been recruiting from among the crew." He looked at me.

Salap stepped forward and looked me over critically, as if I were a peculiar animal, perhaps a scion. "This is . . . ?"

"Ser Olmy Ap Datchetong," Randall said. "A student of Elizabeth. More competent than most."

"A pleasure to meet you, Ser Olmy. The master has always had a soft heart," Salap said. "Fortunately, he's also a good judge of people."

"I'd like to leave as soon as possible," the captain said.

Salap shook his head, clearly disliking the pressure. "Give me two days. We will pack up the equipment I need on the ship, transfer the equipment you are delivering to the station, and finish our measurements of nocturnal weather-born transfers."

The captain looked surprised. "Weather-born?"

Salap gave us a coldly smug smile. "My special surprise. We've learned much about the storm that lies out there now, that chased us both around the Darwin Sea, but never caught us."

"What have you learned?" Keyser-Bach asked.

"That it is alive," Salap said.

CHAPTER NINE

By late afternoon, the last boatload had been delivered, and the captain and Salap stood on the beach, staring out to sea. The storm had swung in close to the coast again, thirty or forty miles offshore, filling the northern horizon almost east to west with pillars and whorls of cloud arranged in spreading, stacked layers. This close, the clouds had a scintillant quality, as if filled with flakes of mica.

Shatro, Thornwheel, and Cassir stood by the boat, waiting to be taken to the ship. I stood beside Randall, a few meters from the captain and Salap.

"He still hasn't explained," Randall said in an undertone. He looked around anxiously. "We should put out immediately or we'll be blown onto the beach or the vine reefs. I'd hate to weather that bastard in any case—but I'd rather meet it at sea."

The captain motioned for all of us to join him and Salap. "We've been talking," he said. "We both agree that things can be finished here by tomorrow afternoon, or by morning if we put our backs into it. We'll need to help rig and test the equipment we just delivered, and then we'll . . ." His words trailed off, and he stared at the storm as if lost in a dream.

"It never comes ashore. It sends emissaries," Salap said.

"Mansur, you have my infinite admiration, but I'd like to know what to expect," the captain said sharply, "in clear language."

Salap seemed to enjoy the captain's discomfiture. "The emissaries are small fronts of cloud, rich with water and materials picked up within the storm itself. Difficult to describe."

"How strong?" Randall asked.

"A few knots of wind. Enough to blow them in gently—not enough to hurt the ship, or rip up the fabric on the prairie." Fabric was what Salap and the station's researchers had come to call the shiny brown tissue that spread over the prairie—and concealed the inner workings of the five types of scions. "In truth, the storm serves many purposes. It stirs the sea, grows nutrients like a gigantic bio-reactor . . . and it controls the weather. For hundreds of miles, there is no storm but the one storm."

The captain was torn between scientific elation, concern for the storm, as a sailor should be concerned about all storms, and what might have been incredulity. "A remarkable discovery," he allowed, "but I think I'll feel more secure when we're all on the boat."

The captain returned to the boat before dark, taking Salap with him to arrange the equipment and specimens aboard *Vigilant*. Shatro had been waiting for this moment, and when Randall was out of sight—walking off the dinner Salap had prepared, a dubious feast of unfamiliar bits of prairie fabric—the three researchers found me on the beach, watching the storm in its unmoving, ever-changing grandeur.

"We have some questions," Thornwheel said amiably enough. He wore a roughly trimmed beard, which gave his high forehead and plump boyish cheeks some maturity, but not a great deal. They sat beside me on the mottled dark sand, picking at the rough rounded quartz and granite pebbles.

"Matthew tells us you have little formal training," Cassir said. He gave me a hard look. "We wonder how little."

"Enough to get by," I said. Their expressions—a little flat, with unconvincing smiles—forecast some sort of trouble.

"We're just curious," Cassir said. "We like to know who we're working with. What you're capable of."

"I'm self-educated," I said. "Lenk school, but no secondary after."

"Shatro tells us you were lost in Liz for two years," Thornwheel said.

"Hardly lost."

"Liz is old and familiar by now," Shatro said.

"I never got *familiar* with Liz," I said.

Thornwheel chuckled. "Our scientific paramours, right? Scholar's mistresses . . . books and dreams of queens."

Shatro was not mollified. "What did you hope to learn? Without equipment, without training . . . We've been trained by Salap and Keyser-Bach. There are no better teachers on Lamarckia."

"I haven't been so fortunate," I admitted, trying to avoid the confrontation Shatro seemed to want. "I spent most of my time trying to track the behavior of mobile scions. Whitehats, vermids, but especially aquifer snakes . . ." I had read enough in Randall's library about the kilometers-long fluid-bearing tubes, part of which I had seen outside Moonrise, that I felt I could hold up an argument for several minutes, at least.

"I tracked one when I was a second in Lenk school," Thornwheel said. "Never found the beginning, and never found the end."

"I tracked one that was three kilometers long, at least. It dipped into the Terra Nova at one end . . ."

"What about the pink shells?" I asked, trying to get the focus off me and my experiences. "I never did see where they came from. Do you think they're remains of scions?"

Cassir took the subject eagerly. "Whitehats," he said.

"We don't know that," Thornwheel said contemptuously. "Don't rely on folk gossip. But we've never seen living things inhabit the shells."

"Salap says he's sure whitehats deposit them as soil enrichers."

Thornwheel shook his head. "They're the cast-off remains of vermids."

Shatro shook his head in turn, more vigorously. The third degree had been averted, at least for now. He took one last shot at me:

"What did you learn that we don't know anything about? You spent two years there—did you *see* pink shells being deposited? Did you see aquifer snakes hooking up to feed another scion, or water a silva bed?"

"No," I said.

"Nobody's seen any of those things," Thornwheel said. "There just aren't enough of us, and too many mysteries."

Randall walked along the beach and joined us as the last ribbon of light in the west faded. "I'd like to try to reach Athenai on the radio, now that it's night," he said. "The storm doesn't seem to want to throw much lightning now, does it?"

"No, Ser," Shatro said.

"Maybe we'll get lucky."

Cassir got up and we retired to the small cabin the researchers shared with the small radio. We were not lucky, however. The radio produced nothing but hiss and voices too distorted to understand.

"The captain could do anything he wanted, under these conditions," Shatro said. Randall gave him a passing glare, but said nothing.

In the morning, before dawn, I came awake from a vivid dream of Thistledown City. The city had been almost empty of people, and the buildings had become like limp balloons. The message was clear enough: a city was nothing without its people.

But what about people, without the city?

I walked along the boundary of the prairie, savoring its extraordinary monotony, wondering what Lamarckia had to offer that could replace a city, or all the components of civilization.

Salap and his assistants seemed contented enough. The captain and Randall found challenges enough to amuse them. But what about me? I wondered what I would grow to miss most . . .

Already I missed Thistledown. I missed the straightforward flirtations and courtships I had been so good at; there was nothing to either constrain or slake my physical needs but willpower, and that left me bluntly frustrated, unable to respond in kind to even the simplest gestures, which were all that Shirla seemed capable of.

Cassir and Shatro met me as I doubled back along the boundary. "Go ahead," Cassir shouted. "Walk on it. It's like spongy wood."

The edge of the prairie resembled knobby melted wax, slumping over the shingle beach. Cassir jumped up to stand a meter above us, hands outstretched, grinning. "Biggest single thing on Lamarckia, what do you bet?"

"Salap said it was made of five scions," Shatro objected.

"All melted together. Only master researchers—such as Salap and yours truly—could discover the components. Come on." Cassir walked inland.

Shatro jumped up before I did, and we both followed. The texture of the prairie was very much like hard cork, springy and pleasant to walk upon. We left no lasting impressions. Cassir ran in a happy circle. "It's been great here, working with Ser Salap . . . But I'm glad to be off, I'll tell you. What are the women like on your ship?"

"Hard-working," Shatro said.

"The mate and a senior A.B. keep us in line," I added.

Cassir grimaced. "Pity we can't go to Jakarta right away. I'd love to spend time in a city again. A real chance to mingle . . . I'd even sign on with a triad, if that's what it took."

"Who knows where we'll be going?" Shatro asked gloomily. "We'll probably end up kidnapped and working for Brion."

Cassir said, "Matthew says you were in a village the Brionists pillaged."

"Pretty awful," I said.

"Sure it wasn't pirates?" Cassir asked. "We've seen ships with no flags. Had to happen eventually. Another thing the Good Lenk didn't consider when he brought us here."

"What?" Shatro said. "Should he have expected pirates?"

"No," Cassir said, laughing. He seemed ready to laugh at anything, refreshed to see new faces. "Fates, I'm giddy just to have company. We've been up all night talking, haven't we, Shatro?"

"And drinking," Shatro said.

"Prairie solvent." He pulled a small glass bottle from his pocket, filled with milky fluid, and offered it to me. I took a small taste. Like pure fire, and still with the bitter aftertaste of all alcoholic beverages on Lamarckia. "We took three scion membranes from part of the prairie, arranged them in a way Lamarckia and Petain did not intend, made ethyl alcohol . . . and without yeast! Salap says we can make all sorts of materials from the scions we've found. We'll make this planet more pleasant, given half a chance . . . And I hope Lenk gives us that chance."

"He's ill, they say," Shatro said. "Getting old."

Cassir suddenly sobered, glanced at the bottle, and pocketed it. "We'll all get old. Nobody asked us whether we wanted to or not."

He lifted up his shoulders, took a deep breath, and swung his arm out to take in the inland prairie. "Quiet, my God, until the rain falls, and then it's like a dull, soggy drum. Do you think it *worries*?"

"I never saw a queen, or anything that seemed intelligent," Shatro said. "I like to think it's alive and thinking, somewhere."

"Oh, it is *that*," Cassir said. "Very much alive and thinking . . . Somewhere. Deep in the interior. Compared to Petain, Liz is a sweety. Petain . . . I imagine it, or *him* if I be truthful, to be a crusty, conservative old miser, except when he sets foot in the sea . . . Then he gets extravagant. If we have time before the boat goes, we should swim out with some masks and look at the vine reefs. Proper big nutrient factory out there. Giant anchored membranes like nets, just bubbling away. *Fast* piscids, dozens of varieties. All of them taste awful. Petain is spectacular out there, but hidden by all that water. That's Petain, however. Rich and not at all generous with his beautiful daughters . . . Fates, I'm drinking too damned much." Cassir reeled dramatically, drew himself up again with a grin, and stamped his foot on the slick tan surface of the prairie. "Rain due in a few minutes, I think." He stared out to the sea, where a low front of oily-looking clouds were moving in rapidly. "Let's get off this or we'll be drummed and sponged. Stranded until it pushes the water and nutrients down below. You can't walk twenty feet when your feet keep getting mucked."

Cassir ran swiftly for the edge of the prairie. We ran after, springing along on the surface, skirting the deep dimples.

"Does the captain make the researchers do sailor work?" Cassir asked as we leaped off the edge, landing in the empty sand and pebbles.

"Only Ser Olmy," Shatro said. "He isn't *quite* a researcher yet, however."

"Right," Cassir said, as if it didn't matter. "I like to climb aloft now and then . . . but not if someone orders me to."

The clouds slid rapidly across the beach, bringing at first a curtain of fine mist that spun in the morning light like whirlwinds drawn in gold dust. A few small brown disks fell and clung to my hands and face. I shrugged them off with a convulsive shudder, as did Shatro, but Cassir plucked them off his bare arms and ate them. "Quite good," he said. "Coins, we call them. Taste like bread, and no immune challenges."

I tried one, biting it in half. It did taste like bread—stale bread. "What's in them?" I asked.

"What the prairie needs," Cassir said. As the clouds blew inland, I saw a haze of coins falling on the broad tan surface. "Sucks them right up. The storm—the *big* storm our captain is so worried about—it makes food for the prairie."

"Salap told us that," Shatro said, blinking miserably against the mist and the tiny slaps of brown disks.

"Yes, but there's more than even that. It makes *lots* of food. Some of it we can eat. Petain keeps its sea creatures pretty unpalatable, but it seems to cater to the prairie—if the storm is really alive, and belongs to Petain, as Ser Salap thinks."

"How could it be alive?" Shatro asked.

The rain fell in thick sheets now. "Run for cover!" Cassir shouted.

We joined Randall and Thornwheel in the cabin, listening to the rain on the prairie, like hundreds of animals running. Thornwheel brewed a kind of tea from prairie skin harvested near the beach. He explained the process as the water came to a boil. "We flense it with our knives, peel a sheet off about the size of a blanket, take it back, cut it up . . . let it dry in sheds. Nothing ever stays dry outside here. The prairie grows it back next day. Amazing polysaccharide complexes, and fast duplication, too." He poured the water over minced skin and handed me a cup. "Go ahead," he said, expression humorless. Thornwheel seemed quite the opposite of Cassir. Handsome, a little somber and sad.

The women on *Vigilant* would have more variety now, and would give their sweets and medical attentions to the new men . . .

Especially Shirla. And what was that to me?

I sipped the tea cautiously. It tasted muddy and rich, like a yeasty broth. "Drop a few coins in . . . lunch," Cassir enthused, lifting his cup in a toast. "When we get to Jakarta and present our papers, we'll be famous. Enough food in Petain to feed millions."

"If Lenk allows it," Shatro said.

"Could use some spice," Randall suggested.

The rain ended twenty minutes after it began, and the clouds blew clear, leaving bright sunshine. The storm had disappeared again, as if following some familiar and habitual track.

CHAPTER TEN

The *Vigilant* put out to sea late next evening. The captain was relieved to be away from Wallace. He walked the deck while deep in conversation with Salap, accompanied on occasion by Thornwheel or Cassir. My elevation to assistant researcher had not yet been approved by Salap; the mate still gave me orders, and I remained with the starboard watch, working hard from just before dawn until just after dusk.

In the twilight, most of the crew rested before dinner. The winds were light, the storm that worried the captain and that Salap claimed was alive seemed to have vanished for good, the air was fresh, and the sea frothed like beer in our wake, hissing softly, a susurration beneath every word, every shipboard sound. I mused over Cassir's description of the offshore membranes, bubbling away oxygen from water . . . completing the two-part respiration cycle.

Shirla stood by the rail amidships, keeping away from the scattered labors of the port night watch, now occupied with binding a crack in the gaff on the spanker. Cathedral tree xyla was liable to split after a few years at sea; the *Vigilant* was ten years old and many of her yards and masts wore tight-wound rope binders to keep the splits from spreading.

I sat next to Shirla, back against the gunwale. She did not walk away, as I had feared she might. She smiled down upon me where I squatted, past irritations apparently forgotten, and said, "It's begun, you know."

"What?" I asked.

"The pairing off," she said.

"Don't tell Soterio," I cautioned.

"It's a game," she said. "You can't stop life even at sea."

"I suppose not."

"Talya fancies the sailmaker, but he's married," she said. "Not that that will stop them if we get more than a day on shore. She likes his voice. They make good music together."

Shirla was finely tuned to the wavelengths of the crew. She seemed in a mood to talk, both a little anxious and a little sad.

"Nobody's after *my* stern, of course," she said, gaze fixed on the horizon. "I've never attracted fast eyes."

"You reward close study," I said, hoping to cheer her a bit.

"*You'll* never know," she said lightly. "You're a loner. You don't want anybody knowing anything about you. So what can a mere woman do to you?"

I laughed.

She wrinkled her nose and flicked one of her ears with her fingers. "I heard Salap arguing with the master yesterday."

"Oh?"

"They were arguing about you. In the research cabin."

"How did you happen to hear?"

"I was painting the lizboo with choker oil. Soterio says I have a velvet brush hand. I didn't hear a lot, but Salap said he'd pick his own researchers."

I lifted my eyebrows. "Oh."

"I didn't know you were held in such esteem."

"Randall seems to like me," I said.

"Maybe you should be after *his* stern," she suggested, not so lightly.

"He's a married man with four children."

Shirla squatted beside me, biting her lower lip. "I could match you with another woman," she said. "The A.B.s in our bunk area talk about you. You attract some of them. Women with fast eyes like you."

"Thanks," I said, "but no. Besides, I favor you."

Shirla stared at me as if mildly offended, then looked away, jaw clenched. "I'm no fool," she said. "It's not as if I can't hold up my end of a conversation."

"I never thought you couldn't," I said.

"Don't tease me."

"I don't mean to—"

She interrupted. "Salap said he'll watch you closely. The captain went back to the radio. He's been listening to it a lot."

"What does he hear?" I asked.

She gave me a cautioning look. "He hears what he chooses to tell us. That's all he hears."

"Oh."

She paused, still squatting on her haunches, and said, as casually as if she hadn't just warned me, "Jakarta might be closed for months. We'll never get in. Salap said he was angry with Randall, but Randall got him to admit . . . that they're going to need more researchers. So I guess you're in."

"Thanks for keeping an ear out," I said.

She shook her head, pursed her lips, and stood. "The engineer is elegant," she said. "A firster. He came over with Lenk. Maybe I'll try him."

Khovansk the engineer was perhaps seventy, the oldest man on the ship. He spent most of his time belowdecks forging old broken metal into new pieces. He also maintained the ship's feeble and primitive electrical system.

"Maybe the Brionists will capture us and we won't have to worry about anything," Shirla concluded. She got up and walked forward, leaving me utterly confused.

Two days out of Wallace, the first mate spotted a pelagic scion floating list-lessly off our starboard beam. It was far from Petain or any other zone ocean territories and seemed lost, its back burned gray and blistering in the sun. We circled, put out the longboat, and investigated the creature. Salap led the boat crew, and soon they had roped the scion and dragged it slowly back to the ship.

Alongside the *Vigilant*, floating in the ship's shadow, we had a much better view of the creature. The crew on free watch—eight of us, including myself, roused from my bunk by Shimchisko—watched from the gunwale as Salap supervised the floating of a xyla platform.

"It's still alive," Ibert said, clucking sympathetically.

"Looking for its mama," Shimchisko said, only weakly sardonic. The scion was a piscid, a slender orange and black torpedo shape with three lines of stiff dark purple fins spaced equidistant on back and sides.

The captain watched from the puppis, tapping his fingers on the rail and murmuring comments to Randall.

"It's a long way from any of its brothers and sisters," Shirla observed from the rigging above.

"No flarking!" the mate shouted. Curious onlookers scraping the decks or clinging to the shrouds, or bellied over the yards, working sails, returned to their jobs—but only for a few minutes. Soon, even the mate watched Salap and the researchers hoist the piscid onto the platform, measure it, and take pictures.

"Good men preserve us . . ." sailmaker Meissner said, peering over the side in passing. He shuddered. "Hope it won't call its queen from the deep."

Ibert scoffed.

Meissner shook his head darkly and walked on.

"Sailor's superstition," Ibert said, but drew his lips tight as Salap prodded the piscid. The creature undulated slowly on the platform, lifting its pink, eyeless snout. It opened and closed a four-part jaw, each part sporting a horny serrated tooth.

"It's just a fish," Soterio said, looking at us with an expression of mixed defiance and guilt, as if he might be blamed for this sacrilege. "A scavenger, I bet. The kind sent out to chew up lost scions from other ecoi or to recycle dead scions."

"What's this?" Randall asked, approaching the group by the rail with a master's concern for brewing trouble.

"Sir, sailmaker Meissner commented we should be leaving this one alone," Soterio said.

"We've never had trouble taking scions on land or in the rivers," Randall observed.

"Rarely take them this far at sea, sir," the mate continued.

"So? Most of them aren't even edible."

"Ocean queens . . ." Soterio said in a lowered voice, shaking his head.

"Ah, that the queens live in the oceans . . . I've heard that," Randall said. "That they'll rise up and punish us someday. Good theory. I'll tell the captain."

"Not my own theory, sir," Soterio hastened to add.

"Of course not."

"It is no longer alive," Salap called up from the platform. He bent down, water slapping at his boots, and lifted the beaked snout. It fell back, limp. "Very far from its home waters. Lost in currents."

"Use it," the captain called from the puppis. Salap looked up, uncertain what the captain meant.

"Our first specimen," the captain said. "Bring it aboard and we'll study it."

"He thinks the queens won't know," Shimchisko said to Ibert and to me.

"Why so afraid, all of a sudden?" Ibert asked his friend. "You don't respect anything."

"Not afraid," Shimchisko said huffily. "The Good Man taught proper respect for things in their places."

"So," Ibert said. "This poor fish is out of its place."

Shimchisko, who had turned very pale, walked to the starboard side of the boat, to be away from the sight of the dead scion.

"What do I know, what do I know?" Ibert muttered, stalking off after Shimchisko.

That evening, Salap dissected the piscid on a table on the main deck, electric lights supplementing the twilight settling over our spot of the Darwin Sea. The water was calm, the wind steady; a light crew tended the ship, while most of us watched Salap at work, circled around the table like an audience at a sporting event.

Salap seemed to enjoy the focused attention. The captain stood by the piscid's tail as the head researcher cut and drew his knife along the thick, tough skin between rows of fins. This took several minutes of effort, drawing grunts from the usually unflappable Salap, but finally he revealed the piscid's interior—ropy, surrounded by pale orange fluid, interspersed with orange and purple grapelike clusters. A familiar gingery, garlicky smell wafted out of the carcass, making the crew murmur and shake their heads among themselves. It smelled like one of Liz's scions, yet Liz was not supposed to venture out to sea.

"We should not draw conclusions too soon," Salap warned, listening to the murmurs. "We have no records of this kind of scion, though it does bear some resemblance to a river whale. Interior anatomy is not unfamiliar for a piscid—these extensive ropy tissues are muscular analogs, but of course there is no cellular structure as such. We call them tissues by comparison only. They are more like bundles of actin or myosin fibrils, surrounded by networks of macrotubules which transport cytoplasmic components, much as do microtubules in our familiar cellular structure."

He lifted the grapey clusters. "All organelles are created and controlled by these, what Shulago called staphyloform masses, which also supply and direct the flow of chemicals and nutrients. Scions are self-repairing, and have sufficient instructional genetic material to carry out that function, but no scion can reproduce its own form. That is left to the reproductive centers of the ecos itself, which, of course, are mysterious."

Salap sliced through the ropes, which sprang aside like stretched rubber bands, flinging orange fluid across his apron and into the captain's face. The captain shook his head and asked for a towel. Salap checked to see if any fluid had gotten into the captain's eyes, but it had not. "Pelagic scions contain many substances that can cause severe chemical or allergic reactions," he warned the crew. "Not only acetic acid in various concentrations, but ethanol, methanol, and organic compounds . . . amines, steroids, enzymes and other proteins, and many types of polysaccharides. Merchant ships becalmed, out of fuel, with starving crews . . ." He shook his head. "Some have tried to eat piscids from the deep waters. Some have died."

This was not news to the crew, of course. Heads nodded around the circle. Meissner, standing with arms folded two meters away from me, shook his head emphatically and said, "The queens protect their own."

More crew gathered closer as dusk deepened. The piscid seemed to hold a fascination even for those disinterested in the ship's scientific mission. "Where's the brain?" asked a tall, nervous A.B. named Wernhard.

Salap turned to the piscid's "head" and took out a small bowed saw with a thin blade. He cut around the head between the beak and fins and pulled the skin aside. "No brain like ours," he said. "Networks of tubules carrying free amino acids, chiefly lysine, and mildly acidic fluids, may act as primitive processing centers. Do they think? Not as we do. Do they see? This one has no eyes . . . It probably tastes with its entire skin.

"No brain, and no digestive system. Its only source of energy, once it is set free upon the ocean, is photoreceptive pigment, an advanced form of rhodopsin, in translucent membranes just beneath the skin of its back and fins. Not as concentrated as similar membranes in phytids and arborids . . . Its main function may be to gather dead sister scions or scraps from other ecoi, and return them to some central analyzer or digester, which then rewards the piscid by replenishing its energy stores, or absorbs it and makes more. Then again, maybe it is a thief or spy . . . a kind of enlarged sampler, like some piscids in the rivers. In some ways, it is simpler than a planarian worm."

Salap pushed his lips out as if about to kiss someone, eyes going slightly out of focus, an expression I had learned meant he was deep in some speculation. "Maybe this is a one-of-a-kind specimen, drawn from some past catalog of designs, sent out on a specific mission. Now it's worn and lost and useless."

I wondered if that could ever describe me.

Salap cut away a grayish membrane and revealed a startling rainbow of components within the piscid's central cavity. The captain became involved. "As Ser Salap tells us," he said, pulling on gloves and examining the organelles before dropping them in jars of water dosed with potassium salts, "scions are more like single cells than multicelled organisms. They have evolved—if I may use that word, with its Earthly connotations—to a condition that has been called *megacytic*."

The captain stepped around the table and dug his hand deep into the cavity, felt for a moment with a squint at the starry sky, and pulled out a marble-sized lump. Smoothing away nacreous connective tissue, he held it up in the lantern light. "Scions carry their genetic material in stony nodules. Ser Salap is famous for being the first to analyze this material, and to discover its chemical and structural relationship to our own RNA and DNA. However, the amounts of genetic material—roughly one tenth of one percent of the DNA in our own cells—and the genetic grammar, even the ancillary support structures, differ from our own.

"Each ecos attempts to hide and protect its genetic material, perhaps with ornate codes or decoys, yet, for the most part, I believe ecoi can sample and analyze scions with fair efficiency. We have seen new scions quickly imitated by other ecoi, and that leads us to believe the ecoi spy on each other, and that they are master genetic engineers."

Salap pulled forth a long translucent tube filled with a gelatinous fluid. "Swim bladder, very fine oily substance," he commented, passing the tube to the captain, who lifted it, weighed it on a scale, and let it slide into a pan for later examination.

"Can anyone tell us why ecoi would want to disguise or encode their genetic information?" the captain asked, treating his crew once again as a class of students.

The A.B.s and apprentices shrugged, glanced at each other, smiled sheepishly. Finally, A.B. Talya Ry Diem ventured her opinion in a gruff voice. "Don't want others stealing their designs."

"Precisely." The captain smiled at Ry Diem, and she beamed like a little girl. "An efficient form requires much effort to design and create, much trial and error. Theft is easier. Baker witnessed scion kidnapping in Thonessa's Zone, a small zone on Tasman, near Kandinsky. He never saw actual analysis—no one has—but found the discarded carcasses in Kandinsky later. Shortly after, adapted copies of these scions from Thonessa were produced by Kandinsky."

Salap lifted his slime-covered hands. "I suggest we name this form *Elizabethae Macropisces Vigilans*—though the connection with Elizabeth's Zone is unproved." He pulled a cloth over the dead piscid. "We have so many questions to answer. How does an ecos deal with death? What is the nature of its energy cycle, its feeding and respiration? Why have the ecoi created an oxygenated atmosphere, yet rely primarily on a non-respiratory photosynthetic cycle? Do ecoi in fact reproduce over long periods of time, or do they merely sex and flux—merge with valuable sub-zones, or with each other? If they do reproduce, since virtually all the land and most of the ocean are already populated by ecoi, where do young ecoi go to grow and mature? Is it possible the young exist within the ecos, and we do not recognize them?" He bathed his hands in a tub of seawater, then removed his gloves. "Many mysteries indeed, and I for one am eager to solve them."

Twenty-three days out from Calcutta, one of the younger apprentices, Cham, standing watch on the foretree top, spotted what he thought were ships to the southeast. The captain came up from the cabin, followed by Randall. Thornwheel and Cassir emerged, then Shatro. Salap came last, and binoculars were passed between them on the forecastle deck near the bow.

"They're coming closer," Randall observed.

Ry Diem was helping me repair a net on the quarterdeck. "Fates and Breath of us all," she murmured, lifting her eyes. "Brionists."

"Not ships," the captain said, loudly enough for all of us to hear. "Moving quite fast, however."

Salap took the binoculars eagerly. He seemed ready to leap into the water.

"Wonderful," he cried. "Speeders, racers . . . largest I've ever seen."

"From where?" the captain asked.

"Petain, perhaps," Thornwheel suggested.

"No way of knowing," Salap said, binoculars focused on the objects, now visible to everyone about a mile from the ship and bearing down rapidly. "They are moving faster than thirty knots."

The captain took the binoculars again. "Pelagic scions big as longboats. Biggest I've seen except for river whales."

Four of the creatures zipped across the ocean's choppy surface, sending up spray from wavetops, bouncing like speedboats and alternately singing and droning. "Baker observed these," the captain said, as if that might make them less interesting.

"I have seen smaller ones myself," Salap said.

"What do they *do*?" the captain asked. "Where are they *from*?"

Throwing long rooster-tails, the high-speed scions circled the *Vigilant* at fifty or sixty meters. They seemed little more than a tall sail or stabilizer mounted on a flat body. The forward part of the body dropped two limbs or fins into the water, where they spread to form hydroplanes. The aft section of the body whirled long bladed cilia like propellers, driving the animals over the ocean at high speed, at least compared to the *Vigilant*. They circled us for ten minutes, then one darted closer, flashing by the port beam. Its colors were blue and dark purple across the stabilizer, gray and white along the body and fins, with red trim on all forward edges. It was breathtakingly beautiful.

Shirla took my arm as we watched. I glanced at her and saw her face flushed with an emotion I knew I shared, but which was difficult for either of us to express.

"Blessings upon Lenk for bringing us here," she said. She held my hand to her lips and kissed it, biting a knuckle gently, and ran aft to trim the maintree skysail with other A.B.s.

The captain and Salap argued over the sighting for hours after, reaching no conclusions they could agree upon.

Meissner spread a sail across the main deck to check his repairs. "Messengers, tattletales," he muttered for the benefit of no one in particular. "Checking things out across the Darwin, reporting back to their queens."

CHAPTER ELEVEN

At the end of the fourth week, Martha's Island lay three miles off the port bow, due north, visible beneath puffs of gray evening cloud as a sawtooth of six jagged mountains. Dark spits of lowland connected the rugged main island to headlands east and west, giving the broader mass the look of a bird with a feathery head prostrate upon the sea, its wings spread flat with tips raised weakly for flight.

The *Vigilant* proceeded slowly over shallow sandy banks devoid of apparent life, topsails and spanker taut in a steady breeze and all others furled. The sea spread calm and deep blue for miles around.

We had entered the protected void of Martha's Island, and approached the island's southeastern shore, the only safe place to land a boat on the mountainous main body. If we had tried to land on the lowland beaches or the headlands and hike inland, we would have encountered extremely rugged and barren terrain; so Jiddermeyer had learned on his first visit, and Baker and Shulago had confirmed.

Most of the crew watched our approach to the island, evenly spaced in the middle and port side on the shrouds, masts, quarterdeck, and on the forecastle deck with the master and researchers. The captain had unfolded his portable chair on the quarterdeck and surveyed the coast and mountains through binoculars. Shirla and Shimchisko and Ibert watched with somber expressions.

"What's wrong?" I asked.

Shimchisko hitched up his shoulders and shook his head with a whistling release of breath. "Martha's Island doesn't know us," he said. "We'll be getting acquainted."

Ibert nodded grim agreement. "Samplers aren't always the same," he said. "Not always small. Not always gentle."

"Nonsense," Shirla countered. "Every ecos is 'polite.'"

That expression found favor among a certain large segment of the immigrants, who idealized the landscape and ecos. A kind of mythology had sprung up. The "many mothers of life," it was said, were "polite, always nurturing."

"That's not what my father says," Kissbegh observed. He had descended from the maintree shrouds with Riddle. Both had pushed their way through the crew to the port rail and stood beside us. "Jiddermeyer lost three of his crew here. Nobody ever found them. My father sailed with Jiddermeyer."

We wondered why he had not mentioned this before.

"He did. Two men and a woman vanished and my father said they were sampled."

"Why didn't you tell us about your father before?" Ibert asked.

"He wasn't proud of me. I'm a clown."

Shimchisko snorted. Riddle and Ibert seemed more sympathetic.

"No, I know what I am, and so did he," Kissbegh said. "But that's how I got my berth on the *Vigilant*. Not every zone need be as sweet as Liz," he concluded portentously. "We should listen to experience."

Shirla shook her head, unconvinced.

Rumors passed quickly. The crew's anxiety increased as we approached the eastern headland and sailed through more stretches of shallow, dead water. We could not make out any scions, even from a few hundred meters; the spits between the island's center and headlands were sandy desert.

As we prepared for our stay on the island, I helped Salap arrange his equipment in the longboat.

"I hear you do not have a strong family," Salap said, helping me carry two crates of specimen jars to the boat.

"No," I said. "I don't."

He was a small man with a face that seemed suited to sardonic opinions, dark eyes set unevenly above strong cheekbones smeared with black-rouge, a finely trimmed, graying black goatee, and square patches of hair trimmed free, like islands, at his temples. He wore loose-fitting black pants and a long black coat that seemed to fill out his thin body. "The master tells me you learn quickly." He gave me a look that seemed at once both unconcerned and challenging, as if daring me to disagree—or trying to provoke me. "So I have agreed to take you on."

"I am honored," I said, climbing the ladder to the longboat in its chocks and carefully lowering the box of bottles.

We loaded a wire-wrapped cube of stacked folding lizboo-mesh cages, for capturing small scions alive.

"Still," he continued, "there could be resentment. If you boast, I will send you back to the apprentices. And your duties will remain those of a sailor when we are not ashore and I have no use for you. Does that seem fair?"

I nodded.

"Good. We will accompany the first party to go ashore." He wiped his hands on a towel and looked across the blue sea to Martha's Island. "Shulago and Baker said the central island and Mount Jiddermeyer were covered with thick silva. Something has changed. Perhaps we won't need so many cages . . ."

The *Vigilant* weighed anchor in a small cove just below the tallest of the island's central peaks, Mount Jiddermeyer. The sun had dropped behind the western headland and the mountains were black against the yellow twilight sky. Electric lanterns were switched on and the deck became a patch of bright stars against the gray-blue ocean and the silhouette of the island beyond. The apprentices and A.B.s were relieved of their duties and sat on deck at leisure, enjoying the warm evening air, yet still keeping nervous eyes on the looming blackness of Mount Jiddermeyer, outlined by stars and faint ribbons of moonlit cloud. Dinner was served on deck as a kind of celebration, and the captain and officers and researchers joined the crew topside.

The other researchers took my promotion from the ranks with fated nonchalance. "It's only what I expect from Randall and Salap," Shatro said to Thornwheel, just within my hearing. "Nine days out of ten, Ser Salap's a martinet and by the rules this, by the rules that. On the tenth he's as generous as a bottomless bucket."

After dinner, a keg of mat fiber beer was shared out on the main deck. I sat on the port gunwale with Ibert, Meissner, Shimchisko, and Shirla. We dangled our feet over the side, backs to the light, facing the darkness and listening to the waves as we sipped the weak, bitter brew, with its faint ginger-garlic tang. From the nightbound shore came the soft grumble of breakers on the black lava sand beaches.

We had not seen any scions at all so far, even on the mountain slopes, and that worried the captain. "It's wrong," he said from his chair as Randall brought him a mug. "Martha's Island had a rich and lively ecos when Baker and Shulago last explored, a full silva both sides of the island. We haven't seen anything. It looks as if the whole island is dead." That seemed to excite him. He turned to Salap, who stood with arms folded a few steps away. "It'll be *primary* science, pure and direct, eh, Mansur?"

"It will, sir," Salap replied, smiling calmly.

"By the Good Man it will," the captain murmured, eyes glittering, and sipped from his mug. He licked his lips with broad satisfaction. "Think of it, friends . . ." He swept the deck with his happy gaze, taking in those of us who sat on the gunwale, his researchers, the other apprentices where they lounged and ate or drank. "How many scientists, how many *humans* over the years, have had a chance to do *primary* science?"

"We will not just clean up little details," Salap said, echoing the captain's enthusiasm.

He rubbed his chin. "Here's to Ser Korzenowski, designer of the Way," he said, lifting his mug. "To his audacity."

The crew sat in silence, all conversations stopped in uncertain embarrassment. Salap's gaze met mine. He was as interested in my reaction as I was in his.

Randall broke the silence. "And to Good Lenk, who used the Way as it was meant to be used, and broke the evil slide of Fate and Pneuma."

"Hear, hear!" the captain said, his face flushing deeper red. He lifted his mug. "To Good Lenk, who guides us all!"

The crew joined the toast. The awkward moment did not pass completely, however. The mood of the evening, set by the warm breezes and the comfortable bright glow of electric lights, the keg of mat fiber beer, broke, and the crew wandered about the deck, finishing up small chores, preparing to sling hammocks abovedecks and sleep in the warm night air.

When the others were settled, Shirla and I still stood by the gunwale, listening to the breakers. "We're awfully confused, you know," she murmured. "I wish I knew what to think, sometimes."

The longboat set out with first light, commanded by Salap; the captain stayed aboard for this first sortie, in case the island might prove dangerous. He clearly did not enjoy this precaution, and gave Salap detailed instructions on what to look for, what to record on both of their slates, and when to return with a preliminary report. On the boat were two apprentices, Scop and An Sking—low-profile types who seldom volunteered, but were picked by Randall for this reconnaissance—and Randall himself. Shatro, Thornwheel, and I filled out the complement.

The boat crossed the few hundred meters to the shore, a narrow black-sand beach scattered with lumps of pumice and broken bits of toughened scion fiber. We dragged the boat from the shallows up onto the beach, then walked up and down the strip of sand, the smooth glassy grains squeaking beneath our feet. Salap ordered us to gather several boxes of samples—the flotsam and jetsam of ecoi from around the Darwin Sea. "The ocean brings them to us for free," he said.

Beyond the beach, a storm-eroded cliff ten meters high revealed layer upon layer of volcanic ash fall, alternating gray and black. Buried within the layers, Randall and Shatro found dessicated remnants of scions, perhaps centuries old. We dug out these delicate specimens with small rock picks and shovels—shriveled brown husks, victims of ancient eruptions from the same volcanoes that pushed up from the sea and gave birth to the island thousands of years ago.

"This much we know about Lamarckia," Salap said, kicking at the black scoria capping the cliff. "It is younger than Earth by a billion years, more active volcanically—but five hundred kilometers less in diameter. There has been much less continental weathering of deposited crust from the era of lime testates, shelly microfossils. Nearly all the metallic ores are volcanic in origin. Likely if we really wish to find rich veins of metal ores, we will have to look five thousand meters beneath the continents, or deep beneath the waves."

We left the boxes of dessicated scions on the beach, atop some low flat lava boulders to avoid the waves. Beyond the beach cliffs, gentle rolling hills—ancient fumaroles, eroded by wind and rain—stretched half a kilometer to the razor-ridged, steep slopes of Mount Jiddermeyer. Lava boulders, scoria, and crumbled, eroded flows of twisted a'a covered the hills. The ground was cool, however, and no vapors emerged from the cracks or from the inland mountains.

Salap surveyed the mountains, sucking on his cheeks thoughtfully. With a small tongue-cluck, as if in moral disapproval, he turned to Randall and Shatro. "When Shulago and Baker were here, they could smell sulfur for dozens of miles out to sea. It's very quiet now, and no smell."

"We'll spend a half hour looking over this sector," Randall said. "Chief objects of our search will be petrids." He showed us a reproduction of a sketch by Baker of hand-sized flat scions clinging to lava, leaving trails of white behind. Serving the place of lichens, petrids or rock-grinders of various sizes and shapes were found in all known ecoi. "We'll also be looking for scion fumets."

Droppings—generally flat, smooth disks, were rarely visible in active ecoi because of collection and clean-up. If this ecos was declining, we might find more droppings—or none at all. "Watch your step. Shulago calls this very treacherous territory—lots of old lava tubes and sinkholes."

We spread out over the hills in the hot sun. I clutched a fiber hat and a bag for small specimens.

I fell twice before adapting to the terrain, skinning my knuckles and knees. The best place to look for fixed scions, I thought, would be inland a few hundred meters. I visualized them soaking up sun between the boulders. *Think energy. An ecos manages energy the way any organism does. Sunlight, air, water, minerals . . . Scions specifically adapted to taking advantage of certain niches for energy and raw materials.*

Treading black sand paths through a maze of fragmented lava, I peered into shadows beneath overhangs, scuffing at the sand with my boots, scraping several centimeters deep with a small shovel. Nothing. When the half hour had passed, we regrouped on the beach. Salap shaded his eyes against the sun and turned down his lips at our empty bags.

"So, the ecos is hiding, or . . ." He shrugged, refusing to speculate out loud. "We will find Shulago's trail, not far from here if it's still marked. There is a small sheltered valley at the base of Mount Jiddermeyer. It is a hike, but I believe we can find it and be back before the captain gets upset." He gave us all an enigmatic look, partly conspiratorial, partly rueful. I detected a hint of rivalry here—Salap wanted to explore the island on his own terms.

As we walked down the beach and searched for the trail-head, Shatro picked up a piece of leathery scrap and passed it around for examination. Dark brown, dried to the consistency of xyla, it still held a few threads in punched holes.

"Part of a shoe," Randall offered.

"Not a scion," Shatro said.

"Disappointing," Salap said, shaking his head sadly. "What has happened here?"

We did not find any trail markings, but a sandy path between the boulders showed promise. The path climbed the side of the mountain and veered around an andesitic outcrop.

"This is Shulago's trail, but the arborids are gone," Salap said, pointing to empty circles of stones and conical depressions in the ground on either side. "When the arborids were here, they pushed boulders away and took root . . . They have crawled away, or died."

We followed the path for a hundred meters, around the outcrop, and then through a tumble of large boulders, some stacked in arches over the trail. The sun warmed my arms and made my scalp sweat within the hat. I felt sad and sleepy.

After four kilometers, a few purple and dark blue stalks showed over a close rise. "At last," Randall said. "Something alive."

Beyond the rise stood a copse of small, squat, palmlike arborids. Spiky leaves spread over round boles in a furry cap. Translucent brown roots formed nets over the ground between the arborids, and along the roots crawled shiny orange vermids—wormlike creatures, each about four centimeters long.

We paused by the edge of this pitifully small and confined silva. Randall, Shatro, and Salap examined the scions quickly, making notes on Salap's slate. I recognized none of them from the illustrations and photos of either the Jiddermeyer or Baker-Shulago expeditions.

"Big differences," Salap said. "Fluxing and reissue of new scions. The island is no longer hospitable."

"Competition?" Shatro asked brightly. "War . . . a sexing?"

Salap looked to the skies and shook his head. "There was only one ecos on Martha's Island, and we're a thousand miles from Elizabeth's Land, fifteen hundred miles from Hsia. Scions from pelagic ecoi stick close to the islands and continental shelves, except for unfortunates who stray . . . And both Shulago and Baker and Jiddermeyer said the ecos on Martha's Island dominated its zone, even out to a hundred miles from land. It was well fortified. How could there be a sexing, much less a takeover?"

Shatro was still hopeful his idea might be proven possible, if not correct. "We saw racers from Petain—or perhaps from Hsia or Efhraia's Land. Why are they out here, unless a zone senses opportunity?"

"What opportunity?" Salap asked, his temper rising. "It is *empty*, Ser Shatro! A zone has *subsided* here. It is in *decline*."

"Old age," I suggested, partly to break Salap's fix on the unfortunate Shatro. Salap rolled his eyes heavenward again but said nothing, walking ahead between the arborids, to the bottom of the small valley.

The air was cooler and moister in the shade of the arborids. It smelled of nothing in particular. I touched the trunks and leaves as we passed, but no stomata opened; there seemed to be only these two kinds of scions, unknown arborids and vermids.

"We haven't been sampled," Randall said as we approached the lowest part of the valley, half a kilometer from the rise.

"That I don't miss," Shatro said.

"Still, it's significant," Randall said. "The ecos may no longer be curious. Unique in my experience."

"We've only been here a few minutes," Shatro said, glancing around. "Maybe they're waiting for the right moment."

The trail broadened into a sandy flat. At the center of the flat, a hip-high wall of lava boulders surrounded a clear, sparkling pool. A spring bubbled to one side, and the waters rippled over a bed of black sand, sparkling in the bright sun. From the walled spring to the copse, a path was marked by smaller lumps of reddish lava.

"Not scions," Randall said. "Someone's living here."

We took the marked path back into the copse. Fifty paces from the spring, a dark gray, weather-beaten house rose on short stilts, surrounded by pink and gray arborids. The roof was made of some sort of gray leathery skin, as were the walls; the rest of the square, ungraceful structure was made of strips and beams of pinkish xyla.

At the sound of our voices, a woman stepped out onto the narrow porch, dressed in sacklike brown robes, face pale, her long black hair prominently streaked with gray. I guessed her to be about seventy years old. She stood with hands on the rail, staring at us for a moment with pale blue eyes. Her skin was dark, her limbs skinny, and she worked her mouth as if searching for words under her tongue.

"I am Liasine Trey Nimzhian," she said in a squeak. She cleared her throat and repeated her name. "I live here. What do you want?"

"Are you alone?" Randall asked.

"Not to alarm you, Ser Nimzhian," Salap said, touching Randall on the shoulder. "I am honored to meet you. I did not know you were still here." He turned and whispered in Randall's ear.

The woman looked at us one by one, eyes wide. "My husband died five years ago. I've been alone since. Human voices and faces quite stun me."

Salap introduced us formally, and then explained, "Sers Liasine Trey Nimzhian and Yeshova Nakh Rassik were feared dead. They were research-ers with Baker and Shulago."

"We did not choose to stay," Nimzhian said. She held out her hands. "Do you have a ship? Of course, you must. I would dearly love to see a ship, to . . . dine with the captain?"

"It would be our privilege," Salap said, bowing his head.

That evening, most of the crew sat down to the best that Frey the cook could offer on board the *Vigilant*. I sat at the table next to the captain's, with Ran-dall, the first mate, and the junior researchers, including Shatro. Nimzhian sat with the captain and Salap and Talya Ry Diem and Shirla, the fe-male A.B.s at table to make her feel at home. Indeed, the women spent much time fussing over her as they might over a revered elder. Liasine Nimzhian seemed to fall into a trance even before the dinner began.

"So long . . ." she cooed as she sat at the head table in the mess. "This seems wonderfully *elegant* to me. It's been years since I ate human food . . . Bread! And so much news! I do not believe all I have missed."

"Your story must be extraordinary," the captain said.

She drew herself up proudly. "I have lived on our island for twelve years now. The first years were good, but after my Yeshova died . . . mostly work." She leaned toward the captain. "You're following in the path of Baker and Shulago. You are going to circumnavigate."

"That we are," the captain said.

"That explains Ser Salap and his wonderful interest in Martha's Island.

Who else would go this far out of the way, to visit such a lonely place? Well, for you all, then, I have a story to tell. It is about secrets, and the death of the only living thing I have come to know and to love, besides my husband.

"Tomorrow, I will show you where it all happened, and tonight and tomorrow, perhaps I can explain why."

After the meal, we returned to the quarterdeck, to sit under the double oxbow and listen to Ser Nimzhian's story.

"When I joined the Baker and Shulago expedition, I was an agro—a farming specialist. I had learned how to care for terrestrial crops, without disturbing the ecos and bringing on a defensive response . . . Something rarely seen now, I suspect, but common enough then. My sponsor was Yeshova, the man who would become my husband. Yeshova." She lingered on the name in silence for a moment, smiling softly. "He thought I could teach Baker and Shulago a thing or two about specialization in ecos populations.

"We put to sea with two ships, the *Hanno* and the *Himilco*. They were smaller than this one, and less well prepared. Baker and Shulago may be heroes and martyrs to many now. I've only just learned they never returned . . . That only Chuki made it back in the smaller ship." She paused and drew several deep breaths, as if to calm herself. With one hand to her neck, absently stroking the brown and wrinkled skin there, she gathered her thoughts. "Not so long ago, it seems. My life has taken on a certain sameness the past few years.

"You know of our journey from Athenai to the northern continent, where no ecos grows, and from there to Hsia. We sailed along the western coast of Hsia, then south to the Cook Straits, and found a passage . . . discovering six more zones on the Cook Islands, small, simple ecoi really, compared to Elizabeth's Land and Hsia.

"We captured specimens, dissected them, and wherever we went, the ecoi were curious. I was personally sampled thirty-three times." She lifted her arms to show us tiny pock-marks, some as large as thumbprints. She also pointed out pocks on her neck and lifted her robe to show several on her ankles and legs. "We followed the eastern coast of Efhraia's land to the southernmost point, which we named Cape Manu, after our navigator. We rounded Cape Manu and returned to the Darwin Sea, rather than face icebound winter seas to the east."

She looked up at her audience, face drawn with memories. "It was a difficult journey. We lost seven to accidents . . . My brother among them. We could not fight the Westers south of the Shaft Island group. We could not cross in that direction . . . We were running out of food. We put into the Shaft Islands. Shulago did not want to return to Jakarta, though it was only six hundred miles away at the time . . . There were small farm towns in the Shaft Islands. We visited them. We were lucky to get enough supplies to go on."

"All the islanders died during the famine of 26," Salap said.

Nimzhian looked vague, as if this bit of history did not have any real meaning for her. Then she mustered what she thought would be a polite response. "I'm sorry. They were nice people, very eager to hear our stories. They thought Baker and Shulago were heroes. They thought we were *all* heroes. But we were just tired and hungry."

Nimzhian seemed reluctant to continue.

"You sailed north . . . so Chuki's journals say," the captain prodded.

Nimzhian rubbed her hands together as if to warm them. "Baker and Shulago had an argument," she said. "They always seemed like angry monkeys in too small a cage. Yet they always insisted on living aboard the same boat. They wanted to keep watch on each other.

"Baker wanted to head west, around Cape Magellan, but Shulago insisted it was the wrong season, that the westerlies would kill us. He may have been right. Eventually, we sailed north, to make the passage west between Tasman and Elizabeth's Land. My husband was arguing with Baker continuously by then. We found Martha's Island by accident . . . Yeshova thought we could profitably spend years studying there. Well, we got our wish."

She stopped again, jaw muscles tensing, and looked around the circle of faces, alternately smiling and shaking her head. "Baker was a very disagreeable man," she said. "He must have felt Yeshova was too much of a disturbing influence. He arranged for us to go ashore together. The ships sailed while we were ashore. I don't know what he told them . . ."

"The journals were lost," Salap said. "Chuki mentions nothing."

"Well, Chuki sailed before the *Hanno* abandoned us. We were very afraid at first. We knew about the three members of Jiddermeyer's crew, lost here over a decade before. We never found them." She rubbed her eyes with the fingers of one hand, then blinked in the light of the electric lanterns. "In a way, Baker did us a favor. We've had a good life here. Martha provides. We never starved, though we were hungry often enough, and sick a few times from eating the wrong things. We came to love her. She never bored us. Sometimes, Yeshova wondered if our work would ever be discovered . . . We wondered why no one returned to Martha's Island. But we weren't unhappy."

"There haven't been any expeditions since," the captain said. "The island isn't on any of the shipping routes—and there isn't much shipping across the Darwin now, anyway. Unless it's Brionists."

Nimzhian did not recognize the name. "Baker and my husband confirmed that the theories of the original surveyors and Jiddermeyer were correct. The only feasible explanation for Lamarckia's biological nature was inheritance from acquired traits . . . And yet, inheritance was the wrong word. Jiddermeyer had speculated about the designers and *observers*, who took the specimens gathered by samplers and thieves and studied them. We have been adding more and more detail to that theory.

"We've seen an ecos die," Nimzhian said. "We've seen its preparations for death. The island disrobed. It revealed its skeleton to us, in a way . . ."

"And was there a seed-mother, a queen?" the captain asked, tapping his fingers on his chin.

"I'll show you in the morning," Nimzhian said craftily. She smiled and rocked back and forth on her chair, enjoying the hold she had on us. "I expect you'll want to explore before you move on."

"You're welcome to travel with us," the captain said.

She shook her head firmly. "Thank you, but no. I'll return to my island in the morning. Much work remains. I do hope you'll take our results with you, and carry them to Athenai or Jakarta."

"We would be honored," the captain said.

Nimzhian let the dark memories pass and was full of cheer now, basking in human company.

Three boats put out the next morning under a low ceiling of thick, knobby gray clouds. Puffs of cool wind and spatters of light rain greeted us as we put ashore where the longboat had landed the day before. With Ser Nimzhian taking the lead, walking along the black sand shore with a practiced leggy waddle, our party of thirty—the captain, Salap and the assistant researchers, myself, and eight of the crew who had chosen lots, hiked over the Shulago trail. The party formed a long line up the slope to the valley. Some of the crew sang songs at first, but the desolation and windy silence, and the gray cast of the day, soon subdued them.

The researchers counted the circles of stones in the old silva and made an estimate of the extent of the silva and the past number of arborids. Nimzhian explained that the silva had declined from the shoreline inward, with scions disappearing night by night, their remains absorbed by ecos cleaners. Rock scrubbers had died after arborids, and then all the smaller forms, month by month . . . and year after year. Inland, the larger scions had died first as well, and then the smaller. "The arborids and phytids gave nutrition to all," Nimzhian said. "We believe they died because of the decline of microscopic scions."

The decline's cause was unknown. At first, husband and wife had speculated that human-borne microbes were infecting the scions, but found no evidence supporting that hypothesis.

"We always blame ourselves," Nimzhian said, approaching the rise with the last stand of arborids visible beyond. "We seem to be guilty about everything, even just being human. But soon we realized humans were trivial."

She could walk and talk easily without losing her breath. We struggled to keep up with her.

"Martha tolerated us, even let us take a few of its phytids and arborids and other scions for food and materials. When Martha was alive, every spring season we would hike inland, into the mountains, to study the blazing red efflorescence, the shedding and bursting of new growth among the phlox trees and divericata, the huge and rare hemohamatids and the coastal halimids. Martha sampled us for five years after we first arrived as if we were new . . . three-legged scions the size of mice springing out of the lower alsophileids, nipping our arms, late in the summer, with the penultimate warming of the Jiddermeyer current. That was unusual in itself . . . We never discovered why Martha needed to sample us so often, and so regularly."

She paused on the rise, bent to adjust her leggings and the socks that had slumped around her ankles. "Then, after eight years, all by itself, Martha began giving up and fading away. At night we heard what my husband called garbage trucks, the size of elephants, rolling down the naked hills into the ocean. There, they exploded like huge balloons, scattering half dissolved remnants to the waves and currents. The ecos took itself apart hectare by hectare, in an orderly fashion. I believe she knew she was dying, and wanted to leave the island clean after she was gone. I realize that is very anthropomorphic of me . . ." She glanced at us, face saddened by these memories. "We missed her being curious about us. We had taken comfort in those seasonal nips, those little samplings.

"We even came to believe the ecos watched over us, that she accepted us as independent parts . . . But that was my husband's idea, mostly.

"Five years ago, Yeshova suffered a stroke, or something like a stroke. Something went badly wrong inside of his head. No doctors, no clues. The ecos didn't save him. He died after twelve days of paralysis. I buried him, but scavengers dug him up and put him with the other scraps, and carted him out to sea. Martha has always kept herself clean, very clean."

We entered the grove as large drops of rain fell, drumming on the fine-fringed arborid leaves and dappling our clothes. "These are decadents," Nimzhia said, touching the fringe of leafy growths with a gnarled hand. "They are barren, of course, like old bees dying on a dry rock."

She pushed on, ignoring the rain, and the captain kept up with her, using his stick to prod aside brown creepers that writhed across our path. Salap peered at the leaves through a pocket magnifier, observing their reaction to the rain. "Ser Nimzhian," he called up the line, just as we reached the house, "I believe this small silva takes all its water from the spring. Am I correct?"

"You are correct," she responded, her voice rising over the hiss of falling drops.

Salap nodded in satisfaction and wiped moisture from his brow.

Nimzhian climbed to the porch and addressed us in the narrow courtyard. We were soaked by now, but the rain was subsiding, though thick gray curtains still cloaked the slopes of Mount Jiddermeyer. "I have something to show you," she said. "You can't all come in at once, but you're all welcome."

We took our turns, in groups of six, climbing the steps and shaking hands with her, at which point she introduced us to her true treasures—cabinets filled with hundreds of watercolor sketches done by herself and her husband. Salap was speechless, and stayed inside with Keyser-Bach as each group came through, staring again and again at the paintings as Nimzhian revealed them, a new group for each party. She glowed with pride.

"When the silva was healthy," she said, "it covered most of the center of the island, in two similar groupings, two silvas actually, as Jiddermeyer and Baker and Shulago saw . . . As we saw when we first arrived. The mountains were more active then. There were even earthquakes a few times a year, and the beach where you landed was rich with fumaroles venting sulfur."

The watercolors glowed with delicate life, revealing as much about their creators as they did about Martha's Island, sketched in with meticulous care using very fine pens cut from the central stalks of arborid leaves, colored by dyes taken from vermids and phlox trees high up in the mountains.

"We recorded all we could on the slate left to us by Shulago," she said. "But it soon stopped taking data. We learned how to make a kind of paper, and taught ourselves how to paint. Martha was very generous. She supplied everything—pigments, stems for brush handles, even brush hairs.

"We ate her scions, and we painted her as a kind of gift . . . Not that it was any true bargain."

A set of paintings showed the vernal efflorescence in the high mountain valleys, when the arborids and phytids shed old growth and produced bright new leaves of vivid reds and oranges, sky blue, and dark purple. The ecos itself seemed to have a painterly plan, the hills covered with zebra stripes of purple against red and sky blue. "The air smelled like the sweetest, finest wine in the spring," Nimzhian said, her fingers caressing the paintings, lifting them from their folders and replacing them with religious care.

Some of the paintings were of specimens of the largest arborids, named yggdrasils: hollow-cored nets of stiff creepers rising in fat cylinders up to a hundred meters high, throwing out tiers of purple-black sun-absorbing leaves. Yeshova had climbed into the hollow trunk of an yggdrasil and depicted it from the inside, like an intricate weavework narrowing to an open circle of sky.

"We used the few pieces of laboratory equipment, over and over again, until all was broken or ruined and we could only look and see and taste . . . And sometimes what we tasted made us sick, and we noted the symptoms." She shook her head ruefully. "Our own bodies became our laboratories. And then . . ." She flipped through sketches of barren lava, slumped and tangled yggdrasils, until the style became much simpler, cruder: the work she had done by herself, after the death of Yeshova.

The captain's eyes filled with tears and he dabbed at them with his knuckles, glancing around in some embarrassment. When all of us had seen the sketches, Nimzhian stood by the unglazed window, staring at the small grove circling the spring, her voice hoarse and cracking with weariness. "I need to rest before we do the next part of the tour."

"Of course," said the captain, and he ordered food brought out of our backpacks. We set up a picnic lunch around the house and on the porch, and Ser Nimzhian presided like a true matriarch, resting on her chair assembled from fallen yggdrasil leaf stems. She wore a broad, battered woven fiber hat to shade her eyes against the infrequent glare of sun peeping between the clouds.

"Captain," she said, "I give all our work to you. I see it all in my head, and it can only be useful taken away from this island. I won't be alive much longer, and the weather would only break in again and ruin everything."

The captain waved his hand as if dismissing her confession of mortality, and was about to speak, but she continued, "Four years ago, we lost fifty-nine sketches when the roof leaked. Months and months of work. Lamarckia is indifferent. And so was Martha, I suspect, but we loved her even so. They were comforting delusions, ghosts of benevolence and care when we were so alone."

We rested in the flowing patches of sun and cloud shadow, alternately warmed and cooled, surrounded by the rustling furred leaves of the grove. Salap and the captain and Randall sat on the porch with Nimzhian, who had closed her eyes and slumped in her chair, her breast rising and falling evenly beneath the folds of her robe and jacket.

Shirla and Shimchisko lay on either side of me, Shirla on her back, eyes tracking the clouds above, Shimchisko dozing lightly.

"I'd like to sneak off and explore," Shirla said. "I've been bunking on the ship too long, with the mate watching every tickle." She rolled on her side facing me. "Shall we run off to the hills?"

I smiled. "No flarking," I said. Shirla surveyed me critically, one eye half closed, and lay back again.

"It's a bold offer," said Shimchisko, waking from his doze. "What do you see in him?"

"I can't help myself," she said lightly. "It's his mystery. Where did you come from? I know . . . from Jakarta, before you lost yourself in Liz. But you don't talk like a Jakartan, and you don't *act* like anybody I know . . . There's a coolness about you."

"If mystery gets me out of cleaning the shithouse, I'll be mysterious."

"Well said," Shirla commented. "Droll defense. Come with me," she whispered conspiratorially into my ear, "inland to the hills," she lifted her chest and tucked in her chin, "and you'll see my tits."

I nearly choked on my laugh, and she laughed with me. But her eyes had fixed on mine. "The old woman's going to walk us somewhere. I'd love to run away behind everybody and sneak back in later. If you don't want to see my tits, okay, but keep me company."

The heat in me almost overrode my sense of duty—if that was what it was now. Duty had transmuted into a burning curiosity and a rush of other conflicting emotions: fascination, anxiety, even a kind of patriarchal concern. "I'd love to," I said.

"Soterio will dock us," she said. "You might be cut back to apprentice. Am I worth it?"

Shirla had never gone quite this far in her coquettishness.

"You are without doubt the loveliest creature on the ship," I said.

"Tell me more," she said.

"Much lovelier than Shimchisko here." Shimchisko opened one eye, then closed it again. "And you're much too smart to ruin a good sea career."

She poked her tongue out between her lips like a forgetful cat and broke our gaze, looking again at the clouds. "One day," she said, "I will see your secret nakedness, and I will gloat."

"You may see my nakedness any time," I said, "by appointment."

On Thistledown, I had been successful with women, too much so. I had come to think of them as delightful and valuable commodities, worth much effort, but not like me in any serious respect. I could see now, middled in this dreamlike experience, that my attitude carried a taint of youth and foolishness. Shirla was very much like me; Shimchisko was not, nor was the captain or Salap.

A steady patch of sun had settled over us, a long gap between clouds making the sun seem to roll down a race course, occasionally fetching up against a wall of cloud and flashing it bright yellow-white. "I'm too stupid," I said.

"See?" Shirla said. "Nakedness. Show me more."

I poked her calf with the toe of my boot. "Don't provoke me," I grumbled.

Nimzhian had stood up from her chair. "I'm rested," she announced. The captain, Salap, and Randall rose beside her like reverent servants. "Come with me," she said, and descended the porch steps.

"You missed your chance," Shirla said, getting to her feet.

"Foolish Olmy," Shimchisko said with a grin.

The billows and runnels of clouds had fled towards the southeast. We marched inland, up the northern rise of Nimzhian's valley, the last preserve of Martha's motherless scions. The grove ended at the rim of the valley, and on the slopes of Mount Jiddermeyer and the hills and mountains beyond, we found the trails and roads of the dismantling. Nimzhian pointed out various features as we walked on the path she and Yeshova had trained through the silva over their first eight years on Martha's Island: here, the site of the yggdrasil that had stood nearest the valley and their house, now a conical depression ten meters across, filled with sterile chunks of lava and a bottom of fine silty mud, cracking in the sun; there, the beginning of the path to the top of Mount Jiddermeyer, where they had found phytids and vermids suitable for making watercolor dyes; here again, a kilometer on, a lean-to they had made in case they were caught in a storm far from the house, now fallen to ruin, with nothing left to lean against. Higher still, in the cup between Mount Jiddermeyer and the central Mount Tauregh, after an hour of hiking, we stood for a moment in what had once been the thickest silva on the island.

"Millions of yggdrasils and tripod oaks," Nimzhian said, shading her eyes at the glare. In a few hours, the floor of this décolletage between the mountains would rise to meet the sun, and all would be in shade. For now it was bright gray desolation, kilometer after kilometer of conical depressions filled with mud.

Shimchisko rubbed his knees as we paused and looked up at Shirla and me. "Suicide," he said darkly. "The queen chose for her ecos to die. Out of shame."

Shirla curled her lip. She had little use for Shimchisko's mystical theories.

The captain, Salap, the researchers, and Randall took in the view with puzzled awe. They could no more explain what had happened here than Shimchisko. I looked to the summit of Mount Jiddermeyer, however, and wondered at the dog that did not bark in the night: no more steam, no more earthquakes, no more sulfur from the fumaroles near the southern beaches.

Nimzhian sighed and waved us on. She took the lead, her long, scrawny legs pumping steadily, her tireless gait marked by a lean to the left with one step, a lean to the right with another. From ten or twelve paces behind, I listened to her exchanges with the captain and Salap.

Shimchisko complained beneath his breath about the altitude and the effort, about the shame of all this destruction; I shushed him so I could listen to Nimzhian, and he regarded me with mild resentment.

"We came to this place two years ago, before Martha finally died," she said. "Yeshova and I toured around the island then, going where we could never have gone when the silva was so thick. With the phlox arborids and most of the phytids gone, we could go practically anywhere we pleased, and it was here we first came upon structures unlike any we had seen before, in any ecos. Yeshova named them *palaces*. I thought it a misleading word. Still, it's his."

Between lava boulders worn smooth by rock grinders and the ceaseless rubbing growth and procession of the silva's tree-forms, we looked out across a deep bowl cut from the side of Mount Tauregh. "There are five other palaces, all similar to this one. When they died, Yeshova believed, Martha died as well. These ruins and the orphaned grove are the only monuments."

The bowl stretched eighty meters edge to edge. Within, curving piers and crossbeams the color of old ivory radiated from the center of the bowl like giant rib bones arranged by an ancient hunting party. Dried shreds of membrane still clung to them. In the bottom of the bowl, beneath the tilted and fallen ribs, hexagonal chambers had been carved in the old lava flow. Rainwater pooled in the bottom of the chambers.

We gathered abreast, in a line along the rim of the bowl. The captain's face was pale. He prodded his jaw forcibly with an index finger and his lips twitched. Salap stood with arms crossed, lost in concentration, as if remembering a long-ago game of chess.

"The queen's chambers," the captain mused. "What do you think?" he asked Salap.

"Perhaps." The more intensely interested Salap became, the less he showed any reaction whatever.

"By the Good Man," Shatro said tentatively, looking to the others to determine the depth of his own reaction.

"Bilge," Nimzhian commented. "Hardly a queen's chambers. I never did like the word 'palace,' so misleading. We found five of these, all dead, all the same. The 'queen' theory allows only one."

"Here," said the captain, pointing to the chambers and vents in the rock along the outer walls of the chambers, "is where the scions are made and released. Given birth . . . There must be outlets. We should search for them."

"Night's coming in an hour, captain," Randall reminded him gently.

"Yes. Of course. But if we found the outlets—or even if we don't find them . . . Here is where the central controller, the seed-mistress, or mistresses . . ." He turned to Nimzhian, who regarded him skeptically. "If there are five, what of it? If there is no central and unique site, no single *palace*, what of it? I'm not wedded to the notion of a lone and exclusive seed-mother. If there were five of them . . . we might think of the others as chambermaids, helpers . . . One might be larger."

"They're all the same size, give or take a meter," Nimzhian said. "All the same structure."

"But you did not see them *alive!*" the captain fairly shouted. "One might have been festooned, *plumed*, with bright decorations, signifying her status, highest of all; the others secondary. There must have been . . . *one* controller, one *head*, one authority!"

He was still wedded to the queen, after all. Nimzhian tapped her walking stick on the ground, irritated in a way reserved for those who have been alone for a long while and are now subject to contrary company. "Have it your way," she muttered.

The captain ordered Shatro and Thornwheel to begin measuring the palace and gathering samples of whatever remnants of tissue remained. Shatro gave me a lizard-lidded glance of satisfaction as he stepped past. I felt like punching him, not because the captain had chosen him for this task, but because he put so much store in it, and seemed to think I might care.

"Water from the bottom of the chambers . . ." the captain mused, oblivious of this brief interchange. "Might be tissues, residues, genetic material there still. We can preserve it now, read it later."

Shatro, Thornwheel, and Cham began to climb down the rough scree to the chambers at the bottom of the bowl. A surveyor's measure was pulled from the equipment box, to be sited on by the captain's slate for later comparisons.

Randall glanced at the sun and then over his shoulder at the long, winding walk back to the beach.

"Captain, Ser Nimzhian probably wants to return to her house . . . And we should get word back to the ship."

Keyser-Bach stopped, his hands and shoulders quivering with excitement. His face screwed up like a little boy's. I thought for a moment he would pitch a tantrum, but he sat abruptly on a nearby lump of lava and clapped his hands on his knees. "All right," he said softly, then, shouting to the men on the path down the slope, "Wait! We'll come back tomorrow. We'll bring more equipment . . . Let's do this right."

Randall nodded. Shirla and the rest of the crew were obviously glad not to be spending a night in this desolation. Shimchisko stared at the palace with dread. He would not tell Shirla or myself what made him so uneasy until we were back on the trail, walking through the empty conical pits in the failing light. "It's ugly," he finally murmured, following a few paces behind me. "I thought they would be beautiful. *Queens.* But it's just like an old collapsed meeting hall. Roof-beams and rooms. Nothing more than a hotel."

"We don't know what it looked like when it was alive," Shirla said. "It might have been lovely."

"Hidden. No one can get to them wherever they are," Shimchisko said gloomily. "That means they're ugly, dead or alive." He would not be persuaded otherwise. "And what killed them?"

I kept my ideas to myself.

In the grove of orphans, the captain inquired whether Ser Nimzhian would prefer sleeping on the *Vigilant.*

"Fates and breath, no, thank you," she said. "I'm an old woman of deep habit. I came here with Lenk when I was a grown woman, and I married Yeshova when I was in my middle years, and now I am old and I have all my work and memories here."

"Tomorrow, we'll return and conduct a full survey," the captain said. "We'll set up a base camp and examine the other palaces. To be sure, we're beginning a long journey, but you'd be safer if you came with us . . ."

"No," Nimzhian said. "I have no taste for another expedition."

"We can provide comfortable accommodations . . ."

"Captain, I've spent the best years of my life here," Nimzhian said sharply. "Baker and Shulago did us a favor. From what you've told me, we've made our world even more confused and contentious. I'm sure you know the profound peace of devotion to research—to *seeing* and *measuring*. I've been present at the end of an ecos—something no other has seen. But the story is not over yet. Why the orphans remain—how they manage to stay alive—why the palaces chose to dismantle themselves and die rather than move . . . so many questions. Enough to fill the rest of my life."

The captain smiled. "I am envious. But there are larger puzzles to solve."

"This is a puzzle on my scale," she said. "Do what you must, take our drawings and results with you. But I am content."

Randall ordered Shatro, Cham, and Kissbegh to stay. The rest of us hiked back to the beach in the last of the twilight and returned to the *Vigilant*.

In the longboat, I took a spot on the thwart beside Shirla, who sat with head in hands, pensive. "Sad?" I asked.

She half frowned, drawing up her cheek and wrinkling one eye shut, then lifted her head and said, "A little lost."

"Why?"

"Queens can die."

"Yes?"

"It's not something I wanted to know, or ever wanted to see."

"Everything dies eventually," I said.

"Back on Thistledown—my father told me—people could choose to live forever. They had machines for inside the head, machines for the body. New bodies. Extra brains. I suppose I'd always hoped . . ." She threw up her hands. "Forget it. I can't even think straight."

"You wanted the queens, the ecoi, to be stronger and better than anything human and to last forever."

She shook her head, though a glint in her eye, a slight nod before denial, indicated my guess was close to the mark. "I wanted to visit a queen someday. I joined this expedition—went to Lenk school and specialized in ecology—and even though I didn't get on as a researcher, I shipped on as a sailor, an apprentice, just to meet a real queen. I suppose I wanted to sit down and talk with her."

"One woman to another?"

"Of course. Mother Nature herself." She grimaced, daring me to laugh.

"It's a lovely myth," I said.

"*Myth.*" She wrinkled her nose. "I wanted her to tell me what was wrong with being alive."

Uneasy myself now, I looked out across the water. The lights on the *Vigilant* sat on the border between the black sea and the starry night. I had never been comfortable around vague dreams and poetic associations. I had abandoned the Naderites in hopes I'd find a philosophy not fogged by uncertain wishes and self-enlarging dreams.

"But whatever they are, the queens here are just *dead*," Shirla went on. "I still think we killed them. A disease or maybe just disgust."

"What did Nimzhian or her husband or anybody else do to disgust Martha?" I asked in a jocular tone, hoping to break her mood.

"I heard what the old woman told the captain," Shirla said. "Baker and Shulago left them here. Abandoned them."

"Even if they were betrayed, what would that mean to a queen?" I asked.

"I don't know," she said quietly.

"A queen has to fight off other ecoi and protect a territory and make her scions. She brings them back when they're worn out and she makes new ones. She has to think about things differently. She couldn't have human concerns. I doubt *she's* a female at all."

"I don't care about that," Shirla said stubbornly.

Shimchisko, sitting on the thwart behind us, had listened without comment until now. "She may not be a female, but she's certainly a mother. That's the way I see her."

Shirla stared at the bottom of the boat. In the light of the lantern on the longboat's bow, I saw tears in her eyes, and I was filled with a sudden urge to comfort her. I put my arm around her shoulder but she shrugged it off.

As we climbed up the rope ladder onto the main deck of the *Vigilant*, I took Shirla aside for a moment and said something that made little sense to either of us, but especially not to me.

"When we go into a live, lush silva," I said, "and you ask me to go with you—if you ask me to go with you—I will go."

She seemed about ready to snap back with some angry reply, and her face flushed in the deck's electric light. Then she pulled away from my touch and walked across the deck toward the forecastle. After a few paces, she stopped and came back, with a deliberate swing in her step. She put her hand on my forearm, looked up at me with stern eyes, and said, "Ser Olmy, I was *joking*."

She swung around again and walked to the forecastle without looking back. But after helping the captain and Salap store the day's specimens in the cabinets outside the captain's cabin, I went to my bunk in the forecastle, and there I found two paper-wrapped sweets sitting on my pillow, given without clue or comment.

It was simply not in my nature to stay aloof and isolate myself. I had to blend in; Shirla would provide a kind of cover. That could be my excuse, at least. In fact, the gift of candy had brought back the hormonal heat. Her sadness, her graceful sway as she returned to give me my comeuppance, put her round face and dark eyes in a new light. By comparison, the women I had known on Thistledown all seemed deliberate and calculating. The comparison was unfair, of course, because my mood was determined by the setting, and the setting was dreamily exotic and more than a little eerie.

I, too, had stared at the ribs and remains of the palace and felt something I could not express. I, too, had secretly hoped that perhaps the ecoi represented something higher and better. But the death of Martha, made even more poignant by the sad grove of orphans, proved to me, as it might not yet have proven to Shirla, that Lamarckia was no heaven spoiled by the presence of humans.

Life here followed the same round of nature as on any other world. Things lived, competed, succeeded for a time or failed, and died.

We had sullied nothing.

Still, some of Shimchisko's mysticism had communicated itself to me. What was eerie, even frightening, as I lay back in my bunk and chewed the first sweet, was the inevitability of conflict, not just between humans, but between the ecoi and humans. The ecoi were curious. Perhaps we irritated them.

Perhaps they had a plan.

I awoke the next morning early with the starboard watch bell ringing. Those not on watch slept through the clamor. I rose and dressed and chewed the second sweet, back to thinking about my mission.

Without reason, these thoughts carried me back around to Shirla, and our flirtation on Martha's Island seemed absurd and not productive. Virtually all of my relations with women had taken on aspects of the absurd; especially my abortive attempt at bonding.

Naderite women—particularly divaricates—seemed a different breed from Geshel women. Somehow, when I had been younger, before and even a little after shifting my attitudes toward the Geshels, the characteristics of Naderite women stacked up in a different way, different results from the same general blend. I had taken up with Geshel women, and found them charming, but somehow less attractive, more deliberate, even harder. All women, I thought, were calculating—even if their calculations took place somewhere south of their conscious awareness. All women weighed and measured; did not always listen to the results rationally, but made efforts in that direction that most men I knew could not duplicate or understand. Naderite women, however—especially those born to the families and not converted—took on a gentler, more innocent approach to this calculation. They did not make you feel inferior when you did not measure up. They simply did not encourage you, or they let the press of social protections discourage you, all the while convincing you it was not their doing or actual opinion that you were unsuitable.

Uleysa had shown me how ignorant I was. In her gentleness, in her shy reticence and quiet style, I had found all I thought I needed. What I learned from her past lovers—for bonding among Voyager Naderites did not require eschewing all others—was that she presented very different faces to different men. She gave us what she thought we most wanted, and she was usually correct.

But knowing who Uleysa really was . . . that I saw would never be possible. Her attempts to please hid something that disturbed me: a kind of underground disapproval, as if I might be a small boy who needed her, but whom she did not truly respect.

I knew of better places to search for uncertainty and mystery—and disapproval, hidden or overt.

But I still had a weakness for Naderite women.

An old story, I thought as I prepared the equipment and longboat for the third journey to Martha's Island. I saw Shirla, who would not go ashore this time. She regarded me wistfully. She could not know my thoughts. Fortunately, we would not be together enough, or alone often enough, for my attitude to make much difference. And I had my mission. Memories and sense of duty could quell the hormonal heat.

Over the next three days, we tramped the slopes of Mount Jiddermeyer, and I accompanied a team to the summit, where William French surveyed the island, took elevations and compared them with measures made by Baker and Shulago. Nimzhian observed our comings and goings from her porch, accompanied teams on some hikes, and looked over our results. Her critical eye and experience was invaluable.

Working from the maps she and Yeshova had made, we walked the denuded mountain valleys flanking Mount Tauregh and examined the five other palaces, all in ruins, even more decrepit than the first. As Nimzhian had told us, there was very little difference between the debris-filled bowls. The captain took this information with a disappointed persistence I found irritating. If the evidence contradicted theory, I thought, then the theory should be discarded. Keyser-Bach was unwilling to discard his pet theory yet. He even came up with one of those smoke-screen revelations that hide a weak theory in clouds of unverifiability.

"The additional palaces may be decoys," he suggested blithely on the quarterdeck of the *Vigilant* one evening. "Only one may be the real queen's domicile . . . shell . . . whatever."

Salap seemed constantly irritated as the days passed. He barked his instructions to the junior researchers, and received their results with a nod and a scowl. Randall talked with him infrequently, and walked away grumbling that the island was not good for us. "Too damned bleak," he said. "I'd just as soon leave."

Shirla came ashore with Ibert and Kissbegh, but there was little contact between us. I was inland, measuring palace two; and by the time I returned, a day and a half later, she had been sent in a boat to accompany Thornwheel as he surveyed the western wing of the island and its bulbous headland.

In late afternoon, with the junior researchers and Randall off to the eastern wing of the island and the captain on the ship studying the results, Salap came to find me in the grove of orphans, where I was resting and eating a spare lunch.

"I think we should go dip our feet in the spring and talk," he said.

Puzzled about what he was up to, I followed the head researcher through the arborids to the pond, which lay pale and still in the afternoon shadow of Mount Tauregh. "Erwin insists there is little for us here, and he may be right," Salap said, removing his shoes and sitting on the edge of the pond.

The gravelly basin of the pool was empty, visited only by the roots of the scions. Nowhere on Martha's Island would we find any of the profusion of life that Earth's ecosystem would have quickly provided, given such a broad opportunity: no seeds, no microbes, no birds.

"I am afraid the palace chambers will be clueless, as sterile as the rest of this island. I do not enjoy being here, even among these orphans." He gestured at the arborids. "She still has her place," he continued, waving his hand around to the house, where Nimzhian sat alone, dozing on the porch. "She will happily die here. But . . ."

His voice trailed off. He splashed his feet in the water for a moment. "This place makes me feel my mortality like a knife in my ribs. And you?"

I shook my head. "It affects us all differently," I said. The island did not disturb me as much as it did others. Salap had never before confided in me— or to my knowledge, anyone else. I was intrigued. The head researcher never did anything—even engage in casual conversation—without having some goal in mind.

"If this can die, then other ecoi can die as well—and perhaps they do. Can you imagine the effect on Calcutta or Jakarta if the zones were to die?"

"Disastrous," I said.

"French tells me you are the best with the surveying instruments. Better even than my researchers."

"I enjoy the work," I said. "My privilege to help."

"Yes, yes." Salap dismissed that as so much camouflage. "Randall believes you should join the researchers. I have not been satisfied with them in all respects. You have only tagged along so far. Perhaps we should make it formal?"

"I wouldn't want to cause friction," I said.

Salap gave me a piercing look. "Randall also says you seem to have some goal in mind, and it is not necessarily with the ship . . . or with us. But I would like to speed up our work on this island before we all succumb to the bleakness. It is like conducting a huge autopsy. Will you agree?"

Salap looked away from me and stared across the pond, his toe making ripples in the clear water.

"I would be honored," I said.

"Good. Do not worry about crew resentment. The captain will query you about your background again. He is ever proud of his own education. But I believe in native talent as well, as valuable as native ore. I will convince him."

I nodded as humbly as possible. Salap dismissed my act with a wave of his fingers. "Sit here and tell me about this pond. I have my suspicions."

"About the pond?"

"The spring *and* the pond. The orphans. Every so often, sitting here, I smell the faintest traces of hydrogen sulfide. The pool is mildly acidic."

"I've tried not to advance opinions ahead of time . . ." I said.

"Yes?" Salap encouraged.

"We know so little about what an ecos needs to survive."

"I suspect we think along the same lines, Ser Olmy," Salap said, using the respectful form with me for the first time. He waggled his fingers, encouraging more.

"Vulcanism has died here. Mount Jiddermeyer was the last volcano to die. In time, the ecos would leach out whatever trace elements it needs—"

"Chromium, selenium, cobalt, zinc, manganese," Salap suggested. "All found in scion tissues in stable concentrations, whatever the ecos, but seldom found in native soils."

"And for an isolated ecos like Martha, there's no place else to go."

"She withers," Salap said. "But this spring . . ." He dipped his toe again.

"The last source of trace elements. A small fissure below ground, still warm."

"She leaves her orphans here," Salap said. "Perhaps for Nimzhian? A last gift between friends?" He sighed, the closest to sentiment I had seen him come.

I matched Salap's pensive silence for a while.

He looked up, dark eyes steady. "My greatest regret, living on Lamarckia, is the poverty of intellectual variety. It might take us several more generations to build a base of intellect sufficient to understand Lamarckia, to solve the biggest puzzles. When intellect is found, we cannot afford to ignore it." He turned away and pulled his feet from the pond. "I will convince the captain."

The captain had for the past two days been spending most of his time on the ship, taking advantage of unusual radio conditions and listening with some concern to messages between Hsia and Elizabeth's Land. He hadn't revealed the content of these messages to anyone but Randall, but Randall seemed twitchy and drawn as well. It did not take much foresight to recognize signs of growing tension in the small but extended political world of the immigrants.

The pools in the palace chambers had turned dark and opaque with debris from the leaking, brittle walls. One apprentice, Scop, had fallen into the pool when a wall collapsed, giving Randall the idea of cutting holes in the chamber walls to drain them, creating a kind of canal across the bottom of the palace.

I helped set filters to catch solid debris, and Salap took samples of the liquid in all the chambers before the breaching began. The water smelled of mud, coldly musty.

I spent half my time the next week ashore, and half on the boat, where my new status caused some ribbing among the crew, good-natured and otherwise. Shirla was polite, but little more. Was I above her, or still equal to her, in rank? Would I shun a mere A.B., even one with scientific pretensions?

For my part, I was much too busy to do more than sleep and eat on ship, and make preparations for the next trip to the island.

Around a cold camp dinner on the island one evening, we named the palaces after ancient royalty: Cleopatra, Hatshepsut, Catherine, Semiramis, and Isabel. On our twelfth day on the island, Salap and I presided over the draining of Palace One, Cleopatra. At the same time, Randall, Shatro, Cassir, and Thornwheel began to drain the other palaces.

The water from Cleopatra cascaded down the dry, rocky slopes for twenty minutes. A few centimeters of liquid remained in the chamber cells. Rising from the water, surrounded by watery reflections of the sky, lay the remains of the last scions of Martha. Salap climbed along the top of a chamber wall, beneath the curve of a dark ivory roof-beam, snapping pictures of the decrepit, half dissolved remains. We then brought up ropes and climbed into the chambers.

The melancholy that filled us was universal and difficult to explain. In a sodden mass at the bottom of the chambers lay half formed larvae of arborids and phytids. Leached of color, mingling with their silvan cousins, were pterids with thin segmented bodies and leathery wings as delicate as sodden tissue paper, hundreds of them, each no more than twenty centimeters across. Salap lifted one on a piece of close-weave net and said, "These might have been Martha's eyes and ears. I think they are the same as Nimzhian's arthro-pterids."

"Samplers," I suggested.

"Perhaps. But are they all nascent, or were they brought back here for disassembly?"

"Nascent," I said. "Remember, Nimzhian saw the dead scions being tossed out to sea."

"Did Martha still have hope enough to make more children, then?" Salap asked. Ridjel and Kissbegh and Cham, standing in the pools or on the crumbling walls, said little as we passed up fragments of carapace, lengths of rubbery muscle cable, horny claws, brown "bones" arranged as long slender rods or delicate basket weaves, hanks of fibrous insulation. Clearly, some of the larval forms were pelagic. They might have patrolled Martha's offshore waters, guarding against intrusions and maintaining the sterile zone around the island.

Equally clear was the strong relationship between these scions and those in other ecoi; however independent the ecoi might have been, through convergent design or copying, many scions resembled their counterparts.

When Baker and Shulago had visited the island, however, years of isolation had produced many unique scions, some of unknown utility. We found early-stage remains of some of these in Cleopatra's chambers: legged balls connected by tough cables to form ambulatory chains; great drums with ridged grips along the rims and tight-fitting lids, perhaps to haul nutrients from one location to another, or to convey volumes of microscopic scions from the palaces; tiny four-limbed creatures with three equilateral snipping jaws that Salap called muscids.

By the end of the day, when we crawled out of the palace and rested on the barren hillside, we had cataloged seventy different kinds of scions, and found fragments of perhaps twenty more, too difficult to quickly reassemble and visualize. Of the seventy, twenty had been cataloged by Baker and Shulago, and forty-five more by Nimzhian and Yeshova. Five no one had ever seen before.

"Martha was creative to the very last," Salap said, back propped against a boulder, lifting a jar filled with bony fragments and feather-edged scraps.

Early the next morning, Shatro stumbled into camp in the dark, awakening Salap first by nearly falling over him, and then shining his lantern on all of us. "Isabel," he said, sucking in lungfuls of air. "Number five. Ser Randall says come quickly." He knew nothing about what was so important, and his hike in the darkness across the rough terrain had taken his breath away. We packed quickly and refilled our canteens; there had been little rain the last few days, and there were not likely to be water-filled reservoirs in the rocks. Shatro led us back along the path in the dawn light.

Mount Bedouin stood between us and the sunrise, a black serrated triangle against the brightening sky. One small moon rose over the northern slope of the old volcano, and after a kilometer or so, we turned toward the moon and that slope, where Isabel lay. It was a ten-kilometer hike from Cleopatra, through what had once been impenetrable silva, and we reached the fifth palace by late morning.

Randall and his team had drained the chambers and surveyed most of them by the end of the previous day, leaving only three chambers to breach.

With a little energy left over, Randall and Cassir had decided to knock a hole in the wall of an inner chamber, to get a head-start on the next morning's work.

"We were about to return to our tents when Cassir shined a lantern into the chamber," Randall explained, taking us down into the bowl. We carefully avoided the crumbling supports for the roof-beams, crawled through a succession of holes knocked through the chamber walls, and came to the second-to-last chamber.

Randall had no words to describe what they had seen. He entered the chamber reluctantly behind Salap. Above, standing gingerly on the walls, Shimchisko—the only sailor present—waved down at me, but with little energy and no cheer.

"I've never heard of ecoi eating humans," Cassir said, his voice quiet in the shadowed stillness. We splashed carefully between piles of odorless, delicate brown and white bones. From the walls, uncataloged scions the size of soccer balls, shriveled limbs tightly curled close, like dead spiders, hung from twisted brown cords. Drops fell from these into the dark, cloudy puddles below.

Salap pushed aside the piles to see what Cassir and Randall had spied from above. It lay half submerged, empty eye sockets staring at the sky, toothless lower jaw slumped to one side, giving it a grimly joking expression. Salap hesitated before stooping, and held his hands out for several long seconds before touching the round shape, or the scatter of slumped and broken bones and a section of feeble gray carapace, like a tarnished cuirass, covering what might have once been a chest or thorax.

"It's small," Salap said. "Less than a meter long."

"A child," Randall said, his voice shaky.

"Never a child," Salap said, shaking his head. "Not a human child."

"The skull," Shatro said loudly, lips curled as if offended.

"Leg bones and . . . hands," Cassir said.

I knelt beside Salap and turned my attention to the hands. They had five fingers, but the fingers were unjointed, flexible as rubber. The wrist was likewise one unit, and the joint that connected it to a long, two-boned forearm—the bones given one twist around each other, with a smooth cartilaginous material between—was not the joint of any human.

"I've doubted her story from the beginning," Shatro said. "Why would they leave her here? What could she and Yeshova have done—or did she bury her husband—"

"This isn't Yeshova, or any other human, and there's been no murder here," Salap concluded, standing and coughing. "Whatever it is, it isn't fully grown. It's unfinished."

Randall's face became even more pale, his eyes staring at us as if we were dreadful angels. "My God, what, then?"

"Made here," Salap said. He held up his left hand imperiously, palm up, and coughed again into his other hand. Something in the cloudy water irritated him. Then he looked between Randall and me, and said, "Get the largest jars. Throw other specimens out if you have to." He suddenly swore under his breath and glared at the men and woman standing on the walls overhead, and peering through the hole gouged in the chamber. "Not a word of this to Nimzhian, and not a word to anyone on board ship. We will tell them after we've studied the specimen, and in our own good time. Master Randall, will you guarantee this for me?"

Randall nodded, face still pale.

"Good."

Digging around the bottom of the chamber, within an hour we found three of the unfinished scions—if indeed that was what they were. I helped Salap photograph the remains, using our hands and a metric ruler for size comparison, in case the specimens disintegrated, as some already had. "Send down some hot wax," Salap instructed as the glass jars were lowered. I filled the jars with water from the chamber, and one by one, we lifted the fragile remnants and lowered them delicately into the jars, through the muddy fluid to the bottom.

As he sealed the jars with paraffin, Salap looked up at me and said, "A fair imitation, no?" He gave me a grin that seemed more than a little ghoulish.

We stored the specimen jars in a small volcanic cave near the beach, out of the sun, and covered them with wet tarps to keep them cool. Leaving us to guard them, Salap and Randall took the longboat to the *Vigilant* and spent several hours offshore. Shatro and Cassir became involved in an argument about what the humanlike remains signified. Shatro was arguing for some sort of conspiracy between Nimzhian and the ecos queen; he had made some ridiculous elaborations on the captain's obsession.

Shatro, I saw, would always limit himself to the opinions of those in authority, and rather than improve upon those opinions, he would make them seem ridiculous.

Shimchisko had fallen into a silent funk, head bowed, staring at the sand between his feet as he sat near the cave entrance. I sat beside him, concerned that his cynical cheer had vanished so completely.

"Olmy, this is the worst thing that's ever happened," he confided.

"Why?"

"It's going to tear us apart. Salap can't keep it secret forever. Randall doesn't like it; I don't like it." He shook his hand loosely at Cassir and Shatro, as if dismissing them. "The first time we're in port . . ."

I was content just to listen for the moment. In truth, I was stunned myself.

"It shakes my faith," Shimchisko said. "First, that this island has died. Now, that it was trying to *make* one of us . . ." He shrugged. Shimchisko was crafty, but not a quick thinker about large issues. "Why?" he stared directly at me.

"I don't know," I said.

"They *all* sample us," Shimchisko continued, frowning deeply. "They steal from each other—are they going to steal from us now?"

The captain came ashore with Salap an hour later. They entered the cave alone and Salap showed him the jars and described what was in them. When they emerged from the cave the captain seemed feverish. His face was flushed and he lurched a little and took Salap's arm. Looking at Randall and me, he said in a gruff voice, "We need to set sail in two days. We'll take a direct course to Jakarta. We don't know what we have. We could stay here and study for years. Primary science. But we don't have the luxury. Tell Nimzhian we'll be leaving. We'll deliver the supplies we promised tomorrow."

"Should we tell *her* anything?" Shatro asked, deep into his suspicions of conspiracy. Everyone ignored him, and he lowered his head, staring at us sullenly.

The captain whispered in Randall's ear. Randall turned to Shimchisko and Shatro, lifted his hand, and swung it to include Cassir and me in the sweep of his orders. "Back to the boat. We need to talk in private."

Thornwheel did not seem happy to be left behind.

"Let Olmy stay," Salap said. "I'll need him." The captain blinked at him, but did not argue. When Shatro's eyes met mine, he closed them and looked away in pure disgust. He joined the others as they walked toward the captain's boat.

"I wish I could talk to the Good Lenk or some of his officers about this," the captain continued. He pounded the black sand with his walking stick, staring out across the blue expanse of sterile sea. The sand made little barking noises with each poke. "What the radio messages say is that Lenk is on a ship to Jakarta right now. Brion himself is going to meet him there. There's going to be a conference. For now, we can't talk to Lenk, even if the airways are clear."

Randall had apparently heard of this, but Salap had not.

"Why should we consult with Lenk?" Salap asked cautiously, puzzled by the captain's line of reasoning.

Keyser-Bach's face reddened to a shade of sienna, his cheeks and chin a brighter pink. "We have a responsibility here, and not just as scientists."

Realization dawned on Salap but still eluded me. I had not worked with the captain very long and did not know his attitudes. Salap was ahead of me and Randall as well.

"You perceive this as a threat?" Salap asked.

"What else would it have been, if the ecos had survived? And for that matter, how do we know it hasn't merely gone dormant? Hidden the queen somewhere, *encysted* to ride out some condition or another . . ."

"I do not agree these are possibilities," Salap said. "The grove is truly orphaned."

"The danger is immense," the captain said. "We've learned more on this expedition than any before us, in all the decades we've been on Lamarckia. And what we've learned *burns*."

"Perhaps it is innocuous!" Salap argued, heat rising. Randall saw the argument coming and tried to intervene, but Salap and the captain both raised their hands, fending him off.

"Ser Salap, how can it be *innocuous* or *innocent* that an ecos seeks to mimic us?"

"They have always been curious!" Salap said. "We are strangers, a new kind of scion, but we do not evoke the responses that guard against thieves or spies . . . We do not smell as a scion from another ecos would smell, perhaps. The samplers study our shape, take samples of every individual, carry them . . . someplace, we assume for analysis. But these samples are much more enigmatic than the tissues of a scion from another ecos. The language of our genes is different in its very grammar. It takes a long time to puzzle out, even for a master . . . or a mistress." Salap's eyes burned with enthusiasm, as if he expressed his own secret dream or nightmare—a religious hope, perhaps. "Somewhere, there is a part of the ecos, a seed-mistress or queen, or many of them, examining the problem, studying our genetic material, laboring over the puzzles of human DNA, trying to understand the functions it codes for and duplicate them, beginning with the simplest proteins. They have so many problems to solve—there is an immense gulf between a megacytic scion and a many-celled organism."

I pictured secret factories hidden in the silvas—perhaps in organic fortresses much like the palaces—where unknown intelligences worked tirelessly for decades . . .

We might as well call them queens.

"That much is obvious," the captain said. "They feel threatened by us. We steal their scions, we cut them down and make *ships* of them, or we harvest them and eat them. We have the potential to fill Lamarckia and take all resources . . . A queen would sense this, with whatever instinct she has. She would know. Ser Salap, didn't you expect to find something like the palaces, someday?"

"Yes, yes, of course! It was my great hope," Salap said.

"I know what we have to do," Keyser-Bach insisted. "We cannot take chances. We must make certain that Martha is dead."

Salap seemed ready to spit. He walked back and forth on the beach, glaring at the captain, at us. "You would have us destroy all we have studied?"

"We keep our own samples, to show Lenk. But we burn the grove and try to find the hidden queen."

"There *is* no hidden queen!" Salap shouted. He had lost all of his restraint and spittle flecked his black mustache. "Martha is dead!"

The captain flinched at this outburst. He set his stick down on the sand

and squatted, laying his arms across his knees. Salap knelt beside him and put a hand on his shoulder.

"It is not necessary to act with such brashness," Salap said, some of his calm returning. "Whatever Martha set out to do, clearly it has come to a stop for now. It appears at least to be dead, or so weakened and reduced that it might as well be dead. We have time to think and to consult. We go to Jakarta, we explain our discovery to Lenk. You can request an audience, even when he is busy with Brion. And you can ask Lenk and his councilors what should be done.

"They cannot deny us now," he said. "Our own curiosity is not a luxury. We must answer our questions. We *must* understand these processes."

The captain's face had come back from its dangerous color, and his anger and anxiety had cooled. "Do you think Nimzhian knew?" he asked.

"Shatro is a fool. She knew nothing," Salap said. While the captain had cooled, Salap had become infected by an enthusiasm that he took some pains to hide. He knew he could win this argument and gain an advantage in a larger war. He approached me and said, loudly enough for the others to hear, "How ambitious are you, Ser Olmy?"

"I'm eager to learn," I said.

"The captain and I, and the master Randall, have tried for ten years to make our case, that ignorance is dangerous, that we live on a dangerous world, however calm and benign it may seem. There are many more dangers than starvation."

The captain looked up at his chief researcher with an expression mixing irritation, puzzlement, and wonder, one eye squinted, one hand pulling on his chin. Whatever his connections, Keyser-Bach had never been much of a political thinker. Salap, however, more than made up for that lack.

"We have fought and been denied too many times," Salap said. "Our victory with this expedition—one ship, and a crew barely adequate—was a small one. But Martha has left a legacy more frightful than anything seen on Lamarckia. And more precious to us than any mountain of metals."

The captain returned to the ship with Shimchisko, Shatro, and Cassir. The necessity for silence had been impressed on all by Salap. Shimchisko took the warning with a somber expression.

As they pushed the boat off, the captain said, "Give my farewells to Ser Nimzhian."

"I will," Salap said.

"Tell her . . ."

"I will tell her what she needs to hear," Salap said. The captain seemed satisfied, and relieved not to have to come up with the words himself.

"Why doesn't he want to talk with her?" I asked Salap and Randall. Randall shrugged, but Salap's energy had spilled over, and as he went to prepare Nimzhian for our departure, he gave a long discourse on the captain's character.

"He is a scholar," he said. "He is a shy man, actually, and sometimes a fearful one. He was raised by stern parents, as I was, but by and large my parents were correct; his were a little mad, I think. He has a fondness for hidden motivations that surfaces during the worst times. It's made his talks with Lenk's administers even more difficult. I believe he still holds the opinion that Nimzhian must be involved with this."

"How could she be?" I asked.

"It is not my opinion, so I will not explain or defend it," Salap said. "Although Shatro expresses it succinctly. Sometimes, he is like a younger, stupider version of the captain, with few of his redeeming qualities." He glared at Randall. "You should not have brought him aboard."

"Well, perhaps Ser Olmy makes up for my lapse in that regard," Randall said.

"We will see," Salap said.

Nimzhian seemed taken completely by surprise. "There's so much more to study," she said to Salap, her face wrinkled with concern and disappointment. "Surely we don't have the broad picture yet."

"No," Salap conceded. "Yet greater storms are brewing. We believe our time is better spent elsewhere."

She walked to the door of the porch. For a moment, I thought she might cry. "Half our drawings and paintings are still here."

"They will be picked up tomorrow. And your supplies will be replenished from ship's stores."

"I need so little, actually. I've enjoyed this company, all this talk. You're going to Jakarta next?"

"With perhaps one or two other stops, if the situation permits."

Nimzhian sat in her graceful woven chair. "Is the captain coming back?"

"He expresses his deepest regrets, and says he will never forget our meeting, our association. Your work brightens our expedition."

"Tell the captain I will miss his company. I admire his dedication. My husband would have enjoyed all of you." She frowned and shook her head. "You seemed so interested in the palaces, so eager to understand them. Why, they could easily take years to study."

"It is not entirely my wish that we leave," Salap said. "As I said, there are pressures."

"When you leave, will the Brionists come?" Nimzhian asked, her blue eyes wide. She lifted her hand and Salap immediately clasped it in both of his, a courtly gesture. Randall stood in the doorway, tall and stooped, lost in his own thoughts.

"I doubt they will stop here if they see the island is barren," Salap said.

"But if scientists arrive, Brionist scientists, would you mind if I am candid with them, as well?"

"Not at all," Salap said. "It is your duty. I hope truth will make us all reasonable. This is no time for division and war."

The third boat had returned, carrying Shirla, Meissner, Ry Diem, and Thornwheel. The replacement party had hiked from the beach to the orphan grove and met us beside the pond as we left the house.

Shirla and I had a moment to talk as Salap relayed instructions to Thornwheel.

"We passed the captain's boat," she said. "He said we're leaving, but to come ashore and keep Nimzhian company. He looks proper serious. Anything you can tell us, now that you're rank?"

I tried for a conciliatory smile. She gave in return a sharp sniff.

"Shatro looked like he wanted to kill somebody, and Shimchisko like he wanted to die. Is everybody crazy?"

I shook my head. "Pressures from across the seas," I said, "and that's the main reason."

"Brionists?"

I nodded.

"Where are we going, then?"

"To Jakarta. After that, to Athenai."

"No lush silvas for me and thee, hm, Olmy, *sir*?"

She was clearly in a dirty mood. I found my own mood too complicated to tolerate any unpleasantry. I patted her arm and got in step behind Salap as we left the valley. Nimzhian watched after us, mouth open, head shaking slightly from side to side. Then she fell to talking with Shirla and Ry Diem.

We moved the specimens from the cave to the second boat and rowed them over mildly choppy waters to the ship. There, we carried them under blankets to the captain's quarters, where they were stowed in a locker behind the boxes of specimens already put aboard. A padlock was provided, and a bolt, and Randall installed them and handed the key to Salap.

"We will sacrifice one specimen to a general anatomical study this evening," Salap said. "Olmy, you will assist."

I went topside and observed the starboard watch performing their afternoon duties, clambering up the trees to prepare the sails for the next leg of the voyage. I felt a strong urge to join them. But I had made significant progress, and there was no returning to the comforts of an apprentice's life.

Twilight would be on us soon, and the sailor's hours of rest.

I thought of the gate opener's words in the Way. *I look for things of interest to humans, Ser Olmy, and I find them.*

If the captain was going to have an audience with Lenk, perhaps I could come along. I would be that much closer to finding the clavicle.

At dawn, one last party of twelve went to the island to deliver Nimzhian's promised supplies. I accompanied the party on the longboat. Shatro seemed resigned this morning to the shift in ranks. He sat on his thwart and pulled his oar with apparent good humor. Shimchisko, Kissbegh, Cham, and French the navigator were also on the boat. French wanted to check a few last elevations.

Nimzhian sat on her porch, barely glancing at us as we deposited boxes of food and supplies. Kissbegh and Cham began to stow the boxes beneath a shelter behind the house. French spoke to the old woman, but she merely nodded, saying little in return. He then went off into the interior for a few hours, accompanied by Shatro.

Nimzhian stood up after they had left and waved for Shirla and me to come up on the porch.

"I've been doing a great deal of thinking," she said. "Could you relay my thoughts to Salap? They are not very complicated, certainly not complete."

"I'll try," I said.

"You're junior among the researchers, aren't you?" Nimzhian asked.

"Yes."

Shirla gave me a wry, brief smile.

"I was junior aboard the *Hanno*, as well. Marrying Yeshova was a good social move for me. You and I haven't spoken much, but I feel it's right to talk with you. You'll take my thoughts to Randall and the captain. The captain . . . may not be very clear about what is actually happening here. As for you, my dear Shirla, it's been so wonderful speaking with the women . . ."

Nimzhian's eyes moistened. "I must stay here. I'll miss the company, but my life is here. Yeshova is still here, his spirit."

Shirla took her hand and stroked it. Nimzhian leaned her head back and closed her eyes. She seemed to have aged ten years since we arrived. Duty had kept her going this long; I wondered if she would pass on one final secret, and then be ready to die.

"Do you realize how simple and primitive all life on Lamarckia is? How delicately balanced? Yeshova and I, the more we explored and learned, became more and more astonished at the delicacy and crudity of Martha. It is all like a dream. And then we wake up."

"Why like a dream?" Shirla asked.

"There is no competition or synergy between animals and plants to propel change. All change comes from within, from the observers, whatever and wherever they may be—queens or factories or palace wombs. And there's precious little competition between the ecoi. Day in, day out, nearly all of life on this planet struggles simply to get enough energy to stay alive . . . Something is missing, some vital strategy or trick. Lamarckia may someday blossom. But are the hidden designers creative enough to supply what is missing?"

"Maybe *we're* what's missing," Shirla said. She did not know about the half formed skeletons. "But now we're here. The queens—the observers have to learn how to use us."

"Admirably homocentric," Nimzhian said softly, eyes staring between us dreamily. "That is part of *our* strength, to always place ourselves at the center. But despite all recent evidence . . ." She looked at me sharply. "Despite that, I do not think we are the missing element. I believe it is a technique, a trick, none of the ecoi have stumbled across. Poor Martha—so reliant on the stingy trace elements . . . Martha did not have the strength to survive when things changed."

She sat forward now, and gripped Shirla's hand tightly. "What is missing on Martha's Island, and everywhere else we've visited on Lamarckia?"

"What?" I asked.

"Green," she said. "Brilliant, lovely green. Shirla, you were born here, and you spend little time thinking about Earth. But Earth was a *green* world."

CHAPTER TWELVE

For two days after we left Martha's Island, the ocean overside and to the horizon lay glass-smooth and the still air hung hot and wet and smelled stale. Thunderheads towered in the west. Each evening, chores done—choke-oiling the decks, tightening the standing rigging yet again to take in a few centimeters slack (mostly, I think, a figment of Soterio's imagination), and spreading drag nets to catch samples (the ocean here was barren and the nets came up empty)—the crew not on night watch ate cold freechunk and dried fruit and drank mat fiber beer in the mess, then lay out on the deck as they had the day before, as they might the next day and for a thousand years after. Each took a piece of the deck for his or her territory. As they lay, flat and still, they watched the few unfortunates still in the rigging or hauling on sheets and braces and halyards, and spoke softly among themselves.

I stood on the puppis, waiting for the stifling laboratory below to cool. The researchers met in the laboratory next to the captain's cabin each day several hours after sunset, working in the coolest portion of the night, sometimes into the next morning, dissecting and measuring the components of a humanoid skeleton. This night, however, the air on deck was not much better than the air below. We all hoped for a cooling breeze, but no relief came.

Randall did not expect the discovery to stay secret for long, and it did not. The ship was dispirited. Randall sensed it; the captain was too preoccupied to care. Shimchisko carried the burden of his knowledge badly. While not telling the truth of the matter even to Ibert, his best friend, he had let on that something very bad had been found on Martha's Island, something important to all of them. The crew picked Ry Diem and the sailmaker Meissner—surrogate mother and father as they had become—to extract more from the captain and the researchers.

I felt guilty at not volunteering the information, but my allegiances had shifted, taking me away from the crew. Ry Diem and Meissner petitioned Randall, and Randall spoke to the captain in private. Finally he gathered a meeting of the entire crew and provided full details of what had been found on Martha's Island, in the palaces of the still-theoretical queens.

They were still digesting this news. It changed the way they thought about Lamarckia.

For Keyser-Bach, I thought, this voyage was at an end. He would sacrifice it for the chance at a larger, grander expedition. The captain was seldom seen without an expression of shrewd calculation, already adding up the pieces of equipment he might order made by Lenk's craftsman, or commandeer from around Elizabeth and Tasman. We had only to proceed to Jakarta and report our findings to Lenk's officers. The captain's cause—the cause of science and exploration on Lamarckia—would be elevated beyond all expectations.

At midnight, Salap climbed up onto the puppis, weary and oppressed by the heat, bare to the waist, brown skin shining in the lamplight. "We might as well get started. It isn't going to get any cooler." Shatro, Cassir, Thornwheel, and I followed him below, to resume our studies of the homunculi.

Cutting cross-sections through the limbs, we found fibrous polysaccharides, not true calcium-rich bone. The "head" was made of three sections, and where the brain would have rested in a human, there lay a soggy lump of oily tissue supported by a mat of thin, translucent fibers. Cassir, who had had extensive medical training in Jakarta, commented: "Whatever Martha learned from sampling humans, she didn't learn how to make a brain."

The captain performed this work with grim resolve. He did not like these poor imitations. They were his ticket, his shining hope, but it was obvious he regarded them less with scientific dispassion than revulsion.

Shatro, Thornwheel, and Cassir arranged these dissections so that I performed the simplest and least elevated tasks. I made sketches of the separated pieces of the pseudoskeleton, laid thin sheets of gridded paper over them, and compared the dimensions with those for human bones. I fetched water for all, and mixed solutions for preserving the specimens.

After another few hours of work, Salap dismissed the researchers. I came up on deck and found the crew as I had left them, sprawled under the bright early-morning stars, the double oxbow rising, one lone moon casting a wan light in the west, sinking fast. They were restless, and most were awake and still talking.

I heard Kissbegh's scratchy tones and walked forward to listen. "If we're all going to be replaced by scions," he said, "then why did Lenk bring us here?"

"He didn't know," Ry Diem said with weary disdain.

"No, I mean, we've all been taught we owe so much to Able Lenk, for taking us away from the 'distortions and presumptions of Thistledown.' That's what my teachers called it."

"They were right," Shimchisko said. "Thistledown would have been worse."

"But we're all going to die here," Kissbegh said. "How could that be better, and why didn't Lenk at least *sense* what he was getting his people into? Aren't great people supposed to be lucky?"

"We don't know we're going to die," I heard Shirla say. She sounded sleepy.

"If the zones rise up against us . . ." Kissbegh persisted.

"We don't know that, either. We don't know what Martha's queens wanted to do," Shirla said. Her voice carried through the night, clear and sensible. I wanted to go down among them and sit next to her. We had not spoken for some days.

I felt more at home with the sailors than I had with any other people in my adult life—but I was no longer one of them. Their talk seemed at once naive and perfect—the talk of humans who lived their lives in a direct and simple fashion, without the kinks and knots I had twisted into mine.

"I wish I had a woman who loved me back home," Kissbegh said. "I've always been too much the clown to make friends or attract serious women."

"I'm your friend," Ridjel said.

"You're no woman," Shankara observed placidly.

"Thank our fate," Ry Diem murmured.

"Yes, you're my friend," Kissbegh said, "but you're here, and if I die, you'll probably die, too. I want someone alive to remember me."

"My wife's a good woman," Shankara said. "But she's a perfect sailor's wife. Right now that makes me sad."

"Why?" Shirla asked.

"If I don't come back, she'll miss me for a while, but she'll get along. My being gone won't tear her heart out."

"It's the way," Ry Diem said, in a voice intended to soothe.

"I'd like someone to always miss me, always think of me," Shankara continued. "My wife will find another husband and he'll fill her heart as much as I've ever filled it. Not that she's uncaring . . ."

"If I had a good woman on shore," Ridjel said, "I'd love her so hard and so long she'd never forget me. Her heart would break if I didn't come home."

"All memory's like this ocean," Ry Diem said. A short silence followed as everyone thought this over, and then decided to ignore it—it could not be riddled quickly enough.

"Will Lamarckia remember us?" Shimchisko asked.

The talk turned to how much Lamarckia knew about each of us, and how much the queen (or now, the *queens*) of Elizabeth's Land or Petain would keep us in some sort of biological memory if we did not return to Calcutta or Jakarta . . . or, by implication, if they actually did get around to replacing us. Shimchisko began to speculate wildly. He wondered whether they would duplicate us so completely we might live again, even if we died.

Randall stepped up behind me. "They're getting far too metaphysical," he complained in a low voice. "Shimchisko's become a very religious fellow. But it's infecting us all."

I nodded, but asked myself who, back on Thistledown, would ever remember me . . .

On Lamarckia, I would leave no impression at all.

My homesickness for Thistledown had become a dark shadow, mingling doubt and dream, wish and self-disgust. The flaws in my armor multiplied and were glaringly apparent: I did not know who or what I was, my past seemed a confused jumble, my present a mess I would never successfully resolve.

If I was any example, I doubted Lamarckia's ecoi could learn anything useful from humans, yet Nimzhian's last words before we left the island haunted me.

Lamarckia's marvels were truly simple and delicate, as if she had suffered some natural handicap at the beginning of her time. She had flowered in a wonderful but hesitant way.

Our natural passengers—the selected bacteria and viruses humans found valuable—had left no mark on Lamarckia's ecoi. But we ourselves were a kind of infection, injected into the planet's tissues by the most sophisticated of delivery systems—the Way itself, an infinitely long syringe with infinitely many openings. What would I report to my superiors in the Axis City and on Thistledown, if I could make a report now?

Lamarckia is still healthy. But humans and the ecoi will change each other immeasurably, and very soon.

Lamarckia is not for us.

We are far too robust.

We come from a green planet.

I did not have the luxury of time. To preserve Lamarckia, I had to act quickly. I had to locate Lenk's clavicle and report my findings to the Hexamon soon.

Fifteen days out from Martha's Island, our batteries drained, our windscrews idle, sharp-eyed Ibert stood his watch on the maintree top. Late in the morning, he spotted something on the horizon, and called down to the master. I sat repairing a dragnet on the forecastle deck near the bowsprit.

Soterio pulled himself out of his hammock belowdecks and groggily followed Randall forward. The captain stayed below. Randall surveyed the horizon following Ibert's directions—fine on the starboard quarter. I stood and shaded my eyes against the steady beat of the sun. At first, I could not see anything, but soon I resolved a thin line of smoke, and then another.

"No land here," Ry Diem said, coming forward. "Couldn't be fires." Shirla and Shankara followed, then Cham and Shimchisko. Soterio trailed Randall like a faithful dog, a worried expression on his dark-bearded features.

Salap emerged on deck, as elegant and seemingly unconcerned as ever. He glanced at the group of us near the bow, then sauntered around the skylight to join Randall.

"Is it a racer?" Soterio asked.

"Racers don't smoke," Randall said. "Two ships. They're burning something."

"Steamships, then," Salap said.

"Likely."

"Brionist," Soterio said, hoping he would be contradicted.

"Sure as hell not out of Calcutta or Jakarta or Athenai," Randall said. "Get the captain up here."

Keyser-Bach came on deck in an apron, hands still gloved. He shed the apron and gloves and handed them to Thornwheel, then took the binoculars from Randall. After a few minutes' scrutiny, he said, "No flags. Of course, that may not mean anything." He looked up and shook his head. "We didn't set our flag after leaving Martha's Island. They're ten miles away. They've seen us." He lowered the binoculars. "They're turning to cross our course."

Shatro took the apron and gloves from Thornwheel and handed them to Cassir. They all needed something to do. Nobody spoke for a few minutes. Keyser-Bach watched the lines of smoke with a face as blank as a child's. Then he pulled his chin with three fingers and said, "Ser Soterio, bring her about and we'll hope for some wind."

I looked up at the sails. A puff of wind had struck my back, and I saw the limp, sad cloths bat and slap. Every morning at this hour, winds of varying speed and direction would slip up on us, forming fine small chop on the water but neither refreshing the air nor offering much speed to the *Vigilant*. The wind did not mean much. There had been no good wind for four days.

The captain, however, started to whistle through his teeth. He strode to the bowsprit and watched the four of us gathered there. Soterio followed him and said, "There isn't enough wind to bring her about."

"There will be," the captain said, pulling the whistle back through his teeth, then sucking on the teeth speculatively, making a small, sharp hiss-squeak.

"He can feel it," Randall said. They both looked up at the sails, and for a moment, I felt as if I were in a dream, an entertaining muse about being lost among superstitious savages somehow more deeply connected to nature, able to feel the presence of gods and spirits . . . and wind.

"Can't you catch it?" the captain asked, as casually as if we were discussing tonight's dinner in the mess.

"The sea has the color," Randall said.

Soterio peered over the gunwale, then straightened. He looked lost.

"If those are Brionists, and they're riding steam, they don't need any wind," Shatro said, just to be part of the conversation.

The captain raised his binoculars and peered southwest, four points abaft the port beam. "There it is," he said.

We all turned. A bank of thick cloud had risen beneath the southernmost thunderheads, like a predator stalking immense gray giraffes.

"We've been carried into its circle," Salap said. "It's far north on its accustomed track."

The captain raised his hands to his chest and gripped them there, supplicating.

Salap sat on the butt of the bowsprit. "It's been stroking us with its feelers for three days," he said. "The little puffs of wind each morning."

"What are you going to do?" Soterio asked, licking his lips and glancing around the small circle.

"Nothing right now," the captain answered. "We'll wait until we see who's going to catch us first."

"There'll be more wind," Salap said. "Enough to maneuver. If we wait here, the storm will suck us toward it."

The captain handed the binoculars around for us to see. Shatro took them from Thornwheel; I was still ranked last. He handed them to me after a few seconds, face pale. I looked.

"What do you see?" Salap asked.

"Sparkles," I said. "Like mica flecks in water." I swung the glasses around.

Beneath the lines of smoke I could make out two funnels, one each sur-
mounting long white hulls. The steamships were sailing at about ten knots.
They'd be upon us within an hour and a half.

The storm's cloudy mass was perhaps forty miles away. The feelers, as
Salap called them, had already gained strength.

"Should we hail them on the radio?" Randall asked.

"No," the captain said. "I do not doubt where they're from, or why they're
here. We're a prize if they can catch us." He jerked abruptly, muscles taut in
his jaw and neck, and gave his orders. The sails bellied and Soterio immediately pulled the starboard watch together to bring the ship about. We
would face into the wind and tack across a course headed due south. The
steamships would see the storm and perhaps decide they did not want us
so much.

Soterio called out the port watch. Salap crossed the deck and put one
hand on my shoulder, the other on Thornwheel's. "This is truly going to be
what the captain calls primary science," he said. The wind pulled his black
beard and hair. "I will station all my researchers around the ship, and one
in the tops . . . Ser Shatro, please join Ibert on the maintree."

Shatro put on a face of unexpected hurt, but went to the shrouds. He
had climbed shrouds before, but not for some time. "Ser Olmy, you will stay
at the bow with Ser Thornwheel. Ser Cassir, you and I will stand by the bulwarks port and starboard amidships. We will record wind speed and direction, and anything else that happens to be interesting." He pulled slim
paper notebooks from his pocket, and small carbon pencils.

The captain kept turning the glasses from the steamships to the storm.

"It is going to be very complex," Salap said. "The sparkles in the clouds
must be how it regulates its temperature and pressure. I suggest they are
very light tissues of different reflectivity born by winds controlled and directed by formations in the ocean."

A sharp gust hit us and the ship shuddered, swung around by the fore
course and jibs like a horse on a rope. When the wind was on our port beam,
Soterio ordered the jibs furled, the fore course reefed and the spanker raised.
We practically spun about in the water.

"If we end up in the thick of it," Salap said, "we can learn how it keeps
itself going." He clapped the captain on the shoulder and walked aft with
Cassir. The captain did not seem to notice. The ship heeled over ten degrees.

Salap lurched on the tilted deck, yet still kept some dignity, his long coat flapping out like a tail. Cassir grabbed a brace for support and Soterio snatched it from him. "Not that one, *sir*," he said, chin jutting.

"Sorry," Cassir murmured, and took his position.

Sails set, Soterio put Shirla at the wheel, replacing an exhausted Kissbegh, and stood behind her. Now came the waiting. The distance between the steamships and *Vigilant* briefly increased. Then they turned as one and followed, applying more steam. The smoke from their stacks billowed thick and gray like the breaths of two tiny volcanoes on the head of the sea.

"It's a chase, all right," Soterio called from behind the wheel. Thornwheel, standing beside me, braced himself as the wind kicked at the ship from ahead with increased force. The deck lurched. Soterio ordered both watches to unfurl all courses and the lower topgallants and swing the yards about to take full advantage of running close-hauled. The captain was intent on narrowing the angle of each tack, to give us maximum speed away from the steamships.

But it was clear from the beginning that we were not going to win this particular race. The storm grew tall and showed long, thick black skirts; the sea became a lively green all around the ship, flecked by vigorous tall whitecaps. We veered onto the next tack and the ship heeled to starboard. After half an hour, with the storm barely thirty miles away and the wind increasing to twenty knots, the captain kept the ship on a steady course, running on a beam reach at ten knots, clearly hoping to round the northern extent of the storm and slip away from both storm and pursuing ships. But the ships were not dissuaded by the advance of the storm.

"They're fools," Thornwheel muttered. "They don't know this monster."

"Will the captain take us into the storm?" Thornwheel asked. "You've sailed with him longer than I have."

"He might," I said.

"But it terrifies him," Thornwheel said, raising his voice over the hum and whistle of the wind in the rigging.

I shook my head and smiled. "Better that than Brionists. He's no coward. But he wants to get this ship to Jakarta."

On the main deck, Cassir and Salap stood by the rails port and starboard. Aloft, Shatro clung miserably to the shrouds, and Ibert stared ahead and to the west intently, shouting observations to the captain and Soterio that we could not hear. Randall came forward, grinning like a happy dog. "Breath and Fates," he shouted at us, "we're in the claws now, if not the teeth. Time to show more courage, eh, Olmy?" I had never seen him in such a mood.

We tacked back and forth for another hour. The storm towered above us, having swallowed and decapitated the thunderheads, which spread out above the dark gray and brilliant white mass in long separate streamers of cloud. These were quickly dissipated.

I wondered if the captain had miscalculated. We might soon be faced with winds sweeping around from behind, hitting us from the starboard quarter, and we'd have to fight to keep from being drawn into the body of the storm.

Somehow, it did not seem to matter. I had always known the triviality of my life, something not common among my peers, surrounded by the thick armor of Thistledown's immensity. I had always calculated the risks taken against my basically ephemeral nature, gambling the benefit of sensation and knowledge against the danger. To fall into this storm would be an experience to remember, and if that memory lasted only a short time, fell quickly into oblivion, at least there was the real moment of experience . . . Like nothing I would ever have seen on Thistledown.

I held this brave attitude, stalwart and admirable, for only a few minutes before my unfettered body told me, without allowing for debate, that it was *terrified*. I sweated despite the chill of the winds, and my hands trembled. Thornwheel squinted west and then north, and tied a short coiled rope around the butt of the bowsprit. For a minute, I ran around the deck looking for another coil, cursing my luck, and finally found one hanging from a belaying pin. I wrapped it around the bowsprit and squatted on the deck. Along the length of the ship, sailors stationed on deck were tying similar lines from bulwark to bulwark, or to the hatch tiedowns and the trees. Looking aft, as the fore and main courses were reefed to give the helm more control, I saw Shirla at the wheel, and Soterio behind her, and felt a stab of regret.

Then my calm returned. There was nothing more I could do. I held my pencil and notebook and clenched my jaw. Thick spats of rain hit the deck and blew across the sails.

Behind us, the flying jib tore with a loud bang and was carried out beyond the jibboom like a mad ghost. Kissbegh and Ridjel leaped past us and climbed out along the bowsprit to cut it loose.

Over my shoulder, I saw the sky suddenly dip below the bow, as if pushing hard on the horizon of rough water. The ship shivered and leaped. The sky suddenly retreated at the rise of a wall of water; the bow plunged into a trough between waves and we nosed into that green wall. It slammed against me and I snapped to the end of my line like a fish and seemed to half swim, half crawl along the submerged deck. Then the water fell away like a heavy curtain and sloshed to all sides, running in rivers, and I spread out on my back on the deck, coughing water, wiping my face. My pencil and notebook were gone. Forward, Thornwheel clung to the rail, hair in his eyes, sputtering. Kissbegh climbed back along the bowsprit, very lucky to be alive; Ridjel stood on the jibboom like a sea sprite, arms wrapped around the forestays, and I laughed at his grace and presumption.

"Shit on you!" Kissbegh shouted at me, scrambling onto the deck and helping Ridjel over the tangle of ropes. "Shit on you all!"

Thornwheel got to his feet despite the pitching of the deck. The waves had come on us so suddenly that the ship took several long, tense minutes to turn into them. Both watches reefed and furled sails frantically. The fore course had ripped halfway and snapped its ragged tails like a cracking whip. The wind now came strong from the starboard quarter, as I had feared, drawing us into the storm.

I could see nothing of the steamships. We had made our gamble, and chosen what suddenly seemed the greater of two evils. I could picture myself surviving among pirates; surviving the storm seemed much less certain.

"How many knots?" Thornwheel shouted. He still gripped his notebook, though it was sodden through.

I watched the spray being whipped from the dripping gunwales, and from the forestays and jib sheets. "Forty," I guessed.

Thornwheel tucked one arm under his rope where it was tied to the butt of the bowsprit, squatted, and wrote the figure meticulously into the limp notebook. Then he looked up and cried out, "What time is it?"

I did not know.

Our world seemed confined to the forecastle deck. The storm and sudden waves had knocked loose all sense of minutes or hours. I could not get to my slate, still secure—I hoped—in my bunk a few meters below. "Afternoon," I said. Thornwheel screwed up his face and shook the dripping notebook in disgust.

The wind quickly grew to fifty knots. The *Vigilant* was now rigged for a storm, all but her fore and main courses furled and those reefed close to their yards, straining alarmingly at their gaskets. I could see men and women running along the deck, a few descending the shrouds with exquisite slowness, hanging on for life, but could not pick out their features through the stinging spray. Personality did not seem to matter in the noise. So long as I kept my position, I could not be accused of shirking my duty— and that mattered suddenly more than I would have believed it could. I *did* owe everything to my shipmates, my captain, the ship itself; if I did not owe them all, then I was not part of something strong and capable of surviving. I might as well be lost in the foam on the waves. I could picture that vividly. I saw myself surrounded by volumes of cold water. My lungs halted in the sudden whoop of spray-heavy wind and my body thought I was drowning; it no longer trusted my senses.

The captain sidled forward, gripping the ropes tied at regular intervals between the mast bits and the gunwales. Salap followed, and at one point we shipped another sea across the port bow and both of them had their legs swept out from under. Standing again, tightening their safety ropes about their waists, they made their way to the forecastle desk, climbed up, and came to the bows.

Salap saw that I had no notebook and shook his head sadly. "Ser Olmy, how will you pass this on to posterity?" he chided. "I hope you've kept a record," he shouted to Thornwheel.

"We don't know the time," Thornwheel said.

That stopped Salap. He looked at the captain, who looked at all of us, and then broke into a braying laugh. "My god, it's half past sixteen hundred," Keyser-Bach said. "I think." We all seemed to be made equals by the storm, like small children at play.

"Cassir just dropped a note stuffed into a spare deadeye. Damned near brained the mate," Salap said. "They claim to see still water ahead, about a mile off the starboard bow."

"They're out of their minds," Keyser-Bach yelled, straining to see through the spray from waves slapping at the striker and parting along the bow. The waves had declined a little in the past few minutes, however.

"Do they see any ships?" Thornwheel asked.

"No," Salap said. "I hope the bastards sink!" His smile was broad and wild, his eyes black and wide like a man caught in a fight he deeply enjoyed.

The wind blew as strong as ever—the gauge registered fifty-five knots—and the ship climbed and bounced and cut through waves, but the waves were diminishing even more. I saw floating objects in the glistening hills of water flying past, gray and pink shapes like closed umbrellas rising from the water. We shipped another formidable scoop of ocean and clung miserably to our ropes and whatever else we could grab. Thornwheel raised his notebook triumphantly above a rushing floor of blue sea, then rose sputtering and whooping. Salap slipped and was washed along the deck until his line snapped him to a halt; he swung at the end of the line, his robe drenched and wrapped around scrawny, scrambling legs, his face and beard streaming. The captain managed to stay on his feet, but he looked battered and kept his eye out for the patch of calm as if it might be our only hope.

I looked up at the trees and yards, the furled sails, the rigging, the greenish-gray sky beyond. All leaped and surged but the sky, which formed thick gray bands perpendicular to the length of the ship. Within those bands I saw a constant twinkling, a coruscating flow of myriads of corpuscles one moment brilliant white and the next black.

The ship spun about like a skater suddenly thrown down and sliding on his rear. With a shudder, the *Vigilant* seemed to leap over the border between one kind of madness—the sea that threatened any second to break her back and kill us all—and another.

Astern, as the hull settled, its pitching and rolling much reduced, we saw furious waves and a haze of driving spume. But all around and for hundreds of meters ahead, the waves were flattened, subdued, by thick layers of brown and red and yellow pads. In the center of each pad rose a growth like a folded umbrella, and at the tip of each umbrella, a fan or paddle spread, perhaps two meters in diameter, black on one side, white on the other. We seemed caught on the field of some impossible sport. The wind still blew unabated through our rigging, but it could not ruffle this tightly controlled field of sea within the storm.

The wind blew off the starboard quarter. I turned and the wind whooped through my half open mouth, making me a living bottle-organ. I struggled to pull air back into my lungs. Salap gripped the gunwale and leaned out to peer into the water beneath the bow. I did the same, and saw the cutwater pushing through the broad pads, shoving aside the fans, some of which bent and spun before our faces, just beyond the forward rails. On the edges of the pads, thick flattened growths like gear teeth meshed with adjacent pads and propelled them as they slowly spun. When the ship's bow forced the pads apart, with a sound like tiny suckers popping, the water between was black as night.

Above the ship, great flocks of silvery triangles from a few centimeters to half a meter on a side blew through the sky, half hidden, and then entirely revealed, in thick curtains of moisture. The air blew alternately freezing cold or hot and moist, as if the ship were caught in some uncertain gradient between winter and tropic summer.

"It *is* alive!" Salap shouted above the steady, shrill scream of the wind. "It's in control!"

"What?" Keyser-Bach shouted back. "What's in control?"

A flight of triangles caught up against the masts, shattered, and slipped away in the storm. Pieces fell and whirled forward, blowing and flipping across the deck like leaves.

"It's a storm-beast! It's master of the warm water and the rising and falling air. We're not yet anywhere near the middle of it. We're on its outskirts. What must it be like farther in?"

Thornwheel scribbled quickly in his notebook. The pages bunched and tore beneath his pencil. Still, he kept writing: wind speed, pressure, the things we saw in air and water around us. He looked up, lips pulled back, squinting into the hot and cold winds.

Salap pointed dead ahead. "Everything in here is alive and growing, prospering! A garden in a whirlwind! Even so, if this is a cyclonic, there must be a calm center!"

Randall worked his way forward, stepping carefully over each safety rope, fastening his line, tugging it free with the secondary loop-line, refastening. He climbed onto the forecastle deck. "We're taking water like a colander," he shouted at the captain. "Every board's been jarred. I've got half the crew below pumping and caulking, but I don't think we can last more than another hour."

"Set the fore course and main lower topgallants," Keyser-Bach said. "Keep the wind on our port quarter."

"That will put us right into the center!" Randall shouted.

"That's where Salap wants to be!" the captain replied. The winds nearly drowned him out.

"Fine!" Randall said, raising his hands and preparing to head aft. He shook his fists at the chaotic sky until he reached the ladder, then glanced back and said something that nobody heard.

I turned to sight along the bowsprit. The waving and whirling fans had passed. Ahead, the ocean seemed covered with silvery grass taller than our upper topgallants, making great steady clockwise waves like cilia on the skin of a cell.

"Storm cell!" I said to Thornwheel. Salap turned to me. Both called out, "What?"

"We're inside a storm cell," I said, but I could not convey my joke, if it was a joke; it might have been a serious observation, a clever metaphor, a crazy way of dealing with incomprehensible phenomena. I did not care. I felt so battered and dazzled, beyond fear, sliding smoothly into exhausted disengagement. The waving silvery grass ahead could have become the hair of some huge giant, rising from the sea like old Neptune, and I wouldn't have been much surprised.

With the sails set, our speed increased, and *Vigilant* moved at fifteen or twenty knots toward the immense rolling wall. The crew worked steadily on deck and in the rigging, Soterio guiding them as best he could from the main deck. Randall had climbed halfway up the shrouds, inspecting something on the foretree. I wondered if Shirla had been relieved on the wheel. I saw Ry Diem and Meissner hauling the tattered remains of a blown-out sail aft.

The fore and main trees and sails stood out brilliantly in a shaft of light like a searchlight beam, and I turned into its dazzle, high above the wall of grass. The sparkles had coalesced into a concentrated shimmer, throwing light on the sea around us like a lens or concave mirror. The whole storm was a system of reflection and absorption of sunlight, the scions in the atmosphere encouraging the heating or cooling of the surrounding air even as they flew through it, turning silvery white or dark black. The scions on the ocean's surface shifted and controlled the surface winds, and perhaps also conserved or radiated heat from the water itself.

Salap marched back and forth across the forecastle deck, staring hawk-like port and then starboard, trying to see and understand everything. The captain paid attention to little but the ship and its immediate obstacles. He lifted his arm, bellowed something, and we all turned to look off the port bow. If we could turn the ship a few points more on the starboard bow, we could pass through an opening in the wall of grass, a space of wide water like the gap left by a swinging scythe.

Randall came forward and the captain gave his instructions. The crew worked—Ridjel took a starboard brace with Shankara and Kissbegh and turned the fore course yard—and slowly, as the wall approached, *Vigilant* aimed for the opening.

"We're going into its belly," Thornwheel said. "How far in are we already?"

"I don't know," I cried. "Seven, maybe eight miles."

"Twenty at least, with that wind," Salap said.

On either side, the grass rose around us, silvery tops swaying. *Vigilant* sailed into the gap. Abruptly, the wind stopped and the sails hung slack.

Keyser-Bach looked at them with a furrowed brow, obviously stumped. What to do next—put on more sail to take advantage of what little wind remained, or drift and wait for another blow? Salap offered no advice. We were all beyond any human experience.

Alternating red and black disks covered the water around the ship, a polka-dot sea as lurid in the glittering light as any child's drawing. The disks rose and fell on a gentle swell, while above the grass, and beyond the opening of the gap, the wind wailed like a fading echo.

The sky above filled with thick black streamers of cloud. Rain spattered down. A warm wind blew from directly ahead and the ship yawed to starboard. The wind ceased as abruptly as it began.

We lay in stillness, if not complete silence. A current in the water around *Vigilant* pushed us slowly, smoothly ahead, along the curve of the gap between the walls of grass. Randall went belowdecks to supervise the pumping. I felt guilty at not pitching in; but Salap shook his head at the look on my face, pinched his lips together, and said, "Eyes and ears. Let the muscles work now. We'll pitch in if the master demands it."

This did not make me feel any more comfortable, but it was an order.

A few hundred meters into the gap, we heard a steady thumping sound, like the beating of a huge heart, though rapid as a bird's. The sails had been set to the captain's satisfaction, the hand pumps seemed to be gaining on the water in the hold, and both master and mate were on deck to take in the scene around us.

Thornwheel had made all the notes there were to make at this point. The wind was light and steady at about five knots, the grass undulated as it had for the past ten or fifteen minutes, and he had recorded the beginning of the sound. We glanced at each other, nodded as if making acquaintance across a busy boulevard, and returned to gazing at the grass, the polka-dotted water, the bands of cloud and spinning scions high above.

"Is it worth it?" the captain suddenly asked Salap. We had grown so used to shouting that his voice boomed across the deck.

"You mean, is it worth my life, to experience this?" Salap asked in return.

"We've seen a lot together," the captain said. "It would be fitting to die like this."

Lamarckia is a good place to die. Swallowed by a living storm, with no chance to be of any use to the Hexamon, no longer seemed the best end to me. I had answered their question hours ago, but had changed my mind since.

"I have a lot more I'd like to see," Salap said. "Things even more remarkable. And to die without telling . . . With what we know . . ."

"I don't intend to die," the captain said. "But my intentions don't mean much here."

Salap said, "Cassir and I are going to take a few specimens at the stern." He descended the ladder and walked aft, taking Cassir from his post. Pieces of shattered wind-driven scions lay brown and withered on the deck, their glory of white and silver fading quickly. Cassir retrieved a few and bottled them, then stowed the bottles belowdecks and returned with a specimen net and gaff to join the head researcher.

The thumping grew louder. Ahead, the walls of grass turned reddish brown, though each blade was still silver-tipped. The tips became flattened, and the stalks shorter, the rhythm of undulation more rapid. Breaks in the walls to either side allowed strong breezes to blow across the ship, heeling and pushing it one way and then back the other.

Soterio came forward. The captain asked who was steering, and the mate replied that Shimchisko had replaced Shankara, and that Ry Diem was on backup. Shirla had been relieved just after the beginning of the storm.

It all seemed more than just dreamlike; it seemed feverishly mad. The light on our faces was mottled white and pink, with flashes of silver from the clouds above. The fore course luffed and bellied in the alternating winds. All around us, the waving blades rose no higher than the yard of the course, and from the tops, Ibert called down that he could see an end to the grass a few hundred meters ahead.

Vigilant emerged from the grass ten minutes later. Ahead, a dense wall of gleaming white cloud churned. In the broad lane of sea before this wall, dozens of different kinds of scions eeled and floated through the water, passing broad black masses like small low islands. Atop the masses rose translucent pillars that gleamed like glass, but shivered with each thump like stiff jelly; within the pillars, long gray and blue cylinders clustered like wires through insulation. The pillars were about twice as high as the truck at the top of the maintree and two-thirds as broad as the *Vigilant*'s length from jibboom to stern.

Above and ahead, the sky filled with detail that eluded explanation, confusing my eyes and mind. I saw pinwheels of darkness spinning lithe as snakes that fell behind the wall of cloud. One of the vortices broke through the wall and fell apart, scattering as sheets of very dark rain into the sea, which seethed like living soup. The thumping began to hurt our ears, a rapid surge in pressure as much as a sound, and we could not talk at all and be heard.

Vigilant would not be controlled. No matter which way we set the sails or steered, the thick mass of scions around us carried us in the flow, leaving the waving grass behind, like brown beach cliffs rising to a silvery prairie on a sloping hill. All behind was wrapped in drifts of brilliant white cloud, pierced by searchlight beams; and above, rising several thousand meters into the air, an immense curtain of black shot with spreading fans of powdery gold. I had never seen anything so awesomely beautiful, not even the advancing wall of a Jart offensive . . .

I felt like a Jonah lost in the belly of a godlike monster, this *storm-beast* as Salap had called it, the captain's nemesis, and my chest hurt with fear and something like shame. My throat clutched and even if I could have been heard, I couldn't have said a word.

Suddenly all my thoughts focused on Shirla. She was the closest thing to a woman and a friend I had on this planet; she was female. Being near her seemed essential. I looked back along the deck, actually made a step to go aft, caught myself and looked over my shoulder at Thornwheel. He had put away his sodden notebook and now lay curled up by the bowsprit, hands over his ears, trying to hide from the pounding trip-hammer pressure. Salap had fallen to his knees beside the port gunwale, his safety line tangled around his legs. The captain still stood, but leaned against the curved black vent over the galley, his face locked in a grimace of pain, eyes mostly shut.

So much energy, I thought. I turned about myself where I stood, taking it all in, for the moment losing all the pain in my ears, my lips calling for Shirla. I wondered if she were dead or alive. If I got out of this, I thought, I would give up everything—my mission, my reluctance to become part of the immigrants—everything, just to be with Shirla.

But Shirla became an abstraction. Suddenly I missed Uleysa, on Thistledown. The faces of several dozen other women, friends and lovers, chance acquaintances, came with extraordinary clarity. I was surrounded by them. I saw my mother, her angular, half angry, half puzzled face unable to comprehend that she had just hurt her small son with a sharp, unsympathetic word, and I loved her, forgave her, needed her.

The thumping stopped. *Vigilant* floated for the moment in comparative quiet. The other sounds—whistle of wind from our starboard quarter through the rigging, sloshing and slapping of water and the confused sliding whisper of scions in that water, came back only gradually, as if having been in hiding and only now emerging.

The quiet seemed like an indrawn breath before a scream, but no scream came.

"We are going to get out of this," Keyser-Bach said, enunciating each word like a schoolmaster. He went to the rail. "I hope to Breath and Fate Cassir is taking specimens." He pointed into the water, lips counting softly. "I can't count how many different types of scion there are. What do they *do?*"

The water around the ship seethed with color and form, as if *Vigilant* had been scooped up in a net filled with the concentrated creatures of an entire terrestrial ocean. Soterio came forward, a dirty white cloth wrapped around his head and ears. He removed the cloth sheepishly and cocked his left ear close to the captain's mouth to receive orders. But the captain said one thing, then belayed it; another, and belayed that, as well. There was no-where to go, no clear direction for safety. We were turned around in the creature, and our compass was of little use. The storm could have shifted course around us as much as we turned within it. We had been inside the system for five hours; we could be as much as thirty miles from the peri-meter, or even forty.

"Shit," the captain finally said, throwing up his hands. He turned, stared toward the wall of mist, turned again and looked down a corridor between the false brown hills and silvery grass prairie, his eye following the curve off into more mist, black shot with gold and silver. "It's pure instinct, or guesswork, Ser Soterio."

"Let it be instinct, sir," Soterio said.

Salap and Cassir came forward. Cassir deposited the contents of a bulg-ing net into a barrel, then poured a bucket of water over the contents, which seethed. With a look of fascination and caution, and a touch of disgust, Cassir clamped the lid down on the barrel.

"What do you see?" Randall shouted to Ibert and Shatro in the main-tree top. I shielded my eyes against another flash of light and saw the two draped limply on the small platform high over the ship. Shatro raised an arm and pulled himself to a kneeling position, gripping the shrouds. He scanned the surrounding sea.

"I don't know," he called back.

Ibert stood beside him. "None of it makes any sense," he added.

"We're looking for a way out! What do you see?" Randall called up an-grily.

"What would it look like?" Ibert asked plaintively.

"A door," Thornwheel said, uncertain on his feet. "With a big brass knob."

A large drop of black ink fell at his feet, splashing his shoes and pants. He stared at it dumbly, then looked up at us, *What next?* More drops fell, steam rising from the spreading stains. One struck me on the back and was hot enough to sting.

"Wonderful!" Shatro screamed from the platform. "We've gone straight to hell!"

We scrambled on the deck to get away from the sudden barrage of hot inky drops. All around, the sea was dappled and roiled with the dark rain, and the mass of writhing scions sank with a chorus of bubbling gurgles. In the tops, Shatro and Ibert screamed. Ibert came down the shrouds as fast as he could, stopping to shriek as a splatter of steaming rain struck his head and back. He nearly fell. Shatro lay on the platform, hands wrapped behind his head, yelling incoherently.

There was no place to hide on the forecastle deck. I saw Meissner run forward with scraps of ruined sail, throwing them at sailors cowering on the deck. Ibert tumbled the last few meters from the shrouds, landing heavily on the deck, and snatched a shred of canvas from the sailmaker. Everyone, covered or not, made a dash for the hatches and pushed and shoved their way below.

In the press of bodies, I found myself standing beside the carpenter, Gusmao, in her workspace in the ship's waist, beneath the upper deck. She blinked at the unwelcome intruders. She had not been on deck since we entered the storm. She was not a curious sort.

"My god, you're a *mess*," she said to the four of us. "What's going on up there?"

Nobody answered for long seconds. "Black rain," said Kissbegh, his face covered with thick splotches, almost unrecognizable beside the stocky, oily-black figure of Ry Diem.

"Who's steering?" Shirla asked, walking down the aisle between the carpenter's shop and the sail locker.

"Shimchisko's still up there. Soterio's with him," Shankara said.

The ship rolled. The deck drummed with heavy rain. The air became stifling, and moisture thickened it until we could hardly breathe. Shirla put her hand on my arm, solicitous. I laid my hand over it and felt like a young boy. Thornwheel came down the aisle, calling my name. "Salap's forward," he said, "in the lab. They got the specimens inside."

I wiped black goo from my face. Where it had thickened, not quite dry, it caked and fell away, leaving no stain on the skin beneath. I touched Shirla's face and tried to wipe it. She held my hand and drew back slightly, but smiled. "It's in my eyes," she said.

Gusmao recovered enough to order us out of her workshop. "I don't know what's happening topside, but the captain wants his barrels and boxes." She shooed us into the corridor, where the air, away from the shop's vents, was even thicker.

"You're going to work in this?" Kissbegh asked, peering around the door into the carpenter's tiny workspace.

"I'm going to breathe, dammit," Gusmao said, and shut the door in his face.

After a few minutes, the drumming stopped. We heard the wind pick up, and the creak of the trees and rattle of yards and rigging. We delegated Ridjel to poke his head up and see what there was to see. He climbed the steps, lifted the hatch cover, and said, "Salap's out there. The black stuff's stopped falling, but it's all over the deck. There's the captain—and Randall."

We hastily climbed out on the quarterdeck and returned to where we had been before the black rain began, all but Ibert, who stood by the shrouds, calling up to Shatro. Shatro answered and said he was coming down. Soterio passed by, half inked, half clean, like a festival harlequin. He did not comment on Ibert's reluctance to go topside again.

All around, the ship drifted through twists and curls of fog. The air temperature had climbed at least ten degrees and our stained clothes clung to us. My throat was parched, but the water butts on deck had been bumped, losing their caps, and were fouled by ink. Leo Frey, the cook, and his assistant Passey emptied the contents of the butts and went below to bring up more water.

Salap's face and beard glistened with ink. His vivid white eyes stared from his black face, the ink glazed and cracking on his skin. "This warm water," he said, "will be pushed outward, to power the outskirts of the storm. If we stay with it, we may get out."

The captain stood beside Salap, a blackened towel in his hand. "Why do you think that?" he asked.

Salap lifted his hands. "Somewhere high up in the storm, scions spray black pigment into suspended moisture, and the pigment absorbs sunlight. When the clouds have reached their maximum temperature, they drop hot rain into the sea, warming it. It's part of this monster's infernal engine. Scions in the water absorb the black pigment, turn the sea milky, and . . . it is pushed outward, full of heat . . ." He shrugged, as if this were elementary. "I imagine at the heart of this beast, there are great sheets of ice, like the inside of a freezer . . . The air cools and falls." He took the captain's towel and wiped his face. "The ship looks sad," he said.

The captain shook his head. "We just follow the current?"

"It will get rough again, I imagine," Salap said. "But perhaps we can get out, and get washed clean in the process."

All around the ship, the sea was beginning to take on a milky pallor. Salap nodded his satisfaction. Thornwheel smiled and shook his head, as if amused by another magic trick.

The captain stood deep in thought, fingers tugging at his chin, eyes distant. "The storm will put this water on the outer edge sometime after dark. Is that what you're thinking?" he asked Salap.

"Precisely," Salap said. "The night air will warm all around the edge, and rise rapidly as the surrounding air cools. The air over the center of the system will fall . . . And the storm will build up enough energy for tomorrow."

"We'll have two miracles to present to Lenk," Keyser-Bach said.

The wind began to pick up again. Around the ship, processions of eel-like black scions, drawing long, thin curved lines following the direction of the wind, channeled the milky sea. We turned the ship to go with the wind, and slid between the lines as if following the surface of an immense chart. The waves grew as we sailed toward the wall of fog, now in ragged patches, revealing depths of tortured, billowing white cloud beyond.

Our passage out of the storm was little less remarkable or strenuous than our journey in. We were blown with the milky sea for dozens of miles, through rank after rank of mists, enveloping clouds, fleeting rain showers that left long streaks and smears and whorls of black stain on our deck and hull. The spanker, christian, and all the courses, unfurled to push us swiftly, carried smeared and bleeding meanders of black.

Behind us now, the thumping started again, trip-hammer pounding that cooled my blood. I did not want to ever hear such a sound again. I felt like a germ invading a huge pulsing heart.

I still expected to die. So did most of the crew, I think, and their behavior was a credit to them. They worked quietly, focused on the ship. There was certainly the temptation to stare at the mysteries, the powers surrounding us, until we were filled like bottles with terror.

Flights of batlike pterids filled the sky, piercing the boiling, ragged cloud-ceiling, rushing to some unknown place in the storm's scheme. The milky sea thrashed with eight-meter waves like peaks in living meringue, slapping pale spray and silvery rivulets across the deck; the waves increased to ten meters, and then became formless, all-consuming monsters again, the lines of eel scions vanishing in their fury.

Blasts of cooler air poured down through rents in the clouds, making the seas steam, until we could see nothing in a general white-out. Thornwheel and I continued to make measurements with the barometer and thermometer, holding the instruments up to our eyes in the impenetrable fog, trying to write them down in fresh notebooks, or calling out figures to the captain, who recorded them on his slate.

After a tense half hour, the fog cleared.

Outside the storm, night was falling, but within, the sea scintillated with a pale radiance that bounced from the clouds. For the first time, lightning flashed in the clouds above us, silent and vague, like candles behind draped windows. These brief glows popped up here, there, ahead and behind, warm orange in the general lividity.

The water crashing across the bow and sloshing over the decks smelled remarkably like wet soil, and then began to give off an offensive stench, combining molasses sweetness with ammonia. We wrapped our faces in whatever fabric was available, including the crusty, smothering sheets of canvas Meissner had brought up to protect us against the rain of hot ink, but the smell persisted.

Since the black rain, the air around the ship, and across the sea, had generally been warm, topping out at thirty-two degrees. Now, more frequently, we sailed through the cool masses of air the sea was intended to warm. But in its silvery pallor, the sea could not release its heat efficiently. The next step—if I followed Salap's reasoning—would be for the ocean to turn black again, or to effect some other artifice to release the heat more rapidly.

The mate had gone below and checked the ship's clock. He told us it was eighteen thirty hours—twenty minutes past sunset. We sailed in ghostly twilight, barely able to see across the deck, lanterns coming on fitfully as the engineer managed to put the windscrews to work. The ship's batteries had been soaked during the heavy seas; their membranes would have to be washed and the distilled water replaced before they would function again. We were working on circuits connected directly to the windscrews, and their vanes were wet and whirled uncertainly in the steady wind.

All I could see, staring ahead, were dull flashes of orange behind greasy black clouds and luminous wave peaks. The plunging and leaping of the ship made my knees and head hurt. I felt sick to my stomach—whether because of the stench, the pitching, or exhaustion, I could not decide and didn't care. Salap handed me a small thermometer and I read off the temperature every few minutes, and Thornwheel replied with the barometer. Atmospheric pressure at sea level on Lamarckia was about nine-tenths of Earth normal, rich for Thistledown's citizens, who were used to quite a bit less than that; and by consensus that was called one bar.

Thirty degrees and nine hundred and forty millibars. Thirty-one degrees and nine hundred and forty-three millibars.

The captain recorded our figures when he wasn't shouting orders to the mate, and we tried to keep them in our notebooks. After a while, sick as I was, I couldn't help laughing as we shouted out new figures. Thornwheel grinned as well, his face a smudge in the obscurity.

The lightning grew brighter just as we emerged from a thick wall of cloud. Ahead, lost in the miasma, we heard a chorus of chirrups and whistles, crossing from off the port bow to off the starboard bow, as if a flight of unknown birds taunted us in the dark.

Flashes of forked lightning revealed serpentheads rising from the water, outlined in pale blue, bobbing, chirping and singing.

"Sirens!" I shouted to Thornwheel. The captain glared at me, but the sound grew louder. I tried to see the serpents more clearly, but they were always featureless, smooth, rising and uncurling slowly, or sinking with tips half curled, like limp hooks. Again we saw low, flat islands floating between the crowds of serpents, but lacking towers, covered instead with rounded bumps.

What little thinking I could manage was half delirious. I imagined cybernetic control systems within the storm, sensing and guiding, the queens of this storm-beast, sending forth flights of pterids this way, ordering the shoals of scions that way, bringing up serpents and lining eels across white seas, making the waves rise and the winds blow hot and cold. Somehow my thoughts became tangled and when I called out temperatures, the air seemed to respond; I believed myself in control, orchestrating all that we barely saw and did not even begin to comprehend.

We shipped a particularly large wave right over the bow, which plunged us all into a darker and deadlier night. Again I lost my notebook, slid to the end of my safety line and spun, then hit and rolled over the deck. In the water, I heard muffled sounds like murmuring, bubbling whispers, and felt something explore my leg. I reached down, blind, to push it away, and my fingers closed on a smooth, cold surface like hard rubber. It shifted beneath my fingers, and then, it stung me. I almost opened my mouth to scream, but some instinct kept my jaws shut tight.

Eyes burning in the sea water, trying to find my way to the surface and safety, my head suddenly bobbed into air. I thought I had gone overboard for sure. The safety rope had broken. I hit hard on deck again, got to my feet, and resisted the wash of water into the scuppers. Lights burned above and to each side of me. I had been swept off the forecastle deck, onto the main deck. My crewmates huddled around me. "Where's the captain?" I shouted. "Where's Thornwheel?"

The nearest person to me, Meissner, had been washed against the bulwark and huddled there like a frightened child. I glanced at my hand in the light of the swaying lanterns, vision blurred, saw a thin trickle of blood from my palm, wondered if I was going to die, and then realized, *I've been sampled.*

That made me laugh again. Hearing Thornwheel call from the bow, and hearing the captain cursing loudly and shouting orders to keep the ship steady, I began to bray like a mule. Shatro rushed past, glanced at me, shook his head, off on some errand. That seemed even funnier. Cham and Shimchisko poked their heads over the edge of a hatch cover. Shimchisko came around the hatch and took my shoulders in his hands.

"Don't shake me," I shouted. "I'm not hysterical. It's just funny." To prove myself sane, I instantly made a sober face and poked my nose against his, peering with bloodshot eyes.

"The water's black!" he yelled, pulling back. I looked around, and indeed, the deck was covered with ink, as was I.

"What does that mean?" he asked.

"I think it's good," I answered. Then I yanked one of his hands from my shoulder, shook it vigorously, smiled, and headed forward to my post.

I didn't much care about anything for the moment but being alive. If someone had asked me about my mission, about any other secret I had ever held in sacred trust, I would have revealed everything.

Nothing mattered but the laughter and being alive.

CHAPTER THIRTEEN

The water's sudden blackness seemed to calm the waves, or at least reduce them to frisky youngsters no higher than the bulwarks. These hit the ship like a drummer's pounding fists, but the deck did not leap and roll nearly as much, and we had a chance to clear the broken yards and tangled rigging. Everybody pitched in, even the captain and Salap.

Soterio had broken his wrist in the deluge of water that had parted my safety line, but he let Cassir and Ry Diem set and wrap it, and gave us as much help as he could with his remaining good arm, though his face was gray with pain.

The black water carried the ship through dancing pillars of rising fog. The air was almost unbearably humid, and the wind came from the starboard quarter, no faster than the current that gripped the hull, so we seemed suspended in motionless air.

Through gaps in the thick deck of clouds, I could see patches of stars. French the navigator was quick enough at sighting constellations to get a rough idea which way we were being pushed—due south. No one was certain what that meant; the horizon was blocked by an impenetrable darkness, unrelieved by lightning or any other detail.

The water grew calmer still. We stood about the deck, wobbling with exhaustion; Kissbegh and Ibert lay where they fell, sound asleep. I managed to find Shirla in the dim light of the few functional lanterns and put my arm around her. She did not push it off; instead, she reached up and gripped my hand in hers, tugging on the fingers like a child. It was such a casual, familiar gesture that one might have thought we had been lovers for years.

"Did you know it would be like this?" she asked. Her eyes were lovely, brown and alive.

"No," I said.

"Do you think it's over?"

"No."

"We're still inside of it?"

"I think so."

Randall walked slowly along the deck. The work that could be done had been done, he said; it was time to get whatever rest we could.

Most of us collapsed where we stood and curled up on the deck in the thick, sticky puddles of black water and the wretched heat, sweating. Shirla lay beside me, knees drawn up, and immediately slept. We had been inside the storm-beast for nine hours.

My own need to sleep had fled. I was exhausted yet wide awake. My mind, however, became as clear of thought as a fine summer sky. I stared up at the patches of stars and watched them be obscured, one by one. The clouds were thickening overhead.

Far to the east, the trip-hammer pulse continued. It did not shake the air or upset our bodies, though Shirla twitched and moaned.

Somewhere aft, the generators whined faintly and the windscrews stilled. I recognized the sounds of their gearing being disengaged. The remaining electric lanterns immediately went out. Someone, I could not see who, walked past with a small electric torch, whispering a string of curses.

Still inside. Still Jonahs.

The black water gave off its heat around the ship and, by morning, as grayish light filtered through the clouds and curls of mist, the sea acquired a dusty greenish color. I got to my feet, leaving Shirla to sleep as long as circumstances allowed, and looked around to see who else was up and about.

Salap stood on the puppis, facing forward. He saw me and nodded but did not smile. Cham squatted in a half doze by the mizzen tree. The rigging pulled and caught with little popping sounds and the remaining yards creaked and rattled. The ship was riding in a normal sea—waves about half a meter at their crests, racing past us in long swells as if eager to win a race. Peering overside, I was left with the impression we were sailing backwards.

I joined Salap on the puppis deck. He had just finished trailing a net in the water, back and forth over the stern. He showed me the net: empty. The captain had gone below; Randall sat near the stern, behind the wheel, which was tended by Ry Diem.

"Do you have any idea where we are?" Salap asked.

"No," I said. "How would I know?"

Salap chuckled humorlessly. "You're a smart man. I thought you had some consoling theories."

"Well, I don't," I said. Our time in the beast had changed me, at least for the moment, and I felt respect for no man, and no sense of discretion, either.

Salap seemed to find my new tone unexceptionable. Clearly, he did not care much for rank or protocol. "I would have guessed we'd be outside of the storm by now."

"I'm surprised we're still alive," I said. Ahead, the blackness had changed to an almost equally uninformative charcoal gray.

"There is a pattern, a process," he said. For a moment, I expected him to reveal some religious belief, but he continued, "The storm is a well-organized system, maintained by hundreds of types of scions. I wish we could have captured a sample of each. We have a few of the flying forms, a barrel or two from the rich sea, and whatever else washed up on deck."

"Something sampled me," I said, holding up my hand. Salap stared at the gouge with interest.

"The storm is not part of zone five, then," he said. Nearly everyone on Elizabeth's Land had been sampled by a river scion at one time or another, and these all came from Petain, so it was believed.

"I guess not."

"It is a separate ecos. Yet it feeds the prairie."

I nodded.

"So we learn more and more. The zones cooperate with sub-zones, as at the Chefla waste . . . And the storm has some connection with Petain, though not a part of it. I am proven wrong all the time now." He took a deep breath and smiled broadly. "It makes me feel young to be wrong so often."

"The water here seems empty," I said. "There were so many scions back there . . ." I waved my hand astern. "Why none here?"

"Even though we are not out of the storm, we must be near its farthest extension, its *caudal* portion, if I may be anatomical. There may be little of importance here."

"I thought the black water would just push toward the outside of the cyclone, not toward the rear."

Salap shrugged. "It was just a theory. A hope, perhaps."

The grayness ahead parted as the dawn advanced. We seemed to be near land—a long dark line of hills rose on the horizon. Ry Diem said hopefully, "We can find a harbor and fix the ship."

The captain climbed to the puppis, his head wrapped in a black-stained strip of cloth. "Good morning, if it is morning," he said.

"It seems to be," Ry Diem said. Randall pointed out the hills on the horizon. The captain stared at it, jaw clenching and unclenching within the bandage. He glanced at me, hooded his eyes, and said, "Slammed my jaw last night. Ruined a few molars. Soterio up and about?"

"His arm's giving him hell, but he swears he'll be on deck as soon as he can get dressed. One of the women is helping him," Randall said.

"That is not land, whatever it is," the captain said. "There is no land in this part of the world." He lifted his binoculars, then handed them around. All looked but Ry Diem. When my turn came, Shatro and Thornwheel and Cassir joined us, and I barely glanced at the formation before passing the glasses on to them. I could not make out any detail, just low knobby protrusions like hills, all of a uniform dark brown. The grayness above them seemed lighter, rent here and there to reveal darker, thicker clouds beyond.

"It's part of this damned beast still," the captain said.

"We're coming up on it rapidly," Cassir said.

"Cast a logline and let's see how fast we're going," the captain told Randall. Randall assigned the task to Shankara, who came back a few minutes later with a speed of four knots. Keyser-Bach examined the distant mass, lips moving as if in calculation. "Our speed with respect to whatever *that* is, is about nine knots. And I'd guess it's no more than five miles away. Erwin?"

"Six at most," Randall said.

"It's part of this beast and it's going to ram us."

"Or we'll beach on it," Randall said.

"It is not a solid mass, that I guarantee," Salap said, shaking his head. "It must be divided into smaller structures."

There was little wind to maneuver in. The captain ordered two boats put out with lines attached to the bow. This time I had to volunteer, if only to keep my sanity, and I clambered into the longboat. Neither Salap nor Randall objected. Shatro volunteered just after I did, loath to let me one-up him in any way.

Shirla climbed into the longboat and sat beside me, favoring me with a faint smile. Her skin was pale, however. She was terrified.

The mass was less than seven miles away by the time we had rowed the line taut and swung the *Vigilant* about. Twenty in the longboat, twelve in the captain's boat, we pulled with all we had.

Vigilant seemed mounted on the top of an underwater mountain, immobile. The sea barely stirred past the cutwater. The gloom all around had lightened to dismal light gray. Sweat stood out on my brow in the moisture and heat. My shirt clung to me. It seemed all wrong; I wanted to be anywhere but where I was. Shirla beside me, pulling with me on the oar, was small comfort. I knew, with an animal instinct I had not felt even during the storm, that something bad was coming.

Behind us, Shimchisko and Ibert shared an oar, swearing steadily and rhythmically under their breath, as if singing a sportster's chant. Across from us, on the same thwart, Shatro and Cham concentrated on their oar. Shatro glanced sideways at me, but our eyes did not meet for long. We worked too hard to care about anything but moving *Vigilant*.

It was useless. Half an hour and we reduced the ship's speed in the current by perhaps a knot. The captain ordered the boats back, but did not haul them aboard. Leaving crews of four in each boat, he ordered the rest of us to our stations. Soterio followed at the crew's heels, voice sharp.

Less than a mile away, the long dark mass *whispered* like children in a room, heard through a half shut door. At its base, water foamed like breakers hitting a shore. The knobby surface now clearly resolved into vertical corrugations, not so much a range of hills as an irregular wall, cut like sliced cheese, bearing down on us. It extended to either side as far as the eye could see, no escape.

All around the ship, the water suddenly filled with scions. They rose and twisted and rolled like breaching whales, spraying thick dark plumes that floated off as brownish mist. Above, the cloudy ceiling showed patches of blue. Light shafted down through these patches across the awful fecund waters, and I thought of an ancient engraving, a phantasma of Earth's seas, filled with bat-finned, slack-jawed, many-eyed grotesques. These scions—what detail we could see in the masses—did not resemble any particular baroque creatures, sticking instead to the storm's steady run of designs: serpents of many colors; long black or purple piscids, featureless except for smoothly tapered fins; writhing hollow cylinders a meter wide, lined along their inner length with coarse bristles like hairy nostrils (and some of them turning inside out as I watched); three-cornered flat shapes reddish brown trimmed with blue that filled the interstices between all the others. I did not have the concentration to keep track of other designs; there were hundreds.

"They're spitting *blood!*" Shimchisko screamed. Before the advancing wall, the scions' expelled vapors turned brilliant red. Less than half a mile away, we saw the wall push against the scions, bunching them at its base where they leaped and thrashed against the swell, then rushing *over* them it seemed, though they may have merely submerged and swum away. But before they vanished, they spewed plumes of brilliant red fluid that stained the wall. And when the wall whispered, the stain vanished, sucked within the sliced-cheese corrugations.

I last saw Captain Keyser-Bach on his knees, praying. We had abandoned our lines despite Soterio's yells, and finally even the first mate stopped his frantic shouting, for it no longer mattered. William French, Frey the cook, and Gusmao the carpenter—who had finally come up on deck—stood by the gunwale, transfixed. Shankara rushed past, heading forward.

Shirla and I met in the middle of the deck, as far from the bulwarks as possible, as if trying to stave off the rush of the sea. Salap I caught a glimpse of, heading to the bow with a bag in his hands. I suddenly realized the bag contained the remains of a humanoid skeleton; he was trying to save it.

Shirla clung to me. We knew we were dead. The wall's whisper, less than a dozen meters away, sounded like shrill fluting. The corrugations had become blades, the edges of knives pressed tight against each other and arrayed into an endless wall taller than the ship's highest mast by at least a hundred meters. The shadow of the wall fell over the ship and, almost gently, it bumped the stern. With a jolt, it pushed the ship, and for a few moments, we began to cheer, despite our terror. It had all been a false alarm: our fate was simply to be pushed along by the wall, perhaps forever. I imagined climbing the vertical face, seeing what was on the other side. I looked down at Shirla, folded in my arms, and she looked up, and we smiled.

Then the knives grabbed the stern and chewed it to splinters. The ship shuddered and lurched up and down, back and forth, caught in grabbing, grinding blades. Shirla and I fell down. Chips and splinters of xyla showered down on us. I heard the suck of a breached hull, water rushing in, and some of the hatches lifted or were blown aside as air pushed out. Cracks in the deck ran along board seams and puffs of caulk rose along their lengths.

Hauling Shirla up with all my strength, I held her hand and we both ran forward, to where we imagined the boats still were, somehow managing to stay on our feet as the deck tilted five, then ten degrees. Others had the same idea. Cham, Ibert, Kissbegh, Riddle, the sailmaker Meissner and cook Leo Frey and Passey and Thornwheel, Gusmao, Pyotr Khovansk the engineer, all ran with us. I saw Khovansk slip into a crack, which clamped down on his leg; he shrieked in agony. The ship rolled to port and Kissbegh fell and rolled with it, behind us.

The masts and rigging that had survived all of the storm-beast so far now gave way and yards fell, their parrels strained open, striking people to each side. Cassir was crushed. The fore course yard writhed on the fore-tree, then broke loose and fell directly before us, pulling blocks and sheets and shrouds down about us. I lay stunned under a web of fallen ratlines and shrouds. Shirla cut me free with her knife.

"No boats," she said, pulling me out. Ahead, we saw both boats loaded with five or six crew, pulling for all they were worth.

The ship had been half chewed to pieces. The deck canted back at twenty degrees, awash behind us, scions crawling and flopping across the wreckage before the grinding wall.

"We'll have to swim," I said, and Shirla shook her head, lips tight. The deck rolled to starboard this time, and we came up hard against the splintered shaft of the foremast, then fell and rolled to the bulwarks. Shirla's face was bloody. Water sprayed over the gunwale and sluiced her clean. Immediately her nose and a cut on her cheek began to bleed again.

"Jump!" I shouted.

"We're dead!" she screamed. She did not want to join the thrashing scions. Neither did I, but *Vigilant* had no future. We could last a few seconds or minutes longer in the water. I grabbed her by the upper arms and jumped, carrying both of us over the bulwark.

We went in headfirst. Water filled my nose and I thrashed through rubbery, slippery masses, trying to fight my way to the surface. Shirla and I came up at the same time. She gasped and screamed as a large gray shape slithered through the water between us. Bloodred spray shot up a few meters away and drifted across us, a choking mist that smelled of sour breath and fresh bread.

Shirla could swim as well as I, but the scions blocked our efforts to move away from the *Vigilant*. I managed to push through the welter to her, and together, we fought to stay afloat and to get away from the hull, now more than halfway chewed. I had no time to think of anyone else; Shirla seemed an important obligation, but I was willing to give her up, give up anything to keep my head above water, to keep from being dragged under by the mash of frantic bobbing, slapping creatures around me.

We managed to stay afloat independently. Facing each other, separated by a couple of meters of hissing, bloodspraying, multicolored soup, she cried out, "Where?"

"I don't know," I said. A massive eyeless snout poked up beside us, striped blue and gray lengthwise, its slashed skin flapping back in ribbons. It sank with a sucking wash that nearly pulled us under.

"The ship," Shirla called after spitting out water. I turned my head around to see what was left of the *Vigilant*, still uncomfortably close—five or six meters away. The packed, oscillating knives that formed the wall had chewed it to within seven or eight meters of the bow, pushing ropes, yards, and chunks of cathedral xyla into a tangle that threatened to topple on us at any moment. I could see no one on deck. Everyone had leaped off, yet I saw no one around us. We seemed to be alone.

Bloody spray shot up on all sides. I reached for Shirla, one last touch before we died; and then the waters swirled violently and we were pulled apart. Unable to breathe in the thick red vapor, I spun in an eddy, choking and thrashing my arms and legs. My eyes filled with the yeasty mist, leaving me almost blind.

I gained a dark and blurred impression of walls rising, masses passing to each side. Shirla moaned and I heard other voices now, some praying, others simply screaming. My vision cleared to see the *Vigilant*'s stempost looming over me, rising and falling with majestic slowness. Ridjel clung to the shattered bowsprit like a monkey, eyes tight shut.

The hull turned between two advancing walls, dragging me in its wash.

Everything whirled violently and I sank for a few seconds. Eyes open, I saw pale shapes around me, some sinking into darkness, others twisting and writhing in the water. I had no doubt at all that I was dead. All I had to do was open my mouth and I wouldn't prolong the agony.

My mouth stayed shut. I kicked and waved my arms. The water around me seemed clear; I could not feel the passing bodies of scions, or anything else. I rolled in a universe of bubbles and lancing beams of sun. Gradually, I oriented myself and floated toward the brightness, arms hanging limp, legs dangling, my body an enormous burning hunger for a single breath.

I lay my head back, and my face broke the surface. I exhaled, felt my lungs catch as if a tight band constricted them, and then my chest filled like a balloon. I became giddy with air.

I floated on my back, rising and falling in a gentle swell, the sky above cloudless and blue. When I rose to the crest of the swell, I saw a sloping shore, dark brown and corrugated, capped by a thick brownish mist. In the water around me, tiny brown disks floated like chips of xyla. At first, I thought they were remains of the *Vigilant*, but small piscids rose and plucked them from the surface, leaving spreading ripples across the smooth rolls of ocean.

Still alive. Still breathing, still floating. None of it seemed real. With a lazy nonchalance, I turned over in the water and tried to look around. I could not remember at first what had happened. I knew there had been a ship, and crewmates in the water, but nothing else seemed clear.

I found the ship—the bowsprit and prow rising and bobbing in the water a dozen meters away, ropes dangling. Ridjel had vanished from the bowsprit. Bits of wreckage slid down the gentle slopes of sea. I reached out for a long yard, perhaps from a lower top-gallant, but it passed by and I could not grab it. A flat piece of xyla, part of a hatch cover, caught my attention, and I swam toward it, grabbing the frame and crawling halfway out of the water. It made a fair raft, two meters on a side, two edges chewed, but floating even under my weight.

Memory came back as I realized I did not need to die soon. I thought of Shirla and clumsily pushed up onto my knees on the chewed hatch cover, shielding my eyes against the sun's glare. A body floated facedown about thirty meters away, on the other side of the ship's bow and the swaying bow-sprit. I recognized the thick shoulders and short hair of Talya Ry Diem. I moaned and turned again, hoping to see someone alive.

I looked back at what Salap had called the caudal end of the storm. More wreckage drifted in that direction, a trail of broken planks, snakes-nest rigging, a few round objects that were either fiddleblocks or deadeyes . . . or bobbing heads.

I tried to get to my feet, but the hatch cover tilted dangerously and I fell back on hands and knees. "Shirla!" I yelled. "Salap! Captain! Anybody!"

Two or three weak voices answered. Among them, a woman—too hoarse to identify immediately. I grabbed a splintered lizboo plank and began to paddle toward the bobbing heads. Awkwardly, I whirled this way and that until I found the best part of the hatch cover to assign as a bow.

The storm still filled the eastern horizon, columns of brown mist rising in air currents, parting in distinct streams, and being sucked back into gray masses of clouds on either side. It was about six miles away. I rowed and watched the remaining brown disks being plucked from the surface by stray scions, and tried to piece together what had happened, how we had survived, but my thinking was too ragged.

Three people hung along the length of a slender skysail yard. They could not all rest their weight on the yard or it would sink, so two were swimming and a third was resting. They called to me hoarsely, voices mere squeaks above the slosh and hiss of the wreckage in the gentle waves.

"Olmy," said one, and left the yard to swim toward my hatch cover. I saw it was Shatro and was very disappointed. But then I saw Shirla clinging to the yard, her face smeared with brown, hair in sticky strands, but alive, and I welcomed Shatro aboard as if we were the best of friends. Together, we paddled with hands and the single plank toward the yard, and Salap, wearing only black pants, swam weakly toward one side of the hatch. Shirla held out one arm and I pulled her onto the other side. Four were too many, and the hatch began to founder, so I jumped into the water and let them settle themselves as best they could while I clung to one side.

We were all too exhausted and emotionally drained to say much. Shirla took hold of my hand and patted it, looking at me with wide, haunted eyes and a weak smile. "Where?" she said, and coughed.

"Wherever," I answered.

Shatro stared over our heads blankly.

"Have you seen Randall or the captain?" Salap managed to ask, balancing himself half on, half off the unstable raft.

"No," I said.

"The others," Salap said. "They might have been swallowed . . ."

"We were spit out," Shatro said. "I saw it. The wall broke in two and let us slip through."

"Not before it ate our ship," Shirla said.

"A tiny morsel it did not want," Salap said. Resting on the hatch cover, breathing for once without swallowing water, they seemed to revive a little. The water was cooling rapidly in the wake of the storm. Soon it would be chilly. The sun, on the other hand, was brilliant and would soon toast us.

Salap studied the departing mass of clouds with half closed eyes. "The whole expedition," he said, and shook his head, his face hard and eyes narrowed.

For a long time nobody said anything. I tried to feel something, grief or elation at having survived, but my thoughts were jumbled and I felt nothing clearly.

"Where now?" Shirla asked again.

"Nowhere," Shatro said.

From a few dozen meters away, another voice called. With a sudden burst of energy, we arranged ourselves to swim and push the hatch cover toward the new voice. Erwin Randall clung to a large piece of hull, five meters long and two meters across, still attached to several ribs. This floated planks-up and he lay flat on it. With a quick reconnoiter, we lashed the hatch cover to the larger piece of hull and all climbed from the water.

"The captain's dead," Randall said. "I saw his body before the storm spit us out."

Salap rubbed his cheeks wearily with his palms and nodded, downturned lips and deep black eyes asking without words, *What is there to be done?*

We lay back to contemplate our last hours in this, or any, world.

Night came as a great relief. We were very thirsty and the sun only made our condition worse. We bobbed gently under the pure welded-metal smear of sunset, in a cloudless twilight sky, the water splashing us, stinging cold at first, then numbing. Salap and Shirla slept for a while. A few small meteors lanced the starry night. I felt dead weary but not sleepy. I realized with a calming certainty that we were as isolated as could be, on a sparsely populated world, and that death was the only likely outcome.

Randall did not agree, however. He responded to my unspoken gloomy certainty with, "You know, there's still the steamships."

Shatro grumbled. I did not want to argue the point. My mouth was dry and my tongue stuck to the roof so tightly that I thought I might choke. The ocean waters of Lamarckia were notoriously drying. Potassium salts and other minerals crusted on my legs and arms.

"We could catch a scion," Randall continued, his words thick. "We really should paddle around and look for others."

I made no response. We had no tools, no bait a scion would go for—all the brown disks left by the storm had been gobbled before nightfall. We could have eaten them ourselves, had we had the presence of mind to scoop a few out of the waves.

"Thirsty," Shatro murmured. He curled up on the far end and slept, snoring loudly in bursts every few minutes.

I had heard that disaster bred a wonderful clarity of thought. All I felt was layers of thick tangled fuzz pulled through my brain. I would die comfortably enough: as I was too dumb to remember anything, death would merely snuff a dull instant of unconnected being. Olmy was already gone.

I gave little thought to my responsibilities back on Thistledown. Family, Nexus, the Hexamon itself—secret duties—seemed like half remembered dreams.

"The captain was a fine man," Randall said.

Salap had awoken. "He was."

Shatro and Shirla still slept. I pulled her close for warmth, and she moaned, but shut her eyes tighter.

"I wish there could be more like him on this world," Randall said.

"Lenk chose it so," Salap said, his tone neutral. "The best divaricates. Few like the captain or like us."

"Pneuma forbid," Randall said, and he repeated this several times, voice fading, before he fell asleep.

"Olmy," Salap said. "Are you curious about the storm-beast?"

I did not know whether Olmy might be curious or not. I cared little, myself.

"I see a diagram of its anatomy in my head," Salap said. "A loose anatomy. It came to me while I napped."

"Good," I croaked.

"A central void, like the eye of a storm, filled with bergs of ice. Air and ocean are brought together, mixed violently, churned to control the energies used to grow the scions within. The caudal portion must be a vast factory of nutrients, nourished within the storm and harvested by the wall of knives. Scions, perhaps those no longer useful—worn out by the action of the inner storm—are sacrificed, transformed into the brown disks, which are whisked away to the upper reaches, and spread out much later over land . . . or wherever the storm has forged alliances with other ecoi. I am sure the storm is a separate ecos, all to itself. Master of its circle of the Darwin Sea."

I thought vaguely that he had been talking a very long time.

"We weren't tasty, I assume," he concluded, and fell silent.

More meteors. That meant there were comets and other latent debris in the Lamarckian system, as well as the five planets spotted by the original surveyors. No asteroid belts; all swept away by gigantic Pacifica, visible to me now as a brilliant blue point, brightest of all the points in the sky. This level of thinking astounded me. I did not know where it came from.

"Do you know much about Ser Randall?" Salap asked later, interrupting my survey of the stars, which I had done many times already, forgetting the patterns I saw each time.

"No," I said. "I like him." It seemed a pleasant thing to say, if meaningless.

"He speaks highly of you. But then, he believes you're special. He believes you're recently arrived from Thistledown."

This was interesting enough to arouse a few brain cells, and I tried hard to focus on what Salap was saying.

"He heard this from Thomas the disciplinary at Calcutta. Many people in positions of authority have been expecting an appearance such as this . . . as this might be, at any rate. Randall told me you're different, that you have a quiet about you not found here. He used a few code words . . . Yes, I know them. I used to be one of the Adventists, years ago. In my student days at Jakarta."

"Adventists," I croaked.

"Waiting for the Hexamon to open another gate. I imagine if a gate was opened, Lenk would know about it, since he has the remaining clavicle. Keeps it always close to him."

"There was an old man in Moonrise," I said. "When I found him, he thought I was from Thistledown." I laughed, making an unpleasant half croak, half bark. "I wish I was," I said. "Somebody would come rescue me now. A gate would open right over us." I sketched the phenomenon against the stars with a trembling finger.

"Randall took you on the ship and elevated you, he was so certain."

"Oh."

"Few know that we were Adventists. It doesn't lead to many promotions."

Randall stirred, and Shirla began to push against my chest. Salap, a blurred shadow in the bright starlight, held his finger to his lips. "Dying people say things. Stupid things. Confidences."

"What's stupid?" Randall asked.

Neither of us answered. Shirla stretched, pushing her foot into the cold water. She jerked it back.

"No ships?" she asked over the slap of the waves.

"No," I said.

Shatro stopped snoring and sat up abruptly. Wide-eyed, he said, "Did somebody try to push me off?"

"No," Shirla said. "But I've been asleep."

"I belong here as much as any of you."

"No denying it," Shirla said softly, as if to soothe him.

"I'm still strong," Shatro said, shaking his head like a tired bull.

Randall leaned over and touched his shoulder, patting him as if he were a child. Shatro gave him a sideling look, eyes hooded, and hung his head between his knees.

Dawn was a long time coming. Shirla and I held each other, and Salap talked now and then of the storm's design, and Shatro kept his silence. Randall sat upright on the planks, twitching his bare toes.

Sometime in the dark, the water all around us whispered, and long, blunt-headed necks or trunks rose from the sea. Curdlike clouds dappled what old cowboys would have called a buttermilk sky, swimming in star-thick black whey. The tall shapes glittered in the broken starlight, and they stood steady, patient, and I could not help but think they were interested in us. I lifted a hand and said, "Take a bite. You'll know who I am."

But they slipped back into the water, and the whisper in the low waves stopped.

With morning, a feverish clarity gripped me.

CHAPTER FOURTEEN

The sky to the east grew yellow, then copper, and spread its smooth sheet of faded blue westward. A few dying shreds of clouds lurked to the south, none overhead. The steady weather in the wake of the storm-beast was becoming more changeable.

I saw my companions, the planked remains of the *Vigilant*, the somewhat rougher waves around us, with the sharpness of a fine line drawing, each line vibrating faintly and seeming to zizz in my ears. I knew with absolute certainty that we were not going to die. There was a great drama playing itself out here, and we were in the center of it: the gate opener had placed me in an event of great *interest,* the humanizing of Lamarckia. Humans would populate the planet to exactly one-half its capacity, and humanoids would fill the other half. The dividing line would be the equator. I chose the northern portion for the humans, to avoid inconvenience. I seemed to hear Shimchisko telling me details. Time smudged itself and some things happened before their proper place in the sequence of second to second, and some happened after.

What came late was Salap's hoarse cry that he saw a ship. *Of course he does*, I thought. *It's inevitable. If we're not going to die, there must be a ship.*

"One, two, three," he said. "Four ships. Two steamships, and two schooners, fore and aft rigged . . . Must be from Athenai. They like schooners there."

I looked with little interest in the direction of his finger. Two stripes of smoke rising high over the cold stale sea, and in tow perhaps, sails slack or furled, two sailing ships. They were quite close—perhaps a mile off. Salap stood. Shatro tugged on his ragged black pants, imploring him to sit down.

"If they have steamships, they're Brionists," Shatro insisted, hunching his neck.

"They're our only hope, wherever they come from," Randall said, and stood awkwardly, making the raft sway, to join Salap's arm-waving.

Shirla watched them, mouth open to keep from pressing and splitting her dry lips. We were ghostly things, crusted white with salts, hair standing up thick from our heads.

"They won't see us," Shatro said miserably.

"They're turning," Randall said, and grinned down at us like a small boy who sees his father coming home.

"I believe they see us," Salap agreed.

All inevitable.

It took the ships half an hour to surround us and send out a lifeboat to pick us up. The steamships were a hundred meters in length and about twenty-five meters across the beam, the largest ships I had seen on Lamarckia. Their broad, bulbous white-painted hulls were made of thick planks, but long sweeps of metal formed much of the superstructure. Each ship carried two-barreled guns fore and aft, and a single smokestack put forth an opaque cloud. Within their hulls sounded the great thumps of powerful engines. The ships were blocky and ungraceful, but they looked sturdy.

Men and women in gray and black uniforms stood by the rope railings and near the bows, watching and talking among themselves as a boat was lowered from one of two schooners.

The schooners had dropped the tow lines. The wind was picking up, and crews were setting the broad sails on each of their three trees, getting ready to proceed once we were aboard. They were longer than the *Vigilant* but not as thick across the beam, and they looked fast, like slender greyhounds beside the powerful barrel-chested mastiffs of the steamships.

Shirla kneeled on the planking as the boat approached, her arms crossed over her breasts. Five occupied the boat, four rowers and a plump man in the prow, dressed in white and wearing a small black cap.

The steamships displayed numbers on their white-painted bows, *34* and *15*, but no names. The schooners were simply labeled *Khoragos* and *Cow*. *Cow* seemed an odd name for so graceful a ship.

The plump man in the bow of the boat waved to us, smiling cheerfully enough. "What ship, and from what port?" he asked as the boat came within twenty meters.

"From *Vigilant* out of Calcutta," Randall said.

"What happened?"

"Sunk in a storm," Randall explained.

"How long ago?" the man asked, face showing great sympathy.

"A day. Maybe two."

"Three-treed full-rig?" the man asked.

"Yes," Randall said.

"We saw her, and we saw the storm. A terrifying thing. We pulled out of its paws just after we lost sight of you."

"Your ships?" Randall asked, and the boat pulled up beside our raft. "We did not see any schooners."

"We were way behind. The steamships look ugly, but they're fast, especially when the wind's asleep."

"Who are you?" Shatro asked.

"We're out of Athenai," the plump man said, looking uncomfortable. "Bound for Naderville. The steamships are escort. They came from positions off Jakarta, I understand. My name is Charles Ram Keo." He offered his hand and Randall shook it. Then they helped us aboard. Once on the boat, we saw how flimsy our raft had been. But it was the last we saw of any of the *Vigilant*, and as the rowers pulled us toward the *Khoragos*, I felt sad at the sight. Shirla stayed close to me, accepting a cup of water poured from a jug, while a thin woman with a worried face asked about our health, what we had had to eat, and other questions. She was Julia Sand, a physician aboard the *Khoragos*.

"They wouldn't have sunk us," Shatro murmured. Salap seemed very solemn, unwilling to speak much. I wondered if he had guessed at something we were missing.

Randall was ebullient. "You're a true gift of the winds," he told Keo, sipping from his cup as instructed: small swallows.

We were near the larger of the two schooners when Salap leaned forward and whispered in my ear, "*Khoragos*. That means a leader of a chorus. She is Able Lenk's boat."

He pulled back. Keo and Randall had caught part of his whisper and the plump man looked even more uncomfortable. "You'll have to come with us, of course," he said. "You know what's happening, I suppose."

"Is Lenk on board?" Randall asked.

"He is," Keo said.

"Going to Naderville . . . to negotiate with Brion," Salap ventured.

Keo did not reply.

We were brought aboard in slings and deposited on the deck of the big schooner. The other ships had already pulled away. They were now spread across nearly a mile of water, the two steamships leading the way.

Lenk was going to parlay.

CHAPTER FIFTEEN

The *Khoragos* was a solemn ship. Of the seventy aboard, her crew was made up of thirty A.B.s, five apprentices (all children of Athenai citizens of rank, we were told), and fifteen craft rates and officers. The remaining twenty were advisors, diplomats, and aides, and there was of course Lenk himself. The *Cow* carried a crew of forty and fifteen more diplomats.

No restrictions were placed upon us, other than that we were not to bother Able Lenk should we meet him on deck, which was unlikely. He spent most of his hours in the largest cabin, the captain's quarters in the forecastle, in the company of his advisors and diplomats, working day and night, Keo said. From this Randall and Salap surmised the ships were indeed going to Naderville.

Officers and selected guests of rank bunked in the stern. The crew bunked amidships. The berths on *Khoragos* were all filled. We were provided with new clothes, and Randall, Shatro, Salap, and I were given places in a private cabin formerly occupied by three junior A.B.s. Where they went we were not told. Shirla shared a berth with two female A.B.s.

We were being treated with remarkable politeness, and I soon discovered why. Keo, assigned to make sure we were comfortable, informed us that the Good Lenk was greatly upset at news of the loss of Captain Keyser-Bach and the *Vigilant.* "He believes the captain could have opened our eyes about Lamarckia," Keo said, standing in our cabin, handing out shirts and pants. Salap surveyed these fresh clothes with some displeasure—they were not black, and not loose—but put them on without complaint. "Able Lenk looked forward to hearing about his discoveries in person."

"We have lost all of our evidence," Salap said. "Still, I request an audience with the Good Lenk, on behalf of Captain Keyser-Bach."

"I'm sure he plans to meet with all of you," Keo said. "You will dine with the officers and crew this evening. Food will be brought to your cabins this afternoon, should you request it." He smiled at us rosily, as if he were a steward welcoming us to a luxury cruise. "I'm glad to hear you are little the worse for your ordeal."

Shatro fingered his red face delicately and winced. "What's going to happen in Naderville?" he asked.

Keo shook his head. "Not my place to say. Eventually, we'll return to Athenai."

Randall finished buttoning his shirt and stood, stooping to avoid the beams of the low ceiling. "I need to make a report on the loss of a ship to the captain and first officer," he said.

"Of course. I'll arrange for a formal hearing tomorrow."

"There's no blame, no reason for an inquest," Randall said softly. "The storm killed our ship. The captain did the best he could."

"I'm sure of it," Keo said, appearing as solemn as was possible for him. "We need to assess the losses for the shipping board in Athenai, of course."

Randall nodded gloomily.

Keo asked what else we required. Shatro wondered if any lizboo sap was available. "For our burns," he said, poking at his arm and wincing again. We were all red, our skins in sad shape from sun and exposure to the water.

"I'm sure we have something similar," Keo said, and closed the door behind him.

"It's all funk," Shatro said as we heard Keo's footsteps down the corridor outside.

Salap patted the thin mattress and blankets on the upper bunk, peered through the single porthole, lifted a ceramic washbasin.

"Are you going to tell them about the skeletons?" Shatro asked.

"Yes," Salap said.

Shatro's face suddenly seemed to collapse and he covered it with his hands, not crying, but rubbing fiercely, as if to wipe away the burn and all that had happened in the past few days. "Everything we worked for. My training, education . . ."

"We're lucky to be alive," Randall said.

I touched Shatro's arm, pained by what he was doing to himself.

"Leave me alone," he growled, jerking away.

"Please," I said. "Don't rub your face like that."

"What do you care?" he demanded, standing up from the lower bunk and bumping his head on the rail.

"Enough," Salap said. "Why are you so angry with this man?"

Shatro stood in silence for a moment, hands limp by his sides.

"We're all equal now," Randall said dryly. "Let's make the best of it."

"It will be a long time until we are back in Calcutta," Salap said.

Shatro went to the porthole and looked out at the ocean, his face peachy-red in the glare.

"I request to be relieved from my contract," he said. "I may seek employment in Naderville." He glanced around at us. "I'm sure they need researchers."

"They probably do," Randall agreed. "Though I doubt that Good Lenk will appreciate it."

Shatro dismissed this with a wave. "He's going to Naderville to surrender," he said. "Brion isn't coming to him."

Again, Shatro stated what seemed obvious to all.

In the afternoon, after a lunch of real wheat bread and salted redbriar cheese—a delicious specialty from Tasman's silva—I walked with Shirla around the ship, examining the *Khoragos*'s graceful lines, admiring the craftsmanship of Lenk's personal ship. It was said that Lenk had turned down his advisors when they suggested such an appurtenance, and it had taken them years to convince him to change his mind. He needed to be able to travel in comfort with the people necessary to the growing government, of which he was still spiritual and political head. His presence on the ship gave the *Khoragos* a special quality that *Vigilant* had lacked: a sense of grandeur. In design and rig, however, she was simply graceful, and very well-appointed.

In truth, I devoted less attention to the ship's details than I did to Shirla. Between meetings with curious crew, who exchanged greetings and asked about our health, we walked in silence, shoulder to shoulder. There was no longer a Soterio to catch us "flarking" or a Ry Diem to cluck at us in her motherly way, and no real sense of direction or duty; we had been relieved of that.

Nearly being relieved of our lives had sparked something in me I could neither deny nor justify—an immediate need for confirmation. My life was too flimsy not to get on with basics, and Shirla satisfied one very real basic: female companionship.

How far we were to go, I did not give much thought to. The direction seemed obvious. If and when the time was right, I would make love to her.

As we walked, I examined Shirla with different eyes. She was not beautiful, not ugly; face and arms red with exposure, skin shiny with ointment and beginning to flake, hips ample, legs short but well-shaped, trunk long, neck long, head and face round, hair of course ragged, brown eyes small but intense and focused, she seemed ready at any moment to become satirical or critical, but she did not. In her motions and few words she seemed very vulnerable, very open.

On the bow, away from the general activity of the crew, we watched the broad blue ocean and cloudy, milky sky, the blurred ball of the sun. "Do you ever think we should have died?" she asked, eyes crinkled, lips drawn up in a half grimace.

"Why?" I asked.

"They were our shipmates. Our captain died."

"No reason for us to join them," I said, with perhaps too much briskness.

"I wonder . . ."

"Don't," I said, irritated. "That nonsense just makes things worse. We're here because we survived, by chance and our best efforts. We can't be blamed for their deaths."

"Will you ever be part of anything?" she asked, glancing at me with quizzical eyes.

I could give no honest answer.

"You have always been a terrible risk, Ser Olmy," she said, looking away.

I tried to steer our talk in another direction. "I've been incredibly lucky, actually," I said.

"Why lucky? And why do you never—"

"I was lucky to find a berth on *Vigilant*. I was lucky to survive its sinking. And now I'm lucky to be sailing to Naderville with Able Lenk."

She could not guess how true this was. If I was to be at the center of things, I had been placed in remarkably apt situations many times. The gate opener had found his mark with supernatural skill.

She puffed out her cheeks dubiously. "You don't make any sense," she said.

"I'm lucky to be placed beside you." There; the maneuvering was fairly begun again.

"You want to see my tits?" she asked, totally serious.

Again I laughed, and this time her eyes narrowed in pain.

"You are remarkable," I said.

"Do you know what I mean when I say that?" she asked.

"Not really."

"The obvious. I'm joking, and this time, I'm not joking. All right?"

She had me baffled.

"Ser Olmy, whoever you are, whatever you really want, I think I know one thing about you, one thing certain right now. We almost died. That makes us horny. Your body wants me. You want to take me someplace private but we'll do our little social dance on the deck first. Your mind thinks you'll make a small commitment and that'll be enough, and that I'm weak enough and my body wants you enough to make it happen." While she said this, a little smile formed. "And you're not wrong."

"Your body wants me?"

She nodded. "When the time is right. It isn't right now, of course, because we're very tired, and I'm sad. But I'll get over that. And when I do, you'd better say yes and make your move the next time I ask, or you'll never get a chance again."

In all my experience with women, I had never encountered such an analytical and verbal approach. In the company of lovers on Thistledown, the graces of centuries of spaceborn civilization, of the highest of technologies and the closest of associations, the most sophisticated of cultural educations, had finally produced so many easeful ways for partners to join in the physical act of love that, it now seemed to me, much of the interest in such proceedings had been drained away.

I had some small clue for the first time why I had broken my proposed bond in Alexandria.

I stared out over the rail.

"I put you at a loss," Shirla observed.

"Not for the first time," I said.

"My tits," she said, "are not my finest feature."

"What is your finest feature?" I asked.

"My heart," she said. "It is a strong heart. It *could* beat with yours."

The warmth spread from my cheeks through the center of my chest, to my groin. I was in the presence of natural genius.

As castaways, we were treated with a delicate deference, as if we were ghosts or small gods of ill omen. Castaways rarely survived on Lamarckia. Humans were few and far between on this world. Losing a ship was tantamount to losing your life. Still, the officers and politicians treated us politely enough, and around our first dinner, in the rank's mess, Randall told our story to the assembled officers and craft rates.

The captain, Lenk himself, and most of his aides were not present, but Lenk had sent his second, a slender woman of middle years named Allrica Fassid, who listened to Randall's telling with solemn fascination.

He did not mention the humanoid skeletons, by prior agreement with Salap, who thought that news should be reserved for Lenk's ears only. I suspect they still thought they could get another expedition out of the news, once these troubles blew over. After the story, the first officer, a tall, well-built woman named Helmina Leschowicz, called for a toast to "survivors, one and all."

Three stewards cleared the tables efficiently and sharp Tasmanian wine was served in crystal goblets. I had still not developed a taste for Lamarckian alcoholic beverages, but Salap, Randall, and Shatro savored theirs with an intensity that brought smiles from the assembled men and women. Shirla accepted her glass, but barely touched it.

The lights over the long table swayed in the gentle sea. Around the walls, A.B.s and some apprentices had crowded in to listen to the proceedings.

"Your story is grim," Fassid said, as we worked in traditional fashion toward another toast. "Your survival is surely a gift of fate. Your courage is an example to us all."

Lifted glasses around the table.

"Beyond the loss of good humans, the greatest loss is wit and knowledge," she continued. "Lenk himself funded Captain Keyser-Bach in his endeavors."

I studied Fassid, but she was too practiced to reveal much about herself. As with the best politicians I have known, she seemed at once present and real, yet gave out little useful information. She had learned her trade in rough times, at the knees of a master.

As we left the officers' mess, she approached Salap and whispered something in his ear, then hurried off. Salap approached Randall, who stood by Shirla and myself in a corner. Shatro stood in the shadow of a doorway. When we were on the deck and alone, a firm cool breeze blowing on us all, Salap said, "Able Lenk requests our presence later this evening, about midnight."

Shirla sighed. We were all still very tired.

Salap continued, "He wishes our advice. There is disturbing news from Hsia, from Naderville. Lenk only brought one expert researcher with him, thinking this would be purely a political journey. We may be of use."

"Shall we tell them tonight about what we've seen?" Randall asked.

Salap frowned and cocked his head to one side. "I do not know. None of this feels right."

We had four hours between the end of dinner and our scheduled appointment with Lenk. The deck was lightly crewed at night, in such fine weather.

Shirla and I walked the deck again, saying little, but keeping our eyes open for privacy. At the bow, behind an equipment locker, a bale of mat fiber lay in shadow. The moons were down and we sat in starlight only, and after five minutes talking undisturbed, we undressed each other to the extent that caution and need demanded.

She accepted me with a tense and earnest eagerness that I found very exciting. I had seldom made love with such simplicity and speed—fashions and centuries of development on Thistledown had given sex a rich clutter of nuance as formal as a ceremonial feast. Shirla knew none of this. As she had said, her body wanted me, and that was more than enough. When we finished, her face was slick with both sweat and tears and gleamed in the starlight. We caught our breaths, then fumbled to clothe ourselves in the dark.

"You haven't done this in a long time," she said.

"How do you know?"

"Have you?"

"No," I answered.

"I didn't show you everything," she said.

"What, your tits?" I asked, but my face was in shadow and she could not see my smile.

"No, idiot," she said gently. "In my village, when a woman chooses a man—"

"Not the other way around?"

She put her finger on my lips. "When that happens, we make a fine picnic and take it in a basket into the silva, find an open place, maybe beneath a cathedral tree, spread a blanket . . . I ask about your family, and you ask about mine. We talk about mutual friends, what our plans are. The rule is that we have children soon. We talk about that."

"I've met a woman here who resented being made into a brood mother." After saying this, I realized the phrasing might seem odd. I was speaking like a newcomer. Shirla mulled in silence before asking, "Who was that?"

"The master's bondmother. In Calcutta."

We sat up on the makeshift mattress. Shirla idly poked fiber back into the bale. "Some women feel that way. Maybe more than just a few."

"And you?"

She lifted her eyes. They glittered faintly in the dark. "I think Lamarckia will be the next Earth," she said. "I don't know why, but I see us prospering here . . . And I still do, despite what Salap found."

"So you won't mind having many children."

"I've never had any," she said. "Would you mind?"

I had never given the least thought to having children. On Thistledown reproduction was if anything more ritualized and nuanced than sex; most Geshel couples chose *ex utero* births. Many Naderites did as well; it was cleaner and certainly less painful. But none of that had ever seemed real to me. I was much too young to be a father. The one artificial capability not removed from my body was conscious choice of whether or not to be fertile.

"I asked you first," I said. My throat caught and I coughed.

"Makes you nervous."

"I suppose it does. It certainly should."

"Me, too. I've always been a little odd. I don't know whether the world needs children like me."

"Everybody feels that way," I said, though I could hardly know that.

"Not my sisters. They're already lost in thickets of kids. At any rate . . ." She held my shoulders and squeezed lightly. "I do not do this to obligate you."

I said nothing. I could not tell her how unobligated I was forced to be.

"But I've never protected myself, either. I follow Lenk's dictates. I'm a little in awe that he's on the same ship with us . . ."

I had a sudden image of Lenk personally encouraging Shirla to propagate.

"He'll be such a somber man now," she said. "And old. All this must wear him down."

"What, meeting us, out here?"

She pinched my nose. "I've always had bad taste in men."

Salap, Randall, Shatro, Shirla, and I walked forward along the corridor to Lenk's quarters. Keo met us midships. The craftsmanship on the *Khoragos* was particularly beautiful as we approached the forecastle. The walls gleamed black and gray and brown, using the inlaid cores of some Tasman arborid I could not identify. Electric lights gleamed steadily every two meters, shining down on elegant carpet woven in Earthly floral patterns. Our muffled footfalls alerted a male guard, who came to stiff attention, a short, broad rifle cradled in his thick brown arms.

"This is the first time in our history on Lamarckia that Able Lenk has felt it necessary to keep armed security around him," Keo explained, nodding at the guard, who glanced at us with flat, emotionless eyes. It was warm in the corridor and his face beaded with sweat.

Keo knocked on the door twice. It was opened by a thin, graceful young man dressed in a formal gray suit. He swung his arm wide with a cautious smile. "Able Lenk is just finishing a nap. He'll be with us in a few minutes. My name is Ferrier, Samuel Inman Ferrier." We shook hands formally.

A mechanical clock mounted on the bulkhead over the door chimed midnight. Salap sat on a couch. Shatro sat beside him, eyes darting nervously, as if he were a little boy about to see a doctor. Shirla, Randall, and I sat in individual chairs spaced around the cabin, which stretched across the bow of the ship. The cabin beyond, Lenk's sleeping cabin, was much smaller. I thought it odd that he would choose the bow; apprentices much preferred to stay out of the bow, especially in heavy seas. Perhaps he had a perverse sense of asceticism.

Shelves on the bulkhead opposite my seat contained a few dozen books, none of them ornately bound, and all of them well-used. They seemed to include statute books and city record summaries.

I wondered where the clavicle was kept. Would Lenk take it with him on a journey as uncertain as this?

Ferrier served us mat fiber tea on a black lizboo tray. As we drank, I heard faint shuffles behind the door of the sleeping cabin.

The door opened, and Jaime Carr Lenk entered. I had seen pictures of him from forty-five years before. Then, he had been a vigorous man of natural middle age, handsome and conservatively dressed, with a presence even in the records that radiated assurance and power. Now, Lenk was still tall, unbent by his years, his hair still mostly dark, his face deeply wrinkled but in all the right places: laugh lines at corners of lips and eyes, lines of sternness near the laugh lines, and a brow that seemed monumentally smooth and untroubled, a tall, unfurrowed brow whose owner had slept cleanly and in assurance of the truth for many decades. He wore a simple long green robe. His sandaled feet, peeking from beneath the hem of the robe, were broad and splaytoed. He slowly turned to face us and shake hands all around.

"Thank you for being patient," he said, staring at us one by one as if we were old friends. "Ferrier, I'll take a cup of that tea." He sat in a large black high-backed chair bolted in the corner, beneath the books, and when he was settled, he looked up in sadness and said, "I deeply regret the loss of Captain Keyser-Bach and his researchers. The loss of a ship full of men and women is one thing, evil enough and hard to bear, but the death of such a man . . ." He shook his head and accepted the cup of steaming tea, then set it on a side table, ignoring it. "I am gratified, of course, that you survived. Sers Keo and Fassid have told me some of your story—about the storm, how our escort of Brion's ships may have frightened you into its winds . . ." He swallowed, his Adam's apple bobbing in his wrinkled, corded throat. His sadness was genuine. Despite his clear brow, he had obviously experienced a lot of sadness recently.

"You could not have known, Ser Lenk," Salap said. "It is remarkable fortune to be rescued by you."

"These seas are so rarely traveled . . . If any ships would have picked you up, that they would be part of this absurd entourage only adds a peck to the improbability. And that is the main part of our problem, no? I go to Hsia, to Naderville, precisely because we have had so little traffic with the people who live there." He examined us closely, his jaw working. He lifted the cup and sipped from it. The warm liquid seemed to invigorate him. "You are Ser Salap." He turned his head to Randall. "And you are Ser Randall. Both of you sailed often with Captain Keyser-Bach. When he made his request, he spoke of you as necessary members of the expedition."

Randall inclined his head, then looked up at Lenk with calm, large eyes.

"We've made important discoveries, Ser Lenk," Salap said.

Lenk followed his own line of thought. "I'll read your reports when they're written. Now, there's so little time . . . I have been in need of more researchers. Questions of considerable importance have arisen. Difficulties of some magnitude."

Salap, rebuffed so smoothly, stared a little pop-eyed at Lenk, but even he lacked the gall to interrupt Jaime Carr Lenk.

"The Naderville researchers claim to have made great strides with the ecos on Hsia. The researcher on my ship does not credit these reports. I don't know what to think."

"What sort of strides?" Salap asked.

Lenk looked over our heads and lifted his cup. He smiled as if at some great joke, too large to deserve laughter. "Queens and hidden masters, palaces in the clouds, Cibola, Atlantis, the Afterlife. I do not know which Brion means. But I see his ships, and I know the power that he shows us, that he's amassed in the past two years and has used against us." He made a little shrug and lowered the cup. "He is not mad, whatever his generals do."

"Blockades, sieges, piracy," Randall said.

Lenk leaned his head to one side, scratching at the lobe of one ear. "General Beys accompanies us," he said.

"He raided nineteen villages before we left Calcutta," Randall continued. His face colored with anger. "Stole tools and metal stores. Took children. Killed some or all of the citizens."

"It pains me to think of the children and citizens," Lenk said softly. "I hate to bargain under those circumstances, but there was no choice."

"Brion denies it all, of course," Allrica Fassid said, entering the cabin on soft slippered feet. She closed the door behind her, nodded casually to Lenk, gave Randall a stern, half puzzled look, and apologized for being late. "I've just come back from number fifteen. Beys and Captain Yolenga say they've received their final instructions. May I speak before our guests?"

Lenk gave permission with a lift of his hand.

"We're to sail to the main port and up a canal to an inland lake. Our charts indicate this canal has been modified by the ecos, and that the lake is isolated from Naderville proper. It may be the site of these alleged researches. Ser Keo, have you told our guests what to expect?"

"As much as we know," Keo said. "A magnificent lack of detail."

"Good. We'll have little time to talk once we arrive, and not much more on the way there. But you must keep your eyes open and digest what you see. It may be crucial to our negotiations."

"We need to know if it's a bluff," Keo said, then his face flushed as if he had spoken out of turn.

"No bluff," Lenk said, shaking his head.

"Not everyone agrees with you, Jaime," Allrica said. "I personally regard Brion as a compelling liar."

"He is a force of nature," Lenk said. "I unleashed his kind when I brought us all here."

"We shouldn't confuse Brion with the Adventists." Her glance at Salap seemed particularly significant. "Brion has no honor. He's interested in power and position. He uses Beys as his iron fist, and hopes to isolate himself from the moral consequences." Fassid stood beside Lenk and examined him solicitously, touching his wrist like a doctor. "You're tired, Jaime," she said. "Time for a good night's sleep."

He stared at us with a wry smile. "I do not sleep the night through. That leaves me with far too much time to think. But Allrica, Ser Salap seems to have something he wants to tell us . . ."

"Can it wait?" Allrica asked Salap, eyes flashing a challenge.

"I would prefer to speak now," Salap said calmly.

"So important?"

"We believe so."

"What is it?" Lenk asked, leaning forward, elbows on knees, clasping his hands.

I glanced at Shirla and Shatro. Shatro seemed lost in his own thoughts, staring at the richly woven carpet on the floor. I wondered about his quiet concentration.

Shirla appeared out of her depth, frightened by the social altitude, yet fully alert.

Salap told them what we had found on Martha's Island, concluding with the loss of all our specimens in the storm. Allrica's lips pressed together until they formed a grim straight line. Lenk's shoulders hunched around his neck.

"Dear God," Lenk said. He gave no sign of either believing or disbelieving.

"That doesn't make sense," Fassid said, though without conviction. Keo and Ferrier stood in silence, as if absorbing news of the death of a loved one.

"It is true, whatever we wish to believe," Salap said.

"Some misinterpretation . . . Remains of humans, not scions," Fassid murmured. "You said three vanished from the Jiddermeyer expedition . . . and her husband's body was exhumed and carried off by . . . scions."

Salap shook his head, and Randall finally spoke. "The captain and I saw them. They were not the remains of humans, and they were real. Are real. There may still be specimens on Martha's Island."

"We all saw them," Shatro spoke up, still staring at the carpet.

"Another expedition," Fassid huffed. "The captain pressed us hard for years . . . Now after hearing this, we're to start all over again. This sounds much like Brion's idiocy."

Salap let this pass without reacting. Randall edged forward on his seat, but Salap touched his arm and he remained silent.

"We'll be in Naderville in two days," Lenk said softly. He stood and Ferrier and Fassid each took an arm, helping him toward the door to his sleeping quarters. Ferrier opened the door, and Lenk turned to Salap before passing through. "Was I mistaken to bring us here? Are we to be rejected like a plague by the entire world?"

No one spoke. Fassid saw him through the door, and Ferrier accompanied him. Then she turned to us and her eyes drilled into Salap. "How dare you," she spat. "How dare you bring us such nonsense for your own political gain!"

Salap's eyes became hooded and dangerous and he gripped the arms of his chair until his knuckles whitened.

"This wonderful man has the weight of the entire planet on his shoulders, and you bring him *ghost* stories! All to maintain your beloved *scientific* stature!"

Randall sat up, his voice harsh in the small cabin. "Ser Fassid, you're very mistaken—"

Fassid pushed her hands out in disgust and turned away. Keo seemed in an agony, caught between supporting Fassid and remaining a genial host.

Randall squared off with her in the middle of the cabin. "I have had enough of ships and the sea for a lifetime. I will gladly retire to Jakarta or Calcutta, or Naderville, if it comes to that . . . But that will not stop the truth of what we saw.

"You opposed all our research out of ignorance and devotion to some faded philosophy that has served none of us well," Randall continued, his words sharpening to hisses or dropping to growls. "Captain Keyser-Bach debated you over and over, hoping to find some shred of sense. You have poorly advised Good Lenk, Ser Fassid. And if you continue to play the fool, *I will bring you low.*"

The grim pronouncement carried an element of comic opera, but it was heartfelt.

Fassid's eyes seemed lost in shadow. "There's no time for this," she said smoothly. "Whatever happens in the next few days may bring us all low. Compared to General Beys, your threats are small rain." She walked around Keo and left through the port side door.

Randall took a deep breath and looked at Keo as if he had a little more anger to vent should anyone want to challenge him. Keo raised his hands. "I think we should all rest," he said. "It's been very tense."

"I'm sure it has," Salap said, taking Randall's elbow. Randall took a deep breath, stared around the room, and lowered his head. "Let's go."

We retired to our own cabins.

Randall joined Shirla and me on the deck the next morning to survey the ships and the surrounding waters. The weather was calm, the ocean smooth. "Salap's asked for notebooks. He's preparing a full report for Lenk," Randall said. He shook his head sadly. "I should have kept my mouth shut. I've just made us a stronger enemy."

CHAPTER SIXTEEN

Hsia became a dark line on the horizon early in the morning, half obscured by thick patches of cloud heavy with rain. As the four ships drew closer to land, we were hit by several squalls, and with their passing, *Khoragos* and *Cow* took advantage of a fresh, vigorous wind, set their sails, and cast loose of the steamships.

Ten miles out, all four ships were met by three fast sloops. One carried two pilots for our schooners, and they boarded to guide us into the harbor. Our pilot took his post by the wheel and gave quick, precise orders.

I knew their type. Young, earnest, nervous, terribly afraid of making a mistake. They had been raised under harsh conditions, I guessed, in a society pushed to the very edge.

Shirla stayed by my side. "I don't like it," she said. "The steamships, the crews, the pilots . . . They all look *stiff*."

The clouds blew south. Lenk's ships put on a glorious show, sails brilliant white in the morning sun, and even pulled ahead of the steamships for a time, until the pilots ordered us to furl our sails.

Us. Our. I had taken sides in this dispute. Perhaps from the moment I arrived and saw the slaughter at Moonrise, I could not be objective. The more I saw, the firmer my commitment became. Yet I could not simply dump all my objectivity. I owed nothing to anyone but the Hexamon, and all of these people were equally in violation . . .

The coast of Hsia was painted by bright sun. From the sea, the shore had appeared deep brown, spotted with red and dark purple. Now, from less than two miles, Hsia's zone showed itself as a forbidding hedgerow tangle fifty or sixty meters high, dark and uniform, its upper surface covered with leathery growths that screened all sun from the ground below. The dark thicket stretched back to far mountains topped by white clouds.

Baker had believed that Hsia was older than most other ecoi, and had developed early in the biosphere's history, before oxygen had reached current levels. The leathery covering on the hedgerow silva might have protected against ultraviolet light, which penetrated the atmosphere easily before the buildup of an ozone layer.

I thought of the immigrants surveying Lamarckia from the hastily opened gate, trying to pick the best place to settle, choosing Elizabeth's Land because it most resembled an Earth landscape, even though the colors were wrong.

Salap came on deck, notebook under his arm, and looked at the coastline, black hair tossed by the wind. He squinted and pointed a long finger. "It is like this everywhere on the continent," he said. "Dreary. A terrible place to settle. Hoagland's followers had to hack their way in, do without sun for months at a time, live like beasts in a cave. Still, for all that, they founded a city."

Naderville was smaller than Calcutta; even now, according to the best guesses, it contained less than four thousand citizens. I had to adjust my sense of scale to regard such a limited population as a military force to be reckoned with.

Shirla and I sat near the bow, a little awkward that there was no work for us to do. The habit of the sea had gotten into her more than into me, and the nervousness of being on a ship and not working made her open up as she never had before. She told me about her family in Jakarta—actually, in a little village called Resorna at the tip of a spit of land five miles south of Jakarta. The past did not come out of her easily, and she frequently had to pause, eyebrows drawn in concentration, not because her memory was faulty, but because she had expended so much effort to forget the hard times.

During the fluxing, when she was a young girl, her family had taken her from Calcutta and traveled with a dozen other families to Jakarta, in Petain's Zone, where edible phytids grew in more abundance, and where some land had sufficient natural minerals and was easily cleared for farming. The winters in Jakarta were always mild, but there had still been hardship. Petain's Zone had prepared itself for some onslaught by the newly united zones, and most of its scions—arborids, phytids, and mobile types alike—had coated themselves with waxy armor and gone dormant for three months.

"We had enough food from our own crops, by then," Shirla said. "But I was scared. My brothers and I kept a pet scion, a dipper, and I found it sealed up on the porch in front of our house one morning. The next day it was gone. It had broken its rope somehow . . . It had never done that before. Then, Petain returned to normal. I guess it decided Elizabeth wasn't going to attack."

She told me about her family: uncles and aunts, first father and first mother—her biological parents—and her second father, and second mother, who had no children of their own and treated her and her brothers with doting kindness. She remembered no third set of parents. That made sense; triad families, designed by a society where children seldom numbered more than two to a set of parents, became unwieldy when there were six or seven children to each mother and father. She was lucky, she said, to have had a second set, though she felt sorry for them, not having biological children.

She talked about several women in her village coming down with an odd malfunction, not exactly a disease; some sort of immune challenge that caused their ovaries to become inflamed. Several had had to have their ovaries removed. "The rest were fortunate," she said. "They kept their ovaries." That seemed to her more important in a way than their survival.

Something had changed in the divaricates on their arrival in Lamarckia. Lenk had encouraged new births, of course. But divaricates had generally had no more children on Thistledown than other Naderites, no more even than most Geshels. On Lamarckia, having children had become a ruling passion, as if some hidden drive had been awakened, and the human race—isolated as this weak little seed on a huge world—had needed to spread its limbs and foliage far and wide once more.

The ships were guided into Naderville's harbor in the early afternoon. The city perched on a headland on the northern side of the harbor, its back to a wall of thoroughly tunneled hedgerow thicket; to the south was a natural spit of rock and sand that served as a breakwater.

Naderville looked remarkably like Calcutta, golden and beige and white buildings rising on low hills facing the harbor. On the eastern extension of the headland, however, in the crater of a small extinct volcano, a military encampment had been established some five years before. The *Khoragos*'s physician, Julia Sand, had been to Naderville some years before as part of an abortive diplomatic effort, and explained these features to Shirla and me. Farther inland, the harbor connected with a wide canal, which may have once been a natural river, but had been adapted by the ecos to its own needs.

Sturdy little tugs took us in tow, then pulled us to the western extent of the harbor, and the mouth of the great Hsian canal. I watched the steamships as we drew apart, wondering if I might ever meet General Beys in person.

A sharp, buttery scent mixed with something herbaceous, like oregano, and an undercurrent of tar, blew with the wind from inland. It was not unpleasant, but I thought in time such a smell might grow irritating.

We cruised with great dignity behind the tugs for several miles, then were taken north through a narrow brickwork gate into a small lake. Hills rose on all sides, covered with dark, ancient thicket; on the higher hills, a few small white and sky-blue buildings seemed to clamber up the thickets and perch on top. I could make out holes hacked through the thickets like tunnels where roads might pass; on a bluff at the northern end of the harbor, the thicket had been cleared completely, leaving chalky barren soil and buildings, a watchtower and storage sheds.

Julia Sand had not seen this part of Naderville in her last visit. "It's all new to me," she said. On one side of the lake, ramps and large drydocks stood, a shipbuilding and repair site now idle.

Randall and Salap came forward to join us. Shatro was still belowdecks. He seemed to be depressed and we had not seen much of him for a day.

"It's a dreary land," Randall commented.

Salap scanned the small lake and announced, "Three ships. I was expecting many more."

The three ships in the lake were not even steamships; two were sloops, and one was a catamaran with tattered fore and aft rigged sails hanging on two masts. It was not much of a navy.

"They're all out raiding or keeping a blockade on Jakarta," Shirla said.

"Perhaps," Salap said, but he seemed dubious.

The pilots guided us past the empty drydocks, toward a small pier at the northern end of the lake. I estimated there was room for perhaps five or six ships the size of the steamships, no more. That would be a substantial navy on Lamarckia, but there was no way of telling how many steamships had been built. I looked for fuel bunkers—whatever the fuel might be—but could not find any. A few dozen men and women stood on the docks, watching us, but the pier was empty. No formal reception committee awaited Lenk's arrival.

The tugs let us loose. The light breeze was sufficient for our schooners to moor at the pier.

Ferrier and Keo came up on deck dressed in dark gray pants and long black coats, formal wear for a solemn occasion. They surveyed the pier with wounded expressions, like dogs who half expected to be struck. Both shook their heads at the indignity. "This is no way to treat the Good Lenk," Keo said. "I wonder why we came at all, if they're going to rub our noses in it."

"It's weakness," Ferrier said with an edge of anger he had not revealed before.

Keo took his arm and they assumed their positions by the gangway. Lenk came up from below on the stairs, aided by Fassid, who blinked at the bright sunshine. Lenk wore sunglasses. He seemed for a moment to have gone blind, stumbling slightly, smiling, reaching for Fassid. But he removed his sunglasses after a moment and stared at us owlishly, then studied the dry-docks south of us, the western shore of the lake, the pier.

Five men and three women stepped out of a gray shed and waited for our ships to maneuver close. Three young men near the bow tossed lines to them, and our ship was pulled in and tied up. All sails were furled.

We waited several minutes. The lake was still and quiet; the silva had not made a sound since our arrival. A single road stretched from the harbor through the hills to a tunnel in the high thicket beyond. It did not look promising.

"Are they expecting us to walk?" Ferrier asked in disgust.

"Intolerable," Fassid said, but Lenk raised his hand.

"He's feeling his power," Lenk said. He pressed his teeth together and drew his shoulders up. I thought I saw a brief spark of anger, but it might have been some internal twinge, a sore joint or other infirmity of age. "Let him have that much."

A reception committee, of sorts, was just now coming down the road. An electric truck passed through the main gate to the harbor and pier, followed by four small electric cars and a wavering line of men and women on bicycles.

Shirla whistled at all the vehicles. "There aren't that many in all of Calcutta," she said. "Except for tractors."

What had seemed at first glance, then, to be a paltry show of ceremony, was sufficient to impress the people around me. The gangway was pushed across to the dock and secured. The dockhands arranged along *Khoragos*'s moorage craned their necks curiously, looking for Lenk. Whatever Brion's social changes and political pressures, the citizens of Naderville still expressed an interest in the Good Lenk who had brought them here.

The truck and cars and bicycles rolled out onto the pier. The truck whined to a stop. The cars parked behind, and the bicyclists, all dressed in gray and brown, braked to a halt around and between them. Everybody paused for several seconds, waiting, and then the doors of the truck opened and a man and a woman got out. The cars' drivers opened their doors and got out as well. They all wore black, with little round hats pulled tight on their heads like swimming caps.

The man and woman from the truck were dressed in white formal suits. They resembled socialites at an early first-century Thistledown full-dress occasion. Producing a walking stick, the man stood beside the woman, and they advanced together toward the gangway, where they paused. Clearly, they expected our party to disembark now. Up to this point, however, not a word was said on either side. The only voices were those of the crew, arranging the sails and rigging, and even they spoke in hushed tones.

Ferrier and Keo crossed the gangway first and bowed to the man and woman in white, who returned their greetings with slightly reduced bows. Allrica Fassid came next, advancing her hands along the rope guards in nervous arcs, gripping the ropes carefully, as if someone might tip the platform and make her fall into the water between the dock and the ship.

After them came Lenk, marching across to the dock by himself with a good show of assurance and vigor. Five men and four women followed, all wearing green and tan, the colors of Lenk's personal guard. Last of all, three men we had not met—elderly enough to have served Lenk since the immigration—joined the party on the dock, giving and receiving brief bows.

We were not going ashore, apparently. Salap smiled his most philosophical smile and turned back to go below. Randall watched the crew reclaim the gangway and close the gate in the bulwark. "I'll be damned," he said.

Shirla sighed as much with relief as disappointment. "I don't like being at the center of things," she said.

Randall said, "I feel about as necessary as a man's nipples."

A few minutes later, a train of four gray electric buses hummed through the gate to the docks and parked by the *Khoragos* and *Cow*. Twelve grim-looking men in gray and black stepped down from the buses and spoke to their colleagues on guard by the gangways.

Guards came aboard the ships and informed the masters and mates that all but a skeleton crew of four would have to get on the buses. The ships were going to be impounded, it seemed.

Randall watched these activities with a heavy frown. "That's not diplomacy," he muttered. "It's an act of war."

We sat crowded three to a seat, two seats across and seven deep, on rough unpadded benches made of pithy thicketxyla. The buses were driven by older men in white and gray. Seeing the preponderance and variety of uniforms, I felt a shiver of recognition: a regimented society, each job given its rank and place and dress, ancient grand schemes reenacted on Lamarckia.

The buses took us into the tunnels through the thickets and we were surrounded by intense gloom. Shirla huddled close to me, Shatro beside her. In the gleam of headlights reflected toward the back, I saw Shatro staring grimly ahead, sweating though it was cool. He had said very little the past few hours, and did not look at anyone for very long.

Randall sat on the bench ahead of us, and Salap two benches behind. We did not talk. We all felt as though we were going to an execution, perhaps our own.

The tunnels formed a kind of road network through the thicket and the drivers seemed to know the routes well. After twenty minutes, we saw daylight ahead, and the buses emerged into a broad natural clearing. Behind, the thicket rose up in a gentle curve like the rim of a bowl, and we seemed to be in a broad crater painted with red and brown foliage.

Ahead, across a level plain covered with a carpet of mottled orange and brown phytids, the interior of this part of Hsia's ecos was hauntingly terrestrial. We might have been crossing a tropical grassland, but instead of trees, tangles of thicket woven from meter-thick vines rose like watchtowers, capped with spreading branches whose tips lanced skyward. Farther inland, after another ten minutes of travel, we saw great purple hemispheric mounds like mold growths, but each perhaps two kilometers wide and a kilometer high. At the top of the mounds, a single monumental black spike rose, a thorn to prick the thumb of a god.

The guards on the bus took this all in without excitement; this was their landscape, familiar for decades. Salap seemed as little interested. Shirla, however, leaned forward and looked past my chest through the window.

"They're taking us to a *grand* hotel," said the man behind us, dressed in a white uniform—one of *Khoragos*'s stewards. "They'll feed us like kings."

"Tom's the joker," grumbled a woman across the aisle. The bus lurched and we turned onto a dusty bare dirt road. Ahead, another wall of thicket loomed, but this was brilliant green—the first green I had seen in a Lamarckian silva, topped with red lances. Above this thicket flew batlike pterids with wingspans of at least a meter. As we approached, the pterids all dropped and grabbed hold of the red lances, like flies alighting on the bloody points of swords.

The buses swung into another dark tunnel, following closely through the darkness, lights blooming and fleeing on the backs of our heads. "Inner compound," the bus driver called over his shoulder, voice husky. "We'll all get out here and walk into the Citadel."

"Citadel," Shirla repeated, eyebrows raised.

The buses drew up in single file beside a road paved with broad flat black stones, white cement between. We left the buses and stood in groups on the edge of the road, the sun brilliant and hot overhead, the sky tinted orange. Shading my eyes, I saw the sky was filled with tiny flying things, orange, yellow, and brown, each no more than a centimeter square, flocking in thick clouds about twenty meters over our heads.

At the end of the road, a blocky stone wall rose high enough for its top to be blurred and half obscured by the yellow and orange clouds. The wall reached across a gap between two stretches of green thicket.

The guards took us from the buses with a minimum of cordiality, lined us up in two rows, and urged us forward, toward the stone wall. Shirla stayed resolutely beside me, Shatro, Randall, and Salap ahead.

"Excuse me, is this where Able Lenk is staying?" a sailor from the *Cow* asked a bulky, thick-faced guard. The guard shook his head, raised his lips in what might have been a smile but more resembled a grimace of discomfiture, and pointed to the wall. I studied the faces of the guards without catching their attention. Flat expressions and muscle predominated. Hair cut short but for a lock on the left side, which trailed to the shoulder. Uniforms neatly pressed, but judging from their movements, only fair military order. Some managed to talk or smile briefly to the two lines as we were marched, but their character and behavior did not reassure me. I felt as if I were back in the slaughtered village of Moonrise, and my neck hair bristled as it had not even during our time in the storm-beast.

The longer I stayed on Lamarckia, the more I felt sure I was going to die here, in an ancient and degrading fashion. I longed for Thistledown and could not imagine why I could ever have accepted such an assignment.

"I wish the storm had eaten us," Shirla muttered.

I touched her elbow with my hand, a brushing gesture that still caught the attention of the thick-faced guard. He gazed at me out of the corners of his eyes, pulled his lips together, and shook his head slightly.

At the gate in the wall, a small deep-sunk pair of doors barely wide enough for two to enter abreast, the lines were halted and the guards milled about, making last-minute checks for anything we might be carrying. They poked and prodded us like animals, conferred, and then the senior officer—a tall, stoop-shouldered fellow whose uniform sleeves rode up on his arms—called out, and the doors swung wide.

We entered the wall.

CHAPTER SEVENTEEN

Dark stone, cool shadow for several meters, then an intense milky green light that seemed to hang like a canopy of fog. The air smelled sweet and slightly bitter.

"Don't be alarmed," the stoop-shouldered senior officer called out as the lines marched into the greenness. "It's no worse than taking a shower. We've all done it. Your Able Lenk has done it and said it was a pleasure."

Small scions, no larger than midges, filled the air in a swirling mist and lighted on our skin and crawled beneath our clothes until we each wore a pale green coat. Shirla squirmed and tried to brush them off, but they clung tenaciously, like living green oil.

"Do not be alarmed," the guards repeated, and the thick-faced fellow reached a xyla stick past me and poked Shirla in the back, bobbing his head at her. I restrained a strong urge to grab the stick and shove it back. "These are servants, not pests. They clean you up for your visit with Ser Brion."

After a few minutes of mild discomfort—more at the thought than the actual sensation—the tiny creatures rose into the air again and hovered above our heads, filling the upper reaches of a large, white-walled cell, open at the top to the sky. I turned to look at Randall and Salap. Salap lifted his arms, the last of the tiny scions rising from him like green steam. He seemed stunned, his face slack, more surprised than he had been upon seeing the humanoid skeletons.

Never, in the history of the immigrants on Lamarckia, had scions ever *served* humans, or strongly interacted with them in any way.

Randall stood stiff as a board, eyes half closed, and shook his shoulders to make sure he was free of the creatures. The guards moved us through the door at the opposite end of the white cubicle, and we came to a broad courtyard surrounded by densely packed, flat-fronted gray brick buildings. The courtyard, except for us, was empty, and it quickly became obvious that we were not in Naderville proper, but in some special compound—the most likely conclusion being that this was a kind of prison. Shirla took hold of my arm despite the poking stick of a guard. When the guard poked at her hard, making her flinch, I could not stand still any longer. I turned and grabbed the stick, wrenched it from his grip, and broke it in two.

The thick-faced fellow stared at me in dumb surprise. Around us, the other guards began to break us into groups of four or five. Still, I met the thick-faced man's stare for several seconds, until he pointed to the broken stick on the ground and said, "Pick it up."

Shirla stooped to do so, but I brought her back to her feet with a not-very-gentle jerk. She looked between us with eyes squinted, but took hold of my arm again.

"Pick it *up*," the guard repeated, his face reddening. He advanced a half step. None of the guards had guns. All my senses sharpened and I examined the situation almost dispassionately, seeing how many guards were close, judging how my fellow captives would react to an incident.

Randall intervened. "What in the name of the Good Man is this about?" he shouted, charging between us and standing stiff-legged, arms held up, fists clenched, as if he meant to fight the man himself. "What is this *brutishness*?"

The tall, stoop-shouldered officer had also seen the brewing confrontation, and strode to Randall's side. "Pardon this, please," he said, his voice soft. "No harm is meant. No harm is meant." Thus soothing and separating us, the incident was brought to an end, and we were divided peacefully enough and led through different doors around the compound. Shirla and I were separated, but there was nothing we could practically do, other than provoke another incident, which I felt we would not be able to conclude in our favor. Shirla looked at me, eyes wide, then swung her head away abruptly and walked with her group of women through a narrow xyla door. I could not tell whether she felt betrayed or simply had resigned herself to whatever was going to happen.

She hated confinement. I dreaded the prospect myself.

The rooms within the gray brick buildings were uniform, four on the ground floor and I presumed four on the upper floor, accessible through a stairwell rising from the middle to the rear. Each room was equipped with a single small square window, two double bunks, a table, and chairs. They smelled clean enough, but the sanitary facilities were primitive: a hole in the floor in one corner, a single tap for water that also served to flush the hole.

"You won't be here for more than a few hours," the thick-faced guard said. He closed the door on Salap, a steward named Rissin, myself, and a young sailor named Cortland.

We settled ourselves as best we could, introduced ourselves, tried to pass the time. Lying in my bunk to doze, I saw something scratched into the bricks of the wall: a crude drawing, a head with round eyes and a down-turned mouth, arms and legs sticking out of it, hair in jags. Beside this figure, five crude letters: B-O-B-R-T. We looked for and found other drawings scattered around the room, on the floors or walls.

"Children," the young sailor, Cortland, said.

Salap let his shoulders droop, and lay on his bunk with a sharp expulsion of breath. "Ser Olmy, I am ashamed," he said.

I shook my head, but could not think of anything to say.

The hours passed, and it grew dark outside. No one came for us, and no one brought information.

A single light bulb came on within the room, casting a dismal pale pink glow, a sick and depressing color under the circumstances.

"Do you think they're going to kill us?" Rissin asked.

"No," Salap said.

Rissin began to fidget on his bunk above mine. "This is not what I thought would happen," he said. "Not as long as we were with Lenk."

I tried to puzzle the situation through. Either the Brionists were savages on the order of the worst human history had produced, or we were simply in crude detention, until Brion and Lenk had finished negotiations. I tried to imagine what strengths Lenk would negotiate from.

CHAPTER EIGHTEEN

The door opened and the thick-faced guard watched as a man and a woman in light blue aprons brought four covered plates. The guard was now armed, I saw—a small pistol. We took our plates and the door was closed. The plates contained a thoroughly cooked green vegetable and a scoop of paste-thick wheat gruel.

The light went out. The steward and the young sailor did not notice; they were asleep. Salap gave a little grunt and moved around in the darkness.

"Olmy, are you awake?" he asked.

"Yes."

"Lenk said Brion had a great secret. Do you think he meant using the scions as servants?"

"Perhaps."

"Do you know what that implies?"

"I think so," I said.

"It could dwarf the importance of our little skeletons," Salap said. "It changes the way we have to think about the ecoi . . ."

He lapsed into silence, standing in the middle of the room, facing the dim glow of the square window. "I am lost," he said. "Everything I knew is turned upside down. All my studies . . . Everything the explorers found, or thought they found. Brion has gone beyond us all." Salap came closer to my bunk and whispered, "What are you going to do?"

"I'm going to stay here, like you, until they come and get us."

"Unless you're from the Hexamon."

"What do you think, that they'd send some sort of superhuman? You want me to break down the walls and let us escape?"

Salap chuckled dryly. "If you were from the Hexamon, would you reveal yourself to Brion, or to General Beys? It could make a significant impression."

"This is stupid talk," I said. "The disciplinary was crazy. Randall was gullible. I'm no superhuman."

Salap stood. I heard him rubbing his hands together in the dark. "I have no wife and children, no alliance with a family," he said. "I have never cared much for family life. But I have always taken care of my researchers, my assistants, my students. I've failed."

"We're all helpless," I said.

"You don't get my meaning. I have always seen a single bright thread of destiny stretching ahead of me. And I've felt those around me would be safe, as long as that thread stretched taut . . ."

"We're not dead yet," I said, finding this line of talk no more useful than the last.

"I have never known what to think of the Good Lenk," Salap said. "When we followed him here, he seemed all-knowing, very thorough. But he has not handled the factions well. So much rancor, so little resolve . . . Unwilling to crack heads, I believe."

"You think he should have cracked a few heads?"

"I think he should have been prepared to do what needed to be done. Ready for what happened. Perhaps the dream is over for Lenk."

Cortland stirred and poked his head over the edge of the bunk. "Have some courage," he said in a harsh whisper. "Don't speculate about things you can't know. Brion may be in for a surprise."

"What kind of surprise?" I asked, suddenly intensely curious. The situation had been entirely too simple, when history demanded that it should be complex and dynamic.

"I'm just a sailor. I don't know much of anything. But Lenk never plays from weakness."

Salap made a small chuff of disbelief. "Let him surprise me, and I will be in his debt even more."

"We're all in his debt," Cortland said with little-boy confidence. "He took us from Thistledown. General Beys doesn't know everything."

"You were born here," Salap said. "You never saw Thistledown."

"How old were *you* when you came here?"

"Twenty," Salap said.

"And you?" the sailor asked, aiming his voice in the dark to where I sat on the lower bunk.

"I was born here," I said. "I never saw Thistledown. I've read about it."

Salap said nothing.

"I never liked hearing stories about Thistledown," Cortland said. "Too much for any human to think about."

"And Lamarckia is not?" I asked, chuckling.

"Lamarckia is like Lenk," the sailor said. "Benevolent, but full of surprises."

"The green," Salap said.

"Yeah," Cortland said. "Why green?"

Salap did not answer.

Rissin the steward snored on.

I dozed a few hours and came awake just before morning. Through the window, I saw a reddish natural stone surface mottled with drooping dark green shapes like melted fern fronds. Banging noises in the courtyard of the compound awoke Salap, Rissin, and Cortland. They used the meager facilities and we stood expectantly near the door, awaiting breakfast, freedom, or whatever might present itself.

The thick-faced guard opened the door and waved us outside. We stood blinking and stretching in the brightness, watching others emerge from the doors around the courtyard. Salap adjusted his long shirt and pants, saw me observing him, and smiled at his pretensions.

Tables had been set up in the center of the courtyard. Shirla stood by one, and I glanced at the guards, who seemed to have their attention on other matters—conferring with more servers in blue aprons, or counting the people coming through doors. I walked across the stone floor of the compound and hugged Shirla.

"Not a comfortable night," she said, clinging to me. With a small shudder, she let me go and looked around the courtyard, lips pressed tightly together. "But we aren't dead. This seems to be breakfast . . ."

Servers brought plates on rolling carts and food in big ceramic bowls. Randall, his stiff brown hair awry, sat at the table across from Shirla and me. We were served more greens and gruel. The guards stood back as if we were not important, or perhaps not even there. All were armed.

Randall ate his serving in silence, staring at nothing in particular. Shirla spoke about the accommodations, no different from ours, and then asked, "I see Salap, but where's Shatro?"

"Not here," Randall said.

"Why?"

"Said he had something to tell Brion. The guard let him out last night." Randall gazed at me over a poised spoon. "He's going to tell them about you."

Shirla turned and asked, "What about you?"

I frowned and shook my head in disgust. "A stupid story," I said.

Randall focused on nothing again.

The stoop-shouldered officer walked to the northern side of the compound, followed by another guard carrying a small crate. The guard placed the crate on the ground and the officer stepped up onto it, shifting one of the odd curved batons from hand to hand. The thicket above and behind the western buildings of the compound glowed brilliant gold-green in the morning sun.

All around the compound, a distant whirring alternated with faint, high-speed chuckle-clucks—the first sounds I had heard that seemed to come from the ecos.

"Hello," the officer said to the assembly around the tables. He shifted his weight from one leg to the other, clutching the baton in both hands now, ill-at-ease. "I realize this part of your visit has been a little boring, but I hope you understand. I can tell you that talks between Ser Able and Ser Brion have been going well." He stopped here, and we glanced at each other, clearly not feeling much encouraged.

"There is no danger. Our manner may seem harsh, but we mean no harm. We have reacted to very difficult circumstances with increased re-solve and order. You should not believe all those stories . . . those things that we have been accused of." This awkward phrasing seemed to irritate him, and he drew his eyebrows together, slipped the stick into a loop in his coat, and clasped his hands before him. "Now that you've finished your meal, we will clear the tables, and you will . . ." He conferred with the guard, who whispered in his ear. "You will gather in a single group in this corner of the compound." He withdrew the stick again and used it to point to the north-western corner.

"What the hell is that?" Shirla asked. "A whip?"

"Looks like a thin boomerang," said an older woman A.B. beside her.

"So please, let us begin," the officer concluded. Then, as an afterthought, "My name is Pitt, Suleiman Ab Pitt. Your host attendants will answer individual questions."

Shirla's concern of the night before had dissolved into quiet contempt. "What a cargo," she muttered. "They think we're idiots."

All around, with fatuous smiles, the guards urged us to our feet and we followed them to a broad double door at the far end of the courtyard, still in shadow. Brion must have had some reason for subjecting newcomers to this passage through door after door, I thought, but none came to mind. My old cynicism returned in force. Nothing made sense. I tried to keep my mind blank. The only positive in this personal cloud of negative emotions was Shirla's closeness. It seemed that through her, I could attach myself to the simple fact of being human; however much bad examples came to mind, she countered them.

But Shirla was not in an optimistic frame of mind, either. We followed the stoop-shouldered officer, Pitt, surrounded by guards, through the broad door, four and five abreast, and came to a flat green space on the other side. For a moment, my eyes refused to believe, but then I saw it for what it was: a well-manicured lawn, covering perhaps fifty acres. Trees—terrestrial varieties, oaks, maples, elms—rose all around, throwing their shadows through a rising, patchy ground mist. At the borders of this garden, intensely green thicket rose in a tortured wall to a height of twenty meters, casting its own shadow over the grass. The guards encouraged us to walk onto the lawn. Salap bent down and touched the grass, and across the nine or ten meters between us, his eyes met mine. He seemed now always to seek out my face when confronted by the unexpected, as if I might explain things to him.

But he called out, "Not grass."

Shirla's shoulders trembled and she shivered all over, as if touched by a ghost. "I've never seen grass," she said.

"We didn't bring this kind of grass with us," Randall said. The sailors and other members of the crews stood like sheep on this unexpected sward, uncertain what was expected of them.

"Brion shows you the beauties of the world he foresees," Pitt called out.

The role of master of ceremonies did not suit him. His eyes remained flinty, his shoulders drawn down, no matter how broad his smile and generous his tone. "We have formed an alliance with the ecos, and it works with us, for us."

Salap shook his head, still disbelieving. One by one, embarrassed but gaining in courage, the crews kneeled and felt the grass, or walked over to the nearest trees and touched the apparent bark, the branches and leaves.

Not a leaf out of place, the lawn as perfect as a carpet.

I kneeled and touched the blades. They were cool and stiff, much stiffer than the grass I had walked across in parks in Thistledown.

A commotion began at the south side of the garden. I looked up from several blades of grass I had pulled loose: they writhed slowly in my hand like tiny worms.

Keo and Ferrier were arguing with several guards. Pitt walked over briskly like a tall gray crow, pointing his baton straight down by his side. More words were exchanged. Salap and Randall came closer to Shirla and me. "Someone's upset," Salap said.

A tall woman with golden-brown skin and long black hair, wearing a rich white and gray gown, entered the garden and took Pitt aside. Pitt listened intently.

Keo and Ferrier looked on in some satisfaction. The crews stood frozen, scattered across the false lawn, watching the woman and Pitt as if their lives might depend on the result.

Finally, Pitt approached a group of four guards, gave them quick instructions, and shouted, "There has been a misunderstanding. The following people will come forward." He took a list from Keo and read: "Nussbaum, Grolier, Salap, Randall, Olmy, Shatro."

Shirla let go of my arm and stepped away. I glanced at her, puzzled, but she nodded toward Ferrier, Keo, and Pitt. "Go," she said.

I did not want to leave her. Salap walked a few paces and stopped, looking back. Randall joined him, and Shirla gave me a nudge. "Maybe it's something important," she said. "Come back and tell me."

Keo and Ferrier greeted Nussbaum and Grolier, and then turned toward us. "Able Lenk didn't suspect they'd take you off the ship," Keo said, walking toward the gate. "He's very upset." We all followed. The tall woman in white and gray stayed behind, still talking to Pitt. "He's calling for his researchers. Where's Shatro?"

"He left the compound last night," Randall said. "We don't know where they took him."

"Well, we'll find him. We've seen pretty terrifying things. Changes our perspective, I'll tell you."

We passed through the doors and crossed the compound.

"Grass," Ferrier said, shaking his head in amazement.

CHAPTER NINETEEN

"Brion's confessed to sending the pirates," Keo said. We walked between three guards and behind the auburn-haired woman, whose ubiquitous presence had not yet been explained. We did not even know her name. "Everybody else denies it. I think he may be a little mad."

"He is not mad," the woman said sharply. She carried herself erect, footsteps delicate and precise, gliding over the ground, her dark-red gown swishing around her ankles with a sound like little rushes of water. Her skin was a rich, pale brown, and her eyes deep black, surrounded by ivory-colored sclera. She did not seem at all impressed by us.

Keo cleared his throat and raised his eyebrows. We came to a wall made of round stones the size of a human head and smooth as pearls, glued together with a translucent, glistening mortar. The wall rose almost fifteen meters and was capped by the drooping, melted fern shapes I had seen through the window of our room in the compound. A hole had been knocked in the base of the wall, and a smoothly planed xyla door had been set in the hole. It looked out of place. Salap touched the surrounding stones lightly as we passed through.

Our eyes adjusted slowly to the dark beyond the door. The auburn-haired woman took a lantern from the wall and switched it on. From all around, the stones returned muted reflections, surrounding us with thousands of dim, sleepy eyes. The stones rose in a free-form arch that came to a point about ten meters overhead. Beyond the arch, pillars marched unevenly into gloom relieved only by a few lanterns. The floor felt resilient underfoot.

I strongly doubted that Brion's people were responsible for this construction. It seemed poorly adapted for human use. If the architecture called to mind anything, it was the palaces on Martha's Land. While these chambers were empty, however, they were not in ruins. Hsia seemed to build for the ages.

The woman guided us through the pillars toward a point of orange light, surrounded by a peculiar granular halo, twenty or thirty meters away. The light and halo resolved into a large lantern mounted on the pearl-stone wall beside another inset doorway. The wall around the door glowed faintly, sunlight seeping through the translucent mortar surrounding the stones.

A guard stepped forward and opened the door. Temporarily blinded by daylight, we stepped through into a rich vegetal tangle of green vines, smooth branches, spreading leaves, helical creepers and aerial roots, melted ferns, pendulous waxy fruits: an orgy of green growth.

Bright late-morning sun cast speckles of tinted light on a carpet of discarded and shriveled leaves and branches. Randall muttered something I did not hear clearly. Salap wore a wise half smile, as if nothing would surprise him now.

"This is the vivarium," the woman said. "My sister spent much of her time here, before she died."

"It's wonderful," Salap said.

The woman walked ahead.

A few dozen meters down a trail, we came to a broad clearing covered with the same stiff, well-manicured "grass" we had seen before. A lattice of smooth bright-green branches, like the weave of a wicker bowl, overarched and shaded three square gray brick buildings on the edge of the clearing.

"Some of your people are quartered here," the auburn-haired woman said. She stopped at the door to the nearest building, still refusing to look directly at us.

The guards stood aside and we passed through the door. Inside, a small, square room with narrow windows, lighted by two electric lanterns on poles, was furnished with couches and two chairs.

Allrica Fassid entered through a door opposite the entrance, skin pale, deep lines around her nose and lips and across her brow. She whispered a few words to Keo, then faced Salap, Randall, and me. She pushed her shoulders forward and inclined her head, looking to one side, like a young girl about to perform some unpleasant chore. "One of your researchers tried to visit Brion. It appears Brion received him. We don't know what they talked about." Her face tensed and her eyes bore into us, but that passed and her weary expression returned. "Did Ser Keo tell you what we've learned?"

"Only that Brion has done some confessing," Randall said.

"Of a sort," Fassid said. "I'd call it bragging. He has a smile that makes me want to kill." She sniffed and drew her head back, speaking more force-fully. "He's made some unbelievable claims. We need all the expertise we can muster to evaluate them."

"They've done extraordinary things with the ecos," Salap said. "That's obvious."

Fassid faced Salap squarely and took a small, shivering breath. She was swallowing pride, anger, and frustration, and the effort made her seem like a marionette in the hands of a nervous puppeteer. "My apologies. I wish I could apologize to Captain Keyser-Bach, as well."

Salap's grin faded. He stared at her with the complete lack of emotion that I had learned to interpret as extreme irritation. "Why?" he asked.

"Brion has caught us by surprise," Fassid said. "If we had known more . . . about Lamarckia, about Hsia, we might have anticipated some of what we've seen the past few hours . . ."

Salap folded his hands, taking no obvious pleasure in this triumph. "How can we help the esteemed Lenk?" he asked quietly.

CHAPTER TWENTY

Lenk stood by a broad window overlooking the vivarium. The furnish-ings and decor of the large but spare rooms assigned to Lenk and his aides fit the deliberate air of drabness seen everywhere. Brion did not revel in luxury.

Lenk showed all of his eighty-four natural years, and more. With his slumped shoulders and inclined head, his chin drawn deeply into his neck, he looked painfully old.

"Brion keeps referring to his triumph," Fassid said, pressing the window with one extended finger, until the adjacent knuckles met the glass. "He also calls it his mistake. He says he made Hsia an offering. Somehow, he's collaborated . . . allied himself with the ecos."

"Is that certain?" Salap asked. We sat on frame chairs opposite the window, suffused by the cool green light of the vivarium's lush growth.

"It's what he says," Lenk murmured.

"What does your researcher say?" Salap asked

"Ser Rustin won't venture an opinion," Lenk said.

"Brion and his wife somehow persuaded the ecos to grow them food," Fassid continued. "They brought Naderville out of the worst famine they had experienced, but according to our intelligence, Brion very nearly had a rebellion on his hands. Some of his people thought a sacrilege had been committed."

"We did not hear *that* from Brion," Keo said dryly.

"Brion's tenure here has not been all that smooth. But our information about Hsia has always been fragmentary," Fassid said. "We learned even less after Brion gave almost all government authority to Beys."

Salap shook his head, plainly trying to get past what were to him irrelevancies.

"There was so much of our own pain to deal with," Lenk said, his deep voice quavering.

Randall asked, "Do you know where Shatro is now?"

"No," Keo said. "Our chief negotiator says he's offered his services to Brion."

"He's been through a lot of trouble," Salap interceded, like a mother protecting a wayward child. This sudden mildness surprised both Randall and me. Salap regarded us with eyes half closed, the elfin smile back on his lips. "He would not be much help to us now. Strictly a technical fellow. No brilliance in him." Salap folded his hands in his lap.

The door to the room opened and a tall, loose-jointed man about my age, with sandy brown hair and a broad, sheeplike face, came in, followed by a short young woman with intelligent eyes. Fassid introduced the man, Lenk's head researcher, Georg Ny Rustin. Salap and he seemed to know each other, and Rustin was not comfortable in Salap's presence.

"We've learned nothing new," Rustin said to Lenk, Keo, and Fassid. "Nothing more surprising, at any rate."

Salap turned toward Lenk's researcher. Rustin had been on the *Cow* and, until this moment, we had not met. "Ser Rustin, I assume we will be working together . . ."

"I disagree that I've reached my limits," Rustin said quickly, glancing at Fassid and Lenk. Then, realizing he had showed his suspicions too plainly, he said, "Of course, I welcome your opinions."

"Is it your opinion that the ecos here has understood our genetic language?"

"Not at all," Rustin said. "All we've been shown so far could be adaptive imitation. We've seen it before. Imitation of the outward physical form of scions, but not the internal structure."

Salap leaned his head to one side. "These forms that resemble terrestrial plants . . . are purely imitative?"

"I've only been able to make preliminary tests, and that woman Chung has hovered around us . . . but yes, I'd say they're purely imitative, with little deep-structure resemblance."

"Have Brion's researchers learned whether these new forms . . . these *collaborations*, let's call them . . . use our genetic methods? Terrestrial genetic syntax?"

Rustin shook his head again. "They do *not*. They're megacytic, with fluid-filled spongelike tissues rather than true cellular structure. We've confirmed that positively with samples put through our own lab kits." The dark young woman lifted a black case that presumably contained the lab kits. She seemed eager to speak, but protocol held her back.

"Have you given any thought to what Brion intends to do with these new forms?"

Rustin shook his head. "Other than what we've been told . . . no."

"Well," Salap said. "You were never one for going beyond the immediate evidence and drawing far-fetched conclusions."

Rustin did not know whether to receive that as a compliment.

"Are these new green scions similar to the food varieties Brion claims saved them?"

"I don't know," Rustin said.

"You have found chlorophyll in these imitations?"

"We've examined the entire pigment range. Besides the usual varieties of Lamarckian pigments, they contain chlorophyll alpha and beta. These pigments do not occur elsewhere on Lamarckia," Rustin said.

"And what does that imply to you?"

Rustin blinked nervously. "It's new," he said. "It's possible Brion's somehow managed to . . ." He raised a hand, waved it vaguely. "Pass on clues to the ecos. But I don't see how."

Salap turned his gaze to the red-haired woman. "You are Jessica McCall, or do I remember incorrectly?"

"You have a marvelous memory," the woman said, clearly pleased to be in his presence.

"What do you think, Ser McCall?" Salap asked.

McCall swiftly studied the faces of Fassid and Rustin, glanced at Lenk, who had his back turned to us, and said, "I'm very concerned, Ser Salap. If the ecos understands the benefits of these far more efficient photosynthetic pigments—"

"I am also concerned," Salap interrupted. "Ser Rustin, you have done your job well."

"Brion's people are not at all cooperative," Rustin said. Then, in a frustrated rush, "This Hyssha Chung in particular has been very difficult. She claims the vivarium is a memorial to her sister. She refuses to let us conduct thorough studies on the remarkable scions it contains."

Salap made a humming noise and nodded. "Able Lenk, I would like to reorganize this team of researchers . . . to take advantage of all our talents in the most efficient manner."

"Why?" Rustin asked, Adam's apple bobbing, dismayed by the sudden request.

Lenk looked at Salap sadly, one eyelid twitching. "If it's necessary," he said.

"It is," Salap said.

Rustin began to stammer a few words about resigning. Salap laid one hand lightly on his shoulder and said, "We have no time for social games."

"I have earned this position, and I have always relied on the confidence of Able Lenk!" Rustin cried out, tears rolling down his flat, red cheeks.

"We can all be useful," Salap concluded after a moment of painful silence. Rustin wiped the back of his hand across his mouth, blinking rapidly.

"I would be honored to have Ser Salap tell me what's happening here," Lenk said.

"Clearly, Brion reveals part of the truth," Salap said. "Some form of collaboration has occurred."

"Are they capable of doing more?" Fassid asked.

"What do you fear them doing?"

"You mentioned Martha's Island making human-shaped scions."

Salap shook his head. "That may mean nothing here. What Brion has done could be much more dangerous. Brion may be right—it could be both triumph and mistake."

"He's not an easy man to understand," Fassid said.

"I understand him well enough," Lenk said.

"What else did Brion confess to?" I asked before I gave the words much thought.

Fassid looked at me as if I were some sort of noisy insect.

"Ser Olmy witnessed the death of a village, not too many months ago," Randall said, neatly giving me a reason for speaking up, stepping out of my place. All but Lenk and Fassid nodded sympathetically. There were many undercurrents in this room, and I could not track them all.

Lenk turned back to the window.

"It's a good question," Keo said. "Brion has given military and even most civilian authority to General Beys. Beys has been making most of the major policy decisions for at least two years. He began sending ships out to gather supplies—that is, raid villages—last year. This year, he accompanied the raiders personally, planning to force Able Lenk to concede authority. He raided all around Elizabeth, and he stole children. He built sail barges along the coast and sent the stolen equipment and food and children back to Naderville. They're alive, Brion says, and are being well-cared for."

"Their parents are dead," Fassid said bitterly. "I despise the man."

"Why did Beys take the children?" I asked. Lenk looked directly at me, as if to reevaluate what he had seen earlier. Randall and Salap regarded me with a fixed intensity that might have been fascination, or a warning.

"They lost over half of their children in the famine," Keo said. "It was that bad."

"He did not come to me," Lenk said. "If we had known, we would have shared what little we had."

"He didn't want your help because it would have made him look weak," Fassid said. "Beys may not have acted on his direct orders, but he knew what Brion wanted. A future, a people to rule."

Randall said, "Children were kept in the compound where we spent the night."

"Yes. Some of the children are here," Lenk said. His throat bobbed and his eyes narrowed. "Makes things very complicated. Hostages now."

The children could not be considered hostages unless Lenk was being pressured to do something, to agree to something—or unless he planned to exert pressure himself, and felt Brion might refuse.

"I don't see that this talk gets us anywhere," Rustin said. "We're here to discuss the ecos and what Brion has accomplished."

"So we are," Salap said, eyes languid.

Lenk's face became lax, almost dead-looking. I saw again the features of the soldier on the prow of the flatboat. In the grip of overwhelming history. Not all the truth was being told; perhaps very little.

I had hoped to admire Lenk in some way, for his leadership and presence, as a force of divaricate society. Instead, he made me uneasy. I felt his power, could not help but respect his presence, but it seemed only half the man was truly with us. The other half was hidden and would never be shown.

"We have no further meetings scheduled." Fassid said. "Brion canceled tomorrow's meeting with Able Lenk. He's suggested we discuss certain issues with General Beys—"

"I will not meet with that man," Lenk said.

"No, we've agreed that Brion is who we must talk with," Keo said with a regretful sigh. "He is an enigmatic and difficult man, and this Chung woman is another enigma."

"She escorted you here," Fassid explained. "Caitla Chung, Brion's wife, was her sister. I think she's also Brion's mistress, though that's hard to judge—he could have so many of them."

Lenk's face underwent a sudden and very brief transformation. In what had, until now, been flat weariness, I saw pass a shudder of deep anger. In a blink, the weariness returned.

CHAPTER TWENTY-ONE

I awoke in darkness and did not immediately know where I was or where I had been. I remembered being in brightness going down a long hallway, perhaps into another room. That was a dream. Finally the dreaming had begun.

I did not welcome the returning memory of where I was: still in Brion's nightmare. I felt strongly that another gate would open soon and I would be taken to the presiding minister for debriefing. It would be a grim story but not so grim as the fear I had felt in the dream at the thought of going into that other room. I rolled over in the bunk and pinched my earlobe until it hurt, struggling to sharpen my thoughts.

An electric light came on in the darkness.

I sat up. The room seemed even more drab and impersonal than it had the night before. Salap, Randall, and I had each been given private quarters near the compound, away from the palace of stones and the vivarium. There were no windows; it was little different from a prison cell, but for the furnishings, which were at least comfortable, though worn.

The electric light on the ceiling sang faintly. Through the door, a woman's voice said, "Ser Olmy, you are expected." It was Hyssha Chung.

"By whom?"

"Ser Brion and General Beys."

I swung my legs out of the bed. "I'm getting dressed," I said. "What time is it?"

"Early morning."

Chung regarded me with some interest this time, as I came through the door. "Your shirt is out in the back," she said. From her, that seemed a statement of great affection. It almost made her charming.

I tucked my shirt in and followed her out of the building onto a dirt path between high brick walls. Beyond, the tall, dense thicket began, and we entered a tunnel through the densely woven growth. The walls of the tunnel rustled slightly as we passed through, dark intertwined branches moving less than a centimeter as the great mass of the thicket above our heads made minor adjustments.

"Do these tunnels ever fill in, or grow back?" I asked Chung.

"No," she said.

We met up with Salap and Randall at a juncture of four tunnels. They were accompanied by two male guards. Each guard wore a holstered pistol. Electric lights hung from the roofs of the branching tunnels, suspended from dry, hard vines as thick as a man's leg. Chung took the left-swinging branch—I believed it headed south, but could not be sure—and we followed, the guards close behind.

Fifty meters down the tunnel, we came to a bend, and around the bend we saw daylight. The tunnel ended, and we emerged at the bottom of a bowl-shaped crater, perhaps a kilometer across. We stood in a gap where the crater wall had collapsed and the gap had been filled in with thicket.

The air within the crater was warm and still. The thicket above and behind rustled like waves on a distant beach.

In the center of the crater, a mass of shiny black hemispheres, studded with spikes and surmounted by arches, resembled a pile of huge, dead spiders. A path led down the rocky bottom of the crater to the pile. Chung proceeded down the path, and again we followed. I wondered if she relished the role of silent guide.

The crater appeared barren. It reminded me of Martha's Island, but here and there, steam and drifts of sulfurous gas still rose from vents around the bowl.

"Do you come here often?" Randall asked.

"Too often," Hyssha Chung said.

The path skirted the base of a shiny arch, curved between two black hemispheres as perfect as blown glass bubbles, and we stood before a small, low white stone building that had been hidden until now.

"This part we made," Chung said. She opened a double door of thicket-xyla, cleverly fitted and interwoven, and we entered a cool, dark room that smelled strongly of cut grass. A radiance of long gaps in the ceiling allowed sun to draw bright lines on the lava gravel floor.

I looked up from the sunlines to see two men standing in shadow by a table at the center of the whitewashed block-walled room. We crossed the room, feet crunching in the lava gravel, dazzled by the brilliant shafts of sun.

This room contained shelves lined with large bottles of liquid, most of them green or dark brown in color. The smooth concrete floor sloped to a drain at the center. The floor was covered with green and brown stains, despite its appearance of having been recently scrubbed. Damp spots and a rivulet of water darkened the concrete.

The air smelled overpoweringly of vegetation. Three electric lights in the ceiling came on, and I saw the two men clearly for the first time, in the center of the room.

A small sinewy man stood to the right of the table, his face thin, pushed-up nose and high, hollow cheeks giving him an exaggerated boyish appearance, verging on the simian. He seemed at first glance to be my height, but he stood a few centimeters shorter. Lank brown hair hung past his ears. His eyes were large and liquid, dark green, and his skin was sallow. He seemed ready to smile with any provocation: glad to see us, as if we were friends long absent. He wore a simple silver-gray coat and pants, the coat laced at the front, half open to reveal a collarless white shirt, and his hands were covered by dingy brown gloves. In one hand he carried a piece of string, which he wound and rewound around the finger of his other hand.

"Ser Brion, General Beys, these are Sers Salap, Randall, and Olmy." Brion looked me over shrewdly, rubbing his shoulder with one hand as if it pained him, then tapped his fingers in a silent tattoo on his biceps. He approached and looked me over as if he were deciding whether or not to buy me. He smiled. "General?"

Beys wore a gray tailored suit. Little taller than Brion, he was thickset and broad shouldered, a small bull, powerful, with thick, ruddy hands. His eyes seemed almost merry, set deep in a milky countenance above reddish cheeks. Beys shrugged. "I can seldom judge men by their appearance. We hide ourselves so well."

Randall stood stiffly, hands clasped behind his back, eyes focusing on the others in the room, one at a time, mechanically. I could sense by his posture and the tight, white-jointed tangle of his fingers his passion against Beys and Brion.

Brion lifted his eyes and stared directly at me, his smile genuine, his eyes gleaming with intense interest. "All right. Show me something. Kill me now rather than wait. I'm sure you've been filled with hatred by Lenk's people."

I think he half expected me to lift a finger and blast him to ashes. He seemed happy with the thought, and a little disappointed when I did nothing. His eyes dulled and his smile weakened.

"You don't want to kill me?"

"No."

"Could you kill me if you wanted to?"

"I don't have any weapons," I said.

He examined me again, as if the first time had not been sufficient. "Inside or out?"

"No weapons," I said.

He focused suddenly on Salap. "You are Mansur Salap. I know your name, of course. Your assistant, Shatro, seems to think he's been useful to me. Actually, I've been aware of Ser Olmy's presence on Lamarckia for some time now."

He turned his gaze on me again and his smile grew, as if he were reading my thoughts. "Usually I hear about poseurs and unfortunates. In your case, my contacts may have stumbled on the real thing." Brion's smile broadened. "How long have you been here?" he asked.

"One hundred and forty-three days."

"Does Lenk know who you are?"

"I don't know."

Brion stepped back but still stared at me. "I expected the Hexamon would send an army to punish us and take us back to Thistledown."

"I never expected that," Beys said mildly.

"Well, I hoped for one," Brion said. He motioned for us all to sit on the thicket-xyla chairs. We formed a circle around the table in the center of the square room. "Ser Shatro thought he would gain some advantage or revenge by turning you in. He doesn't like you. He doesn't like anybody much now. He's a very disappointed man."

"Not my best student," Salap said.

"It's interesting, the first time I have a chance to meet with Lenk, and he brings people far more interesting than himself . . . Among them, key scientists rescued from a shipwreck. A ship captained by Keyser-Bach. I'd have enjoyed meeting that man. I regret his death. I'm honored to meet you,

Ser Randall, and you, Ser Salap. I've received copies of all your journals and publications."

Salap nodded, but said nothing. My admission had thrown this meeting into confusion. Only Brion seemed to have a sense of direction.

He turned to me, hands on his knees, and asked, "Are you here to judge us?"

"I'm here to see if humans have damaged Lamarckia."

"It's taken them a long time to get around to us," Brion said. "Time enough for a new generation to be born—and for a lot of us to die. Is the Hexamon going to descend on us and reclaim our planet?"

"I'm not in communication with them."

"Do you have a clavicle?"

"No."

"No way to communicate with Thistledown?"

"No," I said.

"Did Lenk bring his clavicle on the ship?" Brion asked Beys.

"Yes," the general answered, lifting his chin and scratching his neck. His fingers left pale marks on the reddish, stubbled skin there. His eyes seemed small in such a broad face, one eye brown, one eye pale green.

"It doesn't work anymore," Brion confided. "He still carries it with him, but he broke it in anger years ago. That's supposed to be a secret." Brion sniffed and flicked his gaze back to me with birdlike speed. "So, if nobody comes for you, you can't return to the Way. You're one of us now."

Beys shook his head. "He can never be one of *us*. Shatro tells us you witnessed the destruction at a village on the Terra Nova River."

"I did," I said. "The village of Moonrise."

"Are you here to judge us for that, and pass word back to the Hexamon that we're criminals?"

I did not answer.

Beys shook his head again, slowly. "Something's gone wrong, hasn't it?" he asked. "They don't think it's worth-while to send an army."

"Maybe they can't open a gate long enough," Brion said.

"I was fifteen years old when my parents brought me here," Beys said. "I suffered starvation and illness. I watched my sister and my mother die in childbirth. Lenk did this to us all. If the Hexamon comes, I am prepared to be judged. We have done what we must to survive." He turned away. "He's an agent," he concluded, looking down at the floor. "He has the look. None of the others did. We probably should kill them all."

Brion seemed mildly alarmed by that suggestion. "I don't think they're a threat to us."

The news—or rumor—about Lenk's clavicle was slowly sinking in. If it was broken, and nobody else had arrived on Lamarckia by now, there was little chance I'd ever finish my mission.

Or rather, my mission had become my life.

That disturbed me more than I wanted to deal with now. I had to keep calm before this boyish, simian-faced man and the cheerful, stocky Beys, with his merry cheeks and deadly words.

"Still, you have some interest," Brion said. "I've respected Ser Salap for many years. Some of his works have given me the clues I've needed to make my biggest discoveries. General Beys shares much of the responsibility, as well. He's given me the time to concentrate."

"I hope we have time, later, for a long conversation," Beys said. "I regret I won't be able to stay much longer. I'd enjoy hearing about what's happened on Thistledown and in the Way."

"There's diplomacy to be taken care of, more discussions with Lenk," Brion said. "If they can be called that. The Able Man doesn't do much listening. So many things to plan, arrangements to be made. We all have to be watchful. Ser Salap, why did you come to Lamarckia?"

"I believed in Lenk," Salap said.

"Do you believe what you see here—the vivarium, all our work?"

"Yes."

"A collaboration, communication?"

Salap nodded.

"Ser Randall?"

"It seems real," Randall said.

Brion chuckled. "All of this—the crater, the stone chambers—used to be the home of a seed-mother. Thousands of years ago, the seed-mother moved to another location, up the canal. That's where we'll go. I want to show you some of what we've done. My wife and I. I haven't been up the canal for months. But with such learned gentlemen here, and Ser Olmy, a very special visitor, I think the negotiations can wait." He nodded decisively. "It's more important that you all see what we've managed to do."

Brion leaned toward me, as if addressing a child. "I can't tell what you're thinking. You have some character and discipline, Ser Olmy. That makes you different from most of us. We were brought here by a fool, on a promise that was broken as soon as we arrived. We've been sinking ever since.

"Come with me up the canal tomorrow and I'll show you how much further we have to go before we reach bottom."

General Beys regarded me with his small deep-set eyes and crinkled his pink cheeks in a friendly smile. He nodded as if saying farewell to a fellow soldier.

This time, the guards put us together into a single room along another tunnel, presumably closer to the lake. I did not sleep much that night. I lay in my narrow, hard bunk and wondered what other agents would have done, sent to Lamarckia. Would they have revealed themselves to so little purpose?

Salap stirred on the bunk above me. He descended the ladder. "It feels like morning to me," he said. "I feel like a damned soil tender, walled up in here." At the bottom, he straightened his black robe and ran his hand through his hair, then went to the wash basin and splashed water on his face.

Randall swung his legs over the edge of his bottom bunk and stretched. "What do you think they're up to?" he asked.

"I don't know," Salap said. "I refuse to be surprised."

Randall turned his gaze to me. "Anything *you* can do that will surprise us?" he asked.

"I don't think so," I said.

"How are you any different from Mansur or me?" he asked.

"I've never claimed to be different."

"You were all they could send—a scout, to check out the territory? And nobody after you?"

"I assume that's what's happened."

Salap stood with one hand braced against the brick wall.

Randall looked up at the wall, eyes moist. "All these decades we've been waiting like children for someone to rescue us from our own stupidity. And all the Hexamon sends is one man."

"A mortal, like us," Salap murmured.

"Both of you were Adventists?" I asked.

Salap nodded. Randall said, "I sympathized, but I knew which side to stick with."

Salap smiled like a devil that understands human nature only too well. "Do you think Ser Shatro was listening, on the raft?"

"Apparently," I said.

"It might have been better if you had just told the first person you met who you were," Randall said.

"The first person I met was Larisa Strik-Cachemou," I said. "It didn't seem a good idea at the time."

CHAPTER TWENTY-TWO

The boat waited beside the ministerial dock on the canal, its two-man crew dressed in immaculate white. The boat was ten meters long, made of white-painted xyla with a single metal tree amidships, on which flew a gray flag with a central white spot. Two electric motors waited beneath a bare metal compartment at the rear. A white canopy ahead of the tree shaded a square of padded benches, sunken below deck level. Forward of the canopy, a small cabin and galley waited to serve Brion and his guests.

Salap and I walked down the dock and boarded the boat, escorted by our guards. Randall had not been invited.

What made Brion different—more like Lenk than like any leaders on Thistledown—was his apparent role as the figurehead in a cult of personality. Leaders on Thistledown generally ruled like bureaucratic administrators—hence the unglamorous titles of their higher offices. Brion was a tribal ruler, given unlimited discretion by his people, but with limited resources and limited numbers of people to rule. Understanding him, knowing what to say and to anticipate, could save our lives. I hoped Salap was thinking along similar lines, and I was glad Randall was not accompanying us. Randall had had enough of Naderville and Lenk and Fassid and the mess of Lamarckia's human world-lines. He might not care what would trigger Brion's anger.

Brion arrived several minutes later, with four armed soldiers and a lithe brown man with spiky, short-cut black hair. Brion seemed anxious. "This is Ser Frick," Brion said. "He's been with me for many years, since I came to Godwin."

We introduced ourselves as if we were going on a social cruise, then settled on the padded seats, and our guards and three of the armed men returned to the dock.

Brion wore gloves, khaki-colored pants, and a dark brown shirt. In one hand he carried a piece of string wrapped tightly around his index finger.

Frick wore a thin, loose black coat, faded rose-colored vest, and baggy dark brown pants. "The weather's going to be warm up the canal today," Frick said, settling into the bench seat. "She's been keeping it warm for weeks."

Brion nodded and stared across the canal at the opposite shore, one eyebrow raised. He wound and unwound his string.

"How long is this trip?" Salap asked.

"Two days up, two days back," Frick said.

The pilot switched on the electric motors and the boat pushed out into the stream, which flowed west from the interior of Hsia.

"That woman is awful," Brion said a few minutes later, lifting his chin from his hand and sitting straight on the seat.

"Which woman?" Salap asked.

"Fassid. We had a bad discussion this morning, very unfair. I explained my position yesterday very well, I think, telling them I could do little more even if we negotiated for months. They asked me again to keep General Beys and his soldiers here, and I told them I was unable to do that."

"Beys kidnapped children and slaughtered villagers," I said.

"I do not defend all of his actions, but he is much too useful for me to just recall him. He's a thorn in Lenk's side." Brion would not meet my eye, but his face went through a spectrum of twitches and half frowns as he gazed across the river. "I doubt I would defend my own actions, if you decided to challenge me in a Hexamon court," he continued.

Salap sat like a patient cat, face relaxed but eyes alert. We both knew these men could order the crew to kill us and throw us into the canal at any moment, and there would be few if any repercussions.

Clouds moved in above the canal and surrounding thicket silva. The dark cliffs of arborid growth declined to heights of less than a dozen meters as the boat pushed up the canal, and broad areas had been burned and cleared for farms. The open fields of chalky rubble beneath the thickets had apparently yielded little in the way of crops, however, and the land seemed to have been abandoned, leaving sad, naked scars along the canal.

A white-jacketed steward stooped out of the forward cabin and served us glasses of water and slices of sweet green melonlike fruit. Frick persisted in asking for details on Thistledown as we ate.

"What's it like there now? I've tried to grasp the possibility of time lags in the geometry stacks . . . How many years have passed there, since we left?"

I saw no reason to dissemble. "About five years, Way time."

Frick's face fell. "That's all? I've spent my whole life here and I'm less than five years old . . ."

"No one understood what we would be facing, least of all Lenk," Brion said.

"I think Able Lenk recognizes his mistakes," Salap said softly. "It is too late to wallow in accusations and recriminations."

"If we judge who will lead, and who will prevail when major decisions have to be made," Brion said, "surely we must judge. Mistakes matter."

"Lenk regrets not sending more help to you," Salap said.

Brion's eyes narrowed to slits and his lips curled with contempt. "It was a policy, not an oversight. First Godwin, and then Naderville, was an affront to his legitimacy, to his *record*."

"I am concerned with what you are going to show us," Salap said. "I am less concerned with how you and Lenk disagree, or who is going to overcome whom."

"I appreciate your bluntness," Brion said. "It's what I expected of you, Ser Salap. So few people care to speak directly to me. I'm treated like a willful child. I'm not all that temperamental." He seemed to relax. "I don't worry about my mistakes with Lenk, or the mistakes of my predecessors. Though they truly established our isolation before I ever arrived . . . But perhaps you're right. There's no end to that kind of recrimination. Lenk is no saint. No saint at all."

I quelled the urge to ask about the orders given to General Beys, and whether there would ever be an accounting and reckoning for him. However well Brion took Salap's words, he might react quite differently to mine.

The steward laid out breads and small, bluish grapelike fruit on a tray.

"We have fundamentally misunderstood this planet," Brion said. "I'm as much to blame as anyone. We looked at it with blinkered eyes, expecting simple relationships between simple organisms, however large. We thought in terms of central authorities, self-aware intelligence or personality. There has been neither self-awareness nor personality on Lamarckia. There has been vital direction, order, and of course change. Sometimes frantic change. But not what we could call a *self*."

"What were your mistakes?" Salap asked after a moment of silence. I wondered if perhaps Salap had not been such a fortunate choice after all. Randall might have shown more discretion. I hoped he knew what he was after, and what it might cost us.

"I was grieving," Brion said. "I was not rational. I felt I had no friends on this world, except for the land, the ecos. I felt very close to it. I still do. My greatest mistake."

"Why grieving?" I asked.

"Caitla died," Brion said. "My wife. Hyssha's sister. We were born in the same triad family on Elizabeth's Land, grew up together, lived together practically all our lives. We were the first to travel to the head of the canal. I depended on her."

Frick, out of Brion's view, lifted his fingers to his lips and shook his head slowly, warning us away from these topics for now.

I suddenly cared little for Lamarckia's secrets, as if Brion's interest and passion had tainted them.

Hour after hour, kilometer after kilometer, the canal threaded due east into Hsia's interior with a series of barely perceptible bends and jogs, faint curves on its steady journey. The waters, Brion said, had been flowing here for at least ten million years; the canal and the hundreds of branch canals that drew from these waters, suffusing them into the inland reaches like blood into tissue, had once been parts of a natural river system, but had been adapted by the ecos to its own purposes.

"Until recently, these waters carried replacement scions in floating clusters, like rafts," Brion said. "The canal was thick with them."

The waters flowed clear and empty.

"What happened to them?" Salap asked.

"They stopped coming down about a month ago. Something's going on, perhaps a fluxing. I haven't been up the canal to the Valley of Dawn in several months . . . I left Caitla there, and . . . I suppose I didn't have the courage to return. Besides, preparing for Lenk's visit has distracted me. Now that he's here, I wonder why I've worked so hard."

Frick tried to change the subject, to steer him back to affairs in Thistledown, anything to keep Brion occupied and his mind off this subject, but the small man gravitated back to it.

"I've become lonely without my wife." His face went blank as he stared in my direction. "Being with *her* is a different kind of loneliness."

"Your wife?" Salap asked, puzzled.

Frick's face went pale.

"No," Brion said distantly. "Caitla died."

"I'm most curious about the current Nexus's attitude toward Lamarckia," Frick said, fidgeting on the bench. Brion turned to him, his large liquid green eyes filled with hurt as if Frick had somehow insulted him. Frick's jitters became serious. For a moment I thought he might suddenly spring out of the boat.

Brion looked away from Frick, and his eyes focused on mine.

"I get very dark, thinking about it," he said. "It makes me feel so inferior. And I've worked hard to earn this pride. I've taken the wreck I found in Godwin, and patched it, and steered it through bad storms. It's a miracle any of us are alive—and no thanks to Lenk.

"I should be free to have my pride, but *she's* taken it from me. I'm sure she has. The canal's been empty for weeks now."

Salap gave me a lidded, dubious look. Conversation lapsed, much to Frick's relief.

The sun emerged from behind clouds and the air became thick and humid. We had passed the barren gaps of old farmland. Along the shore, the black cliffs of the thickets towered thirty and forty meters above the canal, and the water echoed and splashed as it raced down side tunnels like so many swallowing throats.

———

The steward laid out padded sleeping mats on the deck and we slept under the double arc of stars. I stared up at the stars through a thin night haze over the canal, wondering if I would dream again when I slept.

My mother would recognize me now. Helpless, mortal, sleeping, and with dreams.

The canal water lapped at the hull of the boat, lulling me. Toward the bow, Brion and Frick slept, one of them snoring faintly. Salap lay on top of the cabin. If he slept, he did not snore.

"Unless you know where you are, you don't know who you are."

I began to know where I was.

We awoke in a golden fog. The mist-thick morning air burned gold over the canal. The steward brought a hot, yeasty decoction in a silver pot and poured it into cups, then served warm, crisp cakes for breakfast. We sat beneath the canopy as the fog burned off, all but Brion, who kept to himself near the bow.

Frick chatted lightly about incidentals, filling the time with stories of trivial social events surrounding Brion. I did not find his stories amusing, but what he said filled the time and offended no one.

My butt became sore with sitting. I stood and walked aft, standing near the stern to watch our wake in the empty water.

On the shores of the canal, the thickets became gnarled, their black clipped edges turning light purple and irregular, lumpy. Only once did I see something moving through the branches, like a huge brown earthworm. Salap came aft to sit beside me as the hours passed into evening.

"The captain and I studied this coast years ago," he said. "Though we never went up this canal, or even as far as the lake. Within the thickets, there are many dozens of types of scions. That was back when Lenk was trying to romance the women who ran things in Godwin. Bring them back into the fold . . . But I don't see much scion activity now. Perhaps Brion is right, and some sort of fluxing is imminent."

"Are you sure there's no other ecoi on Hsia?" I asked.

"None that have been discovered. This one is old, old, perhaps older than any other on Lamarckia. Baker thought it might be the ancestor of all ecoi. I believe it covers the entire continent."

That afternoon, we passed a large flatboat loaded with mounds of dark, fine dirt—some sort of ore. Brion sat on the bow with knees drawn up and watched it pass down the canal. Several bare-chested men on the flatboat waved cheerfully, and Brion waved back once. He said to Frick, "A lighter haul again. She's not piling it up like she used to."

Salap squatted beside me and frowned. "Who is this 'she' he keeps talking about?" he whispered. "What does 'she' have to do with piles of dirt? I'm sick of mystery."

"It's his show," I said, and thought of the Fishless Sea and its mystery attraction.

As evening came, we passed another flatboat, half loaded with piles of brown and red logs like stacked sausages.

"Food," Frick said. "More than we could ever hope to grow ourselves." But something bothered him about the boat, and he went forward to stoop beside Brion. They talked in whispers for a while, and Brion became agitated, finally waving Frick away.

Ahead, the canal broadened into a small lake. All around the lake shore, long dark structures like huge cocoons, with fibrous gray walls, protruded halfway into the water. Between the cocoons lay flat open spaces, and offshore from one of these spaces, a floating crane with a shovel attachment was busily clearing four mounds of ore and loading them into a third flatboat. The ore lay in diminishing piles in a clearing that might have once held a dozen or more mounds of similar size.

"Are you curious?" Brion called back to us.

"Very curious," Salap answered.

"Let it build, let it build," Brion said. "It's seldom I have so many intelligent witnesses. Allow me a little drama."

Salap tapped his fingertips on the rear gunwale, head lowered. "Pity us, Ser Olmy. Lenk has always behaved like one kind of child. Brion is another."

There had been a maxim in Thistledown political science classes: that the governed shaped their governors. This was not quite the same as saying that the people got the government they deserved, but it pointed in that direction. What galled me was the pain and suffering of the innocent, those too young to make a choice, those born on Lamarckia.

But Brion had been one of those, too.

"If I had been a scientist on the Thistledown, or in the Way," Salap said, "how many more intelligent, more capable men and women would stand ahead of me, occupying the finest positions, making the greatest discoveries?"

"So?" I asked, puzzled.

"I know myself, Ser Olmy. I am one of the most intelligent people on this planet."

"And that worries you," I said.

"It terrifies me. I long for my superiors." He peered across the calm waters at the shores of this strange lake. "Who mines the ore? Where does it come from?"

"*She* does," I suggested. "His dead wife, Caitla."

Salap mused, "We are in a land of dreams, Ser Olmy."

The lake passed behind, the canal narrowed and deepened, and we saw no more flatboats, or any other boats at all. The pilot pushed us against the slow steady waters, the electric motors humming, the screws leaving a shimmering wake behind, set with jewels of fire from the westering sun. The sunset light made Salap a gilded pirate. We said little to each other.

I think both of us expected to die soon; either Brion's premonitions of change would be true, and the change, whatever it was, would kill us, or Brion himself would change and kill us . . .

Our chances seemed slim.

I thought often of Shirla, and hoped she was being treated well, but in truth, all the people we had left behind—dead or alive—seemed to retreat in memory as well as time. My universe narrowed to the boat, the canal, Salap, and Brion. All others—even Frick and the boat's crew—were supernumeraries.

Frick crept aft often enough and spoke to us. He seemed even more acutely aware of his mortality. His nervous chatter became an irritation, and was seldom informative. He would not answer direct questions, deferring instead to Brion, who sat near the bow like a sad, unappeasable monkey.

Before our dinner was served, I walked forward and stood beside him. I was catching some of Salap's attitude and feeling impatient, even reckless. He peered up at me expectantly.

"You make everybody nervous," I said softly. "Is that what you want?"

"I am a powerful man, Ser Olmy. But I'm not capricious. I've ruled this part of Lamarckia with a steady hand and done well, under the circumstances. Rough times make for rough decisions."

"At the risk of displeasing you, I'd like to describe what I saw upriver from Calcutta."

Brion turned away with a roll of his eyes. "No doubt some of General Beys's doings," he said.

"Not one of his successes."

"I haven't spoken about such things with General Beys," Brion said.

"You gave him orders to look for resources, to gather children and equipment from undefended villages?"

"I know him well. He is not a monster. I appointed him after the worst famine, after he had lost his children and his wife . . . He had no family at all then. He had a look in his eye that told me he would be useful. So little left to live for."

"I arrived on Lamarckia near a village called Moonrise. Nearly everybody in the village had been killed. They would not agree to give Beys small deposits of ore. I presume Beys wanted to take the ore without working through Lenk . . . and that the ore you get here was not sufficient."

"Are you going to put me through some sort of inquisition? I gave up self-criticism after Caitla died."

"I just want to pass on this bad memory."

He blinked slowly. "If you have to."

I told him about the bodies piled high within the buildings in Moonrise, the implacable soldiers on the flatboats on the Terra Nova, about the trap above Calcutta and the children spilling into the river. I described the expression on the face of the soldier as he methodically and dispassionately fired his rifle from the prow of the flatboat. "He was shooting at everybody. Even at the children in the river."

"He was frightened out of his *wits*," Brion said.

"He was your hand," I said. "Your killing hand." My anger had built so suddenly I heard a hissing in my ears, my heart pounded, and I bit my lip until I felt under control again.

Brion had been saying, almost unheard, "I don't understand what you mean. He was a soldier."

"You made him," I said, voice low. Salap came forward, concerned. I was putting us in danger. *I* was the one who should have stayed behind.

But Brion's face was bright, almost cheerful. "Tell me how you think I am responsible for everybody on Lamarckia," he said. "That's a curious idea."

"What good does it do your people when you set loose monsters and fools, who kill without need, who destroy what you can't use?"

"I expect better from the Hexamon. Are you sure you're not a pretender?" He chuckled and shook his head.

He was right, of course. I was not expressing myself clearly. "General Beys did nothing to help Naderville or you," I said. "You have caused people to be killed for no reason. You've opened the gates to old, evil history. You won't be able to close them when Lenk is gone."

Brion leaned forward, eyes wide and sharp, lips drawn back in a feral grin. "I have thought long and hard about these things, Ser Olmy. What you call 'old, evil history' is the growth and maturation of small groups of humans. If Lamarckia were ever populated to the density of Thistledown, we'd behave very differently. Lenk opened the doors to history when he brought us here, four thousand people alone on a huge world. If you want to find the father of that poor bastard on the flatboat, don't look to me . . . Look to Lenk."

He waved his hand then, and Frick hastened us back to the benches amidships, under the canopy, telling some inane story about how many celebrations there had been when the food on the flatboats first began arriving.

A light shower fell as evening set in. Brion stayed out in the wet, staring at the northern bank of the canal, now and then wiping the rain from his face with a measured and exactly duplicated swipe of his hand.

The steward, a man whose qualifications were efficiency, quiet reserve, and such a presence that he would fade from memory and pass unnoticed, served a dark sweet beer and cold cakes with a tangy syrup. He switched the lights on around the boat. We kept to the center of the canal, the motors humming and pushing us along at seven or eight knots, the boat a small spot of light in fixed and endless obscurity.

Brion came back to the seats beneath the canopy, dripping and soaked, his hair hanging dark and shiny, and accepted a towel from the steward.

"I'm no monster," he said.

"I'm no monster," he repeated after he sat, hoisting the glass of sweet beer. "I did not come here to impose a single mind's philosophy on strangeness and wonder. I did not convince four thousand people that my every word was truth and that the world they had grown up in, that had shaped their thought, was an evil place full of evil schemes that had to be escaped from."

"You blame all this on Lenk," I said. "Even what you do, or order done." Frick sank back into a shadowy corner. Salap murmured that this discussion was useless.

But Brion flared. "Do you know how this all began, Ser Olmy? Has anyone discovered *my* little personal bit of history in Lenk's private domain? Caitla and I loved each other from a very young age. We went to Athenai as Lenk school teachers, and were privileged enough to meet with Lenk himself, *Good* Lenk, *Able* Lenk. Lenk became enamored of Caitla and her sister—"

"Ser Brion—" Frick attempted to interrupt. He seemed ready once again to leap overboard.

"This is *my* story, damn us all," Brion said, reaching out and pushing against Frick's outstretched hand. "If Ser Olmy is from the Hexamon, then he plays a judge—he must! he cannot do otherwise—for the people I would most like to emulate. I was very young when my parents brought me here—seven years old. I had no choice. Neither did Caitla."

He leaned back against the rear pad of the bench and glared at me, then cursed under his breath and leaned forward, folding his hands as if in prayer, touching his nose to his thumbs. "Lenk became enamored of Caitla. He paid formal suit to her. He was already married, of course, and she refused him. He would not take her refusal. He was an old and revered man, to us. Hyssha knew we were in love and went to him. He took her . . . But that was not enough. He wanted Caitla. Finally, Caitla and I had no choice but to leave Athenai. We could not go anywhere in Lenk's domain without being found and brought back. He would not kill us, no, he was not that kind of monster. But he considered certain things his privilege, his payment for being who he was, what he was to all of his people. He would take a few choice *tidbits* now and then, to make up for the misery of being a leader, a prophet, almost a god. So we stole a boat and crossed to Hsia, to Godwin. That's how it began, Ser Olmy. Ten years ago."

Frick closed his eyes and sat across from Brion, trembling as if with his own grief.

"We grew up in Lamarckia. To me when I was young it seemed a rich and wonderful world that did not actively fight us, but did not accept us, either. I learned early that we are not part of the flesh of this living place. We have suffered and died because we stood between two philosophies— to make this place ours, and make it fit our rules, and to let it develop as if we never existed. Lenk . . . could not decide." He stared at me, the whites of his eyes prominent.

"What have you decided?" I asked.

"I am all for Lamarckia," Brion said. "Yet I have fought against it, ordered its tissue ripped away and the land exposed for human farms making human food—and when the crops died, tried to harness the ecos, to fit my people in to what was available . . . And still we starved. Because I loved my people, I profaned this continent, as others had before me. Until I learned another way.

"I did not bow down to Lenk, would not surrender my wife to him, so he let my people die without lifting a finger."

"He claims you did not ask for help," Salap said.

This finally drew out Brion's full fury. He turned to Salap, face twisted, cheeks red, with red spots and a vein standing out on his forehead. "Dear Fate and Breath, I told him all that was happening! I had responsibilities. I asked for his help despite my hatred. There were no secrets between us about how my people suffered!"

Salap remained cool as ice. His thin black mustache barely twitched at one corner. "Whether Ser Olmy is here to judge us or not, I expressly do not judge, and I have been sequestered from politics for so long I am clearly out of touch."

Brion stared between us with a wild, despairing expression for long, painful seconds. Then his expression returned to alert calm with a speed that could be explained only by great skill, or the presence of a deep chasm in his emotions, a kind of fault-line through his being. I had seen the ability in other leaders, to assume masks so often and with such conviction even they could not know their true feelings. Self-truth is a luxury leaders can seldom afford, or perhaps tolerate. But in Brion, the talent had become something more, even an illness.

I had Brion's measure now. He was not a great man, not even in the impure sense of prompting or guiding great events. He was a man of small, specific talents. And he had been badly scarred. Whether he told us the truth, I could not judge, but the pain was real.

"Lamarckia is about to flower," he said softly. "Caitla and I did that, at least. And when it does, what place will *she* give us, what place can we have?"

The countryside covered by thicket, the black or purplish edges of which rose along the sides of the canal like topiary walls, came to an end as the boat pushed into morning. I awoke having dreamed of a hall and the unpleasant door again, to the smell of cakes sizzling in a pan, and something else pungent and herbal, like fresh hot tar mixed with black tea, molasses with roses, spruce gum with the scent of new-mown grass—a perfume I have not since been able to replicate either in life or memory: the smell of the living palaces of the great seed-mothers of all Hsia.

We had come into a huge fresh-water inland sea or lake, the southern and eastern shores lost beyond the horizon, the northern close by, perhaps two kilometers off. The waves lapped crystal blue around the boat, and from the shore—a brilliant green shore, low and flat, covered with immense tapering green stalks like the shoots of young plants but without leaves—came a windy, shooshing, trilling sound, as alien as anything I ever heard on Lamarckia.

"*Earth was a green world,*" Nimzhian had said on Martha's Island. Nowhere on Lamarckia had there ever been this immensity of green.

Brion stood on the bow, caught half dressed and transfixed by the sight. Salap calmly washed his face in the lake water, glancing up at me as I put on my shirt and accepted a cup of yeasty broth from the steward.

"Look at all she's done!" Brion called out. "It's been only three months, and how many thousands of hectares she's changed!"

Salap stood beside me forward of the single metal tree and stared at the shore, eyes narrowed. The steward brought a tray of cakes forward and offered them. Frick leaned on the canopy. A light wind blew through his hair, his white shirt hung open beneath his faded rose-colored vest, and he grinned as if drunk.

"How do you claim to have done this?" Salap asked Brion.

"I don't just *claim* it," Brion said. "I know the truth, because after *she* made the ones in our own shape, and we showed her where she had gone wrong . . . After *she* made the food we could eat and filtered from her ground the ores and placed them where we could gather them, I paid her back. I have studied her for years, and I knew her weakness, her inefficiency." He stared at Salap, eyes blinking rapidly.

"What did you give her?" Salap asked.

"What is *she?*" I asked simultaneously.

Brion shook his head, plainly awed and even a little frightened by what he saw on the shore. He scrambled aft and grabbed a cake from Frick's tray, gobbling it like a hungry child.

"More than I could have imagined," he said. "Forget trying to replace our dead children. Forget trying to teach her scions to speak. None of that meant anything to her. She did not understand. She could imitate, but she could not understand. It was our bottle that she took and gloried in."

"*We* don't understand," Salap said patiently.

"I distilled it and purified it from weeds in a pond outside our sleeping quarters. Decorative weeds Lenk brought from Thistledown, lovely simple things. Easy to isolate what she needed and present it to her in a bottle, concentrated, unmistakable."

"Chlorophyll," Salap said.

Brion smiled. "Lamarckia's weakness," he said, crumbs falling from his mouth. "Not just chlorophyll, but the chloroplasts, the whole intricate photosynthetic structures of our plants, isolated and in context. Starches and sugars and the entire cycle, all in a bottle. And she understood. She gave us the experiments you saw in Naderville. Caitla's garden. The cleansing airborne phytids. More food. I could have signaled Beys to return home, because I knew then that we had won. We would be able to feed our people and make machines and create our little enclave . . . We did not need anybody else."

"But you didn't call him back," I said.

"No. Caitla said we had to be true to our promise. We had to look for *you*, Ser Olmy, the agent or agents of the Hexamon, and we had to bring

Lenk low, to make it clear that humans could not survive here. And then we would leave Lamarckia with the gift we had given her."

"You keep mentioning a *she*. Who or what is *she*?" I asked again. "The seed-mother, the queen?"

Brion pointed to the east. Above a blue horizon haze, we saw seven huge black trunks or towers rising inland. Each was at least four or five hundred meters tall, and seventy to a hundred meters across at the base. "I don't know what she is, exactly. What part she is, with a new shape, I mean . . . Or whether she's something completely new. She may not have even been created yet. But we will know her when we see her."

Brion turned toward Salap and me. His eyes wavered between us, then fixed on me with a look of both determination and desperation. "The Hexamon *must* come and take us back. She has what she needs. No other ecos can challenge her now."

The pilot pulled the boat into a narrow inlet that curved east and then north from the shore of the lake. We motored quietly between dense walls of intense blue-green growth, broad fernlike leaves with water glistening on the myriad tips, thin helical stalks corkscrewing through the growth and rising dozens of meters above this moving, shuddering mass, the immense green stalks or shoots we had seen from the distance, sprouts the size of giant sequoias. Salap wore an expression I had not seen on him even when we found the homunculi on Martha's Island: baffled wonderment. "It is a new silva," he said. "Everything is different."

The late-morning light reflected from this new ebullience of green made us all look like creatures swimming in ocean shallows. Brion's pale skin in particular took on a greenish cast. He crouched on the bow, elbows on his knees, fingers straightening and folding like spider's legs, and licked his lips constantly.

"I hope we can find the landing," he called back. "It's not far now . . . I hope she hasn't knocked it down in her enthusiasm."

The scions in the vivarium had imitated specific varieties of terrestrial plant life. Here, the imitation was superficial or parallel. Clearly, whatever controlled the new growth was starting from simple beginnings and creating new plans and schemes at a prodigious rate.

Shadows passed overhead: immense balloons trailing long black cables passed over the new silva, their undersides festooned with lacework baskets filled with green balls the size of my fist. The cables curled and danced over the silva, touching down, contracting, pulling the balloon in one direction, and then another cable jerking it at a thirty or forty degree angle in another direction. The balloons traveled at five or six knots, and three passed over us before we reached the landing Brion was searching for.

The pilot worked the boat carefully back and forth to bump against the tip of the xyla dock, which had almost been overgrown. Brion jumped onto the dock and lifted his arms. A thick tangle of fernlike leaves and yellow-green stalks curled up and parted at his feet like grass rolled in a man's palm.

"She remembers!" Brion said. "Come on. It's a brisk walk from here—three kilometers to the towers."

The crew of the boat, and Brion's guards, would not be coming with us. They seemed relieved.

Frick took several bags of food and four canteens from the steward, who looked at the teeming silva nervously. Before we stepped off the boat, Frick pulled a slate from his pocket and unfolded it, then gestured for Salap and me to look at the screen. A dark-haired woman, somber and coldly beautiful, with a distinct resemblance to Hyssha, looked back at us with skeptical eyes. "This was Caitla," he said softly. Then he nodded for us to proceed.

Brion plunged through the parting growth with manic energy, like a boat plowing its own wake in reversed time. After several minutes we could not see him, but followed on his path through the new silva. Salap asked Frick, "How does he know which direction to go?"

"It's making a trail. It shows us where to go," Frick said, sweating in the humid heat. I caught a faint whiff of sulfur—more volcanic activity. Every few dozen meters, we passed through a kind of clearing where the new green scions clung low to the ground, and we could see the towers. They were hung with a thick pelt of creepers and growths not green, but purple or black. We made steady if not beeline progress toward them.

Another dark balloon jerked and glided overhead, bearing its cargo to the west.

"It experiments with the new green forms," Salap said, "but keeps its central parts unchanged." He pointed to the towers. "Is he taking us there?" he asked Frick.

Frick nodded. "I've been here with them five times," he said. "It's never looked like this."

After fifteen minutes of steady walking, we caught sight of Brion. He stood facing north at the top of a hill rising ten meters above the level ground, covered with a knee-deep tangle of long green creepers little thicker than strings. He turned to call down the slope to us, "You can see what she's up to. You can see the whole plan from here."

We climbed the hill and stood beside him. The smell of the creepers, pressed against our shoes, was intensely fruity, and tiny puffs of red dust shot up above our knees. On a level now with most of the new silva—only the immense green shoots rose higher than the hill—we saw a spreading carpet of intense blue-green, banded with concentric loops of lighter yellow-green. We could see the edge of the growth to the north, and a boundary between old silva and new—green supplanting brown, black, and purple thicket. Across the ecoscape, emerging from between the seven pillars, an effervescence of hundreds of black and purple and red transporter balloons tugged and drifted to the outer perimeters, replacing dying scions from the air with new green growths.

"How long until this reaches Naderville?" Frick asked.

"I don't know," Brion said.

"A week or less, I estimate," Salap said. "Are your people prepared?"

"I don't know how we can be prepared," Brion said. He stalked down the opposite slope of the hill. I turned and surveyed from our relatively high vantage, locating the inlet, the waters of the lake reaching to the horizon in the south, and back around to the pillars again. A breathy warbling whistle, soft and plaintive, came from the south, perhaps from the lake shores. The sound made me shiver. That so much power and moving *change* would make such a simple, birdlike noise, seemed both typical of Lamarckia, and terrifying.

To the west, cumulus and glowering thunderheads built soft mountains. Brion called from the margin of the silva, as it again parted before him, "The ecos makes its own weather. There will be rain within a few days—wait and see."

"Yes," Salap muttered. "We've experienced that phenomenon."

We caught up with Brion again five minutes later. He stood in a blind alley, the scions ahead refusing to part. He paced back and forth, sweat streaming down his face. Frick handed him a marked canteen and he drank deeply and wiped his mouth on his sleeve. Frick handed us other canteens. Brion drank from his own and nobody else's.

Brion took a deep breath. "It wouldn't lead us this far and no farther . . ." He continued pacing, brushing past me. Again, from the south, the breathless warbling. Salap took advantage of the pause to more closely inspect the morphology of these new green scions.

"I think they are all experimental varieties of food-makers," he concluded. "She—the ecos, I mean—is experimenting with the most efficient structures. Storing nutrients, using them to promote scion production in the center . . . Where we are going."

Beneath our feet, brown tangles and shreds like twisted and splintered dead branches formed the floor of the silva. Pale white tubes pushed through the detritus. Where one of us had stepped on a tube near the surface, it leaked a milky fluid in steady drips. Salap applied a drop of the fluid to his tongue. "It's sweet," he said.

A new machine, a new experiment.

"Would you have done this?" I asked Salap as Brion restlessly stalked back along the trail, out of hearing.

"I don't know," Salap said thoughtfully. He cocked an eyebrow at me. "If I had thought of it, who knows what I would have done? We do not know what he was bargaining with . . . What sort of form, organism, he and his wife were communicating with. Or how they communicated."

"I saw them," Frick said, hunkering down to wait. He nodded and wiped his forehead with a cloth. "They were small, black worm things, on seven or nine legs. They made sounds like human speech, and they took things from us, our food and equipment, and brought back other things in exchange. Brion and Caitla showed them plants in pots and in bottles, and in days, the black things brought back imitations. Caitla was ecstatic. Later, on the third trip, I saw the first one that tried to look human. It even tried to speak. We communicated by gestures, but it didn't have real eyes. It—she . . . it tried to appear female—tracked us by our heat, I think. Ser Brion and Caitla showed it more plants. Caitla's favorites. It made even better imitations and we took them back with us to the vivarium.

"But I've never seen *her*. The one he's hoping for. When we were last here, after Caitla died, I stayed on the boat. None of this jungle was here."

"Is he hoping for something like his wife?" I asked. "An imitation?"

Frick didn't enjoy that thought at all. He shifted from one crooked leg to the other and wiped his eyes with his fingers, grimacing. "I knew Caitla," he said. "She was a stern but fine woman. She suited Ser Brion wonderfully. When she died, we all felt her loss deeply. Ser Brion was devastated. Hyssha, too."

I could not equate any of this with the raids and murders. In the middle of so much change, death and cruelty and incompetence might lose all their importance. My own death might be completely appropriate, or meaningless. I would give up trying to reconcile those cruelties. After my outburst in front of Brion, I had lost any sense of mission or role; I was no better, no more powerful, than Frick. I had finally earned my humility, my perfect sense of mortality.

I wondered what it would be like to be in the middle of this greening, growing silva, alone, for days or weeks.

Shirla provided the only frame of reference I could not shake myself loose from. I wanted to see her, to make sure she was well. If we could meet again, I would have new bearings, a new sense of purpose, free of Thistledown and the Way.

Brion returned to the trembling barricade again and stood silent, head bowed. "I am patient," he murmured. "I am patient."

Still, the barricade remained.

"We have enough food and water," he said. "We'll wait here until tomorrow. I'm sorry. This hasn't happened before."

"None of this has happened before," Salap said.

We slept on the detritus with the silva shivering and growing around us. Every few hours, a sudden rush of motion through the walls around the path made a sound like wind blowing through trees. I slept fitfully and did not remember any dreams, and awoke feeling groggy, not prepared for anything. Several minutes after waking, after eating a cake and drinking from the canteen Salap and I shared, I regained my alertness. The ration of water was not sufficient and I felt thirsty, but not parched.

Brion knelt before the barricade. "She's preparing something," he said. "She would not lead us this far just to block us."

"*She* is intelligent, then?" Salap asked.

Brion laughed and shook his head. "How many times have I asked that question? How many times did Caitla and I talk about it? And after Caitla died . . . Of course, I would like her to return. That would be wonderful. To have her somehow absorbed in all her beauty, her thoughts . . . by something larger. Intelligent."

I thought of the discussion on the *Vigilant*. Lamarckia would be a poor substitute for eternal bliss, but a fair compromise compared to the nullity of empty death.

In the cleared path behind us, we all heard simultaneously the tones and gutturals of human voices. Brion jerked his head sharply around. The look of panic that came to his face, and the searching of his eyes across the whispering, trembling walls flanking the trail, struck me almost like a knife. Here was the face of a man who did not actually want to see the ghost he desired above all else.

Frick's conscience might have been clear. At any rate, it was he who first recognized the voices. "It's Hyssha," he said. "And Grado, I think . . . And Ullman."

A tall man with close-cropped black hair and suspicious black eyes came around the corner ten meters from the path's dead end, saw us, and stopped. He glanced to his right down the path and made a small gesture with his half raised hand, as if he had come upon wild beasts and whoever followed must be as quiet as he.

The stately, somber woman with auburn hair, Hyssha Chung, walked around him without hesitating and approached us, or rather, approached Brion, for she did not pay any attention at all to Frick or Salap or myself.

"You shouldn't be here," she admonished. "Damn your breath, you should not be here, and certainly not now!"

Brion raised his hands as if in defense. "There's nothing happening back there," he said.

"What is more necessary and immediate *here*?" she asked. For an instant, she seemed to acknowledge that I at least existed, with a flicker of her eye in my direction, but then her scowl deepened and she leaned toward Brion, whose hands rose higher. "Lenk is packing up his people and preparing to return to their boats. Fassid says your absence leaves them no choice."

"They won't talk with Beys?"

"What made you think they would?"

"Beys handles all that. What difference does it make where I am?" Brion asked. "And what can Lenk do, anyway?" Before this resolute woman, his voice took on the tone of a defensive child.

"How do you know what Lenk can or can't do?" Chung pursued, pushing her nose almost into Brion's face. "There's more than this monstrous silva at stake."

"Look how it's changed," Brion said, holding his ground against the taller woman, but hoping to persuade, not chastise.

Frick looked on this exchange with something like boredom. Chung did not overawe him—at least not when she had her attention on Brion.

"I don't give a damn how it's changed." Her voice broke and she took his hands in hers. "What *can* you do here?"

"Our legacy is here," Brion said. His face creased like soft leather and he shook his wrists gently, not to break her grip on them, but to make some obscure point physical. "*She* is here. I hoped to convince the Hexamon—"

Now Chung rounded on me, with utter disdain and contempt. "Fassid told me about this pretender," she said. "They've been embarrassed by him and by this foolish man's gullibility." She pointed to Salap. "Even Lenk couldn't think of a way to use him against us. But you believe!"

"He has no proof," Frick said in a mild conversational voice, "but he is very convincing. I think Ser Brion is justified—"

She threw her hand out and nearly struck him in the face. "Who or what he is doesn't matter. Where are the armies, the forces that would pull us out of here?"

"They haven't come," Brion said, as if that were a trifle.

Her brown eyes narrowed and her lip curled again. She regarded me from the corner of her eyes. I could not help my reaction. I had never been the most gentlemanly when faced with rampant female anger. In truth, histrionics of any kind had not been a regular part of my life on Thistledown.

I laughed. Chung did not move or change her expression.

"You are dead men," she said quietly to Salap and me. "You will not carry any of our words back to Lenk."

"Hyssha," Brion said, pulling her hand from his wrist. "None of that means anything. What Lenk does means nothing, and what I do . . . Nothing. Look at the green. I've given her the tools. The advantage. I made my request clear."

"Caitla is dead," Chung said. "My sister won't come back."

The wall of green at the end of the path trembled violently, a cleft forming in the middle and deepening, while the edges pushed to either side. In this parting green sea, our biological Moses seemed as surprised as any of us. A haze of red dust lingered in the air, drifting slowly back to the ground. The path soon extended a hundred meters beyond where we stood, to the inner edge of the new silva, and the beginning of the grounds whose boundary posts were the pillars.

"It wouldn't open for me," Brion said to Chung. "It's opening for you. She smells you. You smell like Caitla."

Chung stared down the trail, far less contemptuous and angry than a moment before. Her dignity broke and her arms shook, and she looked to Salap. "That's ridiculous," she said.

"Let's go and see," Salap said, following Brion, who had already resumed his walk.

"She *is* dead," Chung said to Frick and me, with no certainty. "Nothing can bring her back."

CHAPTER TWENTY-THREE

At the end of the trail lay a desolate stretch of broken lava chunks no bigger than my hand, as regular as gravel in the bed of an ancient river. This field of broken lava stretched across several kilometers, interrupted by six squat dark reddish-brown mounds, each fifty or sixty meters high, capped with craters rimmed with pale yellow, like miniature mountains tipped with impure snow. Hot springs flowed from the center of these mounds and made irregular darker slicks down their sides, pooling around the bases.

Spaced around the perimeter of the lava field, the vine-covered purple and black pillars cast long late-morning shadows over the gravel and two of the mounds. Surrounding the field, the new green silva contrasted sharply with the flat dark colors of lava and the brilliant yellow-white caps of rime on the mounds.

In the sky over the field, their numbers increasing with the warming rays of the noonday sun, hundreds of balloons lifted their cargoes of larval scions, cables dropping straight to the lava plain, only their tips moving, touching delicately on the inhospitable gravel and jerking back like the weary ends of octopus tentacles, pulled from a familiar sea. The balloons rose from the center of the field, hidden from our view by the nearest mound.

Salap could not conceal his enchantment. "We have seen a great many things and survived, Ser Olmy," he whispered to me. "But we have never seen anything like this."

Directly in front of us, a pool of steaming reddish-brown liquid—not lava, but supersaturated, mineral-rich hot water, the consistency of molten glass—rose between the chunks of lava and solidified with small crackling sounds, its smooth surface darkening and fogging. Beyond that pool, a number of pools had already hardened, making a series of smooth trails across the rugged gravel. Brion stood on the fogged brownish surface, then walked lightly to the next.

The vitrified pools led us around the nearest mound. Sulfurous water, steaming, bubbling, slipped down the side of the mound barely ten meters from us. On the other side, we had a clear view of the center of the field. A dark red hemisphere as large as a stadium lay at the end of the trail like an immense bubble of blood, but solid and glistening in the sun.

Around the hemisphere, the laden balloons rose slowly, doggedly, from red-rimmed craters, and began their aerial crawl to the greening silva and beyond.

"It's no different. Except for the balloons, this hasn't changed," Brion called over his shoulder, jumping from step to step.

All of our faces took on a bloodred tinge as we approached the dome. Chung's earlier bravado had subsided; she watched everything with quiet, nervous alertness. Brion, on the other hand, had become manic, darting back and forth in the red glow of the hemisphere, eyes flashing with tears, as if he had finally come home.

Salap walked apart from all of us, lost in his own contemplations, planting his feet carefully, as if the brownish steps of the trail might crack and suck us all down. Frick stayed close to me.

The trail ended at a puckered line like a scar drawn in the dome. Brion touched the long scar in the dome's side, but by himself could not get it to expand.

Salap took Chung's elbow, pushing her to stand beside Brion. "Your place," he murmured as she resisted.

"She smells you. She believes in you," Brion told her. "She believes in us."

With Chung by his side, the scar parted with a tiny sucking noise, and the edges withdrew like a curtain to form a smooth round orifice in the side of the hemisphere.

We walked through. Inside, our eyes adjusted to a blood-colored shadowy interior. Translucent arches lifted from the floor on our left, supporting the dome's perfect exterior. A few dozen meters to our right, another set of arches rose. Between the arches, suspended on thick knotted slings, or depending directly from the inner curves of the arches, enormous sacs like deflated balloons hung, their lower extremities bulging round with deposits of dark fluid.

To left and right, translucent blisters interrupted the resilient floor, each three to four meters broad and rising above the level of our waists. Within the blisters, coiled tubes and flattened oblongs pressed together against the membrane, pale in themselves, but surrounded by a dark, thick fluid like petroleum.

A dozen steps ahead, the arches met at an inner chamber, its walls curved inward, like the cubic intersection between six enormous bubbles. All the surfaces within the hemisphere were sections of large bubbles, expertly fashioned and cut or intersected by other bubble surfaces of varying diameters. We might have entered the interior of a vast radiolarian, one of the silicate-skeletoned microscopic sea creatures of Earth's oceans.

We walked slowly between these mingled wonders. A new odor filled the air, sweet as perfume, musky.

"The outer veil. Smell it," Brion said, waving his hand. "There are eight veils, eight airborne layers of scent. I carried a small scion here once, six months ago. It struggled in my arms, and when it passed through the third scented veil, it collapsed in a thick liquid and fell through my fingers. What lies within tolerates none of its children . . . unless they have permission. And the only scions who have permission are the spies, the samplers and gatherers that bring information. What lies within is always hungry for patterns, blueprints, diagrams . . . information."

Halfway across the interior, we saw a storage area for slabs and chunks of rock—slates, sandstones, conglomerates, flints, and other varieties, arranged in piles with little apparent sense of order, covering perhaps a hundred square meters in the overhang of a main supporting arch. The piles rose over our heads in the center, and just to one side, an elephant-sized, many-clawed scion stood unmoving except for a slight trembling of its forward limbs: many-spiked-gripping claws as long as my legs, some with sharp chisel-shaped tips. At its base lay split sections of stone, revealing beautiful impressed fossils. Brion stepped between two stacks and pulled out a shallow slab of limestone about thirty centimeters on a side. "She had these rocks collected and brought here. She uses them as a kind of library."

He held the twenty-kilogram slab out to us. Embedded in the limestone was a black outline, a many-legged arthropod surrounded by broad feather-shaped feelers. "When my wife and I first came here, *she* couldn't see. She stored these fossils and studied them without eyes, tasting and feeling them."

Salap stood beside Brion, hands held out, fingers greedily spread. He took the fossil, eyes nearly starting from their sockets. "Was this a scion?" he asked.

"I don't know," Brion said. "It's at least tens of millions years old. If it's older, it comes from the era of shelly creatures that covered so much of Lamarckia with thick layers of limestone and made it so difficult to find metals and other minerals. How old do you think the ecoi are?"

"I've guessed hundreds of millions of years . . ." Salap said.

Brion shook his head. "Hsia was the first, and it may be less than twenty million years old. As for the rest, at most they're only a few million years old. Life was small and very simple before Hsia.

"When Hsia ventured out on land, there was very little oxygen, and no ozone in the upper atmosphere. It covered itself with a thick, protective layer. It may have taken fifteen million years for oxygen to reach its present levels."

From ahead came a sharp, sweet smell. As we advanced to the inner cube, we passed through several varieties of this same smell, like veils of scent surrounding the body of a revered saint.

Brion stopped. The shriveled husks of what appeared to be human bodies lay crumpled at the spreading foot of an arch. The arch rose at least sixty meters to the vague red-suffused heights of the dome. The bodies ranged in size from less than a meter to over two meters, desiccated tissues stretched over internal frames that only crudely resembled skeletons. Blank hard-tissued faces stared at us with glazed eyes, the heads of dolls manufactured by a toymaker who had failed, and cast the inanimate results aside.

"These were experiments," Brion said in a low voice. "She showed some to us the first time we came here. She knew what she wanted—something to communicate with us. She knew we weren't part of any ecos, and she desperately needed to discover what we were. The best way for her to learn . . . her way of learning . . . was to imitate us."

The cubic frame ahead was larger and farther away than I had first thought. It lay fifty or sixty meters beyond the graveyard of rejected human-shapes. The last of the distinctive scents wafted around us, this one at once primally offensive and startlingly attractive: baking bread, hot tar, methane and hexane, smelling salts, and much more.

Brion approached the frame at the center of the hemisphere, walking like a tired old man. I tried to imagine his emotional state and could not. What he expected, what it was possible he might see, would have driven many men mad. As he walked ahead of us, he gave a broken explanation, in slow fragments, of his last visit. He had brought his dying wife inside the blood-bubble hemisphere, stayed with her, listening to her last breaths, her last words.

"She was in pain," he said, voice shaky and hoarse. He wiped his face with the back of his hand, the string still wound around his finger. "Nobody could save her." He touched the membranous wall of the frame and looked back at me. "She was extraordinary. We both prayed for the Hexamon to come and bring the medicine of Thistledown that Lenk left behind. He finally had his revenge on us. A lot of my people died the way she did. She lasted longer than most. Her liver and kidneys were rotting away. Such a simple disease to cure on Thistledown. But you did not come. When she died . . . She died." He pulled his hand back. "It was a relief. I felt as if I had died with her, and that was a relief, too. I placed her on the floor, inside . . . I left and camped for five days on the edge of the lava field. Ser Frick brought me food from the launch. Nothing happened; nobody came out of the dome. I couldn't go back inside. We all returned to Naderville."

Frick stared at the deepening shadows on all sides with a fearful squint. Hyssha Chung stayed close to Brion. Looking at me, she had only hate in her eyes. I represented all lost hope, final disappointment. I was a failure to all of them: no rescue imminent, no change and explanation, no reembracing in the arms of secure and all-knowing parents.

"She's in there," Brion said huskily. "I mean, *she's* all around, but the heart of her heart is in there. Heart of Hsia's life."

Outside the hemisphere, clouds must have covered the sun, for shadow enveloped us. All around, faint gleams pricked against the deep red and brown gloom, like stars in the heavens. Violet luminosity flickered within the frame. A low sound grumbled beneath our feet. Meters away, beyond several ranks of translucent walls and braces, something swelled like the throat on an enormous bullfrog, then subsided, expelling a sweetly repulsive scent of tar and burning resin.

Brion leaned against the wall of the frame, a pale shape against the darker membrane. This time, there was no preference for Hyssha. The wall seemed to absorb him, and the tissue beneath our feet grumbled again.

We heard a remarkable voice, and Salap jumped as if poked in the ribs. High, sweet, like the chirrup of a large insect mixed with a whistling flute, childlike, yet mannered and mature, it came from within the frame.

"Names clear now," it said. "Names all are and clear?"

CHAPTER TWENTY-FOUR

Time has become very unclear. My recovery is going smoothly, the attendants tell me. I am a celebrity in the Hexamon. Yanosh floats beside my couch.

"Was it Brion's wife?" Yanosh asks me.

We are in the Way, in free fall, in the hospital unit of the Axis City. I do not know for certain if I am dreaming or even dead. I remember telling my story to Yanosh and perhaps to others, but it has taken some time—some indefinite time—to reach this point. Events are jumbled.

Yanosh has changed. He has assumed an older face, to give the appearance of many decisions made, of political maturity. Only a few years have passed here, perhaps ten. What does that mean?

"Was it Brion's wife?" he asks again, patiently. He is first assistant to the newly elected Geshel presiding minister but has been spending much time in my unit, talking to me, awaiting the return of all my memories.

I know I am an old man, ninety or ninety-one Lamarckian years. I must be dead, or dying, and this is all a shrinking fragment of imagination.

"She was dead," I manage to say.

"What spoke to you, then?"

His curiosity offends me, as if his wishing to know what the seed-mother or the queen looked like betrays a childish and trivial frame of mind. So much else of more importance. What Lenk did, or allowed his people to do. The greening, a wave of change, a fluxing across the generations, Hsia's use of Brion's gift, his *name*.

All seems compressed to me, and I have to regather my thoughts and find the thread again. Flight added to pain and starvation. The migrations from wherever the greening struck, wherever Hsia dominated. And how the name of Brion's wife was given to this tide they had begun, this transformed ecos now called Caitla, a vast vibrant specter that had so much to do with that voice, and nothing to do with Caitla herself, for she *was* dead. Her body lay untouched where Brion had placed it, within the frame, in the depths of the seed-mother's arena, the huge foam-bubble the color of blood.

"Nobody behind the voice," I say.

"You mean, no intelligence."

"No me, no you. No her." I remember pain in my legs, in my arms, all my joints burning, having burned for years. That pain is gone now. I move my fingers and their joints bend with a purity, a smoothness, I have forgotten.

"I *do* have work to do, Olmy," Yanosh says. "I can't stay here forever. I *did* order the massive effort to open the geometry stacks. I won't take credit for proposing you be given a second incarnation. You earned that and the Nexus approved it, and it will not even count against your allowed re-births . . ."

I am not grateful. I understand the value of death. My body—the body I no longer have—prepared my soul by decaying across a full and natural span of life. Because of so many years of starvation and flight, of grief and trial, my body became tough, and refused to die easily. But my mind knew the value of death. I am not grateful if life is what has been given back to me.

I had outlived two wives. My people had settled in the Kupe Islands, embraced by Cape Magellan in the south of Elizabeth's Land. I only remember broken pieces of Yanosh's agents entering my hut and finding me on a soft cot of mat fiber reeds, a special bed for dying.

"Elizabeth knew how to die," I say to Yanosh.

"The ecos," he says.

"Yes. The ecos. My wife's name was Rebecca."

"She would not leave to come here," Yanosh says. "She told us we were angels and we could have you, take you back to where you were born."

"Yes."

"She was your third wife."

"Yes," I say. "Do you want me to tell you everything that happened? I've lived a very long time, Yanosh."

Yanosh appears genuinely distressed. "It was not our intention to abandon you, Olmy. You must believe that. The Naderites came to power and we could not mount the effort for years. When the Geshels took power again, the Jarts pressed us back. And when we finally returned, the geometry stack had become even more tangled, and we could not open a gate. We thought Lamarckia was lost."

"I understand," I say. My tone is still that of a tired old man, though my voice sounds young. I do not care to press blame. I have had a long and full life. I knew Shirla, and after her, Sikaya, and finally, Rebecca, who was an old woman when I discovered her beauty and loved her.

With my death, I will finally be human. *I will know where I am.*

"You want to know what she looked like," I say.

"Nothing of the field or the dome exists anymore," Yanosh says. "The pillars are bare, the dome is gone. The jungle took over everything. Only what you saw and remember remains."

He calls it a *jungle*, not a silva. And that is what it had become. "All green. The last of the old on Hsia."

I see ghosts around him, incorporeal images of others listening in. I am telling all the Hexamon. I am a celebrity.

CHAPTER TWENTY-FIVE

I approached the frame. Chung would not enter. Frick followed Brion next, for he had been here before. He did not like being here, but he was loyal to Brion. Salap was having an epiphany. His face glowed with enthusiasm, skin creamy with brown shadows in the redness and murk as blocks of storm clouds crossed the sky above the dome. He patted my shoulder, smiled broadly, and passed through the curtainlike membrane, into the inner chamber. The membrane sealed smooth behind him, like the inverted wall of a thick soap bubble.

The voice spoke again, perfect and high. I heard Brion sobbing like a child. I pushed my hand against the membrane, felt it rush around my fingers and wrist and arm like a lip of slick flesh.

Within the frame, she stood in the middle of a mass of shiny black hemispheres, studded with black spikes and surmounted by black arches. She wore no clothing and her skin moved, rippling slightly as if she were a badly projected image.

Brion stood two steps from her, Frick by his side. Brion shook his head, chest wracked with sobs. Salap came closer to the female shape, chin in hand, studying her. Her hair hung long and muddy red, motionless and dull, in tufts and spikes to her shoulders. Her face was crudely fashioned, the face of a puppet made by a talented amateur. She paid none of them any attention.

Her mouth did not move as she spoke. "Know not names." Or, "No not names."

"May I speak to it?" Salap asked.

Brion dropped to his knees and lowered his head to the floor, palms flat against the ridged, humped surface that slowly raised and lowered him as if on a swell of ocean.

Frick said, "It isn't what he was hoping for."

Salap approached the shape. "My name is Mansur Salap. I would like to speak with you," he said, as if introducing himself at a soirée.

The shape inclined its head in his direction, but its eyes—pallid gray-blue within fixed eyelids, without expression—could not meet his. It lacked refinements and could not express anything human except in broad strokes. Whatever it had learned, it was woefully incomplete.

"You represent another, don't you?" Salap asked.

"Brion with names not," the voice said, coming from all around. The walls of the frame vibrated like diaphragms, making the sounds, along with other noises: windy flights of whispering, a steady low frog-throat grumble.

"Do you recognize Brion?" Salap asked.

"Talks."

"I talk and my name is Salap."

"I brought Caitla here. Where is she?" Brion asked. Another membrane of tissue withdrew, and the body was visible on a raised hump in the living floor, slack with death, months into its own private decay.

"You understand us," Salap said.

Chung had entered without my noticing and stood one step behind me. "Star, Fate, and Breath," she said.

The figure turned toward her voice. "Two speak gave and use what use. Two now here."

Chung seemed aghast to be confused with her sister again. "I am not Caitla," she said. "You've tried to become Caitla." She shouted at Brion, "She's dead, and you wanted to bring her back!"

Brion had stopped weeping and stood before the figure, examining it critically. "You could try again. More work . . . More detail."

"It will take a long time to understand us," Salap said.

"Why?" Brion asked. "Why so long? It samples us, it must know what we're like . . ."

"We've been mistaken," Salap said.

The figure, I realized, had not taken a step. It grew from the floor and could not lift its feet. It was only a little more sophisticated than the discarded husks behind us.

"Caitla and I gave her the chlorophyll," Brion argued. "She took the bottle and used it. She made Caitla plants for her garden, working with the real plants Caitla showed her."

Salap looked back at me. "Can you tell him, Ser Olmy? Bring the sophistication of the Thistledown to this little exercise in monstrosity?"

For a moment, I hadn't a clue what Salap wanted me to say. Then a thought that had been below conscious expression for some months broke through. "They've never sampled our genetic structure."

"Yes?" Salap encouraged, face seeming to glow again like a beacon. The figure shivered, some rudimentary adjustment in turgor.

"Sampling is a way of identifying other scions. Each ecos carries its own markers, its own chemical scheme. We don't fit any schemes. We don't come from other ecoi. They can't analyze our structure from the level of our genetic material. So they have to copy us from the evidence of other senses."

"But what about the *chlorophyll*?" Brion demanded.

Salap said, "It understands chemistry. It can test and find uses for organic substances. You must have provided the final clues necessary . . . given the pigments a context it could understand. But it can't break our genetic code. We are too different."

"Names," the figure said. "Names know not."

Chung seemed startled. "Does she actually understand what we're saying? Or is she . . . is it just stringing words together?"

"She understands," Brion said.

"That's a miracle by itself," Chung said. She stepped closer to the figure and to Brion, overcoming some of her repugnance.

"What did you talk with before?" Salap asked Brion, pointing at the figure: *before this was created.*

"When Caitla and I came here, this inner room was filled with tissues . . . tools. It was a prototype factory. Part of a scion could be grown here, another there . . . We saw them being carried by giant hairs—cilia—across this chamber, and matched with other parts. And we watched them being dissolved in large pools, turned into jelly or slime. Rejected.

"Caitla realized what this was. She said that we were in a huge cell, all of its parts made large, but because of that, not a cell at all . . . None of us knew why we had been allowed to come in here. On our last visit, before Caitla became ill, the seed-mother . . ." He gestured around the chamber. "*She* showed us the best of her human-shaped scions, still much cruder than this. It could only hum and whistle and make parts of words. Caitla spent a week teaching it, her, before we had to return to Naderville. We knew *she* wanted to communicate with us directly."

"Bring," the voice said. "Know bring names."

"I brought Caitla back here when she was dying. Caitla told me to leave her here. 'Put me where we put my plants,' she said. We knew *she* could do better."

Brion turned, staring up at the red walls of the frame. He seemed uncertain whether to address the figure directly, or speak to the frame, the hemisphere as a whole. "There is so much more you can do!"

"No making more for this child," the voice said, acquiring a cello-like timbre. It had also taken on a quality I might have called *conviction* if it had been human. "New names, no making more, no making more, for this child."

"Why?" Brion asked, dismayed.

The figure swelled again, filling itself with fresh fluids from below. It raised its arms. The color of its skin improved, and the motions in the skin subsided, coordinated, more nearly like the movement of muscles. I watched with queasy fascination the development of its facial features, the refinement of abdomen and breasts, still doll-like, but a better imitation of what Caitla might have looked like. Or Hyssha.

"It's learning from you," Salap said to Chung. She looked up at the gloomy heights of the frame, searching for eyes among the glints and tiny sea-floor glows.

Brion seemed stung by this. He took a step back. "It isn't Caitla," he said.

"It never will be," Salap said. "You've misunderstood what the ecos can do . . . We've all misplaced our nightmares and our hopes."

The figure turned its head, opened its mouth, and the voice issued from the mouth now. "Sounds like smells, names deeper than I know. Two are not one, yet cling. Make third, but within. Third is child, but not like this child. Not of I, not of any I, from where."

Then it added the lilt of question: "From *where*?"

None of us quite understood.

"We're not from this planet," Brion said quietly, as if this were a devastating admission. I think he was trying to shed the last hope for Caitla, and it was costing him dearly. He had some courage or some curiosity left, to speak with the figure at all.

"There only is. There only is." The figure lifted one foot, turned slightly on the other, and placed the free foot down awkwardly, bending forward to compensate. It returned to its original posture, but where the foot had lifted away, a small pucker remained. Though it knew the figure of Caitla/Hyssha would never pass, never enter the realm of a human ecos undetected, it still worked to finish its peculiar scion, the interface for its own selfless and eternal curiosity, the purest and most biological urge to know.

"There's more," Brion whispered. "Planets and planets and planets. In the sky. Wherever there are stars."

At the mention of stars, the lights within the inner frame, scattered in profusion over the braces and walls, dim blue and white, shone out in sudden splendor.

"Stars," the figure said.

Brion turned to Frick and Chung. "I know it isn't Caitla. I know I'll never see Caitla again. But I could stay here and tutor her. I could be happy doing that."

Frick rubbed his hands together in front of him, not relishing what he had to say. "Ser Brion, you are needed. We need you."

Brion's brief resurgence of hope withered. He screwed his face up and imitated Frick's gesture of rubbed hands, then pushed his nose with the tips of his fingers. "Beys can take care of those things," he said.

Chung said, "You put far too much on Beys. Someday he'll discover he doesn't need any of us."

Brion jerked his head up at that, as if to make a sharp reply, but his eyes turned inevitably to the figure, and all expression melted away.

"You have other responsibilities," Salap said soothingly. "Everybody else here has other responsibilities. None of you . . . pardon me, Ser Brion, not even you . . . is prepared to study and teach here. I am."

"What would you teach her?" Brion asked resentfully, unwilling to give up this last possibility of fulfillment, of peace.

"I would study her," Salap said. "And then I would watch her die. I do not think this palace, this field, will be alive much longer, nor any of its kind across Hsia. You and Caitla gave her a very powerful 'name.' I think she uses 'name' to mean the chlorophyll you presented to her. She used the name. And that changes everything."

"The balloons," I said.

Salap nodded. "They carry larval seed-mothers, not just scions. If I'm right, in a few weeks, all this will wither."

"Old names die," the figure said.

"Nightmare," Brion said, words venomous with disappointment. "It's *all* nightmare." Brion turned to me. "Ser Olmy, you know history. That much change means death and destruction everywhere. The Hexamon must come. I've said it . . . I've felt it. You must repair Lenk's clavicle, tell the Hexamon what's happened here."

There was nothing I could say. For Brion to make a plea on behalf of the humans on Lamarckia seemed ludicrous. Yet he was right. There was one last thing left to do: find the clavicle, and see if it could be repaired.

Brion stepped closer to the figure and touched its face. It did not react, but even as he stroked its cheek, it said, "Are more names? Bring more names."

We left Salap with several weeks' worth of food from the two boats, Brion's and the one that had carried Hyssha Chung and her attendants.

"I won't die here, no fear of that," Salap told me, walking back with me through the sea of green. "I'm a tough old vulture, as you doubtless know. Brion, on the other hand . . ."

Brion had returned to the boat in an impenetrable daze, ignoring us all, and squatted on the bow, staring down the waterway. He had let the string unwind and carried it pinched between thumb and forefinger, lying in loose coils on the polished and painted xyla deck.

"Watch him," Salap told me. "He still holds a dangerous amount of political charge, as does Lenk. They must be eased together . . . or apart."

We stood on overgrown dock, with the new silva—the *jungle*—rustling like grass in a wind, though there was hardly a breeze. Salap held me by my shoulders. "Even if you never get through to the Hexamon, even if they never come, some of us can survive."

CHAPTER TWENTY-SIX

"Did you ever find the clavicle?" Yanosh asks. I am finishing my story outside the hospital. Yanosh has been dragged away by greater responsibilities, and has returned to find me making progress. We leave the hospital to see some of the sights of the Axis City.

I am removing myself from the memories of one long and difficult life.

Now we drift and tract beside each other in the Wald, the great weightless and terribly green forest in Axis Euclid. My body is so much sweeter and more comfortable, yet I still miss my old life, my impending death, and still ache so much I have incessant thoughts of suicide. If I return through the gate to Lamarckia and try to find Rebecca . . .

But I can't do that. Yanosh tells me the gate is sporadic, that years have passed on Lamarckia even since I was retrieved. I do not want the new life, but I will not reject it. In this I have a sense of duty to something much higher than the Hexamon.

"I found it," I say. The Wald's green oppresses me, as it did on Lamarckia, where we ran from continent to continent, and finally from island to island . . .

Fleeing the power of the "name" of chlorophyll.

"What did you *do*?" Yanosh asks.

What he really wants to know is, did I finally *act*? The story I have told so far is one of observation and hiding, of trying to put pieces together and understand a pattern. But I never did understand completely. The pieces never fit smoothly.

I made my decision in ignorance and uncertainty.

CHAPTER TWENTY-SEVEN

Brion did not say a word to anybody in the eighteen hours it took us to navigate the length of the canal, back to Naderville. The green had progressed dozens of kilometers through the silva, and along its borders with the thicket, the old growth had wilted, making way for the new. Balloons dotted the horizon and flew overhead, lifting free of the land, blowing with the winds outward.

I watched this with a grim numbness and a sense of abject failure. I could not judge Brion as I once had; if anything, I had become more angry with Lenk. But Lenk was old and could not bear the weight of all blame.

The futility of blame was apparent, but did not lift my gloom. I needed Shirla to bring back my sense of life and reality.

Frick took coded messages on the radio within the cabin, and brought them forward for Brion to read. He read them and handed them back, shaking his head. Frick became increasingly agitated. Something was happening.

Brion sat on the bow, arms wrapped around his drawn-up knees, and stared into the sunset, eyes almost closed, lips drawn into a simian grimace of puzzlement.

We motored past the entrance to the lake. I tried to persuade Frick to return me to the lake so that I could rejoin the ships docked there. He looked at Brion, shook his head as if I were a buzzing fly, and finally just ignored me.

The guards stood on the rear deck of the small, elegant boat, watching me intently. I thought of diving into the canal and swimming to the shore, or up the offshoot to the lake, but knew they would shoot me if I did.

Smoke rose above the tall cliff edge of the silva as we approached Naderville, but for some minutes, the town itself remained hidden. The harbor came into view first, and it was filled with sailing ships. I counted eight, ten, twelve, and as the full harbor was revealed, seventeen—of all types, full-rigs, schooners, big-bodied four-masters, small barks. Flashes erupted from the sides of several of the ships, followed by the heavy blasts of cannon fire and the rushing whistles of falling shells. More flashes from the shore, puffs of smoke, and deep thumps announced explosions.

The pilot immediately increased the speed of Brion's boat, and Chung's boat hastened to keep pace. As the boats cruised out of the canal entrance, I saw Naderville again, hundreds of homes and buildings arranged along several hills, backed by high dark thicket.

Gouts of flame crept from street to street up the hills, and more shells fell, shearing the roofs off buildings and sparking more fires. At least a third of the town had been set ablaze. Shouts and screams carried far and thin across the harbor. Brion stared at the black pillars of smoke with an astonished, hurt expression, then crawled to the middle of the boat and ordered his binoculars.

"Lenk lied," Brion said tightly, swinging the binoculars right and left across the city. "He used himself as a blind."

Brion lowered the glasses and screamed across the water, "Why didn't Beys know? General Beys, *where are you*?"

We swung toward the northern shore and docked in the early evening at a small private wharf. Chung's boat pulled alongside, and Chung stared at us, grim and frightened. Her assistants, Ullman and Grado, leaped from the boat and tied it, then helped her ashore.

A hundred meters away, warehouses burned sluggishly, throwing up thick, sour black smoke. The house adjacent to the wharf was beginning to burn as well as embers landed on its roof.

Brion stood with one foot on the gunwale and stared down at me in utter contempt. "You are *nothing*," he said. "The Hexamon has sent us *nothing*." He seemed ready to order me shot, but he shook his head and took Frick's hand, climbing up onto the wharf wall.

Brion, Chung, Frick, and all the servants and guards ran from the wharf, leaving me alone in the boat. They ran up the harbor road that pointed to Naderville.

For a few minutes, I could not move. My legs and arms tingled. I was mesmerized, watching the fire sweep down toward the wharf and the boats, the xyla burning with slow, curling orange flames, thick oily smoke smearing across the dark blue sky. I climbed out of the launch and stood on the harbor road. Wind blew against my back, rushing to feed the fires in Naderville. A woman in a long black dress with a sash of red ran along the shore road, alone; this part of the town had already been evacuated, probably as soon as the ships appeared in the harbor.

My first impulse was to get back on the boat and cross the harbor, wait on the south shore until the conflagration and fighting had settled. I knew my mission: I was not to interfere, and I was to bring information back to the Hexamon. I could not do that if I was dead.

I searched the ships in the harbor for *Khoragos* and *Cow*, but as I had suspected, neither were visible. Lenk was no doubt keeping them out of the harbor and away from the fighting. I hoped Shirla was with him, and of course Randall.

I was sick of the divaricates and their politics; Lenk's obsessions and calculations, all gone wrong, and his hounding of Brion and Caitla (if in fact that was true). I could not fathom Brion's handing power to Beys, and Brion's gift of green to Hsia seemed to me obscene, the ultimate monkey-play arrogance.

If a gate was to open now and pluck me out of the pilot's seat on the boat, and close forever on Lamarckia, I would not regret leaving—

Except for Shirla. She was essential, an anchor against my drift into this madness. She was not particularly beautiful, not particularly intelligent; nothing about her shone with an ineffable flame. She was merely a woman with a decent set of presumptions and a simple set of goals. She wanted to live a life among friends and peers, live with and love a decent man, raise children to be human beings in a known and familiar place.

I loathed any part of me I had seen reflected in Lenk or Brion. Their smallnesses and failures could easily be my own. Even Brion's grief for Caitla seemed cheapened by his arrogance, his presumption that people of such a high standing could not die, that some magic must keep them alive.

How did that differ from me? On Thistledown I would undoubtedly opt for rejuvenation—life extension and even body replacement.

Caitla and Brion had acted on their beliefs, however skewed or inadequate, and so far, I had done nothing—used none of my expertise, exercised none of my (admittedly few) options, managed to always find myself in positions where aloofness was the best choice.

Lenk's activism had brought his people here and subjected them to immense suffering. Brion's brash militancy and drive had led to war and murder and had culminated in the madness of the spreading green. What had once dwelled in comparative balance was now overturned and could not be set upright again.

My inaction seemed saintly by comparison.

Shirla's face kept popping into my thoughts.

My mission was over.

I had to make a decision, or I would be nothing more than a man filled with vacuum, a nonentity standing always on some thin line.

I stepped back from a rush of flame as the wall of the house collapsed. The gust of burning hot air and embers jarred me and I turned toward the wharf.

With the flames roaring behind me, I studied the harbor, judging the strategic position of the ships and boats, the layout of Naderville itself. There was fighting in the town—I could see troops moving through the streets, hear the crack and continuous popping of small-arms fire.

Lenk had indeed lied to Brion, or expected the worst, and had been prepared. He had kept in reserve a ragtag navy assembled of merchant ships and transports. They were now laying siege to Naderville. The fourteen vessels had crept into the harbor a few hours before, perhaps signaled by the departure of the two diplomatic ships *Khoragos* and *Cow.* The steamships were not visible—Beys must have taken them out of the harbor, perhaps heading back to put more pressure on Jakarta. Lenk's ships had surprised the small defense force and had landed several hundred troops. It had all happened very quickly.

There were no masters on Lamarckia, there were only children. Some of the children, however, were more crafty than I had imagined. Lenk had turned out to be smarter—or luckier—than Brion, after all. I suspected that Lenk had the superior force, selected from the more capable of the angry citizens of Tasman and Elizabeth's Land. Brion's troops—to judge by the poor fool on the flatboat—might turn out to be little more than opportunistic thugs, poorly trained and cruel, no match for that kind of avenging passion.

All of Brion's invincibility had crumpled. The ultimate failings of a frightened, grieving, and angry little man were written all over the hills and streets of Naderville.

As the flattened house behind me crackled and exploded, I returned to the deserted boats and examined their supplies and reserves of power. The batteries in Chung's boat were almost drained. Brion's boat, however, had a spare set, fully charged. I carried the spare set of batteries to Chung's boat—less identifiable than Brion's elegant launch—removed the flag at the bow, and prepared to push off. I cruised quietly through shrouds of dense, choking smoke, not to the south side of the harbor, where there were few if any buildings and no visible fighting or shelling going on, but west, along the shore, under the line of fire of the ships in the harbor.

Twilight was fading fast. I guided the boat around a smoldering hulk that had once been a wooden merchant vessel. Its crooked trees stuck up out of the water like broken fingers. I wanted to thoroughly understand the strategic situation, find the best vantage point, and then walk into the town and join Lenk's troops.

The gate opener had placed me in a very *interesting* time indeed, stuck me here like a fly in amber. There would be no returning.

Naderville rested on two main hills, with a line of smaller hills along the peninsula between the harbor and the ocean to the north. East of the two main hills, between the town itself and the lake and Citadel, a patch of thicket silva had been allowed to remain. The silva would be mined through with tunnels, and if Beys or his subordinates had positioned any last defensive troops—or hoped to fight a final action—I surmised they would be hidden in that patch of thicket, or perhaps at the Citadel itself, and when opportunity arose, certainly after the artillery barrage, storm up one or both of the hills.

I saw a group of soldiers marching down a street on a hill, almost hidden in the shadows of a row of buildings still intact in that quarter of town. They marched about a kilometer and a half from the boat. I could not tell whose troops they were, of course—it was possible that none of Lenk's troops had uniforms, but I couldn't make out the cut of their clothes, or even determine the color.

It was necessary to survey the town from farther south, to get a better view of the streets and buildings, the centers of potential conflict. I guided the boat south, away from Lenk's ships. Locking the wheel for a moment and searching through the cabin, I found a piece of paper in a drawer, and quickly sketched the harbor, the town, and the streets visible. I used the binoculars to gather details—likely administration buildings, a water tower, and what seemed to be a radio mast on the western side of the town. Any one of these could be crucial objectives.

By this time, I was starting to attract unwanted attention from Lenk's ships, less than two kilometers away. A gunner had targeted the boat and a shell landed barely a dozen meters away. I did not know what type of guns they had, and how accurate they might be, but I could not risk staying on the water any longer. I headed for the docks again. Another shell drenched me with spray. I was less than a dozen meters from shore when a direct hit split the boat in two and flung me backward into the water.

Dazed, I floated on my back in the black water of the harbor for several minutes before swimming for the docks. I crawled up a ladder and stood in the darkness between two warehouses, one of them shattered by the shelling but not on fire. I tried to get my wits together. A piece of xyla had cut a bloody groove across my forehead. I wiped the blood away with my wet sleeve. The map was gone, but I had most of the details firmly in memory.

Naderville was divided by four main east-west streets and seven or eight wide streets running north-south from the harbor to the hills. The buildings that seemed most likely to be administrative—still intact, surprisingly—lay on the slopes of the easternmost hill, off of a north-south boulevard. I walked toward these buildings.

A few civilians still lingered in the town, and the scenes I saw, heading for the eastern hill, could have been several thousand years old. Bodies littered a small courtyard where a shell had exploded: two large ones, two small. Children. I wondered if Lenk had killed some of his own children.

Five older men and several women, heads wrapped in cloth against the smoke, pushed their belongings on a makeshift cart through brick and xyla rubble.

I hid in the half open doorway of a hollowed-out building to avoid a straggling line of young men and women, not knowing whether they were soldiers; they crossed along an east-west street, shouting encouragement to each other. A few carried electric lanterns.

By the glare of one lantern, I recognized a face—Keo, one of Lenk's assistants, following close on the line. I called out his name and he jerked around, then raised the lantern and spotted me in the doorway.

"Olmy! Fate's breath," he said. "You're still alive! We were sure you'd all have been killed when the attack started." He shouted at the retreating backs of the young men and women, "Hold on!" They turned and clustered around us, showing the whites of their eyes like startled deer, breathless, at once frightened and cocksure.

"What's happening?" I asked.

"Where's Salap?" he asked in return.

I did not want to waste time by explaining. "Is the town taken?"

Some of the young people shook their heads. Several laughed nervously, milling like dogs. I counted heads and sexes: eight men, five women.

"Not yet," Keo said. "There's an action up around Sun Road. Lots of resistance. Beys was back at sea—missed our ships—but swung around to the northern side of the peninsula, landed troops. They're moving back into the town now, to replace the soldiers who went to the western peninsula. A diversion. Lenk's auxiliaries—we're all auxiliaries now—grounded a small ship there and burned some houses and buildings. I didn't know about this—" Keo's chest jerked. He was hyperventilating in his nervousness. "Randall told us . . . before he left, and . . . about you . . ."

"Is Shirla with Lenk?"

Keo's face fell. "The woman? No," he said. "She and Randall were taken by Brion's police two days ago, just after you and Salap left with Brion."

"We have to go," shouted one of the young men, an apprentice sailor from one of the schooners to judge from his clothing. He confronted me. "Whoever you are, we can't stay here clacking teeth—we have to report if there are any troops coming around to the east of town."

"That's true," Keo said, clearly uncomfortable with leadership.

"He's the Hexamon man," a young woman said, peering at me curiously. Dirt and sweat streaked her lean face and she seemed stupid with fear and excitement. "He was on *Khoragos*. He's the one they've been talking about."

I hardly heard all this. My thoughts raced, trying to think of where they might have taken Shirla. She could still be back at the lake, hidden in the buildings within the old seed-mother palace.

"I've been out in the harbor, and there's no action to the east—not yet," I said. "But there could be a contingent of troops back at the lake. Beys might use them to pinch us all . . . Where are his steamships?"

"North of the peninsula, the last we saw."

Clearly, Beys's most likely plan—the best plan under the circumstances—sketched itself in my head. He had landed the soldiers traveling with the ships in the north, perhaps two companies of well-trained men and women, a fair force under the circumstances, but not enough to have much impact. Troops at the old palace could number in the hundreds. If the town had been lightly defended—concentrating the troops in Beys's ships and around Brion's quarters—then that was likely all Beys had to work with, a few hundred troops. The rest would be working Tasman and Elizabeth's Land.

"How many soldiers does Lenk have?"

Keo stared at me, uncertain, sweating in the lantern light. Stars poked through drifting patches of smoke. The shelling had stopped for now. "You're a soldier from the Hexamon," he said. "Who are you for?"

"Not for Brion," I said. "I need to find Shirla . . . and you need to secure the town. As you said, I'm a soldier—I have a lot better training than Lenk, and probably better training than Beys."

I could almost see the outline of Keo's thoughts. He had been put in command of these young men, but he had no military education—few coming to Lamarckia had. They would make a haphazard force at best. I had no idea of the level of their strategic planning—clearly, Beys had been unprepared for anything like this, but he was likely to put together an effective defense soon. Keo was smart enough to see this.

"Lenk didn't confide in us until the last," he said. "We have maybe six hundred volunteers."

"Seven or eight companies," I said.

"Lenk has them ordered differently, I think."

"Who's his general?"

"He designed the operation. Fassid helped."

I shook my head in disgust. Keo started to defend Lenk's expertise, but I cut him off. "You have to set up a strong defense in the eastern part of town. At least two hundred troops. Beys will almost certainly deploy the forces at the lake. Do you have a radio?"

"Yes," Keo said. One of his men, little more than a boy actually, lifted a small box. "Not a lot of range, unfortunately."

The young men and women clustered around us, no longer protesting. I felt a queasy exhilaration.

Here, among amateurs, going up against a butcher who was sly at best, I could be useful. Lenk's soldiers occupied the cape and headland in strength, Keo said. To the north and west, positions had not yet been consolidated.

"I need five of these good soldiers," I said. "We should split into two groups."

"I have a map . . . of sorts," Keo said, lifting a cloth satchel and pulling out a small, folded piece of paper. He spread it out in the lantern light. It was an original sketch in pencil and ink, and supplied more detail to what I had seen from the harbor, in particular charting the roads through the silva from Naderville to the lake. The Citadel area was not shown.

"We can use it. You take one group and keep watch on the eastern edge of the town. I'll take my five, and we'll reconnoiter the silva between Naderville and the lake. For now, tell Lenk's commanders—or Lenk himself, whoever's in charge—that he needs to post at least one hundred well-armed men to meet you at the edge of town."

"I don't think we have one hundred well-armed men," Keo said. "Not that we can spare."

What had seemed a major coup in the beginning was looking more and more uncertain. *No masters, only children.* "Don't tell Beys that," I said. I picked the five who seemed most fit and enthusiastic, and Keo's group and mine ran in two lines along the street, until we came to a clearing beyond the last of the houses. Beyond lay the cliff edge of the thicket silva and the dark holes of two tunnel roads.

"Good luck," Keo told me.

I felt incredibly alive, and very, very stupid.

CHAPTER TWENTY-EIGHT

We made our way down Sanger Road, through a thicket tunnel. Sanger was one of two parallel roads the map showed going to the lake. The tunnel lights had gone out; we probed ahead with a lantern. I expected to meet a contingent of Beys's troops at any time.

The nighttime thicket was still. We walked down the tunnel road for thirty minutes, then emerged under a brilliant star-rich sky, the double ox-bow rising in the east. A few lights flickered ahead. We were in a broad clearing, once perhaps a farm area, now barren fields. The road crossed the field toward another thicket, perhaps a kilometer off, and entered another tunnel at that point. I guessed the Citadel lay about two kilometers beyond.

I did not know the palace grounds thoroughly; we could easily get lost.

A small young woman named Meg, with a smooth dark face and wide eyes, kept close to me. She carried one of the three guns Keo had been willing to spare. "This is going to be rough, isn't it?" she asked.

"Probably," I said.

"Do you know where we're going?"

"I've been there."

"And you say there are a lot of soldiers."

"Meg worries for us all," said the oldest male, a tall, stooped fellow of twenty-five named Broch.

"There are a lot of soldiers," I said. "But we're going to avoid them. We don't want to fight; we want to learn things."

"How?" Meg asked, licking her lips and staring ahead of us, at the wall of the next stretch of thicket silva.

"We're going to hide between the tunnel openings. That is, the five of you are. I may take one with me. I'm going on to the old palace. Soldiers will likely come through one or both of the two tunnels. You can see both roads from where you'll hide. If they appear before I get back, we send the fastest runner—"

"That's Youk," said Meg, pointing to a small, slender woman with faun-like features.

"Youk," I said, "You run ahead of the soldiers, and report to Ser Keo. He'll give warning with his radio."

"What if they use trucks?" Youk asked.

"Then we'll change our plans. But the troops will probably be on foot." From what I had seen, Beys had concentrated all their vaunted technology where it would be highly visible. I doubted that they had many more transports or tractors than Calcutta.

"What will you do?"

"I'm going to the old palace," I said again. "The Citadel."

"You keep saying 'palace' . . . What kind of palace?" Rashnara, the shortest male, asked.

"It's where Brion lives," I said. No need to explain further.

Closing on the opening to the next tunnel, we cut away from the road catercorner toward the thicket wall between the north and south openings. I stumbled once and Youk helped me to my feet. The ground was hard and chalky and had not been plowed for months, perhaps a year. We hugged the thicket, backs against the smooth outer trunks of the arborids that intertwined to make a flat dark wall.

"Why did Ser Keo turn us over to you?" Meg asked.

"We're not supposed to ask that kind of question," Broch said.

"It's a good question," I said. "Always ask questions."

"Why, then?" Meg asked. We were about fifty meters from either road. We could see the pavement of each road clearly enough, thin lines of lighter gray against the gray-black soil.

"A friend of ours told him I had been a member of Hexamon Defense once."

Broch sniffed in the dark. "Are you *that* old?"

"No," I said. "Not so very old." *Not much older than these kids*, I reminded myself.

"So what does that mean?" Meg persisted.

I saw something block out stars and looked up. Balloons floated across the night sky. One dropped its trailing tentacles onto the field, scraping them across the dirt barely twenty meters from where we squatted.

"What is that?" asked Olivos, a short, bristle-headed man with a brushy beard. Youk stood to run out and investigate, but I grabbed her arm.

"It's from the interior," I said. "A new kind of transporter." I stood and looked down at them. "Ser Broch, you have a gun. Will you come with me?"

"You're asking, not ordering?" Broch said, incredulous.

"Yes, because what I have to do is partly personal."

Broch stood. "You worked in Way Defense?" he asked.

"A long time ago."

"I'll come," he said.

"If we're not back in two hours, you can assume we've been captured," I told the rest. "Meg, you're in charge."

"Thank you, I think," Meg said. "Does anybody have a watch?"

Nobody did.

"Count, then," I said.

Broch and I walked north to the Godwin road and stood in the middle of the stone slab and gravel pavement, staring into the tunnel's impenetrable darkness. We had no lantern. The tunnel was quiet, except for the sound of dripping water. "Let's go," I said.

"What are we going to do?" he asked.

"See what the troops are up to, and rescue a friend," I said. "If they're still there at all."

"You think they might have come by water?"

"Not if they're smart. The harbor belongs to Lenk for the time being." It seemed likely Beys would try to retake the harbor. I hoped we could be back before that happened. "We're not going to talk while we're in the tunnel, okay?"

Broch nodded.

"Brush your hand against the left side. I'll stay to the right."

We walked for fifty meters in complete darkness. The air was getting thick and smelled stale. Broch coughed and apologized in a whisper. Whiffs of an ammonia-like smell, tangy and very unpleasant, met us farther down the tunnel. Sounds from above filtered down to us: rustling, shifting. With some relief, we came to the end of the tunnel and stood in a field. A few lights gleamed across the field, electric lanterns bobbing to and fro, and we heard subdued voices.

From the west, more explosions and the distant pop of cannon. I guessed we were at the northern end of the lake, west of the Citadel. I could barely make out the black shapes of buildings. A light came on in a distant window. A voice called out, and the light was quickly extinguished.

"Brion's soldiers," Broch whispered, standing close beside me.

"They could be evacuated civilians," I said. "We don't know yet."

I doubted anyone would see us if we cut across to the right, where the silva massed again as a solid wall. With a few words and gestures, I made our route clear, and we set out across a flat, empty field that had never been plowed.

"Give me your gun," I said.

"Why, Ser?"

"Do you want to have to kill someone?"

He handed me the gun. It was a heavy, short-barreled rifle of simple design.

We followed the line of the thicket slowly, trying to keep on our feet over the uneven ground. A shape sprawled across the dirt a few meters in front of us, a black blur in the star-lit darkness. I thought for a moment it was a human body, but it gave off a thick ammonia smell. I bent over it briefly and saw a tangle of limbs, a long cylindrical body, sharp digging barbs around its tail. My neck hairs tingled. It was a dead scion. Nothing had come to pick it up and take it away. This was the smell of *death* on Lamarckia. The closeness in the tunnel had also been death.

"Fate and Breath," Broch said. "What is it?"

"A scion," I said. "It's dead."

"Why don't cleaners come and get it?"

"Things are changing," I said. We edged around it. I had little doubt it was one of the thicket's mobile scions, so seldom seen outside the tangle of arborids. The thicket silva, after tens or hundreds of millions of years, was being told to die.

In buildings to our left, we heard footsteps and voices, orders given. Soldiers were getting organized. I heard snatches of conversation. ". . . We'll get them in a vice at Jalipat . . ." "They're fools. Blood-thick fools." "Who's got the squadron radio?"

So these were the troops, comprised of most of the old palace's guards and security. I could not judge how many there were; at least a hundred.

"Form up," a loud, authoritative female voice said. "West in ten minutes."

I stopped and Broch bumped into me. "Hear that?" I whispered very softly in his ear. He nodded. "That's what we need to know. Run back and tell the others to report this to Ser Keo."

"You're not coming with me?" he asked. He was clearly unhappy at the thought of going back alone; unhappy, also, I surmised, at the thought of going back down the strange-smelling tunnel. "I thought you needed me."

"I needed you for this. It's time," I said. "You have your duty. I'm going to find my friends." I handed him the rifle. "Take this with you. I hope I won't need it."

Broch hesitated for a moment, backed away with arms folded, then dropped them by his side, turned and walked into the darkness. He skirted the dead scion and I could no longer make him out in the darkness.

Somehow, I had contrived to be alone again. I had always preferred working alone, even in Way Defense. I wondered if one's life history was the result of world-lines collapsing in response to simple force of character. The dilemma had not been solved in a thousand years of human philosophy.

I walked quietly and quickly between two buildings. A single moon rose and cast some extra light. That was not good. I tried to stay in deeper shadow wherever possible. I had to be within a hundred meters of the old palace complex.

I entered a courtyard through a narrow open corridor. A fountain in the center of the courtyard threw a steady ribbon of water into the air, splashing and chuckling to itself. Staying close to the wall, my feet scuffing lightly on a gravel-covered walkway, I passed a line of doors and darkened windows, through another corridor. A few lights danced in an alley between the courtyard and a wall. I flattened myself against the wall and felt large, smooth round stones: the old palace. The lights—two men gripping lanterns—moved past the entrance to the alley.

If whoever was in charge felt the situation was desperate, and Brion was no longer here, this area might be almost deserted.

In a couple of hours, dawn glow would begin lighting the sky. I followed the curve of the ancient stone wall for fifty or sixty meters before reaching a gate. Three men stood by the gate, talking softly in the darkness. I pitched my voice to just the right volume and tone of concern.

"Excuse me. Don't be alarmed. Ser Frick—"

All three guns instantly pointed at me, and I heard three simultaneous *snick-clacks* as rounds were chambered.

"I'm one of Brion's guests. I'm not armed. Ser Frick left me in a boat at Naderville."

"Who are you?"

"My name is Olmy," I said.

"Frick isn't here," the tallest guard said, a bulky shadow with a gravelly voice.

"Where am I supposed to go?"

"We don't have any instructions about you."

"Ser Brion told me to come back here on the water, but the boat was destroyed . . . I had to walk. It was frightening."

"You were with Brion?" the gravel-voiced guard asked.

"I've heard about you," another guard said, and they conferred in whispers for a moment. "You went with Frick and Ser Brion . . . didn't you? Where did you go?"

"Up the canal," I said.

"Come here."

I stepped up and the tall guard allowed a thin beam of light to play across my face from a slit in his lantern.

"I think he's the one," the second guard said.

"Go inside and find out if anybody wants him."

CHAPTER TWENTY-NINE

Hyssha Chung stood in the vivarium, the early dawn casting a blue and indistinct light over her sister's garden. The smell was atrocious—ammonia and still, stale air. All around her, the garden lay in dark tatters. The two guards who escorted me covered their noses with cloths to filter the dust raised by our feet.

"Have you found your gate back to the Way yet?" Chung asked, her voice tired but still acid.

"No," I said. "I've come back to see where my friends are. A woman named Shirla. And Randall, the scientist who worked with Salap."

Hyssha said nothing for several seconds, then dismissed the guards with a wave, saying she knew me, and I was no risk.

The guards departed, and we were alone in the tainted stillness.

"You managed to get in here without being killed. That's a kind of magic," she said.

"I acted stupid and innocent," I said. "Lost."

"You may be the only innocent person on this planet," Chung said. "Innocence is a luxury for outsiders."

"Why are you here?" I asked.

"I don't want to watch the fighting."

"Where's Brion?"

"In Naderville. Maybe Beys picked him up. Actually, I don't know where he is. Your woman and your friend Randall . . . I think Beys took them with him on the ships."

I felt sick. "Why?"

"I don't follow Beys closely. We don't like each other much." She looked around her, staring at the dead garden with lips set in a rigid line. "A balloon transporter dropped a few larval seed-mothers here yesterday. All of Caitla's creations . . . dead in hours. The food supply . . . gone. Rotted. There's probably very little food anywhere in Naderville by now. The air is filled with instructions from the green seed-mothers . . . orders to die and rot in place, to make nutrients for the new forms."

"You know for sure that Shirla and Randall aren't here?"

"I don't care where they are. We're all going to die, unless Lenk wins and sends us food, or Brion wins and we all sail to Elizabeth's Land or Tasman. *She* did this to us." Then, stepping closer and looking into my face, she said, "You hate Brion, don't you?"

"Yes," I said. The emotions were not so clearly expressed, but to say anything else would have been lying.

"You'd kill him if you could?"

"No," I said.

"And Beys?"

"I'm not here to kill," I said.

"You think Brion's weak now, and Beys is going to return and take over completely."

"He already has, hasn't he?"

Hyssha Chung bit her lip, her eyes filling with tears. "I feel what Caitla would feel," she said. "Everything wasted, all the suffering and dying. She was devoted to Brion. He loved her very much. But love doesn't excuse us, does it?"

"No."

"You *have* judged us, haven't you?"

"Not you," I said. "I don't know much about you."

"An accomplice," she murmured. "Will Lenk take us back with him?"

"I don't know," I said.

She touched her finger to her cheeks and smeared her tears. "You don't believe in drama, do you? Brion believes in drama, too much I think. But Beys is like you . . . He has your woman and your friend. Maybe he'll be expecting you. Go kill Beys."

CHAPTER THIRTY

Dawn had turned the sky gray-green in the east. The guards stood by the main gate into the old palace, saying nothing, holding their rifles with barrels raised a few degrees above horizontal, as I walked away. I expected a bullet in my back at any moment. The path back through the buildings to the road was deserted. The troops from the Citadel had departed hours ago.

On the Godwin road, heading west, I found two bodies in the barren fields: Broch, lying face down in the dirt, had been shot in the chest and jaw. Youk, the fast young runner, lay on the other side of the road a few meters away, on her back, calm eyes staring at the dusty morning sky. Ahead and behind, the thicket silva made ugly groaning and rattling sounds, settling, throwing up billows of gray dust. The tunnel was a nightmare, dust falling all around in drifts like ash, sections half collapsed, the air almost unbreathable. I thought I would suffocate before I stumbled out into daylight again. Behind me, the tunnel collapsed and I was surrounded by a thick cloud of acrid powder and ammonia. I closed my eyes and ran clear, then lay gasping on my knees by the road, eyes burning, covered with clinging grime. My skin itched furiously.

I had sent Broch to his death, I had guided Youk and perhaps the others into death, and I did not know if I had accomplished anything. The soldiers had passed through the roads and might be in Naderville even now, fighting Keo's unprepared young men and women. Lenk would lose; Beys would command.

I pictured Shirla already dead, and Randall with her. As I lurched along the road, rubbing the skin on my arms and chest and head, I stopped my scratching long enough to reach up to the skies and shout, "Come take me now! Where are you? Take me now!"

I think I was asking for a gate to open, but I might have been asking to die.

CHAPTER THIRTY-ONE

Yanosh and I have settled in a secluded district of the Wald. We are eating a midday meal and sharing a bottle of wine. I have paused from my story, trying to keep my composure, even after all these decades and into the full-grown infancy of a new life.

Yanosh fills in for a few minutes with tales of his months as assistant to the presiding minister. Then we drift in silence, and finally, as if to get me going again, he says, "I'm listening."

This is a part I know I will have great difficulty describing. It has been sixty years and more since that day, by the time of my older body, now abandoned somewhere, all of its history so much useless tissue.

"The town wasn't pretty, was it?" Yanosh asks.

"The ships had destroyed about half of it. The soldiers from the old palace fought their way through the eastern part of town to go north. There was still fighting in the north. The battle between Lenk's troops and the soldiers from the old palace . . . quick and bloody. I found Keo, dead, and two of his boys stumbling around through the bodies of their friends. Lenk had not sent reinforcements."

Yanosh looks off across the green expanses of grass and spherical trees and huge thick vines and long, interwoven tree trunks that form a lacework around the perimeter of the weightless Wald. "Some would say that such destruction is trivial, compared to what's happened between us and the Jarts. There was a time two years ago when we thought they would capture Axis City—"

I shake my head in violent disagreement. "Nothing that fills an eye with horror is trivial. It was on a scale that I could almost get used to it. That horrified me."

"Lenk had been building weapons for some time, then," Yanosh says. "In secret."

"He didn't think Beys or Brion would listen. He made cannons out of cathedral tree limbs, hardened by heating over fire and then steaming. They could only shoot four or five times, but he filled his ships with replacements . . ." I don't like talking tactics and logistics. That has all become vague and uninteresting to me. When humans set their minds on something, when we are forced into a corner, we can work miracles of destruction.

"Tell me what happened to Shirla. She must have been a fascinating woman."

"She was simple. When I was with her, I was simple."

"Tell me," Yanosh says.

I am back at Naderville again. It is remarkably the same as my first hours in Moonrise. I am back where I began in Lamarckia.

Bodies lay in the streets, men and women, a few children. Brion had valued his citizens, and especially children, so much, needing them for a future on Lamarckia that he later abandoned, and here were so many, wasted, and the bodies of Keo and his young men and women lying with them. The fighting had been fierce and Keo had taken many with him.

I walked through the streets weeping, and finally I would not look at the dead. Medical teams—I did not know whether they were Brionists or civilians—had set up camps in the center of town, at the base of a low hill, and I carried a few injured people there from the blocks nearby that had been shelled into utter rubble. Nobody asked who I was or where my sympathies lay.

Naderville was finished. Brion's political movement was at an end. All around the city, the silva was turning gray and crumbling. The great dark thickets were collapsing, roads were being cut off by falling debris, balloons were dropping their cargo and some had even fallen in the rubble of the town.

I had to go where the fighting was. I heard shots and more cannon fire to the north, so after doing what little I could at the eastern end of town, I walked north.

Empty buildings, shattered houses and markets, warehouses, the ruins of the administration building, I passed them all, my thoughts clearing again. From the top of the western hill, I looked across the harbor and saw one steamship coming around the western headland, leaving a trail of gray smoke. Most of Lenk's ships had left the harbor. Only four remained, and they immediately fired broadsides on the steamship. Several shells made direct hits. The steamship's guns were still active, however, and it closed.

The big guns boomed once, and the direct hit on the southernmost of Lenk's vessels broke the ship in half.

The remaining three ships had reloaded and fired again. The steamship took two more hits and for a few minutes, it slowed and followed a gentle curve to the middle of the harbor. My heart rose; I hoped it was disabled. But again the guns fired, fore and aft, and two more ships took large shells, one in the middle, one forward, blowing the bow off.

One ship remained. I did not want to see any more, but I could not leave. There was an even chance that Shirla and Randall were aboard the steamship, that they had already been injured or killed by the cannon shells.

The last of the sailing ships in the harbor fired two more cannon shots. The first raised a tower of spray fifty meters in front of the steamship. The second blew the bridge to pieces. The steamship drifted first left, then right, leaving a frothing wake, and then settled against a sand bar and rolled on its side. The stern sank below water.

The remaining sailing ship stood out in the harbor, triumphant, but only for a moment. Fire had started on her deck and was spreading swiftly. The trees and furled sails caught and flared, and smoke drifted across the harbor, to the south. I had had enough.

I walked another block along Sun Street, to where I could see the northern edge of the peninsula on which Naderville sat. A thick fog covered the ocean there, but through the fog I heard more cannon fire, and saw a bright orange flash. A mushroom puff of smoke and flying debris rose above the ceiling of fog, about three kilometers from the shore.

A deafening thud went off, seemingly at my feet. I swiveled and looked to my left, along the northwestern extent of the peninsula. A lazy curl of smoke and the residue of flame still hung from where a large gun had been fired. It had been dragged on a wheeled carriage along a dirt road and was now mounted under camouflage, backed up against thick, low-lying arborids at the top of the hill west of where I stood. I wondered who commanded the gun, and quickly decided it must be Beys's forces.

The fog would soon be lifting. Somewhere out there, very likely, was the second steamship, wreaking havoc on Lenk's sailing ships. The gun was useless for now, firing once just for practice, but when the fog lifted, it would quickly finish the job.

I ran down a street to the east, past bewildered civilians returning to this part of the town now that the shelling and fighting had subsided.

I encountered the first pickets for Lenk's troops on the outskirts of the low hills. I knew they belonged to Lenk because they wore no uniforms, as Beys's troops did, and because their discipline had broken completely.

They saw I was unarmed, and were too exhausted to pay me much attention. The fighting here had also been vicious, and bodies littered the thin scrub of phytids and arborids in the fields around the hills. A few shacks had been reduced to rubble, and men and women—mostly men—rested while others went among them with water and medicine. Moans and shrieks broke out from the wounded, laid out in rows on the ground, watched over by exhausted medical attendants.

It looked like any ancient battle, any fragment of war long past, something I had once thought would never be possible for humans again, and certainly not humans born in Thistledown.

I came upon four men standing together beside a lone stone wall, passing a bottle. They eyed me suspiciously as I approached.

"Who's in charge?" I asked.

"Nobody, now," one of the men said. "The ranks are back on the cape, or dead. We're waiting to be called back . . . to wherever. Who are you?"

I told them my name and pointed out that a gun was in place and would soon be firing on the fleet. I was about to lay out a plan for taking the gun, knowing I had to begin somewhere, when a fleshy man with a patchy beard and thick eyebrows lifted a thick fist and poked his finger at me.

"You're the Hexamon agent, aren't you?" he asked. "You're going to bring a gate down and take us back to Thistledown."

I stared at him for a moment, taken by surprise, not sure what to say or do.

"We're sick of this," the fleshy man said. "I killed four people today. I killed a woman. That's mortal error." He backed away, head dropping. "I killed a woman."

"You *can* take us back now, can't you?" The youngest in the group reached out to grab my arm. Battle shock and hope gave his face a pallid glow. "We need to go home. Something awful is happening here. Can't you smell it?"

"Are you what they say?" the tallest and oldest of them asked. He was about my age, and he had bandages wrapped around his arm and leg. "I don't know what we'd do if you turned out to be a lie."

I heard a commotion behind us. A few men with rifles ran to confront an approaching group of uniformed Brionists, ten or twelve in all. They held several white flags and carried no weapons. They were quickly surrounded, and the shouting died down into tense discussion, gun barrels pushed against hands held up, palms out, heads leaning, subdued words passing quickly.

"They can't be surrendering," the bandaged man growled. "They're just resting before they push us back out to the headland."

I heard wind-blown scraps of the conversation and walked toward the group. Again I felt the queasy excitement, the tingling sense that something significant was happening.

"That's him," one of the Brionists said, pointing at me as I approached the crowd. I recognized the officer who had addressed the ships' crews at the Citadel and tried to remember his name: *Pitt*, I thought. His uniform was torn and covered with mud. He approached me with hands outstretched. "I know who you are. Word has been passing everywhere that you're here." He stared at me with wolflike intensity. "Your name is Olmy. You know what's happening. The silva is dying. You know."

My hands seemed to pulse. "I do know," I said, letting some deeper instinct, deeper personality take over. "You came with the troops from the Citadel?"

Pitt nodded. "We fought west of here." He glanced at the encircling men and women, eyes jerking back and forth between stiff, unsympathetic faces. "The thicket is dying. We can smell it. Scions are crawling out everywhere and dying. The food is rotting in the storage houses."

378 / GREG BEAR

"Are you in charge?" I asked.

"I am a captain, rank second over my company."

"Are you done fighting?"

"What good is it? What can we do?" he asked plaintively. "The food is going bad. The food *in our kits* is turning into dust. Since last night . . . All the food from the silva, all of it. We rely on it. There is so little of anything else . . ."

Most of the able-bodied men and women on the hill, about a hundred and fifty of them, had gathered around, looking to me for explanations. Voices clamored for answers. I saw the gray Brionist uniforms absorbed in the motley of Lenk's soldiers, exhaustion and battle and common fear removing the last barriers.

I felt a roaring in my ears and my vision tunneled for a moment as blood pumped into my head. I found a low broken wall and climbed precariously on top of the ragged stones. "Listen," I shouted, raising my hands. "Ser Brion has let loose something new on Hsia. I spoke with him; I saw it. The ecos is in a major fluxing. In a few days or weeks there isn't going to be any food from the ecos, and very few are going to be able to survive here. The battle is over."

"It's dying," voices cried out.

"We have to let everybody know so the fighting will stop."

"We don't have any more radios," the bandaged man shouted at me. "The ranks have them."

I looked down at Pitt. "Do you have radios?" I asked.

He shook his head. "They're controlled by General Beys's attachés," he said.

"Where is Beys?" I asked.

"On the *15*," Pitt said, pointing north. "They're going to sink the rest of Lenk's fleet. They hope to catch Lenk and kill him, as well."

"*Able* Lenk," a woman muttered. I could not tell whether she was correcting Pitt's disrespect or expressing her own.

I bent over on the wall and put my hand on Pitt's shoulder. I had managed to lose all sense of my limitations. A small rational voice told me, *Now you really are like Lenk and Brion.*

But there was nothing else I could do, nothing else to be done, but follow the inner pressure. I had fleshed out a legend, once half dreaded, a bogeyman of another place and time. I could feel a coalescing, upturned faces, despair and hope and weariness all around me, weaknesses and passions into which I could fit like a plug in a socket and where no one else could fit so well.

"How many soldiers will follow you?" I asked Pitt.

"Fifty," he said. "They're waiting for me to come back. I remembered you when the word started spreading. There was a message from the Citadel, telling about you. Some others saw you walking through the town."

I scanned the crowd again for the face of the bandaged soldier, saw so many bandages, so many wounds and dirty, frightened faces, found the man again. I fixed on him. "How many here will follow me?"

"What are we going to do?" the bandaged man asked.

"There's a large gun on a hill below us. It's going to help Beys sink Lenk's ships. We need those ships. We need to capture that gun."

Pitt's face wrinkled again, this time in genuine anguish. I bent down again and shook his shoulder firmly. "You've come here for a reason," I said. "Beys will never give up, will he?"

"I don't know what Beys will do," Pitt said.

I picked up the phrase the fleshy, bearded man had used. "Beys has led you into mortal error."

Pitt closed his eyes and took a deep breath, brows squeezed together.

"If the ships are sunk . . . What can we do?" I asked.

"They won't need the gun. *15* can destroy most of the ships by itself." Pitt's face gleamed one last time with *esprit de corps.* "Lenk slipped his ships into the harbor when our steamships were out to sea. Beys came back as soon as he heard, and Lenk ordered his ships out of the harbor. But Beys pushed them up against the bight north of the peninsula, and now, the ships are as good as sunk."

"Beys will never give up," I repeated.

A quiet fell over the crowd. Those attached to Lenk knew the truth of this, and the soldiers of Beys and Brion were absorbing the implications.

"Ser Brion did this?" voices among the gray and tan uniforms asked. "He poisoned the silva?" Heads shook, and bitter whispers passed.

Pitt roused himself, making a decision with a quick spasm of his body.

"There was a rebellion two years ago. We felt the ecos might have been pro-faned. We warned him and his Caitla Chung, but then Brion brought us the food. We were hungry."

The crowd absorbed this information in silence. I examined the faces, try-ing to find where the river of consent and passion would flow. A wrong word, a jarring phrase, could shatter this crowd like a crystal vase. The Brionist soldiers would be beaten to death, the battle would resume, and I would be able to accomplish nothing. I thought of common sufferings and deep fears.

"No more food," I said.

"Join us!" the bandaged man shouted.

The crowd coursed around me, arms raised, hands gripping in the air. I could hardly believe what I was seeing. The crowd had become one, and was ready to absorb more.

CHAPTER THIRTY-TWO

The gun, Pitt informed us, was approachable only by the dirt road. The fog north of the peninsula was already thinning, patches of ocean and a few ships revealed, and morning was giving way to noon. We had Pitt's fifty sol-diers and, keeping well behind them, fifty of Lenk's troops, all of them now following me.

I considered the situation carefully. If we put the gun out of action, Beys's steamship could still cause considerable damage to Lenk's fleet. With four ships sunk in the harbor, having taken the 43 down with them, there were ten vessels still in the fog, at severe risk.

The situation was also clear to Pitt. He sat on a rock at the bottom of the hill road, just below a detachment in place to guard the road. The detach-ment had already exchanged a few words with Pitt and recognized him.

I sat beside Pitt. Kristof Ab Seija, the bandaged man, stood behind us.

"I can talk to them some more," Pitt said, "but I don't know what good it will do. They're a special crew. They take orders directly from Beys and no one else. After the steamships, that gun is his pride."

"We don't have much time," I said.

The gun blasted a great gout of flame and smoke from the side of the hill. The shell flew out over the water, sounding like a huge shoe grinding boulder-sized gravel. Seconds later, kilometers away, an explosion answered like the same heavy shoe dropping.

"It can shoot seven kilometers," Pitt said. "Maybe more."

"We may have to kill them," Seija said.

Pitt lowered his face into his hands and rubbed his eyes. "It's not easy," he said.

"To kill them?" Seija asked.

"To be a traitor," he replied sharply, and looked up at me, eyes pleading for some sort of inspiration. I had put myself into this position; I could not back down now.

I listened intently to the conflicting messages inside me, trying to find that conviction of invincibility I had known before.

My neck hair tingled again. *Interest.* The word that described so much and explained so little. I heard more voices coming from the flat between the hills, mostly female.

The bearded man, Hamsun, ran up to join us. The detachment farther up the dirt road began to mill restlessly, weapons raised, sensing something was about to happen.

"Women," Hamsun said, out of breath, panting heavily. "From Naderville. Older women coming back. Now that the fighting. Has stopped."

In a town or city as small as Naderville, everybody should know everybody else. They had shared mutual grief and misery; I tried to imagine the depth of the social connections, the influence some people might wield. Beys might have been a true aberration, his support shallow; the dull calm on the face of the man in the flatboat could as easily have been numb acquiescence.

And now the women were here, perhaps the mother or wife of that man. For a moment I felt lost in this new sympathy. All the energetic loathing I had carried left a confusing vacuum.

"Ser Pitt," I said, "can you explain things to the women? Bring some of them up here?"

"You want them to go up the road first?"

"Mothers, sisters, wives," I said.

Pitt stood. "I'll try to explain," he said. "I know some of the gun crew. I know their families."

Yanosh is trying to absorb this. "So you became a general," he said. "You learned how to move the masses."

His words are ironic, perhaps a little disbelieving. "Pitt and I walked with the women. We walked up the road. The soldiers could not shoot their own women."

"You told them about the food," Yanosh says.

"It was more than food," I say. "It was exhaustion, and thirty-seven years of frustration and recrimination and misery. And now the profanation of a sacred thing."

"That is what I have the most trouble understanding," Yanosh says. "How could anyone revere such a thing as the ecos? Wasn't it part of their misery?"

"No," I say, not knowing exactly how to explain. Yanosh will never see the ecoi as they were. Nobody will ever see them again.

The women walked past the guards and the chain barrier and up to the gun. Lenk's troops stayed behind; they were not necessary.

The gun crew were not the devoted warriors Beys might have hoped. They succumbed rapidly to the pleas of their wives and mothers, and radioed for instructions to 15. Beys could not explain the fluxing to his soldiers, nor why they should continue supporting Brion when the sustenance of their homeland was rotting.

The gun did not fire again. Beys had lost his constituency, and word was spreading against Brion.

Pitt sat with me afterward, and the captain of the gun crew joined us in the shadow of the big weapon, looking out across the ocean at the steamship and Lenk's bottled-up fleet. The captain tossed his hat down into the dust beside the massive wheel. "I have two young ones," he said, glancing at me like a shy, frightened child. "My wife didn't come here with the others." He swung his hand at the women on the road and surrounding the emplacement. "If they're still alive, where will they go? What will they eat? I tried to speak with Beys, but he hasn't answered the radio since we stopped firing."

"Is there a boat?" I asked.

"On the beach," the captain said, pointing down the hill.

The launch had once served the government's needs on the northern side of the peninsula. Less fancy than Brion's launch, or Chung's, it still had a fully charged set of batteries and a sturdy electric motor. Pitt stepped aboard with me, carrying a radio from the gun crew. Hamsun followed. Seija would stay behind to keep the peace between the Lenk troops, the gun crew, and the rest of the Brionist soldiers, many seeing their wives and mothers for the first time in days.

On the beach beside the launch lay wilted gray devastation. The beach-front thicket had died. A balloon had dropped the last of its green larval seed-mothers and now lay half collapsed on the spit of black sand and lava gravel nearby, pushed at by slow, persistent waves. The new, young seed-mother had taken residence in a tangle of phytids the night before and had immediately enslaved them, to protect itself against whatever weather there might be. They had formed a small shelter over its delicate green body, and in the middle, beneath the canopy, it grew and sent forth broad flat green folia, spreading wide in the afternoon sun.

The balloon's wrinkled, rapidly deflating bag rolled back and forth in the low surf. As we prepared to board the launch, the green center beneath the dry, crumbling protection of the phytids exploded and threw out tiny corn-kernel grains. They immediately pushed probing tendrils into the dirt and wet sand.

Pitt regarded the new ecos with disgust. I did not bother to tell him what it was; we had little time.

The steamship sailed in a tight loop four kilometers offshore. The last of the sailing ships that had dropped off Lenk's troops and shelled Nader-ville had gotten themselves into a tight situation, bottled up in a bight that stretched seven kilometers north from the peninsula. It was obvious from the steamship's threatening posture and strategic position that if they tried to leave, they would be shelled, probably demolished. But for the time be-ing, no action was being taken. The sailing ships could not shell *15* at its present distance from them, but it could certainly fire on them, and Beys seemed to be weighing his options.

Hamsun and Pitt insisted that they be allowed to run the boat. "You need time to think," Pitt said. His deference made me nervous. Again, all my confidence had fled. The way Pitt looked at me made my stomach churn.

I dreaded the thought of meeting with Beys. I knew his kind of evil would rise above any small talent I might have at persuasion and politics. He would know I was no prophet; he might simply shoot me, or order me shot. I did not fear that, however. Death seemed the least of my worries.

I hoped Shirla was on board, and Randall. On the other hand, I was uncomfortable at the thought of her seeing me in this new, false role, of diplomat and putative avatar. She would instantly know it for the sham it was. If Beys saw her reaction, he would know, then, also.

And yet—what could Beys do? He could kill us. He could fire on the sailing ships. But Lenk and the *Khoragos* were not in the bight. Without support from Naderville, Beys was nothing more than a pirate. His strength would rapidly wane.

The situation in Naderville was far from stable, however. Brion could reappear at any moment, from wherever he was hiding, and draw his people back together, back to their accustomed ruler and ways. He was far better at playing his role than I could be. Beys might be in touch with Brion; the pair of supposed opposites might again be drawing lines of force between them, north pole and south, on the brink this time of regaining not just Naderville but all the other human settlements as well.

Pitt had told the steamship that we were approaching, and that I was aboard to parley. He stood beside me on the prow; Hamsun piloted the boat from the stern.

"Will he blow us out of the water?" Pitt asked.

"I was just about to ask you the same thing," I said.

"I feel sick to my stomach," Pitt said.

"So do I."

Pitt squinted up at me. "The general is a powerful man," he said. "I think he'll squash me like a bug."

"What does he believe in?" I asked.

Pitt frowned. He was a thin, weary bureaucrat in a uniform that no longer seemed to fit him. His long wrists hung out of the sleeves, and he clasped his bony hands together tightly. "A few hours ago, I would have said he believed in Brion and Naderville. In bringing rational planning and thought to Lamarckia. I was a student in the academy before my enlistment began and the call-up put us all in uniform. I didn't see any duty away from Naderville . . . I stayed here and watched things change. Brion became more aloof. Beys more prominent. I did not disapprove. Should I have?"

I shook my head. If I could not judge Brion, surely I could not judge this man, or any like him. The confusing vacuum persisted.

No right, no wrong, only forces of nature, like winds blowing us back and forth. My stomach knotted tighter. We were less than a kilometer from 15. The steamship had slowed. She had dropped a sea anchor to maintain her position. Pitt rubbed his nose and said that was a good sign.

"15's given us permission to put alongside," Hamsun called from aft.

Pitt arranged his uniform and smoothed back his hair, blown about by the sea breeze. The smell of ammonia and flat staleness was apparent even this far from shore; on the land it must have been awful.

"Some of us worshipped Hsia," Pitt said. "It wasn't her fault she couldn't feed us. Some thought she did what she could, that we had just overstepped our bounds. That's why so many were upset when Brion said he was going to make her fruitful, he was going to change her. Brion almost lost everything then. But he brought the food down the canal in ships, and we had been so hungry for so long . . . The rebellion ended before it really got started.

"The last two days . . . I don't know. I've lived here all my life. The thicket silva's been here for millions of years, so they say. I think if I were someone else, I'd cry. How could Brion have done something like this?"

I could not give any useful answers.

The launch pulled alongside the steamship and a gangway was lowered level with our deck. We lashed the launch to the gangway and climbed the steps. A narrow-faced man with a short stiff cap of brown hair greeted us stiffly at the rail.

"General Beys is busy now. He'll be with you shortly."

We were taken forward, past the big forward gun, sea-based twin of the gun that had been rolled up the hill. It must have taken immense effort to make such weapons, and yet, they had not saved 43 from being sunk by primitive xyla-wrapped cannon. I could not fathom the reasoning behind such a military buildup. Had Brion or Beys anticipated a major showdown at sea?

The bristle-haired man introduced himself as Major Sompha, then sat us under an observation canopy erected in front of the forward gun.

"Is it as bad as it looks?" he asked softly, nodding in the direction of the mainland. From where *15* floated, the stretches of silva looked pale and irregular, the sharply defined boundaries turning ash-gray as the day progressed.

"It's all changing," Pitt said.

"What's the worst of it? We haven't heard much."

"The food," Pitt said. Hamsun described the situation in the storage barns. Major Sompha took it with as much stoic calm as he could muster, but it obviously hit him hard. He asked about his family in Naderville.

"Some are coming back into town, but . . ." Hamsun shook his head.

"Are you with Lenk?" Sompha asked me.

"No," I said.

"He says he's from the Hexamon," Pitt said. "A lot of people believe him."

Sompha nodded, putting facts together and drawing his own conclusions. "I think General Beys believes him," he said. "Why let you come here, otherwise? We're waiting for nightfall, and then we'll sink Lenk's ugly fleet one by one."

"There's *no food*," Pitt growled. "What good will it do to sink the ships that might take some of us away, or bring food from Tasman or Elizabeth?"

"Lenk wouldn't do a thing for us before," Sompha said.

"I need to know if there are two people on board," I interrupted, my patience ending. "A man and a woman. One is named Shirla Ap Nam, the other is Erwin Randall."

"The hostages," Sompha said. "They're here. Beys is keeping them below. Maybe he *is* worried about you." He shrugged and left us sitting out of the milky sunlight, in the shade of the canopy.

An hour passed, and Sompha returned with glasses of water. He stood with us for several minutes, grimly staring across the water at the ash-colored shore. "Looks like a huge fire hit it," he said. "Do you think it's happening everywhere?"

"It will," I said.

"We'll put in to the harbor tomorrow morning, after we sink these ships, if it's clear," Sompha said. "I need to see things for myself."

An hour later, he returned again. The distant shore appeared creamy white in the late-afternoon light. The sun crept toward the western horizon. Within the bight, the remains of Lenk's fleet had anchored.

To the men and women on those ships, I thought, it must seem as if the world was ending. They'd probably try to break out in an hour or so, and chance that Beys's monster would miss a few, not be able to track them down, or that they could return sufficient fire to put the steamship out of action. I imagined myself on one of those ships.

"General Beys says he's ready to meet with you now," Sompha said. We stood and Sompha placed himself in front of me. "If you are the judge, from the Hexamon, I need to tell you something now. My wife and I were ordered to take in three children from Elizabeth's Land," he said. "We were ordered to. We have taken good care of them."

We looked at each other for a long moment, and then Sompha turned away, murmuring, "I just wanted you to know that."

He led us to the bridge, up a steep companionway and around an outside passage to cabins on the upper deck. Sompha opened a door, and an imposing dark woman, taller than I and probably stronger, stared at us with sharp clear eyes, then stood aside.

General Beys sat at a table within the cabin. All was painted white, and the table was set with a white cloth. A glass pitcher of water and several cups had been placed around the table, and folding xyla chairs drawn up.

Beys looked at the men beside me. "You're Rank Two Suleiman Pitt. I don't remember this man's name . . ."

"Hamsun, sir. Tarvo Hamsun."

"Is it as bad on shore as it looks?"

"Yes, sir," Pitt said.

Beys indicated we should sit. His ruddy cheeks had blued to a pale violet in the last few days, and his skin was sallow from fatigue. His left hand trembled slightly on the white cloth of the table until he removed it and hid it beneath the table. "Brion should have killed you all, and Lenk, days ago," Beys said. "We had Lenk in our hands. We both miscalculated badly."

"What good to kill more?" I asked.

"My mistake," Beys said shortly, his voice clipped but calm. "I underestimated Lenk, and in my profession, that's a crime."

He leaned forward. "Still no help from the Hexamon? Lenk's clavicle no good for you?"

"I haven't seen it," I said.

"Brion took you up the canal and showed you more than you cared to see, I'll bet."

"He took us up the canal," I said.

"The scientist, Salap . . . what did he think?"

"He's still there."

"Is Brion responsible for what's happening on shore? He and his wife?"

"It looks that way," I said.

"He knew, damn him," Beys said, looking up at the ceiling, then back at me. "He behaved like a kid whose dirty little secrets are going to come out soon. Do you know where he is?"

I shook my head.

"Neither do I. I can't reach him by the radio, and no one on shore has seen him." Beys leaned back and glared at Pitt and Hamsun. "Get out," he ordered loudly. They stood quickly and the imposing dark woman escorted them through the hatch. "Aphra, shut the door behind you and stay outside yourself."

"Yes, sir," the woman said.

Beys put both hands on the table. "We're equal now. Fate damn either one of us who lies."

"All right," I said.

"The oath assumed," he added, staring at me with brows drawn together.

"The oath assumed."

"Brion gave you the impression that I'm responsible for all the mayhem, didn't he?" Beys asked.

"I believe you carried out your interpretation of vague orders."

Beys thrust his jaw out and leaned his head back. "Did Brion show you the army he wanted to make? Or rather, have the seed-mother make? Designs for scion soldier-weapons . . . ?" He read my features intently.

"No," I said.

His face shifted from a wry smile to disgust. "He wanted to start over again. He wanted all of Lenk's people to realize what Lenk had done to us. Anything to further that cause . . . was legitimate. We were working to stabilize *all* settlements on Lamarckia, to transform this planet. Food was the first accomplishment. The scion soldiers would have been next . . . But his wife died. That broke him. I thought he was strong, or I wouldn't have allied with him, but that broke him."

Beys met my silence with a lift of his lip and a cluck of his tongue. "If I destroy this fleet of Lenk's in the next hour, what will you do?"

I avoided directly answering that question, instead explaining about the larval seed-mothers, the rotting scions of old Hsia. "Everyone in Naderville will starve," I said.

"If I let Lenk go free, and . . . whatever you might think is honorable or just, what will you do?"

"Naderville will need to be evacuated. That could take months. A lot of people will die, but not all of them."

Beys considered this, rubbing his cheek with a short, fat finger. Then he lifted one eyebrow. "What would you have done, if you were me?"

"Why did you kill so many?" I asked in return.

Beys jerked slightly in his chair, but his expression did not change.

"Why kill the adults?" I asked, taking another angle.

"Irrational loyalty to Lenk and all he stood for," he said.

"Yes, but why kill them?"

"To end the old and begin the new. How would you have done that, if you were me?"

"You really don't know why you ordered them killed, do you?"

Beys lowered his eyelids until he resembled a sleepy farm animal, a dog or a pig. "You judge me. Have you judged Brion?"

"I'm not a judge," I said.

"Brion believed you were powerless," he said. "He thought you were a gnawed-off piece of some aborted effort. I told him the Hexamon does not work that way. He laughed and said I was an idealist. I think that all you have to do is wink just the right way, and all this will end. Why not wink?"

I did not answer.

He refused to look me in the eye, and I saw sweat on his lip. "I have something for you. Brion asked that I take your companions, Ap Nam and Randall, with me on this ship. He learned that you and Ap Nam were lovers. They're here."

"I'd like to see them," I said.

Beys clenched his hands on the table and knocked it sharply with his knuckles. "I would have done anything to have never come here. I would have worked my way up in Way Defense." His voice tensed. "I am in a backwater, with nowhere to go. When my family died, Brion was all I had."

"Show me Shirla and Erwin," I said.

"If I give them up to you, and let the fleet go, what then?"

I did not hesitate to tell a half lie. "I will not turn you over to Hexamon justice."

"Where will I live?"

"Wherever you can travel without my help."

Beys mulled this over. "You can have this ship. It's hell to maintain. I can take one of Lenk's schooners and a crew of ten. I can manage with ten. If you want, I'll sink this ship."

"We'll need all the ships," I said.

His once-florid face had taken on the cast of wet free-chunk paste. Beys lifted his eyes to meet mine. "A small ship. A boat. Where do you suggest I go?"

"I don't care," I said.

"Lenk might have shelled his own children, you know," Beys murmured. "They might have been kept in Naderville as protection."

"Were they?"

"If I had thought about it, I would have ordered them kept there, but I was sixty miles out at sea when the attack began. I was going to Jakarta, and then to Athenai."

I shook my head.

"I stay here on Lamarckia, whatever happens. You will not let them take me back to the Way."

"All right," I said.

Beys brought his hands up on the table. Star, Fate, and Pneuma be kind, I shook hands with that man.

Shirla and Randall stood in the shadow of the aft gun, guarded by three soldiers in gray and tan, and Pitt and Hamsun waited nearby. I walked along the passage to the rear deck. Shirla saw me and ran forward. Nobody tried to stop her. She grabbed me and I squeezed her tightly, burying my face in her neck and sweat-scented hair. We said nothing for a time.

"Are you a prisoner, too?" she asked.

"I don't think so," I said.

"Are we going back to Liz now? I keep hearing that we can't possibly stay here, that the ecos is sick."

So word was spreading around the ship. I wondered if Beys or Brion could possibly survive.

"I hope we can go, and soon," I said. "There's a lot of work to do. A lot to prepare for."

"No magic?" she asked.

I shook my head. "I'm afraid not."

"Just you?"

"Just me," I said.

Randall came closer and joined us. "I hope you'll be enough," he said.

CHAPTER THIRTY-THREE

Yanosh and I have made our way to my newly assigned apartment. He has to leave soon; the presiding minister has been affording him considerable time to arrange for my care and debrief me, but other matters are pressing hard, and Yanosh can assign only so many incorporeal ghosts to do his work before his embodied authority becomes necessary.

Much has changed in the Hexamon in ten years. The art of ghosting—of projecting partial personalities to do one's work—has advanced to astonishing sophistication.

"Did you ever learn why Lenk destroyed the clavicle?" Yanosh asks.

Shirla was with me when we went ashore, in Lenk's main party, to pay homage to the dead. Brion, Hyssha Chung, and Frick had been found murdered, their bodies mutilated. Lenk claimed disgruntled soldiers from Brion's army had caught them and killed them. I never heard any reason to believe otherwise. Their alleged killers were going to be put on trial in Tasman.

They were being buried with a full divaricate Naderite funeral, allowing Lenk to show that time and honor can heal all wounds.

A few days later, the *Khoragos* departed Hsia. Because of the extraordinary fluxing, boats were being sent from Tasman and Elizabeth's Land, and some effort was being made to evacuate the citizens of Naderville. It would take months, and Lenk did not want to be there if things went wrong. He insisted Shirla and I accompany him to Tasman.

Beys left Naderville in a small schooner, with a five-man crew, all that would go with him.

None was ever heard from again.

Shirla sat on the deck of the *Khoragos* in a small folding chair, sipping from a bowl of tea. She smiled up at me as I approached, afraid but trying hard not to show her fear. I sat beside her and she offered me the cup. I took a sip.

"When is he going to show us?" she asked.

"Tonight. He's busy arranging things now. He's still Able Lenk."

Shirla gazed out to sea and her teeth began to chatter. With a jerk, she stilled the quiver in her jaw and looked miserable. "You'll be going soon," she said. There had been so little time to talk, so many meetings and arrangements before leaving Hsia. None of this had been worked over between us.

"I don't think so," I said.

"If you can fix the clavicle . . ."

"Ferrier says he doesn't believe that's possible, now."

"But if you can . . . You'll go back to the Way."

I took her hand. "I don't know what will happen."

"You come from a larger place than anything I can conceive of," Shirla said. "I've been taught all my life to be afraid of that place, to despise it. Now you're my love and you come from there."

"We all come from there," I said.

"But I don't want to leave here. You must."

I squeezed her hand. In truth, nobody knew what would happen. "He wants you to be there, too," I said.

"Good Lenk invited me?"

"He did."

"Olmy," she said, putting her other hand over mine, "I wanted—"

She tried valiantly again.

"I wanted—"

Tears dripped down her cheeks.

"I *wanted*," she managed again, and shook her whole upper body to rid herself of this foolishness. "Never, ever, ever want anything with all your life, ever. Never want. They will take it away. You will go away."

"I want, too. I know where I am now," I said.

"Who are you?" she asked.

Lenk sat in the cabin where we had met it seemed years earlier. Allrica Fassid stood beside him, but left as Shirla and I came in. On the table before him was an ornate xyla box.

"Nobody can offer any proof that you are from the Hexamon," he said as we sat in two chairs opposite. "That is remarkable. I accept that you are, because of what you have done. I know the ways of history, and it all smells right to me." He turned to Shirla.

"You are a good woman, and have never wanted more than to have a family and live a decent life."

Shirla blinked at him, then looked at me, too stunned to answer.

"Isn't that so? There's no need to be shy."

She nodded. It was so. Lenk knew his people well.

"You have made love with this man, in a certain way, under difficult circumstances, and that means you are committed to him, and believe he is committed to you. Do you accept him for what he is?"

"I don't think we came here to talk about that," Shirla said softly.

Lenk focused his deep-set, dark-lidded eyes on me. For a moment he looked remarkably like a dead man. "I hear that Brion and Beys thought you could pass judgment, that Beys worried you would split him like a ripe fruit. They were cowards. The Hexamon cannot judge us."

He leaned forward and opened the box. Inside, the clavicle lay in many pieces, some of them melted. Even after years, at the end of two projections within the shattered sphere, a tiny bit of glimmer showed, the last trace of a small finite artificial universe sympathetic with the Way. None of the controls remained, however, and I saw it could never be repaired.

"You were a fool to come here alone," Lenk said. "Whoever sent you here was a fool. I have withstood Lamarckia and treachery and the devils of my own nature. I do not fear you or the Hexamon. Brion is dead, and that is a kind of waste—though he had too much of the Hexamon in him—and Beys is gone. So what are we to do, you and I?"

I stared across the table at the man who had started all this, saw his weary defiance and his strength. I saw that Shirla was still in awe of him. He had his center of power, and the force necessary to oust him from that center would cause more bloodshed and, in the end, with all of Lamarckia changing, do nobody any good.

"You've made a beginning for yourself," Lenk said. "You've gathered a following. You could be like Brion, only I suspect you'd be a little colder than he was, and never trust someone like Beys. You could be formidable, Olmy."

I studied Lenk and felt the remains of my hate dissolve, not because of any lessening of indignation and anger, but because he was part of a river of human history that could not be shifted without immense pain. He was not the worst, far from the best; but inevitably, he was in his place, and for me to oppose him would be another kind of cruelty, not to him—he might relish the battle—but to his people.

To Shirla.

I could guarantee nothing. The Hexamon might never come, and I could not return to the Way.

My mission was over.

After a moment, Lenk leaned back and said, "I thank you for what you've managed this far. I bless you for your work. You're a smart and decent man, Ser Olmy, but you are not like me, and not like Brion. Go and live a life with this woman."

I did not want my children on Lamarckia. Shirla wanted children; we compromised.

Shirla and I lived in Athenai for ten years. It was there we adopted our first boy, Ricca, one of the many orphans called Beys's children. I came in time almost to forget the Hexamon. For weeks on end I thought little or nothing of my past. I was well-known wherever we lived for being the Hexamon agent, but even in the worst of times, nobody resented me, or at least nobody expressed their resentments to me. The Adventists, what remained of them, came now and then, and Lenk did not oppose their coming. He knew I would not encourage them.

When Lenk died, Allrica Fassid took over the reins of power for a while, but the first starvation set in five years later, and she committed suicide. Others followed. The divaricates kept their political scheme, and never did I sense a place for me in that scheme. For this, Shirla was grateful.

We left Tasman after it began its own fluxing. We adopted our second son, Henryk, in Calcutta.

As the years passed, more and more the change spread. So much of the beauty and variety of Lamarckia was fleeing before Brion's gift of green. What replaced it was simple and direct, tiny ecoi, covering only a few acres, and getting tinier. Some of the scions—phytids, even mobile scions—seemed capable of independence, and perhaps even replicating on their own. Randall studied them closely and wrote more papers. We visited often.

Shirla and I and our two sons had our happiest five years together in Jakarta. Petain's Zone resisted the green longer than any but the island zones in the south, where most of the survivors clustered for decades. In those five good years, however, Jakarta became a wonderfully feverish city, an island of creative ferment and relative prosperity in the change.

We actually saw Salap again. Yes!—he had survived, and was back at Wallace Station, but he made a trip to Jakarta.

Many of us were dying from new immune challenges as Petain tried different defenses against Hsia and the green. Salap had been charting the spread of new scion chemistries, and he arrived when Shirla was very ill, making the trip especially to see us, I suppose, but also as part of the research effort.

Shirla and I met with him in her room. Henryk and Ricca, ages ten and fifteen then, came in and out, carrying food, clean bedding, water. Shirla had become a real mother to them, and I had done my best, in my distracted way, to be a real father.

Salap made his tests, took samples from her withered body, told us that there might be ways to turn back such challenges in a few months. Idle hopes, as it turned out.

Salap finally related the story of his last few days with the female figure in the hemisphere. "She struggled to become human," he said. "Having watched the Chung sisters and Brion, and finally paying close attention to me, the only model left to her—observing me while I observed her—we taught each other many things. But she could never think like us, much less understand our shapes. She was never more than a meticulous and crafty observer, without the cycling knot of self-awareness that must always separate us from the ecoi. At the last, though, she broke her second foot free and became independent for a few days. She managed to walk. She did pretty well, under the circumstances."

"What did she want?" Shirla asked.

"The ecos had observed humans having sex. It was curious about the process. Thought it might result in another 'name,' like Brion's gift of chlorophyll. She actually became seductive, at the end." He stared at us, eyes flicking back and forth. For the first time, Salap seemed ill-at-ease.

"Did you?" Shirla asked.

Salap smiled and leaned his head to one side. "Three months after you left, the hemisphere withered," he continued. "The last of the balloons had been manufactured and sent away with the winds."

"What happened to *her*? To the imitation of Caitla?" Shirla asked.

"She withered, too. She maintained her interest to the end, trying to speak, trying to extract biological secrets, hoping for more gifts of 'names.' Finally, she could not move, and she made only shrill whistles and rasping, barking sounds.

"When she died, I cut her open and studied her, but there was nothing particularly novel about her anatomy. I buried her beside the body of Caitla Chung, in the new silva."

"She *was* a queen," Shirla said, and she swallowed and stared up at the mat fiber ceiling, and then looked at me. "You saw a true queen, Olmy. I wish I could have seen her. I don't think we'll ever have that chance again."

Shirla died that winter. So many died that winter, as the weather itself changed, and Petain began its final decline. The green arrived with its own disastrous spring, but by then I was a different man, without Shirla. I flowed with the people, with Lenk's river of history.

CHAPTER THIRTY-FOUR

I go with Yanosh down the Way in a flawship to the gate on the geometry stack. Transport ships are loading the last of the evacuees from Lamarckia. The situation there has become critical, and the Hexamon has ordered that all be removed.

Because of the difficulties of a gate in the geometry stack, fifteen years have passed since I was retrieved. Rebecca has died.

All but three hundred of the remaining nine thousand Lamarckians have been brought through the gate. My two sons are not among them. They have chosen to remain, to ride out the worst of the changes, though their chances of surviving are almost nil. Somehow, I feel that I have given them a part of myself, made them like me, and done them no favor.

I watch from a deltoid craft as the last of the Hexamon agents evacuate the gate.

The gate is closing by itself, the stacks becoming unstable despite the best efforts of the best gate openers.

The wall of the Way glows brilliant violet, then flashes rich, vibrant green. The dimple fills and smooths over, and the surface assumes the color of fresh-cast bronze.

The green flash lingers in my eye.

I become who I am now.